Thank you!
Enjoy the read.

Through Seasons of Fire

Karen J. Hasley

Karen J. Hasley

This is a work of fiction. The characters described herein are imaginary and are not intended to refer to living persons.

ISBN 13:978-1727524536
ISBN 10:1727524535

Thank you, Ann, for your eye for detail. You're a treasure.
Cover photo by Markus Spiske temporausch.com from Pexels

1882 New Hope, Nebraska

Railroad/Train Station	**N**	RR stock pens
Freight office		Livery/Blacksmith
alley		Fire Dept
Telegraph/Post Office		Variety & Groc
alley		Carpentry &
Feed & Grain	**Main**	Undertaker
Boot & Shoe Maker		Jail
Leather Goods	**Street**	Bliss House Hotel
City Meat Market		and
Dry Goods & Notions		Bliss Restaurant
Gooseneck Hotel & Billiards		Bliss Music Hall
Hardware, Agric Implements & Stoves		Meeting /
United Bank of Nebraska		Entertainment Hall
↓Newspaper Office↓		____________
W ←School]	**←Alley/Church St→**	[Church→ **E**
↑Photography Studio↑		↑Tull's Beer↑
←Laundry] Dress Shop		Barber Shop
Nebraska Café		Law Office
Hart's Boarding House		MD/Drug Store
	S	
	River	

“”Thy rage shall burn thee up, and thou shalt turn to ashes…Look to thyself, thou art in jeopardy.”’

William Shakespeare, 1616†
King John, Act III, Scene 1

October 1882

I've lived with fire every day for the last eight years. It's a part of me now, as much as my brown eyes and the ache I feel in my left wrist when the weather turns cold and damp. If I wake in the middle of a fall night, huddled warm and cozy under my quilts, the crackle of flames in the dark corners of the room blends comfortingly with the ticking of the mantel clock. When I walk outside on a winter's day and the air is so sharp and frigid that it steals my breath away, I still feel a tender lick of heat against my cheek. A consuming fire roars much like the raging bursts of wind in a spring thunderstorm, so I hear fire clearly in the spring, even as the rain pours down. And summer? Well, Nebraska under the August sun on a breezeless day is stifling as an oven, and the flickers of hot summer air feel like sparks from a campfire landing on my skin as timid and quick as stolen kisses. I'm a practical person with a head for business and as sane as any other woman, but be that as it may, fire has been my close companion, burning through all the passing seasons of the last eight years.

1

Ogallala slows down in November, the herds of cattle and their wild drovers done for the season, the saloons closed, and the brothels moved on to bigger, busier towns like Denver and St. Louis and Omaha. The girls have to make a living and they need men for that. Once the number of both visitors and inhabitants dwindles, the quiet of the Nebraska prairie turns melancholy, its stillness encouraging memories and regrets. We maintain a single stop on the railroad so Ogalalla House, where I work, still has a modest measure of business but nothing like the summer months. That's why I'm restless from November through May. I don't like time on my hands.

So when John Bliss showed up in the restaurant's dining room in mid-October, I was happier than usual to see him. John and I have known each other for ten years, but we've been friends for only four of the ten. It took a long time for us to make peace, but it's only right that we reconciled because we both cared deeply for the same man, and now we honor his memory together. Because John married last year, I had expected to see less of him, but his wife is a remarkable woman, sure of herself and her husband, and John and I have been able to maintain our friendship. There is nothing carnal between us and never has been. We're bound together by the memory of a man we both loved.

I set his usual steak in front of him, covered with onions the way he liked it, and sat down at the table to keep him company. It was mid-afternoon, and the dining room was empty. John was lucky the cook was still puttering in the kitchen to handle the beef or I would have had to deliver a plate of leftover chicken fricassee instead of the restaurant's signature steak.

When I said as much, John responded, "I've had worse than warmed-up fricassee in my time, Caro, but" – he pointed his fork at me – "I admit to a partiality for the way your man cooks Nebraska beef."

"Better than the Bliss House restaurant?"

He grinned. "I won't admit to that."

"But–"

"But it would be a close contest, and I wouldn't like my odds."

We sat in silence as he ate until I said, "Sheba's well, I hope." At his wife's name, a shadow flickered across his face.

I didn't think I was mistaken, but he replied easily, "Yes. She sends her regards."

"I wish you'd bring her with you next time. As I recall, she favored the steak, too." I had met John's new wife only twice, last fall when she had spent a short time in Ogallala and then again after their December wedding when they'd both come to Ogallala to let me know they were married, but Sheba Bliss is the kind of woman who makes a lasting impression, a woman you take to instantly or you don't take to at all. Fortunately, I had liked her from the start.

"She's finishing up two paintings for Charles Crocker, who heard that Sidney Dillon had one of Sheba's pictures hanging in his front hallway. Nothing would do for Crocker but to have two in his hall. There's enough country for two railroads, but you'd never know it from the way those two always need to get the better of each other."

"There's money in the railroads," I stated.

"At least in the pockets of the men who run them," John said.

"Well, you be sure to tell Sheba I asked about her. The way business has slowed in Ogallala, I have too much time on my hands and I'd welcome a visit."

John, a surprisingly neat man, patted at his mouth with his napkin and set both napkin and fork down onto the tablecloth in a deliberate motion before he spoke. I recognized that whatever he was going to say was the reason he had taken the train west from New Hope and showed up in Ogallala on a slow Thursday afternoon. He was a man who liked a good steak, but not so much that he'd spend a day coming and going on the Union Pacific Railway just to eat one in the Ogallala House dining room, especially when he owned an equally fine restaurant in New Hope.

"I know Ogallala slows down in the fall, Caroline."

Caroline, I thought. Using my full name meant that whatever John had on his mind was serious.

"It does," I said. "Another four weeks and we'll close the kitchen for part of the day. Mr. Gast doesn't like to do that, but it's a practical decision, and I can't fault him for it. We only have the one railroad stop as it is, and when the cattle business slows down, all of Ogallala does the same."

"As I recall, sometimes you stay in town during the slow season and sometimes you go out of town for a few weeks."

"I've traveled some," I admitted, "but not in a while. Nebraska's my home now. I like it here."

I couldn't linger at the Wyoming graves any longer or afford the luxury of grieving the past, I thought. Those earlier trips certainly hadn't been wasted because I had made discoveries and gathered facts I would someday put to use, but now I was ready to make definite plans and follow more meaningful pursuits. I didn't share any of that with John, however, just waited for him to say what he'd come to say. I was curious. John Bliss doesn't have a hesitant or indecisive bone in his body, and it was interesting to watch his expression as he took the time to put his thoughts in order before he spoke.

"I'd like to take Sheba to Paris, but I need to leave Bliss House and the restaurant in good hands when we go. The Music Hall, too, but Benny knows what it takes to keep that place running, and I wouldn't give it a second thought while I was gone. I can't say the same for the hotel and restaurant, though. They need more skill than Benny's got. He's a good man but too rough around the edges for the clientele we get at Bliss House. You on the other hand–"

"Ah," I said. "I see. I wondered where this conversation was headed."

John smiled and plowed ahead. "You know something about my business from the year you spent in New Hope before Gast stole you away to Ogallala."

"I left of my own free will, John."

"I know. I was trying for a little humor." He gave a quick smile to support his words. "You did a better job of running my establishments than I did, Caro. It was clear you knew how to make a place efficient and profitable and keep the help happy at the same time. That's a special talent, as I've discovered to my regret. If you don't have other plans for the slow months, I'm asking you to come to New Hope and run Bliss House while Sheba and I are gone. I'll make it worth your while" – he quoted a figure that was shockingly generous – "and you can live in our home if you like. It's got all the luxuries. Or you can take a room at the hotel if you prefer. Whatever suits you." He wasn't a man to beg, but I heard pleading at the edges of his voice.

"This trip to Paris must mean a lot to you and Sheba," I observed.

"I haven't said anything to her about it yet."

"A surprise, then?"

"You could say that. There's a woman painter in Paris that Sheba admires, and I read about a special exhibition planned after the new year to show some of the woman's paintings. Sheba can't say enough good things about Miss Cassatt. I'm trying to arrange a personal meeting with the woman, maybe a few lessons, too. Sheba would like that."

"You're coming up on your first anniversary, as I recall."

"Yes."

I paused and then asked, "But it's more than an anniversary present, isn't it, John?" I had known the man for a number of years, and while I didn't know exactly what emotion I heard in his voice, it was more than simply a new husband planning a special surprise for his wife on their first anniversary. "Is everything all right between the two of you?" Only our long acquaintance allowed me to ask so personal a question, and I was rewarded with another smile, this one warm and genuine.

"Everything is fine between us, Caro. Better than fine, really, except—" Some emotion sparked in his dark eyes and was quickly quenched. "I don't like mentioning it to you, for more reasons than one, but Sheba lost a child some weeks ago. *We* lost a child, I mean."

"I'm sorry, John." I leaned forward to rest a hand briefly on his forearm before relaxing back in my chair. "Very sorry. Is Sheba recovered?"

"Yes. We never talked much about it before, and we don't talk much about it now. She wasn't very far along, and neither one of us had ever given much thought to being parents. We were just starting to adjust to the idea when she lost the baby. It was a sudden thing. Scared the hell out of me, to tell the truth, but Sheba's back to painting, and we picked up our life where we left off without much fuss."

"But still," I said.

John met my gaze and nodded slightly. "Yes. But still."

He took a quiet breath. "It seems like a good time to take a break from New Hope and see something of the world. Sheba will be beside herself at the idea of meeting Mary Cassatt in the flesh, and all I want to do is make Sheba happy."

"Are *you* happy, John? With marriage, I mean, and settling down in a place as respectable as New Hope?" Knowing him, I couldn't quite see it, but he didn't hesitate.

"I am. Happier than I ever expected to be and sure enough happier than I deserve. Sheba means the world to me, and I wouldn't change one thing about my life with her. Not one." Except the baby, I thought, feeling a tug of quick compassion for this cool, contained man. You'd change that if you could. I understood the feeling well enough.

I studied John's face a while, gauged his expression and his tone, and then asked, "When do you need me to show up?" His unusually tentative smile broadened into a grin.

"In about two weeks. I'll contact the steamship company to reserve tickets out of New York as soon as I'm back in New Hope and then wire you with the details. I expect we'll be gone a while. At least three months. Do I need to talk to Sam Gast about this?" His words made me raise an eyebrow.

"I have a voice and a mind of my own. I'm sure I can manage a conversation with Mr. Gast without your assistance, but thank you for the offer," my tone mild enough, but something in my voice or eyes made him flush. He's a swarthy-complexioned man, but there was no missing the rose color that crept up his cheeks.

"I only meant—" He gave a quick bark of laughter. "I'd better be quiet before I get myself into more trouble. When Sheba uses that tone with me, I know I've opened my big mouth too quick or too often, though she tends to be more direct in her comments." Something about his rueful good humor made me laugh, too.

"You wire me when you want me to come, and I'll be there. I promise," I said.

"That's a relief. Thank you, Caro. I've got a big meeting of Colorado cattlemen and Chicago meat packers scheduled at Bliss House in February that I worked hard to set up, and I'm glad I won't have to cancel it. The Merchants' Association has already begun plans for the arrival of all those important honchos. They're some of the richest men in the country, and New Hope believes they're bound to leave some of their money behind when they leave. I don't trust anyone else but you to keep Bliss House running smooth and steady." Hearing his description of the February meeting, I felt a rush of energy and anticipation, suddenly very glad I had agreed to the request. A stay in New Hope, Nebraska, could prove to be more profitable than I had first thought. Standing, I placed my hand lightly on his shoulder.

"You're a good man, John Bliss. I can still recall the glow on Sheba's face the day you two came to tell me you were wed. It was clear as could be that she wouldn't have any other man but you. Smart woman, that Sheba." I didn't give him time to respond but walked away to find Sam Gast and fill him in on my change of plans for the next few months.

Two weeks later, I boarded the east bound train for New Hope. A smarter woman than Lot's wife, I didn't waste my time on a backward glance at Ogalalla. I had lived there for four years, but it was never home to me, only a means to an end, and an unsuccessful means at that. I was hopeful that the next few months in New Hope would offer a more satisfying experience than all the years I spent in Ogalalla.

Both John and his wife waited for me on the platform when I stepped off the train in New Hope. They were a striking pair and impossible to miss, even with a throng of people hurrying around me, passengers stepping down from or up into the train, others waiting in anticipation for or waving goodbye to someone in particular. Quite a hubbub but not unpleasant. Unlike Ogallala, the pace of New Hope, Nebraska, had not slowed down as winter approached. It was a town continually on the move, progressive and thriving. I could feel its vigorous good health and welcoming nature all around me.

"Hello, Caroline," greeted Sheba Bliss, extending a bare hand toward me in the energetic, purposeful way that defined her nature. At our first meeting just over a year ago, I had recognized Sheba Fenway, as she was then, as a force of nature, a woman impossible to ignore or miss, nothing traditionally beautiful about her but the sum of her parts breathtaking, nevertheless. A fine-boned face all angles and planes, startling blue eyes, and a crown of luxurious hair the deep red color of oak leaves in autumn. No wonder that John hadn't been able to take his eyes off her at the time. Clearly, even after a year of marriage, he remained just as smitten because it took him a moment to shift his gaze away from Sheba and in my general direction.

"Hello, Sheba," I replied, returning her firm grasp. "It's good to see you. You look wonderful." In truth, she did look wonderful. If John hadn't told me of her recent loss, I would never have guessed. "Hello, John," I added as afterthought. He grinned and reached for my bags.

"Never mind me," he said. "You two go on ahead to the restaurant. I'll drop these off at home and meet you there." Sheba and I walked east along the platform as John hefted my bags and turned in the opposite direction.

"It looks like New Hope's thriving," I observed as we stepped onto the boardwalk that led into town, passing first the livery with its side extension that housed the fire engine and then the Variety and Grocery Store. The late afternoon hour, dimming daylight, and cold air had not slowed traffic. Several people exited and entered the grocery store and the post and telegraph office directly across the street.

"Yes, it is." I detected satisfaction in her tone but something less enthusiastic, too.

"A steady flow of business makes everybody happy," I said. "No one I know sneers at prosperity." We continued walking south toward Bliss House, John's elegant and very successful hotel and restaurant.

"No one's sneering," Sheba said. She sent me a sidelong glance. "But the passengers stepping off the Union Pacific don't always have New Hope's best interests in mind. There have been a few individuals John's had to escort straight from the Music Hall to the train station for an immediate and forceful change of locale. It's either that or get our marshal involved, but John prefers not to bother Si if he doesn't have to. Usually John's strongly-worded suggestion that the fellow in question move along to another town on the rail line is all that's needed. It doesn't hurt that New Hope is such a peaceful, understanding, and generous community that the Merchants' Association sometimes volunteers to pay for the train ticket out of town."

The words made me smile. "Ogallala gets those same kinds of visitors, but we tend to welcome them and invite them to stay a while. You recall the general kind of business and entertainments Ogallala offers its visitors." Sheba opened the door to the restaurant and motioned me to enter before her.

"I do, indeed." A pause and then a thoughtful observation, "Maybe we should concentrate on buying farewell tickets that go west as far as Ogallala from now on."

"New Hope's loss being Ogallala's gain, you mean."

Sheba met my look and laughed. "It seems like a practical solution, Caroline, but I can't tell if you approve or not so I won't suggest it in the near future. With Christmas close, the Merchants' Association has other things on its mind, anyway."

From there the conversation moved on to city holiday festivities and Sheba's own travel plans and how surprised she'd been when John proposed a trip to Paris. Her voice softened when she said her husband's name, and I was satisfied to see the same deep feeling I had detected on John's face earlier as we stood on the train platform now mirrored in Sheba's eyes. They'll be all right, I thought, because two people who care so forthrightly for each other can weather anything.

John joined us for dinner and when we finished, Sheba excused herself from the tour of Bliss House her husband suggested.

"John says you're willing to stay in our home while we're gone, Caroline, so I'll make sure your room is warm and see you at home later." She smiled a pleasant good night to me and gave her husband a quick kiss to the cheek, something very natural and appealing in the gesture. To John, Sheba said in a low voice, "Caroline's been traveling all afternoon and would no doubt appreciate her rest so don't keep her too long. You'll have more than enough time to get her settled tomorrow." John and I watched Sheba as she sailed through the dining room and pushed open the door, letting in a small swirl of cold air as she exited. Then he took me by the elbow and steered me toward the kitchen.

"Sheba's right," John said, "so I'll make it a quick look-around. I'm curious how much you remember from your stay a few years ago. How many years has it been?"

"Four," I said, and added, "I remember quite a bit, John, but not this kitchen. Bliss House must be doing even better than I thought. You've updated nearly everything since I was here last."

"About a year and a half ago I managed to tempt one of Fred Harvey's cooks away from him, but part of the arrangement was that the man would be able to cook on the finest appliances money could buy." John gave me a quick grin. “And I still got the better of the deal. I’ve had more than one traveler tell me that the meal they had at Bliss House outdid anything they had at any Harvey House.” I could tell the comparison pleased him and saw that the John Bliss of ten years ago, a man supremely arrogant, confident, and competitive, might have mellowed with time and circumstance but had not disappeared entirely. He always expected to succeed, which was probably why he always did.

From the dining room, we moved through the arched doorway into the hotel’s lobby, an inviting space with two of Sheba’s paintings showing to advantage, one on the wall directly across from the door that led outside so the painting would be the first thing a person would see upon entering and the other painting opposite a comfortable arrangement of stuffed chairs in a waiting area off to the side of the foyer. It’s difficult to describe Sheba’s work. Stirring. Sparkling. Brilliant. Uncommon. All of that and more. She’s very talented. John followed my gaze to the painting on the wall near the entryway but made no comment.

“I never quite know what to say when I see Sheba’s work,” I told him. “It’s so unexpected and so beautiful.”

“Yes.” A single syllable of quiet pride. I wondered what it would be like to love someone possessed of such a gift and passion. Did John ever begrudge his wife her painting? He said he was happy and he appeared to be, but I thought it must be humbling in its own way for him to share his wife’s affections and time with something, with anything, in which he played no part. I didn’t believe the John Bliss I had known ten years ago would have settled for it, but, of course, time and love change all of us, with or without our consent.

After a quick introduction to the young man behind the hotel counter, John and I went outside, took a quick look through the front door of the Music Hall, a place as bright and loud as Bliss House was subdued and elegant, and then made our way north up Main Street to the big house where John and Sheba lived. The night sky was black as coal, the air nipped by winter's approach. The house itself sat in splendor so far back from the street that we had to go down an alley next to the freight office to reach the porch. At night and from a distance, the house reminded me of one of Sheba's paintings: imposing and inviting and lit from within.

"Sheba must be in her studio," John said when I remarked on the brightly lit second story, but when he opened the front door and stepped back for me to enter the house, his wife stood waiting for us at the foot of the stairs.

"Would you like a cup of tea before I take you to your room?" she asked me.

I shook my head. "No, thank you. I think I'm ready to turn in."

"This way, then."

Behind us, John murmured a quiet good night and drifted down the hallway as I followed Sheba upstairs. We passed what I knew must be her studio from the subdued smells of turpentine and paint coming through the partly open door and stopped at the third door down on the opposite side. The room Sheba showed me was warmly inviting, lamplit and made comfortable by a crackling blaze in the fireplace.

"Right next door is the water closet," Sheba said, "indoors and for my money the best invention in the history of mankind." I laughed at the enthusiasm in her voice but didn't argue. "And next to that is John's and my room. No doubt you figured out where I paint when we passed the door to my studio. If there's anything you need, please don't hesitate to knock and ask. John's study is downstairs, not to mention a kitchen, dining room, and parlor we never use. If you wake in the night and want to go exploring, feel free."

"It's more house than I expected," I said. "I'm used to two rooms and a single toilet shared by others on the floor."

Sheba nodded. "I know. I felt the same at first. It took some getting used to, but it's home now." I wanted to tell her that home had much more to do with the people you shared your life with than the size and shape of the building you lived in, but I didn't speak my thoughts. Perhaps she heard them, anyway, because she gave a small smile and added, "Well, wherever John is would be home. He's the only man I value more than an indoor toilet, and that's no small praise." I laughed out loud at that, and Sheba joined in. She may have experienced a recent heartache, I thought, but Sheba Bliss is still a happy woman, and I was glad for John's sake.

"Sleep as late as you like and wander down for breakfast whenever you choose. I like to catch the early morning light so I'll be working, and John is usually off to the hotel first thing to make sure it was a quiet night. We have a woman who comes in to cook five mornings a week, and I've asked her to keep everything warm for you. John and I like to breakfast together, but after that we catch our meals as we can, and honestly, Caroline, why would any woman slave over a hot stove for three meals a day when her husband owns a restaurant with the finest chef north of the Platte? I can paint with acceptable skill, but I couldn't cook a full meal if my life depended on it."

Sheba paused, her expression sheepish enough that I thought she wasn't exaggerating about the cooking. After a moment she shrugged, dismissed that particular defect – if defect it was – and gave me a look I couldn't fully read, a touch of discomfort on her face mixed with a hesitant shyness. Unusual for Sheba Fenway Bliss, who never seemed self-conscious and was as far from shy as a person could be.

"Thank you for agreeing to this. John wouldn't have gone otherwise, and I want—" To go to Paris, I thought she'd say or, I want to see a little of the world, but that wasn't what she said, at all. "I want John to have a little time away from New Hope. It's our home, and we love it, but lately I've felt my husband might benefit from a change of scenery. He has a lot on his mind. Too much. New experiences and new ideas will be good for him. So thank you."

"You're welcome," I said. "I'm happy I could do it. New experiences and ideas might be good for me, too."

We said good night and I shut the door of my room, unpacked my bags, then stepped next door to wash my hands in Sheba's pride and joy. Hot water from a tap really was a luxury! I'd have to find out exactly how it worked before John and Sheba left on their trip in case it needed repairs in their absence because I could tell it wouldn't take long for me to get used to the indulgence of indoor plumbing and ready hot water. With December as close as it was, I looked forward to thumbing my nose at an outdoor privy and the need to boil water on the stove just to wash my hands.

Lying in bed, I thought about the bond between two people who loved each other, who mourned but believed that keeping their grief to themselves was doing the other a kindness. The trip away from New Hope was a good idea because it would give John and Sheba time for each other away from the many distractions with which they surrounded themselves. Surrounded themselves on purpose, I guessed. Grief buried deep inside, grief unshared and hidden away from the world had the same ability to roar up and consume as the undoused embers of a fire. After so many years of contained and nurtured grief, I had forgotten what happiness felt like, what it looked like. There's little enough joy to go around in this wide world, I thought. I hope John and Sheba can find some of their own on their trip to Paris. I fell asleep to the comforting and familiar snap of flames in the fireplace.

2

A small group of New Hope residents waved their goodbyes to John and Sheba Bliss from the New Hope train platform Monday afternoon. I was there, too, but not waving because I had my hands tucked securely into my coat pockets. The weather had turned cold, a warning of the months to come and a kindly reminder from Mother Nature to get ready for a Nebraska winter.

Before taking her husband's hand as support on the steps that led up to the train car, Sheba bent down to plant a kiss on the forehead of a young boy standing in front of her and then stood upright again long enough to rest her cheek briefly against the cheek of the woman who waited beside the boy. From a distance, the two women looked very similar, especially that rich auburn-red hair. Sheba's sister, I realized, and felt something of a shock. I'd known that woman in a different time and place, but she had disappeared one night and because I feared it might open a wound for Sheba, I never asked John and certainly not his wife if they ever found where she'd run to. Now I knew. Right here in New Hope. I'd never have guessed that the woman she'd been would settle in little New Hope. She hadn't run all that far after all. And the boy must be

Sheba's nephew, the child mentioned to me in passing with the affection and pride of a devoted aunt.

With the Blisses gone from view and the train beginning its measured exit from the station, the gathering of people on the platform scattered.

Sheba's sister stopped in front of me long enough to smile and say, "Hello, Caroline."

"Florence," I said, scrambling for a name and coming up with it at the last minute.

But the woman shook her head and smiled again. "No. I was never Florence, not really. I'm Dee Gruber now, and there's nobody else I'd rather be." She looked content and happy. "I hope you'll like New Hope. It's a place that lets a woman alone so she can find herself. That's how it's been for me, anyway. Maybe we can find time for a visit while you're here."

"I'd like that," I said, but we never did. I think Dee was working hard at putting her past behind her and I was a small part of that past. I understood only too well how hard it was to move forward if a person dragged the past along behind her.

As I watched Dee Gruber and her son walk hand-in-hand back toward town, Benny Tidwell, the manager of John's Music Hall, stopped beside me and with an audible sigh said, "It's up to us now, Mrs. Moore."

"Caroline, please," I said, "and the way John sang your praises, it sounded like you knew the business as well as he did. You'll do fine."

Benny was a small, wiry, man at least fifteen years my senior with shrewd eyes and a pair of impressive sideburns that met almost at his chin. He hadn't been in New Hope during my first stay four years earlier, yet I had the impression that he and John shared a history that went well into the past. Not as far back as John and I went, maybe, but several years.

"I expect I will. Since the wedding, John's mind hasn't

been on business the way it used to be. Not that I'd expect anything different from a man newly wed, of course."

"You're not married yourself, Benny?" He shook his head, not nearly as regretful as he'd like me to believe.

"Me? Oh no, ma'am. That wasn't in the cards for Benny Tidwell." At my curious look, he gave a quick grin. "I gambled for a living, Caroline. I mean it when I say it wasn't in the cards." The look of mischief on his face made me laugh as we turned to walk back toward Bliss House.

"Someone's loss was my gain, then," I said. "I'm sure I'll have a lot of questions for you in the weeks ahead. This big gathering of cattlemen and meat packers seemed to mean a lot to John. It's in February, as I recall."

"Yes, ma'am. Last week of the month. Quite the accomplishment for little New Hope to host it, and that's all due to John." He started to expand on the comment but was interrupted by someone calling my name from behind us. Benny and I both looked over our shoulders at the same time.

"Ruth Carpenter," he said. "Did the two of you already meet?"

"Yes, briefly. I got the impression she and Sheba were close."

He gave my remark a thought and nodded. "That's true, I guess, though they're different as night and day. You need anything, you just ask. Between the two of us, I imagine we can keep the Bliss enterprises from going belly-up."

I had to laugh again at his wry tone. "Let's hope so."

He gave a nod and walked quickly away. From what I'd seen in the past few days, Benny Tidwell seemed to do everything quickly. Easy to understand why John trusted him.

I stood on the boardwalk and waited for Ruth Carpenter to catch up with me. The autumn air had nipped her cheeks with pink and added an icy sparkle to her green eyes. I'd never seen a real emerald, but from descriptions I had read,

I thought that Ruth's eyes on a cold day would compare favorably with that jewel.

"I didn't have the heart to interrupt you these past days, Caroline, with John lecturing you like a schoolmaster about ledgers and menus and credit lines, but I promised Sheba I'd make it a point to let you know I was available if you needed anything, even if it's only a listening ear. You may not remember me from your first stay in New Hope."

"You were Ruth Churchill when I was here last."

"Then you must have left town before the bad business we had with Emmett Wolf."

"I left in February of '78."

Ruth nodded. "That was right before the trouble. You were fortunate not to be involved. It was a difficult time. Poor Eddie Barts." Her face, still and grave for a moment, brightened. "But Pastor Shulte always says that God can bring good from bad, and that's what happened. For me, anyway, though not for poor Mrs. Barts, God rest her soul. She took the loss of her son to her grave, but I met my husband because of it, so at least in my case what Pastor Shulte said proved true."

"You think there's some kind of divine balance sheet, then, of good and evil in the world?" I watched her face as she considered my words.

"I do." She emphasized the first word to show she would understand if I didn't. Perhaps my skepticism showed on my face. "The idea is a comfort to me, but I can't speak for anyone else." Her tone picked up, brisker, less serious. "Anyway, I wanted you to know that if there's anything I can do to help you settle in, you only need to ask. And you know my husband heads the town's constabulary—" she waited for my confirming nod "— so don't hesitate to let him know if there's anything that makes you uneasy or concerned. My husband's a good man and John's friend. You can trust him."

"Thank you," I said.

Ruth pulled her heavy shawl tighter around her shoulders. "That's winter breathing down our necks," she said of the breeze that had picked up. "Lucky you to be able to take advantage of Sheba's indoor plumbing." Did the whole town know about it, I wondered. Should I expect people to quiz me about how much I was enjoying my toilet? The idea almost made me giggle, though I was long past giggling age. Ruth Carpenter must have caught something of my thoughts, however, because she grinned. I'll have to be careful around this woman, I thought. She's too observant by half.

"Sheba's not one to stay silent about her enthusiasms," Ruth told me by way of explanation, "but only to her family and closest friends. I promise no one will ask you how you're enjoying indoor plumbing. The citizens of New Hope aren't perfect, but most of us try to maintain the common courtesies with each other." She leaned forward to add in a low voice, "Except for Cap Sherman, the old reprobate who runs the livery. He doesn't care what he says so just ignore him if he says something impertinent. That's what the rest of us do." I thanked her for the information and for her kind offer, and we said our goodbyes.

Ruth Carpenter – Ruth Churchill, as she had been known five years ago – was one of those rare people who radiated a kind of transparent, natural goodness. From my recollection of that earlier time, she had been a more subdued woman then, her smile dimmer with a touch of sadness at the back of her eyes. She'd been a young widow and no doubt still grieving at the time. The new husband had brought about subtle changes in her appearance, a reflection of the changes in her heart, I supposed. For a moment, I felt a sharp pang of some emotion. Was it envy or anger or simply a new take on an old grief? Nothing welcome or comfortable, that was certain, and I shook off the feeling. I had tasks I wanted to begin immediately: hotel reservations to approve, menus to acquaint myself with, workers to schedule, and that was only the beginning. I would be busy for weeks learning the details of Bliss House that John hadn't found the time to mention, and keeping busy was what I did best.

I had managed Ogallala House for four years, so it wasn't as if I was unfamiliar with what it took to keep a hotel or restaurant running smoothly, but where Ogallala House was one building of moderate size that contained both hotel and restaurant, each also of moderate size, John Bliss's businesses were two large, imposing, and individual buildings. There were elegant pillars and a covered porch at the entrance to the three-story hotel and heavy double doors flanked by wide, curtained windows at the front of the restaurant. Inside, an arched doorway connected the two establishments.

On my way to John's office, I stopped long enough to greet the young man standing behind the counter.

"Is there anything I need to know, Les?" My standard question to anyone who worked for me. Why shouldn't people be allowed to use their own brains, ideas, and talents? There was nothing wrong with failing now and again, either. How else do we learn? Besides, Les Woodson had worked the front desk of Bliss House for the last two years. What was I going to tell him on my first day that he didn't already know?

"No, ma'am. We checked in three people from the last train."

"We're not fully booked, though."

"Oh no, ma'am. Not today. Plenty of room for the last train of the day, which is where we get a lot of our business." I nodded. Another particle of information I needed to stow away.

"I'll be in the back," I told Les. He was a pleasant-faced young man, who seemed to enjoy being a part of Bliss House and I was curious enough about him to ask, "John said you've been here two years, Les. Are you from New

Hope?"

"No, ma'am. I was passing through is all, looking for something, I couldn't tell you exactly what now, but something, a place to settle and fit in, I guess. My pa farms north, outside of Bassett, and I knew that wasn't for me, but I wasn't ready for the big cities, either. I heard that New Hope was a place on the rise so I thought I'd take a look, and I guess I was in the right place at the right time. Mr. Bliss was looking for someone to run the front desk, and there I was, just the man for the job."

He seemed endearing and awfully young to me all of a sudden, proud of having a job that demanded he wear a long-sleeved shirt and necktie.

"Mr. Bliss seems to think he's the lucky one," I responded, "He couldn't pay you enough compliments." Les's ears turned a rosy pink and he seemed tongue-tied at the words, further testimony to his youth,

"I'll be in the office, Les, and then I'll take a stroll to the kitchen to see how our cook is holding up."

"Chef," said Les.

"I beg your pardon."

"If you call Mr. Clermont a cook, he'll tell you in no uncertain terms that cooks are for cowboys. He is a chef. Chefs have a long tradition of refined elegance and superior taste—" I enjoyed the slight French accent Les gave to his words; apparently he was quoting directly from Mr. Clermont, "—and must never be confused with cooks."

"Well," I said, "thank you for the warning. John forgot to tell me that important fact. I will do my best to address Mr. Clermont with the respect due a man of his elegant and superior skills." The two of us grinned at each other, and I walked past him toward the office located along the small hallway at the rear of the hotel.

Emil Clermont, a stout man wearing the finest mustache I had ever seen, inclined his head slightly when I eventually entered the kitchen, bestowing permission with a generosity he clearly doubted I deserved.

"Monsieur Clermont," I said by way of greeting. My use of the French address went a long way in assuring him I was worthy of entrance into his personal domain.

"Madame," he replied, acknowledging my presence with another nod.

"I have no desire to interfere with your kitchen," I assured him. "None at all. Mr. Bliss told me there was no need for me to be involved in the running of the kitchen," — not exactly what John had said, but close enough — "but I hope you will allow me to continue the regular weekly meeting you had with Mr. Bliss. I can't think of any easier way to keep up the reputation of the Bliss House restaurant."

Clermont, who had spoken only the one *Madame* since I entered the kitchen, gave a final nod, not a man to begrudge a woman a favor, no matter how unreasonable her request might be.

"Yes, madame, if that is what you wish."

I smiled. "Thank you, Monsieur. Does Wednesday morning remain convenient?"

"Yes, madame."

"Good. I look forward to Wednesday morning and, of course, if you need anything – anything, at all – in the meanwhile, I am at your disposal."

"And I yours, madame," but by that time the expression on Emil Clermont's face said he wished nothing more from me than a hasty exit from his kitchen.

Handling men, I thought as I walked through the dining area that was quickly filling with customers, is the same regardless of their country, language, or age: simply let them think they're the ones in charge and then do exactly as you please. It had been so even with John Bliss for all the years I'd known him, but I thought perhaps living with Sheba had softened his inclination to think he was always right. Love will do that, and there was no doubt that John

Bliss loved his wife. John had once played a grim role in my life, but I knew he carried a weight of regret on his heart that he wasn't likely to lose for a very long while, if ever, and I liked his wife, besides. Sheba was a woman surprised by love and still trying to figure out the changes that marriage had brought.

I made myself banish other memories: a cold Wyoming winter warmed by love and laughter, a man's touch and a feeling of belonging I had never known before. Looking back, I thought that time in my life had happened to a woman I couldn't recognize and didn't know. Now was not the time to indulge in memories, anyway, whether painful or happy, because I had a hotel and restaurant to run and once I was confident in my abilities to do that, I could concentrate on a long overdue reckoning. Settling old accounts was the only way I knew to quench the fire that was my constant companion.

New Hope, Nebraska, bustles at a steady pace. It's a community that shares only one common element with Ogallala, Nebraska, and that is being located in the same state. Other than that, the two towns are as different as night and day, quite literally in some respects. Where Ogallala's enterprises begin to drift toward sleep around sunrise after a night full of entertainment, revelry, and vice, New Hope's enterprises begin to unfurl along with the sun. Signs turn to *open* on the door, shades are raised and curtains pulled, and Harold Sellers and Cap Sherman, two confirmed bachelors, take their regular morning walks – always separately because the two men aren't friends – past the hotel's front windows on their way to breakfast at Ezzie Liggett's Nebraska Café located at the far south end of Main Street. At first amused, I eventually came to appreciate a routine that worked with the precision of a fine old clock. Years before I had worked in Virginia City during the silver boom and at an establishment along the railroad outside of Denver, both busy, clanging places where every night differed from the night before and nothing ever slowed down. New Hope was my first experience with an ordinary schedule among ordinary people. Almost my entire life had been far from ordinary, and I was surprised by how much I enjoyed the daytime pace. Because the last train of the day pulled out of New Hope in the early evening, the restaurant closed at nine and for all intents and purposes the hotel did the same, with everyone booked in that wanted to be booked in. I adopted the habit of making a final round of both establishments, a good night to the kitchen and table girls as they dressed for the walk home, wherever home might be, a final conversation with Kip Messerschmidt, who would man the hotel desk for the night – I should say *boy* the desk because he wasn't yet sixteen – and a stop at the jail on my own walk home to let the deputy on duty, usually Lucas Morgan, the senior deputy marshal, know that all was quiet in the hotel and restaurant, and I was done for the day. Lucas was serious but pleasant, a man a person could turn over the care of a whole town to and then sleep like a baby, knowing you had left the place in good and competent hands.

Not that I slept like a baby all that often. It took me a while to get used to living in that big house all by myself when I was more used to Lucas's life, a single room and my meals at whatever café or restaurant I could afford at the time. I don't believe there was a single night in November that year that I didn't brew myself a cup of tea, pull back the curtains of the parlor's front window, and sit in the darkened room looking out at the night. There's not much to see from the parlor window: the back of the Western Union Telegraph Office, the double doors of the Freight Office warehouse, and the black hole of the alley that ran between them. Still, on a clear night the stars shone like a thousand lights in the expanse of the black Nebraska sky and sometimes, if the weather allowed it, the moon looked right back at me, which always helped to calm my restless thoughts. I found comfort, too, in the picture of Lucas Morgan making his faithful walk down Main Street, keeping a lid on the activities at John Bliss's Music Hall until the place shut down for the night, checking the alleys for shadows that didn't belong there, moving with his easy stride from store front to store front, New Hope's private guardian angel. He was training a new young deputy, too, and sometimes two of them made the rounds. All the better, I thought. All the safer.

I met Ruby Strunk the very first morning after John and Sheba had left for Paris. Frightened the bejeebers out of her, in fact, or so she told me.

"Good lord," Ruby said once she caught her breath. "You gave me a scare, Mrs. Moore. There's never anyone in the kitchen when I come in. To tell the truth, there's never anyone in the kitchen ever. Sheba always says she has an aversion to the kitchen, that's the word she uses: *aversion.* I tell her it's a good thing her husband owns a restaurant, then, because while most women could probably work up an aversion –" Ruby gave the word an amused twist "– to their own kitchens if they were allowed to, we'd have nothing but starving families roaming the streets of New Hope." Her tone made me laugh.

"I'm sorry I scared you," I said, "and it's Caroline, not Mrs. Moore. I'm not a late sleeper and I like my cup of tea first thing." I lifted a biscuit off a plate on the table. "Did you make these?"

She nodded. "Sheba and John like to take their breakfast together later in the morning, and they're partial to my baking. Neither of them's a heavy eater. Living on love, I suppose."

The light-hearted words surprised me, and I caught

Ruby's quick grin.

"It's true," she went on, "though Sheba's not a woman given to sentiment." Ruby walked past me and reached for the skillet on the counter by the stove. "Those two were meant to be together. I've known Sheba a long time, before she was married or ever thought about it, and there's no man but John Bliss she ever gave a second look to in all the years she ran that dress shop of hers. And him, well, when Sheba's around, it's like no one else is in the room."

"Still newlyweds," I said. "I wouldn't expect anything different."

"I suppose that's it. Would you like something hot for breakfast? I can have hotcakes on the table before you know it," the discussion about John and Sheba Bliss finished. I thought Ruby's loyalty to the Blisses wouldn't allow any further comments, and I approved. I was a stranger to Ruby Strunk, sitting in her kitchen for a few months and then gone. Her true allegiance lay with John and Sheba.

I started to say hotcakes weren't necessary, but I changed my mind and said, "Hotcakes sound fine, Ruby. Thank you."

She gave me a slight smile as she tied her apron around her waist, turned to the stove, and reached for the can of shortening.

"Have you met my oldest boy yet?" she asked, still with her back to me. She set the skillet on the flame and scooped lard into the frying pan, then spooned flour into a large bowl and reached for the milk jug.

I stopped to think before answering. "I don't recall so. Should I have?"

"Henry works for Mr. Bliss before and after school. Usually in the restaurant kitchen, but he does whatever needs doing. He's a good boy."

"I'll probably see him today then," I said. "What time does school start?"

"Eight o'clock sharp. Mr. Stenton is a punctual man. Teaches those children more than just book learning. He says good habits are what make a person successful in the long run, and I don't disagree. I don't mind that Henry struggles with his studies as long as Mr. Stenton continues to improve the boy's character. A book education is all well and good, but it's a man's character that makes the difference."

"Sheba mentioned that Mr. Stenton was the schoolteacher," I said. "She seemed to hold him in high regard."

"I don't know anybody who doesn't. Some people don't take to him right off. He can seem a little stern sometimes, but he's a good man and New Hope's lucky to have him. We got ourselves a fine preacher and a fine teacher and probably the best two lawmen in Nebraska watching out for us. That's what makes New Hope a cut above any of our neighbors." By then I could hear the sizzle of the hotcakes in the skillet. Ruby sent me a slight, sly smile over her shoulder. "Even a cut above Ogallala, I bet." I didn't bother to argue. She was right, after all.

"Oh, *especially* above Ogallala," I said, "and more than just a cut." Ruby slid two golden hotcakes onto my plate.

"Honey or cinnamon sugar?"

I was growing accustomed to Ruby's habit of changing the subject without warning and said, "Cinnamon sugar. Is there butter?" She had it all on the table in a moment and after that, conversation declined. Ruby reached for the flour again, raised cinnamon rolls on the menu as I would find out the following morning. After a little while, I finished my hotcakes, refused her offer of numbers three and four, thanked her, and left her to her baking.

Over time I came to look forward to Ruby's arrival Monday through Friday mornings like clockwork. I told her that three days a week would be enough for me, but she stopped what she was doing and faced me.

"John paid me for five days a week through April, and I won't abuse his trust."

"All right," I said, "Five days it is, then." Not just a loyal woman but an honest one, too. Something else I approved of.

When I walked down the alley toward the street, ready to start my day at the hotel, it was often about the time the whistle of the first train of the day announced its approach. The Union Pacific was New Hope's lifeblood, and the town's residents held train whistles in the same reverence as the sound of a ringing church bell. No one ever complained about the racket of the engine or the rattle of the tracks. Music, not racket, to everyone's ears.

From the start, I made it my practice to get to the hotel with enough time to speak to young Kip before he headed home after his nighttime desk duty.

"Did you have a quiet night?" I would ask, and almost always Kip's response was, "Yes, ma'am. Quiet as a cat."

The hotel had a resident cat, a brown tabby with golden eyes that the girls called Gypsy, and Gypsy could startle me with her quiet – padding without a sound into my office and up onto the corner of the desk without so much as a rustle of warning – so Kip's answer made good sense. The few times it wasn't a quiet night, a guest taken ill or someone coming from the Music Hall a little worse for wear and needing help to his room, Kip would adjust his reply to, "Almost quiet as a cat," the additional word a signal for me to ask more questions. An unsettled night was a rare occurrence, however, in my months at New Hope. Something else to chalk up to the quiet presence of a pair of law officers whose reputation was well-known throughout Nebraska. Marshal Carpenter, I had been told, was highly respected by the governor, both the man soon to leave office and the newly elected Governor Dawes. Keep the citizens safe, the money secure, the railroads happy. Marshal Carpenter did it all and then some. New Hope was in good hands as was Nebraska.

When Kip headed home, Les Woodson showed up at the front desk exactly when the first train of the day was unloading its passengers onto the platform. People would soon be checking into and out of the hotel, and Les was the best at room entrances and exits. He arranged them like stage plays that I had no role in, so once Les and I exchanged morning greetings, I moved to the kitchen, greeted Monsieur Clermont and young Klaus Fenstermeier, the chef's apprentice, and ensured that the girls scheduled to wait tables and wash dishes had all turned up before I drifted back to the office. There was usually something waiting for me on the desk to occupy my time – changes to the regular menu, the daily list of hotel customers, invoice payments, bills of lading, and the like – but by and large, John Bliss's enterprises were organized and efficient. Perhaps that was to John's credit, but I thought it was due as much to the inhabitants of New Hope, who realized that when the hotel was full and the hum of conversation in the restaurant was loud, then business must be good. And business being good was always in New Hope's best interests. In general, it was a community made up of open-minded, ambitious, and intelligent people who enjoyed hearing the wheels of progress rumble firmly down Main Street.

3

I missed meeting young Henry Strunk that morning, no doubt because I lingered too long over his mother's tender hotcakes, but caught up with him in the afternoon.

The Bliss Restaurant served supper continuously for roughly five hours. The layovers of the last eastbound and westbound trains were long enough to allow passengers to walk to the Bliss Restaurant, order, eat, and make it back to the train before it departed, with digestion taking place somewhere between New Hope and the next stop. Fred Harvey would eventually perfect the practice of providing tasty and timely meals to train passengers served by friendly young women in genteel surroundings and all of it done in accord with the local railway schedule, but the workings of Bliss House and the quality of its food were as efficient and welcoming as any Harvey House would ever be.

One of young Henry's tasks was to whisk the used dishes off the table so the girls could give the cloth a quick shake before the next guests took those seats. Everything done with a smile, of course, and fresh coffee always arriving before a lady had time to remove her gloves.

By eight o'clock, business had slowed enough for me to

seek out Henry in the kitchen where he bent over a tub of soapy water and carefully washed plates, cups, and utensils. When I said his name, he looked up as if surprised to find himself washing dishes in a kitchen. I recognized the expression: the boy's mind had been wandering far afield from New Hope, Nebraska, even as his hands scrubbed away at the hotel china.

"Yes, ma'am?"

"I'm Mrs. Moore," I said, "and this morning your mother mentioned in passing that you worked at the restaurant after school. I wanted to be sure to meet you."

"Yes, ma'am," Henry repeated. No question this time but still a touch of inquiry in his tone.

"When do you have time to get your studies done," I asked, "or doesn't Mr. Stenton give overnight assignments?"

"Not very often to me. On an ordinary day, I get everything done in school, and if I think I'll need a little more time, I use lunch time."

"And if it's not an ordinary day?" I liked the look of the young fellow, fourteen his mother said, the oldest of seven and since his father's death the man of the Strunk house. Henry pulled his shoulders back like a soldier standing at attention.

"I always have my assignments done on time, Mrs. Moore. Always. Mr. Stenton says men are judged successful when they meet their obligations, and I plan to be successful with my life." Then he squinted at me, which spoiled the effect of his firm declaration, ran a soapy hand across his forehead, and said, "Mr. Stenton believes I have promise," the words and their tone displaying a confidence that if Mr. Stenton said it was so, that's the way it was.

Looking at the boy, short like his mother and lanky, with a face nowhere near fourteen, I found myself agreeing with Mr. Stenton. For some reason, whether from Henry's posture or tone or expression, I believed he did have promise, squint and all.

"Well, I won't keep you," I said. "It was good to meet you, Henry. You'll let me know if you need anything, won't you?"

Henry narrowed his eyes at me as if testing my sincerity before answering, "Yes, ma'am, I will, but I don't need anything except to get these last dishes done and dried." I took the hint and left him to his work.

I wouldn't have given much thought to that first conversation with Henry Strunk except within a week Darla Jones, one of the restaurant's morning girls, stood in the office doorway holding an empty plate in one hand and an empty bowl in the other. The girl said my name and as soon as I looked up from the account book on the desk, she stepped into the office.

Darla seemed a pleasant young woman, the oldest child on her parents' farm and a good worker, quick and alert. She looked slightly uncomfortable as she stood in front of the desk, as if suddenly unsure what to say or at least how to say it, so I tried to help her along.

"Hello. It's Darla Jones, isn't it?" I asked. "I'm still trying to learn everyone's names," which wasn't true because I have a good memory and make it a habit to learn all the names and backgrounds of the people I work with as quickly as possible. By then, I knew the names and faces of every worker at both the restaurant and the hotel. In the past, however, I'd found that people were more comfortable and apt to talk if they thought I was more ignorant than I actually was and at Darla's silence decided that pretending to be something I wasn't might help move this particular conversation along.

"Sit down, won't you?" I invited, then added when she still hesitated, "It looks like you have something you want to show me."

"Yes." Darla was relieved that I had started the conversation in the right direction and sat down at the edge of the chair before carefully placing the plate and bowl on the desktop. "Look at this, will you?"

I gave her a puzzled look, then picked up the bowl with both hands and examined it before I picked up the plate and did the same. When I looked up, she was eyeing my face carefully, apparently hoping that she wouldn't have to point out the obvious.

"Oh, dear," I said. "We wouldn't want to set these down in front of a diner, would we?" Both dishes had small speckles of dried food on them. An unappetizing sight. They must have been washed, just not washed very well.

"No, ma'am. Mr. Bliss says that when someone sits down at one of our tables, we should treat them like they're the President. Listen to their order carefully. Smile. Make sure everything sparkles. Then they'll leave wanting to come back on their next trip through and maybe tell others about us."

For a moment I was at a loss as to how to continue. Finally, I asked, "Is this a problem Mr. Bliss has been dealing with?"

"Oh no, ma'am. All us girls noticed it, but we didn't want to bother Mr. Bliss, him being somewhat distracted lately, and we wouldn't dare say a word to Chef because he can be fearfully sharp with his words if he thinks something's not right. None of us want to get Henry in trouble."

"Henry Strunk? You think Henry isn't doing his work properly?"

Darla scooched forward on the chair. "We all like Henry, Mrs. Moore. He comes in when he's supposed to and he's never nothing but cheerful, but—"

"But he's not getting the dishes clean," I supplied. Darla nodded, relieved at my understanding.

"No, ma'am, he's not, and it's getting worse. It slows us girls down when we have to check every dish before we can put a new setting on the table and that's not good.

We've only got so much time to feed passengers before they're ready to get back on the train, and we work together to get that done. Yesterday a man said to me that he thought I must be able to read his mind because it seemed I had everything set in front of him before he even finished telling me what he wanted. That's how us Bliss girls work, Mrs. Moore, smooth and fast and always smiling. That's how Mr. Bliss wants it."

"Mr. Bliss is a good employer, then?"

"Not a one of us could get a better wage anywhere in the county. Mr. Bliss keeps his distance, Mrs. Bliss, too, but last year when Tillie Fry fell and broke her leg on the ice outside her barn, Mr. Bliss helped her folks with the doctor bills and gave her part-time wages until she came back to work. Last December, he gave all of us a five-dollar bonus. Five dollars! I couldn't believe it myself. We don't want to disappoint him and we're not fools, Mrs. Moore, for all we're young and female."

I saw the wry twist to Darla's mouth with those words and wondered if she found it as difficult to be talked down to by well-dressed customers with a sky-high opinion of their own importance as I did.

"We know that when the restaurant's busy and the customers are happy, it's good business, and that's good for us, too. Susie Malone – she works mornings usually – mentioned something in passing about the dirty dishes to Henry, in a kind way, you understand, but he hasn't gotten any better. I feel awful bad tattling like this, everybody hates a tattler, but I thought maybe if you talked to Henry, you being a lady and all, you could set him straight in a nice way, but," she emphasized a final time, spacing her words with care, "we don't want to get Henry in any trouble. We like Henry."

I listened without comment to Darla's speech and when she finally stopped talking, I smiled.

"I will certainly talk to Henry," I told her, "but the first thing I'm going to do is add some light to that corner where he works. It's awfully dim and that might be part of the problem. In the meanwhile, you and the other girls keep doing what you're doing. Set a neat table and keep smiling. I'll take care of the rest."

Darla rose and reached for the two dishes she had brought in with her, but I waved her away.

"Leave those here for now," I said.

At the door, the girl turned back to say, "You won't turn Henry off, will you, Mrs. Moore? You'll talk to him first, won't you?"

"I don't intend to let Henry go," I said, "and certainly not before I take a closer look at the problem. I promise."

After Darla was gone, I couldn't help but smile. I couldn't recall ever being quite as innocent or as straightforward as Darla Jones, having learned early on to test the people around me, especially the men, much like you'd test a coin to see if it was genuine: apply some pressure and see if it bent. I liked Darla and I liked Henry and I certainly wasn't going to fire the son of the woman who cooked my breakfast. Who knew what would find its way into my pancakes if I did that? This was a simple problem, it seemed to me, and I already had some ideas for going forward. Truth be told, I was glad to have a small puzzle to work on. Otherwise, I told myself, working in John Bliss's organized, efficient establishments wouldn't hold much challenge for me. But there I was wrong. Henry Strunk's poor dishwashing skills would end up changing my life in ways I never could have guessed or imagined.

It didn't take long to figure out that lighting wasn't Henry Strunk's problem or lack of initiative or even a general streak of laziness, to which some boys – even boys of good families or demanding mothers – are prone. I made some slight changes to Henry's work location over the next few days, none of which according to Darla made a difference in the end result. Finally, I was forced to skulk in a darkened corner one early evening and observe the boy bent over the dish tubs. When I did, I saw the problem and was annoyed with myself that I hadn't figured it out from my first meeting with Henry, who had squinted at me throughout the conversation. I had ignored an obvious clue.

At first, I thought I might mention my conclusion to his mother but at the last minute decided to walk out to the schoolhouse, which sat over a small hill west of town. In the alley that led to the school, I met a number of children on their way home bundled up against the cold wind. There was a great deal of chatter and shoving, the latter among the boys especially, and for just a moment I felt something small but painfully sharp poke at my heart. After all this time, seeing a group of children acting like children shouldn't hurt. But it still did sometimes.

The office of The New Hope Union, the town's weekly newspaper, was brightly lit against the dim light of late afternoon when I passed it, and across the street the same held true for George Young's Photography Studio. The Strunks' small house was in the same general vicinity. Curtains on the window and smoke from the chimney made it appear cozy, but I knew that Ruby, as a widow with seven children, had to work harder than most to keep her home lit and warm.

I trudged up the small hill, passed a beautiful hand-finished bench sitting at its crest, a bench Ruth later told me had been placed there in honor of a young man from New Hope who'd died, and then followed the path down to the schoolhouse. When I opened the door, the wind that entered along with me stirred the papers on the large desk at the front of the room. The man seated behind that desk placed his palm on a stack of papers to keep them from blowing onto the floor before he looked up to see who had allowed late fall into the classroom. I pulled the door closed behind me but didn't move any closer to the desk.

"Mr. Stenton?"

"Yes." He stood, as a man of good manners would, and waited. The two of us had never met, and I had the advantage.

"My name is Caroline Moore. I'm helping out at Bliss House while John and Sheba are traveling."

"Ah." Satisfied with my introduction, he stepped out from behind the desk and came toward me, walking with a noticeable limp he made no attempt to hide and acting like he was completely unaware of it. Reaching me, he held out his hand. "How do you do, Mrs. Moore? I heard from Henry Strunk that John had left a woman in charge."

"And Henry didn't approve?" I said the words with a smile to take any sting out of the question.

"Henry added no qualifying statement." No responding smile from Mr. Stenton. I thought he was a man who didn't smile very often.

"It's about Henry I'm here," I said.

"Indeed?" I heard the schoolteacher clearly in the single word.

"Could we sit down, please?" I asked, more in mind of the teacher's comfort than mine.

"Of course." He walked to a corner where a lone chair sat and pulled it closer to the desk. "Please," he said, motioned with his arm toward the chair, and returned to his chair behind the desk.

"Thank you." I sat back comfortably and studied the man – in his mid to late thirties, clean-shaven and thin-faced with clear hazel eyes and a head of thick brown hair. What was it Ruby had said about the teacher? *He can seem a little stern sometimes.* I should say so. But in my past I had of necessity dealt with every type of man imaginable and Arthur Stenton could not intimidate, even if that was his intention. For some reason, however, I didn't think he was trying to be condescending or belittling. I thought it was just his manner, nothing underhanded or sly. In his own way, a transparent man.

After Mr. Stenton sat, he folded his hands on the desktop, leaned toward me just a little, and moved the conversation along.

"What about Henry Strunk has brought you here, Mrs. Moore?" Not a man for small talk, I thought, and approved. Life was short, after all.

"I assume you know that Henry works after school at the restaurant." Stenton nodded. "The waitresses are somewhat concerned about him, about his work more to the point," I explained what Darla had brought to my attention and paused to see if Mr. Stenton would wave the problem away as something beneath his interest, but to his credit he listened attentively until I concluded, "I believe Henry has a problem with his eyesight, Mr. Stenton. Have you found that to be true at school?"

"Yes."

I narrowed my eyes at the single syllable. "And you've done nothing about it?" With no attempt to hide my disapproval, I now sounded like the one trying to intimidate.

Arthur Stenton, however, was not a man to be provoked. Too rational for that, I guessed, too experienced with clever children, no doubt with clever adults, as well.

"I shared my concerns with his mother."

After a pause, I prompted, "And?"

"Mrs. Strunk is a proud woman, Mrs. Moore. She assured me that as soon as she could afford eyeglasses for Henry, she would consider obtaining them for him. In the meanwhile, she asked what could be done for him at school, and I said all I could suggest was to seat Henry at the front of the classroom so he could better see the writing on the chalk board, and I have since done so."

"Did you notice any improvement after you did that?"

"Henry can better see what's written on the chalkboard, and that is certainly an improvement."

"But if he can't see spots on dinner plates, words printed

in books must be difficult for him."

"Difficult, yes. More often impossible."

I sat back in my chair and considered the meaningless blur that education must be for Henry Strunk. And still he came to school daily and faithfully, then showed up at the restaurant to squint at dishes that no matter how much light we set up would never be enough for his diminished eyesight.

"Where's the nearest eye doctor?" I asked.

"Julesburg, Colorado," Stenton's response quick and sure.

"What is that, maybe eighty miles or so west?" I had heard of Julesburg.

"Eighty-four to be exact. Six railway stops."

"You've done your homework, Mr. Stenton," – he allowed himself a slight smile at my small joke – "and you must have confidence in the skill of this eye doctor."

"I know Dr. Conrad, and I can personally vouch for his professional expertise. He's a graduate of the Illinois School of Optometry and is well-known in his field."

"I see," I said, and at the unintended but appropriate phrase Arthur Stenton and I smiled at each other. It was the first time I had seen the man soften. Doing so took ten years from his age and made him almost attractive, or at least human. Perhaps keeping ahead of a room full of mischievous children didn't allow or encourage smiles very often.

"I think you should make an appointment for Henry with Dr. Conrad," I said.

"As much as we might wish otherwise, Mrs. Moore," – I thought the *we* a good sign – "neither you nor I have the authority to countermand the expressed intention of the boy's mother."

I stood and shook out my skirts before glancing across the desk at Arthur Stenton, who had with his gentlemanly manners also stood.

"You handle Dr. Conrad, Mr. Stenton, and let me take care of Ruby Strunk." My own words made me laugh. "My goodness, that sounded threatening, didn't it? I only meant that I understand Ruby's pride and I can speak to her in a way she'll understand. We're both widows and we have that in common."

"You have children, too, then, Mrs. Moore?"

He meant the question innocently enough, a natural follow-up to my claiming fellowship with Ruby, and I intended to answer it with the same innocence. After eight years of practice, I was used to pretending, but to my own surprise I said, "I had a daughter. She and my husband died in a fire several years ago."

Somehow, I knew I could say the words aloud to Arthur Stenton when I could not usually take the chance. He was not a man to respond with any of the emotions I found unbearable: no gasp of pity or horror, no cool remarks about God's will, no curiosity for the details, no awkward fumbling for the right words.

"My sympathies, Mrs. Moore," was all he said, his sincerity and his brevity the perfect response.

I gave a tiny nod to acknowledge his words and dismiss the subject before I said, "I promise you that Ruby will have a change of heart about Henry's eyeglasses in the next day or two. In the meanwhile, you'll wire your Dr. Conrad and set up an appointment for Henry." No question in my tone. It was already apparent that at least in this one particular enterprise, Arthur Stenton and I were of the same mind. "The train ticket will be at my expense. Both tickets, if it would be possible for you to go with Henry. Your doing so makes sense since you know the eye doctor and where his office is, but how you balance your classroom duties with making the trip will be up to you."

For a moment I thought I caught a wry twist to Stenton's lips – was the man laughing at me? – but his response was serious enough.

"I believe it can be arranged without compromising either enterprise, Mrs. Moore, and thank you for the offer of a train ticket, but I can pay my own way." I sent him a quick look, not sure what I heard – if I heard anything – in his voice. Some men were prickly about accepting aid or even advice from a woman, but I wouldn't have pegged the schoolteacher as that kind of man.

"I didn't mean to insult you, Mr. Stenton."

"No more than did I, Mrs. Moore. Perhaps going forward we can each agree to accept the other's words at face value."

"Yes," I said aloud, "I'd like that," and thought how simple it would make my life if that was always possible. But dealing as I did with the paying public, with diners and lodgers as well as the hired help, *face value*, whether in words or emotions, was usually impossible. If I didn't maintain a calm appearance and choose my words with care, the chef might walk out in offended dignity, the traveler decide to press on to the next stop with its more welcoming accommodations, the diner decide to walk a few steps south to the Nebraska Café where his opinions might be more respected. I had been hiding so much for so long.

"Good afternoon, Mr. Stenton," I said, turning toward the door.

"Good afternoon, Mrs. Moore."

That the schoolmaster considered the conversation over was clear in his tone, but with no sense that I had imposed on his time or interrupted his work. It was simply time for him to move on to the next action on his list, and he figured it must be the same for me.

Which it was, of course. Outside it was the dark of early evening and most of the passengers from the 3:30 westbound would be hurrying back to their train, Les would be busy at the front desk booking rooms for the people staying over, and the girls in the dining room would be hurrying from table to kitchen and back to table, getting everything ready for the rush of passengers off the next train. Late afternoon was a favorite time of the day for me, in an odd way satisfying, everything in order, every person with a task and every action with a purpose. I appreciated orderliness. It meant the world was not spinning wildly out of control, regardless of how life sometimes seemed.

Later, the restaurant readied for the next morning and Kip behind the hotel desk, I drew my shawl tightly around my shoulders against the cold air and hurried home, giving Lucas Morgan a quiet greeting as we passed each other on the boardwalk. Once inside the big house, I raised the flame on the lamp in the kitchen, made myself a cup of tea, sat down at the table, and decided exactly what to say to Ruby Strunk when she appeared in the kitchen early the next morning.

We were two of a kind, Ruby and I, regardless of the difference in our circumstances, and getting her permission to outfit her son in eyeglasses took hardly any effort.

"It appears that Henry needs eyeglasses," I said in between sips of morning tea. I didn't look at Ruby but felt her stop her activities and turn to face where I sat. I finally looked up to meet her gaze. "He can't see the dishes well enough to get them clean and it's giving the girls extra work."

"I'll talk to him," Ruby said. I shook my head in response.

"It's not for want of trying, Ruby. The boy's a good worker, but he can't do what he can't do. You understand my meaning." She gave half a nod.

"Mr. Stenton said the same thing and I'll tell you what I told him: I don't have the money for spectacles."

"I need someone who can see what he's doing," I countered. "It's not the boy's fault and I understand that, but if he can't do his job, I'll have to find someone else for it." We stared at each other for another moment. "Here's what I propose," I continued, "I'll pay for the eyeglasses to start with and take the cost a little bit at a time out of Henry's pay. If John Bliss hadn't paid you in advance, we could do the same for you."

"That money's already gone," Ruby said, neither defiant nor apologetic, just stating a fact.

"I understand. I'd have done the same, but instead of money I'm thinking something else. I'm thinking about those fine corn meal biscuits of yours and your raisin buns. If you deliver a basket of either or both of them to the restaurant every Monday, I'll tell Monsieur Clermont to expect them and have him include them on the menu. You can add the biscuits to the laundry you already do for the hotel, and if Henry can work a couple extra hours in the kitchen, the two of you could have the eyeglasses paid off by the time the new year rolls around."

"How do you know that? Eyeglasses don't come cheap and Henry'd have to take the train to get them."

"I talked to Mr. Stenton."

"Did you now?" No offense, but curiosity and grudging respect in her tone.

"Yes. We both have an interest in improving Henry's vision. Mr. Stenton's agreed to accompany Henry to the eye doctor. He's a man Mr. Stenton knows. The trip can be done in a day and I'll add Henry's ticket to the total due."

"I don't need anyone's charity."

"I know that and so does Mr. Stenton. I could tell he was a decent man, but more than that he's a teacher, and he naturally wants the best for his students. It's bred in him. I imagine he couldn't help it even if he tried. And I –" Ruby Strunk eyed me as I interrupted my own sentence to take a sip of tea before concluding, "– just want the dishes clean."

We stared at each other one final time before Ruby said, "All right, then," and turned back to the fritters she was frying.

As easy as that, I thought, satisfied, and decided to make

a return trip to the school that afternoon to share the victory with Arthur Stenton. I knew he would be pleased. Perhaps the news would tease another small smile from him. Looking back, I suppose that was the moment Arthur Stenton first became meaningful in my life, even if only in a trifling way. Somehow, from our brief interaction, I had found in him a kindred spirit, something I had never expected to find again, not ever or anywhere and least of all in little New Hope, Nebraska.

Not a hint of surprise showed on the teacher's face when I once more appeared at school that same afternoon. No surprise when I told him I had Ruby's approval for the eyeglasses, either.

"That's convenient news, Mrs. Moore, because Dr. Conrad replied immediately to the wire I sent late yesterday and Henry now has an appointment confirmed in ten days, a Sunday appointment, which is rare but not unheard of. This morning before the school day began I purchased two round-trip tickets to Julesburg. Henry and I will leave on the first westbound train of the day and be home by that day's end." I tried to find any trace of smugness in his words or tone but found none. Mr. Stenton was simply stating the facts.

"Well," I said, "I admit that surprises me a little." The schoolmaster raised his eyebrows slightly.

"I can't imagine why, Mrs. Moore, since you gave me a clear and definite assignment yesterday afternoon. I was to handle Dr. Conrad – I believe that's how you phrased it – and you would take care of Mrs. Strunk." For a moment I would have sworn that something very like a twinkle sparked in the man's eyes but then decided it must have been the reflection of light from the oil lamp by his elbow. Arthur Stenton was not a man to twinkle.

"A satisfactory grade for both of us then," I stated.

"Yes," ignoring my weak humor.

"I'll let Ruby know. Could you share the news with

Henry?"

"I should *handle* Henry as well as Dr. Conrad, then?" Surely that was an intentional tease, I thought, studying his face, but I would have put teasing and twinkling in the same category when it came to Arthur Stenton.

Still, whatever his intention, the words made me laugh. "Exactly, Mr. Stenton. You didn't ask how I convinced Ruby to change her mind."

"I'm content with the result, Mrs. Moore. I don't need to know the details. You seem a woman of practical competence, and I'm sure you have your own ways, apparently effective ones, to accomplish what needs to be done."

"'If I be waspish, best beware of my sting', you mean?" The words had been a favorite tease of my husband's.

My quoting Shakespeare finally caused a shadow of surprise on Stenton's face, but he replied simply, "Not at all, Mrs. Moore. I see nothing waspish in you whatsoever." He looked down long enough to draw a stack of papers on the desktop toward him, then looked back at me. Our conversation is done, the gesture said, and my work isn't.

"Thank you, Mr. Stenton. Good afternoon."

"Good afternoon, Mrs. Moore."

Trudging home through the deepening twilight, I decided that not being waspish was as much of a tribute as I should expect from Arthur Stenton and must surely be one step above being practically competent. I had learned long ago that women must take their compliments where they can find them.

4

I am a woman of routine, but my husband, my Davey, was as far from routine as a person could be, a man who would take the unknown path simply because it was unknown, who enjoyed change and taking chances, a man who considered every horizon a challenge and every *you can't* a dare. When our Jean was born, Davey sometimes showed a surprisingly cautious side – no trip to town if the weather looked uncertain or a quick peek into the cradle if the baby was too quiet, her blankets either loosened ("We don't want her overheated, Caro") or pulled up closer under her chin ("I can feel a draft from the window") but for all that, my husband's basic nature never changed. He became a man suddenly aware of the burden, a loving burden but a burden nevertheless, of having someone totally dependent on him. At the same time, he never lost his love for adventure and risk, for new places and new ideas. I thought more than once what a marvel it was that the two of us found each other and loved each other and managed to live together with arguments few and far between. But we did. I was a fortunate woman then and I never lost sight of the wonder of it.

For the short time we were together, loving and being

loved by Davey Moore changed me, tempted me with hope and a light-hearted feeling of security that were foreign to me. But in New Hope, once more a woman on my own with duties and responsibilities, I reverted to the person I am at heart: one comfortable with routine and skeptical of good fortune.

Which is why I was happy in New Hope from my first day there. There was nothing special about the place, you see. It was as ordinary as ordinary could be, and it was the town's very ordinariness that made it feel so right this time around, settled as I had back into old habits. It was not my first stay in New Hope. Five years earlier, John had tracked me down to where I was working in Denver and convinced me to return to New Hope with him. He had offered me the same position I now filled in his absence, but then, five years ago, I was not the same woman I am today. Then, I felt hardly healed from the fire, fragile in my body and more unstable in my mind, driven by emotions that could not rest or be relieved. New Hope didn't offer what my troubled spirit needed then. How could it? Too quiet, too normal, its citizens common people with common lives. I had matters on my mind more urgent than bed linens and luncheon specials. Ogallala, loud and hectic and thronging with strangers, raw and busy and often violent, seemed to fit my unsettled state, and when I heard that Mr. Samuel Gast was looking for help to run his newly-opened Ogallala House, I took the train west, met and liked him and his wife, Harriet, and took the job at Mr. Gast's first offer, which was little more than half of what John was paying me at the time. Truth is, I couldn't leave New Hope fast enough, couldn't get away from John Bliss fast enough, either. Not that he was ever anything but respectful and kind, but he and Davey were once as close as brothers and I couldn't look at John without seeing my husband, no matter that Davey had been as fair as John was swarthy. Five years ago, memories still held the power to wound me. Funny how time changes a person. Now there are moments when I can't quite conjure up my husband's eyes or recall his distinctive laugh, and for all the pain, I would do anything to feel the jagged thrust of grief that seeing John Bliss once brought. I fear I'm losing Davey. Losing my Jean, too. No matter what old wisdom says, time isn't a healer. It's a thief.

My first weeks living in New Hope the second time around were as comfortable as an old pair of shoes, and the schedule of my days soon took on that same comfortable air. Breakfast chit-chat with Ruby, cross the street to the hotel, more chit-chat with Kip, wander into the restaurant kitchen, greet anyone I saw along the way, and eventually find my way back to the office. There were times I might examine the hotel rooms for cleanliness or change a menu item – a perilous move to be undertaken with great thought before braving Monsieur Clermont in his den – or walk down to the freight office to inspect a delivery before I decided whether I would accept it or not. (I always accepted it, but it was a necessary pantomime to demonstrate that I was in charge.) For the most part, however, my early days in New Hope were filled with nothing more strenuous than strolling and chatting.

In November, however, I was asked to gather with a few select members of the Merchants' Association to discuss the meeting of meat packers and cattlemen scheduled for February in New Hope, and with that invitation the pace of my life picked up in a way I welcomed.

Joe Chandler, the owner of the hardware store and the president of the Merchants' Association, presided over all the meetings, small and large, and earned my admiration from that very first gathering. He was a young man who somehow managed to keep the attending members talking about the subject at hand – all of the members senior to Joe in years – despite their varied comments about the rising cost of train travel, the likelihood of bad weather, and the continuing effect of the 1873 financial panic on the price of beef. Had I been Joe, I might have felt frustrated at hearing all the reasons why New Hope's Beef Convention, as it had begun to be called, might fail. When John Bliss talked to me about it, he was nothing but positive and hopeful, believing that such an important gathering of wealthy men could mean an economic boon for the town. But other men more cautious than John took a more practical approach. It wasn't their idea, after all, and the man whose idea it was now toured the European continent with his wife. Not that anyone faulted John Bliss for the timing of his departure. Word of the couple's loss had somehow filtered into the community and the members spoke of John and Sheba with affection and regard. Their comments were rather touching, really, and gave me a glimpse of the type of people who lived in New Hope. Respectable people, for the most part, bound together in common decency and hard-working industry. Still, it was a small town dependent on the railroad and the weather, and I supposed opinions about either or both of those topics were understandable. To Joe Chandler's credit, he was never anything but patient, attentive, and respectful as he followed the discussion. Not at all the temperament of a man I later learned had spent time in prison for killing someone. But as I well knew, more people than you might guess have things buried deep in their past that would come as a shock if they were exposed for all the world to see – to see and judge, which is what most folks do. I thought that setting out his own past for everyone in New Hope's small world to see and judge was something else to Joe's credit. It must have taken courage on his part, more courage than I possessed, certainly, and nothing I could ever see myself doing.

Isaac Lincoln was at that first meeting, along with Abner Talamine, Benny Tidwell, and Mort Lewis. Each man had an important role in making the Beef Convention a success. Benny was there in part to represent John, but also because the meeting, to be chaired by New Hope's attorney-at-law Mort Lewis, would take place in the Bliss Music Hall, which was Benny's responsibility. No regular paying customers would be allowed into the Music Hall the day of the meeting, only the men coming east from Chicago and west from Denver, those who had been invited to attend. It would be up to Benny to be sure the Music Hall was set up, cleaned up, and presentable.

Isaac owned New Hope's meat market and while not exactly a key participant, had been tasked with following the planning discussion and making a note of meeting comments he thought important. The invited participants knew things, knew the future of beef commodities and the potential for advanced refrigerated rail cars and what people in the East would pay for western meat. Because Isaac ran a successful meat market himself, it made sense to John and to the rest of the Association that Isaac would follow the topics of conversation better than someone unfamiliar with the business side of putting a steak on someone's plate. Abner Talamine, a founding resident of New Hope who owned the bank, was there because he understood money the way Isaac understood beef, and I – well, I was there because the men coming in February would stay at the Bliss Hotel and eat their meals in the Bliss Restaurant and with John gone, it was up to me to make sure theirs was a comfortable stay. It would only be two nights with a day in between, not even forty-eight hours all told, but I intended to make it a memorable stay, nevertheless.

"We'll meet again in a month or so," Joe Chandler said as he concluded the discussion. "I've asked Val Copco to join us then. Val can let us know about train schedules. I don't expect there'll be a whole lot of changes to what we've got now, but he's the man who'll know, and, Mrs. Moore—?"

I looked over at Joe and met his gaze. "Yes?"

He looked somewhat sheepish when he told me, "I don't believe that John let the participants know that he wouldn't be here in February, so it's possible you might get a wire delivered to the hotel from someone – I'll give you a list of the men John invited – with a question or change of plans or the like. If that happens, we'd appreciate it if you'd send the telegram along to Mort or me. Between the two of us, we'll figure out how to answer."

"Of course," I said, but inside I was shaking my head and smiling a little. It was so like John Bliss to want to keep a finger in a pie he'd put into a Nebraska oven – even if he was an ocean away.

That meeting was the first time I realized how important the Beef Convention was to the merchants of New Hope, how they hoped it might imprint the name of their little town onto the minds of influential men of business and how they believed that if New Hope made a good impression, the town's future success would surely take a great leap forward. It wasn't simply an idea thought up by John Bliss and tolerated by other town merchants. Maybe it started like that, I didn't know, but now John's plan for a Beef Convention was everyone's plan, an exciting, hopeful idea that might literally change New Hope's future forever. At least, that's how the Merchants' Association seemed to view it. Maybe New Hope could become a hub for the transfer of beef or money or maybe a center for a commercial venture as yet unthought of and unknown. After all, the men coming to town in February to parley and discuss and explore were men of invention and progress, who made things happen all across the country, and why shouldn't New Hope be a partner in their progressive thinking?

Not long after, I understood even more clearly the important responsibility I had taken on in John Bliss's absence because I met Mark Saylor, a man as invested in the Beef Convention as any member of the Merchants'

Association, and for a similar reason: the reason being money. In the end, for most people, everything they do boils down to money and what money can do for them. I'm not faulting that kind of thinking. How could I when all my younger years I had believed the same and still do to a point? Money can mean freedom from worry and want and can open the future to all kinds of possibilities. Money can keep the wolf from the door, and because I've had to hold off my share of wolves, I would never pretend money wasn't important. But when I met and married and then lost Davey, I began to see matters differently. And now, years later, my opinion was tempered by the knowledge of all the things money can't give me.

Mr. Saylor was what I noticed first after walking down the hallway from the office one late afternoon and stepping into the hotel's lobby. It would have been difficult if not impossible not to notice him, a broad-shouldered man with brown hair light enough to appear blonde in the lobby lighting and long enough to brush the collar of his dark brown woolen walking coat. He was well dressed, the coat cut away in an elegant curve worn over a jacket, waistcoat, and matching trousers, and a small string tie showing under the collar of his crisp white shirt. Fashionable but not too much so. My first impression was of a man who would always appear to advantage but would never look like he gave a care about his appearance. A sophisticated nonchalance that was quite a trick if a person could pull it off. He could.

Les glanced at me as the man bent to sign the register and gave an almost imperceptible nod of his head. As the visitor straightened, Les turned the book, read the signature, and said, "Welcome, Mr. – it's Saylor, am I right?"

"Yes, Mark Saylor. Saylor with a y and not an i." He looked at Les.

"Yes, sir. For how many nights will you be staying with

us?"

"Just one. This time. I'm traveling to Saint Jo and thought I'd stop for a night and have a talk with Bliss."

"With Mr. Bliss? I'm afraid he's not available now and won't be for quite a while. He's clear out of the country." Les's explanation was the cue for me to enter the conversation.

"Mr. Saylor," I said, using his name as if it were familiar to me. He turned from the desk to face me. Smooth tanned skin, a handsome fair mustache, and very pale blue eyes rimmed in darker blue. There was something unsettling but still attractive in the way those unusual eyes took me in, how they skimmed from my face down to my skirts and then made their way back up to my face again. Nothing insulting or vulgar in his look, but I knew he had missed nothing of my form or face. He was a man used to picking and choosing his way through a variety of women, selecting the ones he wanted to know better, and dismissing any he considered not worth his attention. I had noticed right away that he didn't wear a wedding ring – I could do so without shifting my gaze at all – but, of course, that meant nothing. Even if he were married, it might not be his custom to wear a ring or he might remove the ring when he traveled. I had met many men like that.

"Yes?"

From his smile, I guessed he approved of what he saw and the one word held a pleasant *do I know you?* tone, apologetic and at the same time complimentary, hinting that he would have to be a fool to have forgotten someone like me. He was very good, very smooth, and I found myself smiling at him more warmly than usual. I had loved my husband dearly and still mourned him, but I can enjoy the unspoken flattery of a handsome man as much as the next woman. I put out my hand.

"I'm Caroline Moore. Mr. Bliss is traveling with his wife for several weeks, and he's left me in charge in his absence."

Mark Saylor didn't hesitate to take my hand in his. He had a strong grip and a soft shake, his idea of the proper way to treat a woman's offer of a handshake when engaged in men's business. There was something both careful and endearing in his action. A man who placed value on doing things properly.

"How do you do, Mrs. Moore – it is *Mrs.* Moore?"

"Yes."

"Well, I'm sorry to have missed Bliss. He's the one who sold me on the idea of a meeting between Colorado cattlemen and Chicago meat packers. Do you know about the meeting?"

"I do. In fact, John will still be abroad in February and he's entrusted many of the details of the meeting with me. Well, the details about lodging and meals, I should say. Mort Lewis, New Hope's attorney, will be handling the meeting itself. Have you met Mort?"

For a fleeting moment, so fleeting I might have imagined it, I thought I caught a flash of strong annoyance in Mr. Saylor's unusual eyes, a brief wrinkling of his brows with displeasure, but his answer was easy enough.

"No, I haven't had the pleasure."

"His office is a short walk down Main Street on this same side, just past the barber shop. You can't miss the sign. Once you're settled in your room, you should take a stroll in Mort's direction. He'll still be in his office, I'm sure. Introduce yourself, and if you're both hungry, come back to the restaurant for supper. On the house, of course. That's sure to get Mort's attention." To Les, I said, "Put Mr. Saylor in room eight, will you, Les? The corner room holds the heat better and the weather's turned quite chilly outside."

Mark Saylor nodded his thanks to me before he took the key from Les's hand.

"Top of the stairs, turn left," I said. "The rooms are

numbered."

He reached for his small satchel, probably used to having someone carry his bags, but that was an amenity Bliss House didn't offer.

"Thank you, Mrs. Moore. You seem to have matters well in hand. Come February, I don't believe we'll miss Bliss, at all."

"I can't speak for the meeting, Mr. Saylor, but I can guarantee that you and the other attendees will want for nothing from Bliss House or Bliss Restaurant."

"No doubt." He smiled and turned toward the stairs, then turned back long enough to say, "I'm leaving on the 11:15 train tomorrow morning. Will I have a chance to see you again before I depart?"

"I'll make it a point to greet you at breakfast, Mr. Saylor."

"Good. I can't imagine a more agreeable way to start the day than sharing a cup of coffee with you. You'll join me for breakfast, won't you?" From his first words, I had known he was a practiced man, but I had to give him credit for being even more practiced than I had first thought. Smooth indeed.

"I'd be honored. I hope you enjoy your stay at Bliss House."

"How could I not?" He held his satchel in one hand and his fine, flat-crowned hat in the other so all he could do was nod and smile one last time before ascending the stairs to his room. As soon as he was out of sight, I turned to Les, still behind the counter.

"Hop down to Mort's, will you, Les, and let him know he'll have a visitor in a short while? Give him the details. I'll watch the desk while you're gone. If Mort's not in his office, track him down. I wouldn't want to disappoint Mr. Saylor any more than we already have, and Mort might welcome a little time to figure out what to say to Mark Saylor, though from what I've seen of New Hope's resident lawyer, he doesn't seem to run short of words."

Les was back in hardly any time at all, reporting that Mort was where he should be and looking forward to making Mr. Saylor's acquaintance.

"Mort recognized the name," Les told me. "Said Saylor's a rich man. Owns a big spread north of Denver."

"Let's hope he likes his room, then," I said. "I'm going to go let Deb know she doesn't need to bother either Mort or Mr. Saylor with a tab for their supper. Then I'll be in my office if you need me. Thank you, Les. I can see you appreciate the importance of the Beef Convention, and I know neither of us wants to disappoint Mr. Bliss."

"No, ma'am. He's been a good friend to me."

"And to me," I said, thinking as I retreated to my office that there had once been a time when I hated John Bliss and he had felt the same about me. John believed he was saving Davey from my dangerous influence, and I believed John was poisoning Davey's opinion of me out of sheer malice. We were both wrong. Neither danger nor malice was ever at work. In the end, it was love John and I had in common, always love. But what a long time it took for me to realize that!

The next morning I put on a favorite dress, high-collared and elegant, of light wool in a soft gold color that warmed my eyes and brought out the tawny streaks in my hair, and laughed at my vanity as I did so. If someone were to comment, I would be tempted to say that I was representing John Bliss to an important man of business and wanted to put my best face forward, but there was no one to comment and no reason for me to make up stories. It was the lure of a handsome man at the breakfast table and the almost forgotten pleasure of feeling attractive, however fleeting, that made me conscious of my appearance that morning.

Mark Saylor was not yet at breakfast when I looked into the restaurant from the hotel lobby, but someone was standing at my office door. When he saw me, young Henry

Strunk straightened from petting Gypsy, the hotel cat, who waited for me at the office door, her expression always slightly offended that anyone would dare close a door to a room she might wish to enter at some unspecified time in her busy schedule.

"Good morning, Henry." I pushed open the door, entered the office with Gypsy padding at my heels, and turned to beckon him to follow. "Come in, please. Is there something I can do for you?" I hung my heavy shawl on the hook behind the door and walked toward the desk. When I looked back, Henry still stood in the doorway.

"No, ma'am. I just wanted you to know that Mr. Stenton and I are traveling to Julesburg this Sunday to see the eye doctor."

"Do I need to change the work schedule?" I asked.

"I traded places with Bertie Barts. He said he'll work for me on Sunday, though his ma won't like it he said, and I'll do double duty on Wednesday."

"Which your ma might not like," I pointed out.

"She don't mind. I asked."

"That's all arranged, then." After a moment's pause, I added, "Is there something else you want me to know, Henry?"

"I wanted to say thank you."

"You'd be better off thanking Mr. Stenton and your mother. They're the ones bearing the cost of the trip."

"I already spoke my thanks to Ma and Mr. Stenton, and I wouldn't have thought about you" – those were words guaranteed to humble any woman but especially one who had just spent too long pinning up her hair and deciding what dress would be most becoming – "except they both mentioned to me that you were the one who made the trip possible, so I wanted to let you know I appreciated your effort."

I felt a spurt of affection for the boy. Three months ago I hadn't known he existed, and even now I hardly knew him, but the dignity of his plain face and straightforward words touched a spot somewhere in my heart. Henry Strunk didn't share one common feature with Davey Moore, but for just a moment and for a reason I didn't understand, it might have been my husband standing in the doorway.

"You're welcome," I told him.

Another pause and then Henry said, "Well, I'm off to school."

"Learn something new today," I said, pulling a phrase from my memory that Davey had used sometimes. There was nothing to get my husband more excited than the thought of seeing, visiting, learning something new, something he had never pictured or imagined before.

"Mr. Stenton told me about a man named Ralph Waldo Emerson. Have you heard of him, Mrs. Moore?"

An unexpected and rather abrupt question to which I had to answer, "No, I don't believe I have."

"He's a famous writer from Massachusetts," Henry explained. "Well, he *was* a writer. Mr. Stenton said he died this past spring, but I read something Mr. Emerson wrote and I never forgot it. Mr. Emerson said," – I could tell by the way Henry squinted that he was going to quote word-for-word – "'the health of the eye seems to demand a horizon. We are never tired so long as we can see far enough.'" The young man gave me a serious smile. "That seems about right, doesn't it, especially for me?" I took a moment to repeat the last words aloud before giving Henry a serious smile of my own.

"Yes," I said at last, "I believe Mr. Emerson's words fit you exactly. I'll have to see if Mr. Stenton will loan me a book of the man's writings. Ralph Waldo Emerson sounds like someone I should know more about."

Henry gave a shy dip of his head and disappeared into the hallway. Standing behind my desk, I leaned forward with both palms pressed against the desktop and looked down at my fingers for a long moment. People are such surprises sometimes, I thought. How could you ever know or guess what was going on in someone's head? If Henry Strunk could quote a famous New England writer at the drop of a hat, what other surprises did the people of New Hope, Nebraska, have in store for me?

I might have mulled the thought a while longer except Les Woodson, still unwrapping a muffler from around his neck, poked his head into the office to tell me that at the same time he arrived to start his day behind the hotel desk, he had seen Mr. Saylor descending the stairs into the hotel lobby.

"No impertinence intended, Mrs. Moore, but I thought from your conversation with the man yesterday that you might want to know that he was up and headed for breakfast."

"Good thinking, Les. I'll be right along. Thank you." I gave a final pat to my hair and shook out my skirts before going in search of Mark Saylor.

I saw Saylor before he saw me, stopped in the arched doorway that connected the hotel lobby to the restaurant, and took a moment to observe him. Observe the back of him, anyway, since he was seated in such a way that all I could see was the rear of his head as he stirred sugar into the coffee that Darla poured carefully into Mr. Saylor's cup. When she stopped pouring, he looked up at her and must have said something more pleasant than thank-you because she blushed at his words and gave what looked to me like a curtsy. A curtsy, of all things! But I couldn't blame her. Mark Saylor was a handsome man and any girl might find herself overwhelmed by his undivided attention. Hadn't I taken the time to dig the dress I wore out of the bedroom bureau? Hadn't I used my favorite amber combs to pin my hair? But no curtsying, Caroline, I told myself firmly, you have to draw the line somewhere. I smiled at my foolishness as I entered the dining area and for some reason, likely because Darla saw me and made a point of looking in my direction, that was the moment Mark Saylor turned his head. He stood and waited for me to approach.

"Good morning, Mrs. Moore." He was quicker than I with a greeting. I thought he was a man who would always make quick, spontaneous decisions based less on thought and more on emotion. "I hope I had something to do with the smile I just saw on your face."

"Good morning, Mr. Saylor." Deciding to ignore his comment, I said, "I trust you slept well last night."

"I did." He stepped to the other side of the table and pulled out the chair. "Join me, won't you?"

When I sat down, he did the same – I liked that he was a man knowledgeable of public courtesies – and replaced the napkin in his lap.

"I've already ordered," he told me. "I'm sorry. I should have waited, but I wasn't sure you'd remember my invitation." Which was nonsense and we both knew it. Mr. Saylor was a man used to the effect he had on women and had expected me to show up at his breakfast table, probably wearing a new dress and my best hair combs, too. Nevertheless, I allowed him to pretend he was surprised.

"I keep early hours, Mr. Saylor, and my mornings stay busy. I usually have a quick bite at home before crossing the street to the hotel office, but a cup of fresh hot coffee would be welcome right about now. I'll ask Darla about it when she brings your breakfast." I looked across the table. "I hope you found Mort Lewis to be good supper company last night. Was he able to set your mind at ease about the February meeting?"

Saylor made a noncommittal response that made me give him a curious look and ask, "No?"

"I wouldn't say *no*. Lewis seems savvy enough, but it was Bliss who extended the invitation, and I'd prefer that he was the man running the show."

"Oh, John Bliss will be running the show, Mr. Saylor, regardless of whether you see him or not. He's not a man to leave things to accident or chance."

"You know him better than I do, I guess." An indirect question there.

"John and my late husband were close as brothers," I said, "and I've known him a long time."

Saylor might have pursued the topic – I thought he wanted to – but Darla showed up with a full breakfast plate, that she set in front of him and then refilled his coffee cup.

"Can I bring you something, Mrs. Moore?" the girl asked.

I tapped the empty cup at my place setting. "Just coffee, thank you."

"You like yours black, I know," Darla said and I nodded, not surprised that she knew how I liked my coffee. The girls who waited tables at Bliss Restaurant were as competent and resourceful as any of the Harvey House girls, though they didn't get the same attention. I suppose the difference between little New Hope, Nebraska, and bustling Topeka, Kansas, might account for that.

Mark Saylor ate with enjoyment, something I've always appreciated in a man, especially if I was the one doing the cooking. After a few quiet minutes, he set down his fork and raised his napkin to his lips.

"It must be true that you've got yourself a French chef in the kitchen," he said, "because last night's steak was about as perfect as I've ever had, and these hotcakes" – he looked down at the now empty plate – "were as light as clouds. Very fine cooking, Mrs. Moore."

"Thank you. I'm glad you enjoyed it." Changing the subject, I said, "You have time before your train. You should take a stroll around New Hope in the daylight, acquaint yourself with our little town. Joe Chandler is the president of the Merchants' Association and he runs the hardware store. Stop in there, if you'd like. I'm sure Joe would be happy to meet you. New Hope is a serious, orderly place. A good choice for an important business gathering."

"I hear your sheriff – Carpenter, isn't it? – has quite a background."

"Does he? I didn't know that. I'll have to find out the particulars." In fact, I knew more than I indicated but didn't intend to share the details with Mr. Saylor.

"It's been a few years now, but he apprehended Emmett Wolf right here in New Hope. Surely you've heard the name Emmett Wolf. The outlaw?"

"I've heard the name, yes, and I recall reading about it in the newspaper several years ago, but nobody in New Hope talks about it. It's not a community to dwell on the past."

Mark Saylor said, "I agree with them there. Nothing good comes from living in the past. It's hard to make a future for yourself if you can't leave the past behind." He held my gaze a trifle too long, as if giving some kind of personal advice he thought important for my happiness. And maybe it was important, but I had no intention of taking advice from a man who was little more than a stranger. We sat in silence a few moments more before he pushed his chair away from the table.

"I believe I will take a walk through town. Would you join me?" I shook my head.

"I'm sorry, but my morning is already spoken for." I spread my hands out in a casual gesture. "I have responsibilities here."

"Pity. I enjoy your company, Mrs. Moore." Said simply, a statement of fact that did not expect a response. "I plan to stop at New Hope again on my trip home at the end of next week, however, so maybe you'll find it easier to fit me into your day then." He waited a moment, but I neither agreed nor disagreed, just smiled and stood. Saylor did the same, and as he rose, his coat fell open to reveal a dark blue silk tie on which rested a small piece of jewelry that caught the lights of the restaurant and sparkled with the brilliance of a star against a midnight winter sky. He followed my gaze and lifted the tie slightly away from his shirt front to give me a better view of the glittering pin.

"I own the Anchor spread outside Hot Sulphur Springs in northern Colorado. This is my brand."

"Of course," I said. "Saylor. Anchor. How clever."

I couldn't take my eyes from the pin, a recognizable anchor shape made of two opposing capital J's joined in the center and extending up to a horizontal line fork-pronged on each end. Above the line was a long closed oval, which for a real anchor would have attached to a chain or rope. Although hardly more than an inch in size, the shape was unmistakable because the anchor's gold outline was filled with small, perfect diamonds.

"It's beautiful," I said, looking back at Mark Saylor's face. "Your spread must be doing well."

"Well enough, but I'd do better if I can expand my market east. Other, bigger brands are taking care of California's appetite for beef so it's no use looking west for business."

"I see. Well, in a few months you'll be able to sound out opportunities for increasing your trade east to Chicago, and who knows where it might go from there?"

We walked together toward the hotel lobby. Behind us, the restaurant remained busy with breakfast patrons. Saylor and I had no sooner departed our table than Darla was carrying off our dirty dishes and behind her another girl was giving the tablecloth a soft brush before setting on clean dishes.

Once back in the lobby, I turned to face my companion "I wish you a successful trip to St. Joseph, Mr. Saylor."

"I've been summoned by my father, who lives there, Mrs. Moore. He's a demanding man and very hard to please. Part of my interest in the February meeting is on his behalf so I imagine he wants to make sure I understand and present his interests properly."

Saylor's tone held a touch of peevishness, and I guessed

there wasn't much love lost between father and son. Sometimes when the two men were either very similar or very different, there could be rivalry. Was that the case here? The diamond tie pin was almost too showy. Was it meant to send a message to Mr. Saylor, Senior?

"But meeting you has made the trip worthwhile, regardless of what happens in St. Jo. I look forward to seeing you again. And now" – he glanced toward the lobby doors that led outside – "I believe I'll take your advice and see a little more of New Hope." I watched Saylor as he left, still able to view his figure through the front windows. He looked in both directions and then turned north, toward the jail – maybe he wanted to meet the famous Silas Carpenter in the flesh – and eventually the railroad stock pens. That made sense, of course. Maybe he wanted to see for himself how situated New Hope was to handle great numbers of cattle.

Finally, I turned away. I wanted to see which rooms had check-outs today because after they were cleaned, I gave them a final inspection before allowing Les to book a new person into it. I hadn't made my usual morning visit to the kitchen, either, and there were ledgers to review, orders to place, work schedules to organize, and menus to suggest. Certainly enough to keep me busy for the next few hours. Still, for all the tasks on my list, every so often during the day's activities, I found myself pausing to reflect on the morning. Not on Mr. Mark Saylor, although his open admiration was gratifying, but on that diamond tie pin in the shape of an anchor. For some reason, the beautiful thing had captured my interest. Distinctive and eye-catching, yes, but for me there was an attraction that had nothing to do with gold and diamonds, an attraction I couldn't deny but at the time didn't fully understand.

Months later, I would remember that morning and understand how important a diamond tie pin was to the events that played out in New Hope. I didn't realize it then, however. Instead, I remember laughing softly and taking myself to task for having the eye of a crow, a creature tempted by baubles and fascinated by things that glittered.

5

I crossed Main Street to the restaurant early Monday morning to be sure I'd catch Henry Strunk before he left the kitchen for school. No morning tea in the Bliss's warm kitchen for me that day and no conversation with Ruby. I could always grab a cup at the restaurant and I wanted my information firsthand. I was excited enough to hear about the boy's new eyeglasses that I didn't care one little bit about changing my routine.

Henry was loading cups and saucers onto a tray, counting under his breath as he did so, when I said his name. He looked up and gave me a grin.

"Good morning. How was your trip?" I said, coming closer and making no effort to hide my interest in the wire-rimmed spectacles he wore. I thought they made Henry look older, closer to his age, and gave his thin face more substance.

"It was an adventure, Mrs. Moore. Purely an adventure. I've never been out of New Hope in all my life, and I went all the way to Colorado!"

"What did you think of Julesburg?"

"It was a lot like New Hope." I detected a touch of disappointment in Henry's voice. A decade earlier

Julesburg had been as wild a place as Ogallala. Now, though, to Henry's obvious disappointment, the place must have settled down.

"That's too bad," I said and was rewarded by another grin.

"Can't be helped, I guess," Henry said. "Mr. Stenton says civilization can be slowed down, but it can't be stopped."

I gestured toward the eyeglasses. "It looks like you managed to find your way to the eye doctor in the middle of all that civilization."

"Yes, ma'am. We didn't have any trouble. Dr. Conrad is a friend of Mr. Stenton's and sent him directions ahead of time."

"Do you notice a difference, Henry?" The boy understood exactly what I was asking.

"It's a wonder, Mrs. Moore. Everything's a lot clearer. It's not just that words on paper are bigger, but they seem brighter somehow, too. I won't be missing any spots on the plates now." Just hearing the enthusiasm in his voice lifted my spirits.

"I'm glad to hear it." I looked over at the big clock on the wall. "Isn't it time for you to get to school?"

He followed my gaze. "Yes, ma'am. I didn't realize it was that late."

"If Mr. Stenton scolds you for being tardy, tell him it was my fault for talking too long. And, Henry—"

"Yes, ma'am?"

"Learn something new today."

Later that afternoon, I walked out to the schoolhouse to find out if the trip to Julesburg had been as much of an adventure for Mr. Stenton as it had been for Henry. I suspected not, but perhaps even schoolteachers enjoyed stepping out of the county now and then.

When I pulled open the schoolhouse door to enter, a pesky wind came inside with me and blew down the center aisle between the desks, catching at some papers on the teacher's desk and sending them swirling onto the floor. I was reminded of my first visit a few weeks ago. Same wind but colder now.

"I'm sorry," I said, yanking the doors closed behind me and hurrying up the aisle to offer assistance. "I didn't mean to disturb your work." As I came closer, Arthur Stenton stood from gathering the windswept papers, which he now held in both hands as if he feared they had a life of their own and might try another escape.

"Good afternoon, Mrs. Moore. There's no harm done." In the methodical way I was growing used to, he returned the papers to his desktop, gave them a quick shuffle to make the stack even, and turned toward the lone chair that sat beside his desk.

"Oh, don't fuss, please," I said. "I don't need to sit down. I'm only staying long enough to see if you were satisfied with the result of your visit to Julesburg." Because I remained standing, Mr. Stenton felt obliged to do the same. "Henry seems happy with his eyeglasses," I added.

"Those aren't his permanent eyeglasses. Dr. Conrad will prepare the glass specific to Henry's needs and send the eyeglasses once he's satisfied they're right for Henry. The spectacles he sent home with Henry are only magnifiers."

'Well, for a boy whose world must have been a confusing blur, the substitute eyeglasses must seem like magic to him."

"Yes."

After an awkward silence, I said, "Mr. Stenton, I'd like to give you a bank draft for the cost of the spectacles, as well as the train tickets. That way Ruby and I can settle the matter between us without having to include you." At his look, I added, "Not that including you is a hardship, of course."

"Of course." I heard something wry and almost amused in his tone and had to smile.

"It's just that Ruby and I understand each other." I looked at him. "It was good of you to concern yourself with Henry, Mr. Stenton. People hold you in high regard and I'm beginning to understand why." He flushed slightly at the words but didn't speak. "If you prepare a summary of the costs and send it along to me, I'll be sure you're reimbursed right away."

"Thank you. I'll have it to you tomorrow."

Many men would not have been comfortable talking money matters with a woman, but clearly Arthur Stenton was not one of them.

"Good." I tried to think of something else to say, but when nothing came to mind, I simply wished him a good night and turned to go. As I reached for the doorknob, Stenton said my name.

"Yes?" I stopped and turned to look at him.

He came out from behind his desk and walked down the aisle toward me holding something in his hand. A book, I noted, which he extended toward me once he was closer.

"I hope I'm not being presumptuous, but I thought you might find this interesting," Arthur Stenton said.

Curious, I took the book from him and glanced at the title on the cover: *May-Day and Other Pieces* by Ralph Waldo Emerson.

"Henry told me he mentioned Mr. Emerson to you and that you weren't acquainted with his writings. I thought his poetry might be a way to introduce you to Emerson the philosopher and the ideas he, well, to be honest, the ideas he seems to struggle with."

"Such as?"

That Arthur Stenton didn't hesitate answering my question made me think that the teacher might struggle with some of the same ideas.

"Mortality and renewal. Aging. The cycle of nature and by extension the cycle of human life."

"Those are topics any thinking person might struggle

with," I replied but wondered if I had the stomach, the temperament, or even the desire to dwell on any of those serious matters.

As if he saw uncertainty in my expression, Mr. Stenton said quickly, "I've made the work sound too somber, I think. It's my opinion only. Many of the poems are quite beautiful, and I promise you can enjoy them without looking below the surface." His words were an apology of sorts, as if he feared he had mentioned matters that I might find painful. The quick words surprised me. Maybe there was more to the man than just being practical and stern.

Not sure how to respond, I opened the book and saw an inscription on the inside cover. *Arthur,* it read in a thin, spidery scrawl, *Merry Christmas. Never forget that deep in the man sits fast his fate,* the last eight words underscored. A quote from the poet, Mr. Emerson? Or someone else? I would watch for the phrase as I read. The book was obviously a gift, but there was no name at the end of the message.

"Thank you," I said finally. "This is very thoughtful of you. It appears the book was a gift and no doubt holds special meaning for you. I'll take good care of it, I promise, and return it when I'm done."

"It was a gift from my grandfather. He was a serious thinker who put great store in education."

"Was he a schoolteacher, too?" I asked.

"He was a judge by profession but often said he was a schoolteacher at heart." I heard affection in Stenton's tone and a warmth I would never have guessed. "You may rest assured that I won't quiz you about the poems or any of the contents of the book."

I recognized a light-handed attempt at humor and responded, "You may quiz to your heart's content, Mr. Stenton. I'm the first to admit that I've read very little poetry in my life and certainly nothing by Mr. Emerson. He sounds a bit grand for a beginner like me. I may need your quizzing to put my understanding straight."

"No." A quiet, firm syllable that set aside my words as if I hadn't spoken them. "You need never be humble or modest in my presence, Mrs. Moore. It's clear from the few times we've talked that you possess a sharp and intelligent mind." He said the words simply, but I thought I had never received a finer compliment; it wasn't my mind that men were interested in. "That said," he went on, "if something strikes you as unclear or muddled – Emerson's poetry has been called that on occasion – you may certainly say so. It would be no reflection on you."

I smiled at the words. "You may be sorry you've agreed to that since I have a tendency to speak my mind, but thank you."

"You're welcome, Mrs. Moore."

"Caroline," I said. "Please call me Caroline." This time it was my words that seemed to surprise him but he simply nodded. "I need to get back to the hotel," I continued. "You won't forget about forwarding the bill for Henry's eyeglasses to me?"

"I won't forget."

"I'll hold you to your words, then," I said, pulled open the door – careful not to let in an untidy breeze this time – murmured a quiet goodbye, and left, pulling the door shut behind me.

I clutched the small book along with the ends of my shawl firmly to my chest, almost against my heart. With Davey's death I thought my days of being surprised or touched by an unexpected kindness were over. How odd to think it was Mr. Stenton that proved me wrong! Then I corrected myself mentally: How odd to think it was *Arthur* that proved me wrong! He hadn't returned the offer – did he think I hadn't noticed? – but I didn't care. From now on, I would call him Arthur whether he liked it or not. Just one thinking, intelligent mind speaking with its equal. Whatever Emerson might write or think, that was exactly the way it was meant to be according to the Caroline Moore view of life.

One afternoon the next week, without any warning, Les Woodson told me he was getting married and would no longer be able to work at Bliss House. His was happy news, but I still thought I heard a trace of regret in his voice.

"I didn't know you were keeping company with anyone, Les."

"I been stepping out with Sally Winters almost from the first day I got here," he said and colored a little. "We noticed each other right off."

"Her parents run the grocery store," I said, finally placing the last name.

"Yes, ma'am, and her pa wants me to learn the grocery business so I'm going to start working in the store. Sally's their only child, you see." I did see. A son-in-law familiar with the grocery business would be a practical addition to the family.

"When's the wedding?" I asked.

"Well, Sally would like it before the new year, but her ma thinks we should wait until spring. Mr. Winters says no matter when it is, he wants me to get started working in the store right away, but I told him I can't leave Mr. Bliss – leave you, I mean, since Mr. Bliss is gone – in the lurch. That's why I took it on myself to talk to Lizbeth."

"Lizbeth?" I was lagging behind in the conversation, which must have been noticeable because Les began to look a little worried. Maybe he read my confusion as disapproval.

"Lizbeth Ericson. She helps over at the boarding house. Been doing that for years so she knows about checking people in and out and how to manage a front desk. Except the boarding house is a lot smaller than the hotel, but I know she'll do fine. She thinks working here would be a good way for her to try something new. To branch out is how she put it." His words were coming faster and a small vertical line had appeared between his brows.

"Les," I said, calm and quiet and smiling a little, "are you happy about marrying Sally Winters?"

"Oh." A grin began to appear as he thought about my question. "Oh, yes, ma'am." There was something so sweet and so terribly young in his tone that my heart went out to him. I had loved Davey but couldn't recall ever feeling that sweet or sounding that young about it, having left my youth behind years before I met Davey Moore. "Sally's pretty and smart, and I still can't believe she said she'd marry me. Me, Les Woodson, with hardly a prospect to my name. I got awful lucky."

"I bet she feels lucky, too," I said. "Everything will work out, I promise, so don't let worry about the hotel spoil the happy news. I'll need you here for a while yet, until I can find a replacement, but you let me take care of that. I appreciate knowing about Miss Ericson, but I'd like to talk to Mrs. Carpenter before you talk any further with Lizbeth. Agreed?"

"Yes, ma'am."

"I'll walk over there now." I smiled. "I'm very happy for you, Les."

"Thank you." His cheeks turned rosy once more. "Fact is, I'm pretty happy myself."

When I stepped into the boarding house lobby, Lizbeth was polishing the front desk with vigorous strokes, using something that had to hold a touch of lemon because the pleasant citrus fragrance reached me even before Lizbeth's greeting.

"Hello, Mrs. Moore." With a movement graceful yet discreet, the young woman lowered both cloth and polish out of sight behind the desk without dropping her gaze.

"Hello to you, Lizbeth." I smiled and shifted my heavy shawl from head to shoulders. "I've brought the cold air in with me, I'm afraid."

"I hardly felt it. The fire keeps it cozy enough in here."

She was right. The lobby, with its padded chairs and a tasseled table lamp on a table between them, the lace curtains and pretty flocked wallpaper was a welcoming and comfortable room, but it was the fire in the hearth that kept it cozy.

"That looks like one of Sheba Bliss's paintings." I gestured to the large painting that hung over the fireplace. "Is it a view from around here?"

"It's the Platte in summer. There are several places along the river that might have been Miss Sheba's inspiration, but she's not telling."

"It doesn't matter, though, does it?" I said. I took a moment to give the picture a second, longer, more thoughtful study. "Because it's more about the way it makes you feel than where Sheba stood when she painted it." I looked over at Lizbeth. "Right?"

"Right."

Lizbeth Ericson was a slim girl with a boyish figure, fair hair, light, clear eyes, and a smattering of freckles across the bridge of a sharp little nose. At the risk of being fanciful, I might have said she had the look of the prairie about her, a gaze as open as the horizon but with nothing sentimental or soft in it. A young woman who knew what she believed and like a stand of oaks would not, could not be swayed. She smiled at my comments about the painting over the hearth and it was a lovely smile, one that added a surprising sweetness to her face, softened her somehow and reminded me that she was still quite young. I would have been surprised if she had reached her eighteenth birthday yet.

"Is Mrs. Carpenter here, Lizbeth? I need to talk to her for a moment. I won't take up much of her time, I promise."

Behind me I heard the door open, felt a draft of cold air, and turned to see Ruth Carpenter.

"I'm here now," she said, entering just in time to hear

my question. "Hello, Caroline." To Lizbeth, Ruth said, "Is that rapscallion son of mine still sleeping?"

"Yes, ma'am. Hasn't made a peep since you left."

"Well, drat it all. That means he won't sleep tonight. Couldn't you have made more noise while you worked?" But she laughed a little when she asked the question and Lizbeth laughed, too.

"Come back with me, Caroline," Ruth invited. "We can talk in the kitchen, if you don't mind."

I followed Ruth down the hallway into the back of the boarding house where the Carpenters lived. Ruth dropped her coat over the back of a chair and went immediately to the large cradle next to the table, crouched down, and pulled back a blanket to peer at her son. When she touched the boy's cheek with one gentle finger, her face softened in much the same way Lizbeth's had when she smiled. I walked closer and looked down at the child with his dark lashes fluttering against plump cheeks. He was a beautiful boy, not yet two I knew but sturdy and rosy with good health. A loved child that was clear.

"He'll be awake soon enough," Ruth said and stood upright. "Would you like a cup of tea, Caroline?"

"No, thank you. I can't stay long enough to enjoy it, I'm afraid."

"The Bliss establishments keep you busy." Ruth's statement was true enough, but I thought there was another message behind the words.

"They do."

"Still, I wish you could make time for tea now and then. I'd appreciate the company and you might enjoy getting to know some of your other neighbors, besides. We're not a bad lot, on the whole."

"I know you're not." The fact was that I was used to being on my own by then and trusted my own company, and I didn't know how to explain to Ruth Carpenter that after the struggle I'd had learning to be content with my solitary life, I feared upsetting the apple cart.

"Never mind." She reached over and patted my arm. "I was widowed, too, Caroline, and I understand." I was surprised by her words, then touched. Maybe she did understand much of what I felt, I thought finally, but not all. There was no way she could guess everything that went on in my mind or heart. She hadn't the temperament for it. But I still appreciated the woman's kindness.

"Now," Ruth said, her tone back to brisk, "what can I do for you?"

"You've probably heard that Les Woodson and Sally Winters are getting married," I said.

"By now," Ruth made a point of glancing at the small mantel clock that sat on her sideboard, "every person in New Hope has heard the news. Millie Winters is beside herself."

"Happy with her future son-in-law, then," I observed.

"Happy enough with Les but happier to have her daughter settled with anyone even halfway acceptable, which Les certainly is. Sally's been a handful for her mother this last year, too high-spirited for a woman like Millie, who sets great store by the conventions. Getting Sally settled with a husband and bringing the new husband into the family business has made Millie Winters about to burst from relief and satisfaction, and I'm not being critical, just stating a fact."

"Well, with Les taking on the grocery business, I'm in need of a reliable person at the hotel's front desk." Ruth smiled, but I didn't think her heart was entirely in the smile.

"I know," she said. "Lizbeth's already told me she's considering making a change." I waited without speaking. Ruth took a deep breath, close to a sigh, and added, "And I told her she should talk to you and see if something could be worked out. I can't say I won't miss her. I've watched her grow up and I've loved her like a sister for a long while. I don't know how I'd have managed without her all the years I was cutting hair and running the boarding house at the same time, but things are different now. Even with a baby, I don't need her in the same way I did, and I'd like to see her use the talents she's got."

"You don't think running the front desk of a busy hotel would be too much for her?"

"Too much?" Ruth gave a small hoot of laughter. "I tell you this truly, Caroline. I can't imagine anything that would be too much for Lizbeth if she put her mind to it. She's smart as a whip; I never have to tell her anything twice. And she's good with people, always kind, of course, but she's not a girl to let herself be run over by anyone, either. She can hold her own and then some. You'll see what I mean. Lizbeth Ericson looks like an ordinary miss straight off the prairie, but she speaks her mind and there's not much that gets by her."

If that was true, I thought, maybe Lizbeth wasn't someone I wanted to spend time with every day. But then, with the Beef Convention coming up, I needed a competent person at the front desk and didn't have a lot of time to spend finding Les's replacement.

"Then if you don't mind," I said, "I'd like to talk to her about coming to work at Bliss House. Should I speak to her parents first, do you think?"

A downward twist to Ruth Carpenter's mouth was the only indication of her opinion of my question and Lizbeth's parents. Her words were pleasant enough.

"Lizbeth is only a few weeks away from turning eighteen, and she's been making her own decisions since I've known her. She sends most of her pay to her father, and I'd guess you'll be able to pay her more than she's making here, so you don't have to concern yourself with the Ericsons giving their permission. Of course, that's just my opinion. You do whatever you feel is right and proper."
I didn't know Ruth very well and she hadn't said one

untoward word, but I understood what she was telling me.

"Thank you," I said and turned to leave. "I'll talk to Lizbeth on my way out and see what she thinks."

Behind me, the child made a small, gurgling kind of noise and then began to whimper, waking from sleep and hungry. I recognized the sound, universal to all babies, that would soon be followed by a noisy complaint about an empty belly and maybe a wet nappy, too. By the time I was back in the lobby of the boarding house, young Carpenter was crying with a volume that seemed too loud for such a small person. I stopped next to Lizbeth and we smiled at each other.

"There's a good set of lungs on that young man," I said.

"He doesn't use them all that often," Lizbeth replied, "but when he does, it can sure get a person's attention."

"Les tells me you wouldn't be averse to coming to work at Bliss House," I said. If what Ruth Carpenter said about Lizbeth Ericson's character was true, it would do no good for me to beat around the bush. Lizbeth met my gaze with a steady look.

"No ma'am, I wouldn't. I know the hotel business, " – she gestured around the cozy lobby – "and though Hart's is nowhere near the size of Bliss House, people are still people, and I know my way around keeping folks happy."

"You like it here at Hart's, though, don't you?"

"I do, yes, ma'am. There's no one in the world I think more highly of than Miss Ruth. No better person that I've ever met."

"But –" I prompted.

Lizbeth didn't hesitate. "But Miss Ruth doesn't need me, not like she used to, and I'm ready for something more, something bigger. I'll be eighteen soon and I want to try my hand at something else."

"No young man waiting for you off to the side, then, I take it?"

There was a touch of sadness in Lizbeth's smile, but she

said, "No, ma'am. No young man waiting anywhere."

It would happen soon enough with this smart and pretty girl, I thought. "And your parents will approve of the change?" I remembered Ruth's words and thought I already knew the answer.

"Yes, ma'am. Pa has my brothers to help on the farm and the money I send home is more helpful to Ma than I could ever be."

"Speaking of money," I said. "I'm not authorized to pay you any more than what Les was making. When Mr. Bliss gets back, he'll do what he wants, of course, but until then," – quoted the same wage Les earned and watched Lizbeth's eyes widen at the figure. "Will that do for the time being?"

"Oh, yes, ma'am. That's very generous. That'll do fine. When do you want me to start?"

"I'll want you to spend a little time with Les before he heads down the street to the grocery store, but let me work that out with Les before I give you a date. Maybe Mrs. Carpenter will want to get someone to take your place, too."

A momentary frown drew Lizbeth's brows together, as if the idea that someone might take her place at the boarding house working beside her beloved Miss Ruth hadn't crossed her mind. But of course, it must have, Lizbeth Ericson being a bright, forward-thinking young woman, who would have thought things through carefully before she allowed Les to say a word to me about her replacing him.

"Maybe she will," Lizbeth said finally. "We all have to get used to change, don't we?"

"We do," I said, "and only time will tell whether what we decided was progress or a mistake." From the girl's quick glance at my face, I thought Lizbeth hadn't expected an answer to her question and was surprised as much by my serious tone as by my words.

"Everybody makes mistakes, Mrs. Moore. I don't plan them in advance, but I'm probably going to make a few." She thinks I was talking about bringing her on at Bliss House, I realized, and that I was worried about how she'd do.

"I'm relieved to hear you're human, Lizbeth, the same as the rest of us. There's no shame in mistakes, as long as we learn from them. As soon as I talk to Les, I'll let you know what day and time you can plan to start. And thank you. It's a load off my mind. That big beef meeting is scheduled in February and Mr. Bliss is counting on me to make sure it happens without a hitch. I believe you'll be a big help with it."

"I'll do my best."

"I have no doubt about that," I said and retied my shawl tightly around my shoulders before stepping outside into the late fall cold.

6

Soon after my talk with Lizbeth, Mark Saylor returned to New Hope, arriving on the last westbound train. As I stood in the arched doorway making a casual count of the last wave of diners being served, I was aware of a figure standing, waiting at my shoulder.

"I beg your pardon," I said and turned around, thinking I blocked someone's way, but it was no hungry stranger hoping for a late supper.

"Mrs. Moore," Saylor said, and doffed his hat, "I hoped it was you." He had a fine smile, bright and friendly, and I couldn't help but smile in return.

"Mr. Saylor. How nice to see you again. You're just in, I assume. Are you looking for a quick bite before you continue on your way?"

"Not once I saw you standing in the doorway, Mrs. Moore. No man of any sense would take a quick by-your-leave if there was any chance of spending more time with you." When I remained silent, he added, "Is there?"

"Something can be arranged, I'm sure," I said, smiling, and reached out both hands. "Let me hang your hat while you find a table that suits you. There's always steak on the menu and you can't go wrong with it, but I have to put in a word for Monsieur Clermont's very special veal loaf with mushroom sauce, which is also available today. You can let Deb know your preference." Saylor handed me his hat but didn't move from where he stood.

"And will you join me, Mrs. Moore, or if you've already eaten, at least keep me company? Your presence would turn an already fine meal into perfection." The words were complimentary enough, but it was the sparkle in his eyes that convinced me.

"I have some business to take care of, Mr. Saylor, but I'll join you for coffee at the end of your meal, and speaking of perfection, I'd be remiss in my duty if I didn't recommend the chef's fruit tart for dessert." I carried the man's hat to the front desk where I set the handsome gray Stetson on the counter.

"This is Mr. Saylor's," I explained to Les, who was tidying the area and getting ready to leave for the night.

"Yes, ma'am. I noticed it when he registered." After a moment, Les said, "I want to tell you that it's been a pleasure working for you, Mrs. Moore. It surely has."

Touched by the words, I at first couldn't think what to say, then, "Thank you, Les. I wish you the best in your new endeavors, and I can't thank you enough for putting in a word with Lizbeth about taking your place."

"She's the one who said something to me about it, not the other way around. Lizbeth generally knows what she wants and goes after it."

"And she wanted to work at Bliss House?"

"Well, the way I see it, Lizbeth wanted a change, and Bliss House would do just fine in that regard."

"Whatever the reason," I said, "I feel fortunate to have her starting with us on Monday. She seems to have taken to the job pretty well from what I saw of you and her training together."

"She's an awful smart girl, awful smart." He repeated the words as if slightly nervous about the idea. "I doubt there's anything she can't do if she puts her mind to it," repeating Ruth Carpenter's earlier comment.

"Do smart girls make you nervous, Les?" I asked, grinning at him.

"My Sally's exactly as smart as a woman should be, Mrs. Moore. A man don't want to think he's only a step away from looking like a fool, especially in front of his girl. Not that Lizbeth is ever snooty or unkind or anything like that."

"Just smart, then," I said, trying not to smile. "That's good to know."

"Yes, ma'am." He gave me a look and realized I was teasing him. "I don't have anything against smart women, ma'am," he added, making sure to set the record straight.

"That's a relief, Les. There's probably more of them around than you think." Laughing softly, I turned back toward the dining room. Before I could join Mark Saylor for coffee, something I looked forward to, I needed to visit the kitchen to extend my last tribute of the day to Monsieur Clermont. I was never fooled by the chef's nonchalant acceptance of my grateful praise. The man expected, required, compliments on a regular basis, and as long as he continued being a genius – even a *temperamental* genius – in the kitchen, I was happy to oblige.

By the time I sat down across from Saylor, he had had time to finish his meal – he'd taken my veal recommendation to heart, I noticed – and was placing his napkin next to his now empty plate. His eyes brightened when he saw me, and he made a half-hearted attempt to stand for my presence. I waved him back down and took the chair across from him.

"I hope the veal didn't disappoint," I said.

"It was perfect. Everything's perfect. Now." He gave me his full, warm smile, a smile intended to charm, which it did because I've never been a woman immune to a handsome man.

"I'm glad to hear it." When Deb swooped in to clear away the used dishes, I turned to her and said, "Bring Mr. Saylor a piece of peach tart, will you please, Deb, and a fresh pot of coffee for the two of us?" She was gone and back in just a moment.

I filled two cups with coffee and sipped mine, allowing Saylor time to enjoy the tart, a masterpiece of tender crust and just enough cinnamon in the filling to bring out the sweetness of the apples and peaches.

"Tasty, isn't it?" I asked.

"You've got yourself a treasure in the kitchen, Mrs. Moore."

I laughed. "I can't argue with that, though I admit that I usually appreciate his cooking more than his temperament."

"Great artists have a reputation for being difficult, I'm told."

"I've heard the same," I said. It stayed quiet at the table until Saylor reached for his coffee cup. The lapel of his coat pulled away enough to show the anchor-shaped stick pin on his tie. Its unexpected gleam caught by the wall sconce surprised me enough to distract my words as I said, "I hope your stay in St. Jo was successful." He didn't seem to notice my brief hesitation.

"With my father it's hard to tell," the words accompanied by a shrug, "but I believe he approved of everything I told him. He's not a man for compliments, either giving or receiving them."

"Is he in the cattle business, too?"

"Yes. He owns several ranches. Wyoming Territory. Nebraska. The Dakotas. And Colorado, of course." I didn't ask the question his offhand *of course* brought to mind, but Saylor must have seen it on my face because without prompting he explained, "I own the greater share of the Anchor, but my father still has a say in its running. He doesn't hold a lot of confidence in me."

"Oh?"

"I ran a little wild in my youth, Mrs. Moore, and Trenton Saylor isn't a man to forget or forgive easily."

"From what I've seen, it's not unusual for fathers and sons to share in a few rivalries. The nature of growing up, I suppose. Is your mother still living?" Saylor's face softened at the question.

"No, she's been gone some time now. Which I regret. She always believed in me, but never got the chance to see me – well, grow up, I guess you'd say."

"I'm sorry." He let his blue eyes rest on my face.

"Thank you. My mother was a good woman and deserved better than the men she got," adding with a sheepish smile, "You know how to keep a man talking, Mrs. Moore, but I think it's time to talk about you."

"Oh, I'm a dull topic," I said.

"Impossible. Surely you know how attractive you are. A man could never find a woman with your qualities dull." When I made no response, he said, "I hope my comment didn't offend you. You got quiet."

"I'm a quiet woman by nature, and no, I wasn't offended. Compliments are too few and far between for me to be offended by a few kind words."

"The men of New Hope must be a slow lot, then. Either that or blind."

"Not slow or blind, Mr. Saylor," I spoke with a smile so he'd know I recognized his words as part of the same compliment and not a slight to the local population, "but an industrious group with families and businesses of their own, much too busy to give a second look at a woman whose only role is to make sure John Bliss's establishments roll along as smoothly as they would if he were here. Truly, I'm just a substitute for the real thing." He raised both brows and made a noncommittal sound, something like a *hmmm,* before he reached for his coffee cup.

"I can tell you honestly, Mrs. Moore, that I count myself lucky that Bliss is gone. Otherwise, I'd never have had the pleasure of your company at supper. Likely never have met you at all, in fact, which would have been a pity. Can you pull yourself away long enough for a stroll down Main Street with me? I won't keep you long; I know you're a busy woman. I need to stretch my legs after a long time on the train, and I'd appreciate the company."

"It's dark and cold, Mr. Saylor."

"Well, who'd have thought that a capable, strong-minded woman like yourself would be bothered by a little cold weather? I never expected that."

I opened my mouth to retort and saw the gleam of humor in his eyes. He really was a handsome man, and I wouldn't mind spending a little longer in his company.

"I suspect this is as pleasant as it's going to get for the next few months," Saylor said, continuing his pursuit. "By Christmas, I'd wager you'll remember tonight's walk the same way you recall a summer stroll along the river." His nonsense made me laugh and I pushed back my chair.

"All right," I said. "You've convinced me. Let me get my coat and I'll meet you in the lobby." He grinned, pleased with himself in the way men are whenever they think they've gotten their own way. Whether what they believe is true or not, I've always found it wise not to spoil their triumph.

We had a pleasant walk after all. The November night breeze couldn't really reach me with my hand tucked under Saylor's arm and my shoulder brushing his. It felt, in fact, quite cozy. Nothing like a summer stroll by the river, naturally, but warm enough. I don't remember all that we talked about, but I was curious about his relationship with his father and even more about his wild youth that forced him to remain under his father's control. Mark Saylor was no child and could certainly have struck out on his own if he'd chosen to.

When I said something to that effect, but using more careful words, he responded, "I did walk away, for a few years, but to my surprise my father put the Pinkertons on my trail and when they found me, the old man came himself to talk to me and offer me a deal."

"Deal?"

Saylor and I crossed the empty, dark street and stood in front of Hart's. The light through the boarding house windows shone amber and warm, as welcoming as Ruth Carpenter's smile.

"A business deal. If I bring the herd, he'll provide the grazing land. A partnership he called it, but I could tell he thought I didn't have it in me to settle down and work that hard. Thought I couldn't recognize good beef, either, so a few years later when I wired him to come take a look at my little herd, he was surprised by what he saw. Prime beef, every one of them and all wearing the Anchor brand."

"You must have worked your fingers to the bone," I said in a light tone, "and I bet it felt good to show you could be as successful as your father."

We crossed the alley and passed the darkened bank and the Chandlers' Hardware Store, nearly collided with a man exiting the front door of the Gooseneck's Billiards Parlor, and finally stopped across the street from Bliss House, ready to cross the street and return to warmth.

"Better than good. What it was, was satisfying. Deeply satisfying. Satisfying to the bone." I could tell from his tone that he enjoyed reliving the moment and wouldn't have been surprised if it wasn't the first time in his life he had ever bested his father at anything. Something more than rivalry there but it was late, and I grew cold and lost interest at the same time.

Once in the hotel lobby, Saylor turned to me, removed his hat, and said, "Thank you. I appreciated the company more than you know, Mrs. Moore."

Appreciated the attention, too, I thought. Mark Saylor enjoyed talking, especially about himself, but I didn't hold that against him. My husband had enjoyed talking, too, but in Davey's case, it was always more about his ideas and dreams than about himself proper. I wasn't sure if the same held true of Saylor or if it was the image he had of himself that he liked talking about.

"Will you join me for breakfast?" he asked, but I knew where to draw the line.

"I'm afraid that's not possible, but thank you. Morning is my busiest time of the day."

My words didn't seem to surprise him. With his hat in one hand, he looked down long enough to unbutton his coat with the other and then raised his head to smile at me.

"You've said that before, but you won't mind if I come in search of you to say goodbye tomorrow, will you? I'm out early on the 8:11, and I promise I won't get in the way of such a busy woman as yourself." He might have been mocking me, I couldn't tell.

"I'll look forward to it," I said, "busy woman or not. Good night, Mr. Saylor. Thank you for the walk."

I returned his smile before I moved toward the front desk counter where young Kip stood watching. As Saylor turned toward the stairs, I noticed that his coat, now hanging open, swung unevenly, one side weighted down more than the other. He carried something heavy in a pocket, no doubt a weapon, small but deadly. A derringer of some kind, probably a Remington, which many travelers carried. It was something I'd want to keep in mind as I got to know the man better. I had a small, pearl-handled pistol myself, but I didn't carry it with me in New Hope. I had bought it after the fire, when I moved to Denver and was slowly getting back on my feet, knowing I was too weak to defend myself if it ever came to that. Those early days in Denver, everyone was a stranger and so everyone was a threat, and the little derringer helped me find my confidence again.

Neither Mark nor I looked back after we parted, and yet I knew we were both as conscious of the other person as if we had indulged in a passionate kiss in the middle of the Bliss House lobby. A circumstance I thought Mark Saylor would find even more satisfying than the time he surpassed his father's expectations.

Henry Strunk appeared in the office doorway early the next morning, his face brightened by a beaming smile and shiny new spectacles. Gypsy, curled on the seat of an office chair, opened one eye, saw that the new arrival was Henry, one of the few humans she favored, hopped to the floor, and sauntered over to the boy. Henry took a moment to give the cat the usual back scratch she had come to expect from him, then straightened to grin at me and say, "Do you notice anything new, Mrs. Moore?"

Confronted by so much good humor, I couldn't help but give him a wide smile in return and ask, "Are these the real thing now?"

"Yes, ma'am. They came on the train straight from Julesburg. My name was on the box." I couldn't tell if the awe and triumph in his voice were because of the new eyeglasses or because he had received a package all his own, something I was sure had never happened before.

"Looks like they meet with your approval."

"Yes, ma'am, they do. They sure enough do. It's like a miracle. I thought the ones we borrowed from Dr. Conrad were fine, and I couldn't believe the difference they made in seeing things, but these," he took off the eyeglasses and waved them at me to emphasize his words, "these are just plain–" Henry stopped abruptly and I realized he was trying to find the right word to explain how the eyeglasses made him feel, how they changed his view of life.

"Amazing?" I supplied. "Wonderful? Marvelous?"

He settled the spectacles back on his face and nodded. "Yes, ma'am, all them words you said and more. I still can't believe that this is how people have been seeing things all this time. I never had no idea. I knew I didn't see things like other folks. That was why I got moved to the front of the schoolroom, but I never once fancied that everybody else was seeing the world like I'm seeing the world right now. It's a wonder."

It *was* a wonder, I thought, and a miracle in its own way, too. For some reason, the bright look on the boy's thin face and the sparkle in his eyes, magnified a bit by the eyeglasses, brought a prick of tears to my own eyes. The last time I could remember seeing such pure joy on a person's face was when Davey reached down to lift our newborn Jean, red and wrinkled and swaddled in an old blanket, up from where she lay beside me.

"Well," my husband had said, unable to take his eyes from our daughter, "aren't you something, little girl? Aren't you just something?" Eyeglasses and babies might both make a person see the world differently, but that was all I thought they had in common, that and the way they could spark pure happiness. Perhaps Henry's tone threatened to make me teary because I heard in it an echo of my husband's voice. My big-hearted, true, and faithful Davey. Whatever the reason, I pushed myself to my feet with a brisk movement.

"If you're late to school," I told Henry, "you won't have time to show your spectacles to Mr. Stenton. He deserves a firsthand viewing, don't you think?"

"He sure does." The boy added, "But I wanted to show them to you, too. You and Mr. Stenton – well, I don't know what to say exactly."

"A thank-you is good enough, but you might consider volunteering to clean the chalkboards for Mr. Stenton every so often. I'm perfectly content with clean dishes so you can consider me properly thanked already. Now scoot off before you make me late, too. Monsieur Clermont and Mr. Stenton are not men to be trifled with."

Before leaving, Henry tucked the wires of his spectacles firmly behind his ears, reached down to the patient cat to give her arched back a final scratch, shot me a quick one-handed wave, and disappeared. I heard his footsteps on the wooden floor pick up into a run before the sound disappeared entirely.

There are worse ways to start a day, I told myself and still smiling, headed for the kitchen.

Mark Saylor waited for me at the front desk when I returned from my morning conference with the chef. When he saw me, he straightened from where he leaned against the counter.

"Good morning," I said. "I hope you had a good night's sleep."

"I did. You have a quiet little town here, Mrs. Moore. I don't think I heard a thing all night."

"New Hope tends to shut down early for the night," I agreed, coming to stand in front of him, "and no one wishes otherwise, including me. I spent a few years managing a fine little hotel in Ogallala, which if you know anything about that town, is just waking up about the same time New Hope is drifting off. I much prefer New Hope's hours."

"Have you ever lived someplace bigger, like San Francisco or Denver?"

"I spent a while in Denver."

"Then you know that Denver makes Ogallala look like a Sunday School picnic. Is that why you left?"

"It's true that I didn't much care for Denver, but I left because John Bliss made me an offer I couldn't refuse, and I was ready for a change." Because I didn't want to talk anymore about my history, I continued without pause, "Your breakfast table's all set and you're in luck because we have hotcakes on the morning menu. A word to the wise." I lowered my voice as if sharing a secret. "Save yourself some time and order two stacks right from the start. You won't regret it."

He laughed a little. "I wish you'd join me."

"Thank you, but not this morning." Too much of a good thing can unsettle a person, I thought, and while I wasn't sure Mark Saylor was a good thing, I was sure that too much time in his company had the power to unsettle me and keep me from considering him with a clear head. "But I'll look forward to seeing you in February." I added the words to take any insult out of my refusal.

"Oh, I doubt I'll stay away from the attractions of New Hope until February. I expect to make the trip to St. Jo more than once before then. Lately, my father's been talking about attending the Beef Convention here in New Hope himself and I need to talk him out of that. Having two Saylors at the meeting would be one too many."

"I suspect one Saylor will be more than enough." I gave the words a light touch with just enough compliment to make him smile.

"I suspect you're right." His pale blue eyes caught my gaze and held it. "No one's complained about my company that I've ever heard. Just the opposite, in fact. I'm told I have a knack for keeping people satisfied." Keeping *women* satisfied, he might as well have said.

I took a quick step back and then to his side, saying as I did so, "Goodbye, Mr. Saylor." But he wasn't finished with the conversation yet.

"I hope it's all right if I look you up the next time I'm in New Hope, Mrs. Moore," his words more statement than asking permission.

"Of course. I'd be disappointed if you didn't." I gave him another friendly smile. "Have a good trip home," I said, "and don't forget about those hotcakes."

Not waiting for a response, I raised a hand of greeting to Les, who had just appeared behind the front desk, and then headed toward the side hall. Behind me, Saylor said something, whether about the hotcakes or the trip I couldn't tell, but while he might not be done with the conversation, for the time being I was. I stopped at the office door, one hand on the knob, for a quick calming breath before I went inside. I wasn't sure how I felt about the man, if I was flattered by his attentions or uneasy with them, if I wanted to get closer to him or put more distance between us. I needed time and more information to figure him out.

7

During those first few weeks in New Hope, I was busy adjusting to the demands of Bliss House, learning its routines and learning the names and habits of the people who worked there, something which through the years I have learned is the most important part of making any enterprise run smoothly. I had one main goal at the time: to keep Bliss House solvent and successful so that John's confidence in me was not misplaced. After that, my ambitions had nothing to do with either Bliss House or New Hope. Certainly, I never expected and never intended to grow comfortable there or make friends there or consider it home. I had plans for my future that had nothing to do with the bustle of respectability and progress that was the town's life blood. And yet, with hindsight, I suppose my settling so quickly into a place that accepted me without question or challenge was inescapable. I had been homeless in heart and hearth for a long time, and New Hope couldn't help itself. It offered then, and still offers, all the warmth and welcome and calm security of home.

In an odd way, it was Lizbeth Ericson's arrival at the front desk of the hotel that first tempted me to forget that I was in New Hope for a specific and temporary reason.

Lizbeth had a way about her that was as warm and welcoming and calmly sensible as the town itself, a way that made a person comfortable with her from the start. At least, I was comfortable with her from the start, which shouldn't have surprised me because Lizbeth had, after all, grown up under the steadying hand and admirable example of Ruth Carpenter, the kindest woman I had ever met, bar none. Whatever the reason, it didn't take long for Lizbeth to become a fixture at Bliss House, for the table girls to share their personal secrets with her or for the regular travelers to ask about her by name. Her place at Bliss House was cemented when Monsieur Clermont commended me for bringing "the young mademoiselle," the name the chef always used for Lizbeth, to the hotel.

"A worthy addition," Clermont told me one morning, as if I needed him to approve my decisions. "You have done well, Madame." High praise from a man whose impossible requirements had more than once driven a table girl or dishwasher to tears for some slight imperfection only he could see.

I met Lizbeth's mother one Saturday afternoon when she, her husband, and sons came into town to shop, a weekly ritual that brought people in from the farms and ranches that dotted the countryside around New Hope. Mrs. Ericson stood leaning against the front desk of the hotel as if she needed it for support, talking happily with Lizbeth. Seeing both women in profile made the family resemblance obvious, matching small but straight noses and high foreheads, but Lizbeth's complexion was clear and fair and sprinkled with freckles and her mother's skin showed the effects of age and Nebraska weather.

"You're Mrs. Ericson," I said without waiting for an introduction and put out my hand. "How do you do? Lizbeth certainly favors you. I'm Caroline Moore."

"I know who you are, Mrs. Moore. Lizbeth can't say enough good things about you. You'd never guess to look at her what a talker my girl is."

"Ma!" No serious rebuke in Lizbeth's voice, only a touch of self-consciousness that she was being talked about at all.

Her mother smiled. "Well, it's true, and I'd guess Mrs. Moore already knows it."

"People appreciate Lizbeth's friendliness," I said. "I do, too."

"That's kind of you to say." The look Mrs. Ericson gave me was surprisingly shrewd, her eyes, considerably darker than Lizbeth's, carefully taking in my appearance. "You're younger than I expected, Mrs. Moore. From everything Lizbeth's told me about you, your experience in Ogallala and this being your second stay in New Hope, I expected someone older." One more appraising glance before she finally smiled. "But Lizbeth's nearly grown and she's good at taking care of herself, always has been. Gets along with just about everybody and smart as a whip, besides. The farm was never for my girl, and I can't blame her. Once she found a place with Mrs. Carpenter – well, she was Mrs. Churchill then – she decided she liked her independence, liked working inside out of the sun and the wind, too. I'm glad of it. My Lizbeth has a head on her shoulders that would be wasted on the farm, not that her pa ever understood that."

Lizbeth said, "Ma," again, this time in a low voice and with a touch of the rebuke that had been missing earlier. Her mother heard it, too, and shrugged.

"Well, that's neither here nor there. Speaking of your pa," she took a look at the hotel's big wall clock, "he'll be waiting for me by now and all I'll hear on the way home is how I slowed the man down." To her daughter, she added, "He'd a come over to say hello, but it's dark early now and he don't like being away from home after dark."

"I know, Ma. It's all right. You can say hello to him and the boys for me." For a moment their eyes met, sharing a message between them that was unspoken but clearly understood. Mrs. Ericson pulled her short coat more tightly around her and fastened the button at the very top.

"I'll do that," she said. "It was a pleasure meeting you, Mrs. Moore."

"It was a pleasure meeting you, too, Mrs. Ericson. I'll keep an eye on Lizbeth. You don't have to worry about her."

"Oh, I stopped worrying about Lizbeth the moment Mrs. Carpenter took her under her wing. Wasn't no need to fear for my girl's future after that." She turned away, intent on tying the strings of her bonnet under her chin as she walked toward the door.

Looking back at Lizbeth, I asked, "Does your mother miss you sleeping at home?"

"No. You could tell how much she trusts Miss Ruth so my sleeping at the boarding house is fine with Ma. She feels better about it than if I were making the trip to and from the farm every morning and night, like I used to when I was younger."

I examined Lizbeth's face as seriously as her mother had studied me. She was a pretty girl, nearly grown, and as civilized as New Hope was, I could understand why her mother wouldn't want her out alone on the road, especially on these dark mornings and evenings. Wickedness was always afoot, no matter how civilized a place might be.

"Truth to tell, I feel better about it, too," I told her. "I forgot to ask. Was there anything you heard from Kip this morning that I should know about?"

"No, ma'am. Quiet as a cat he said."

"Good. I'll be in the kitchen for a while." Behind me I heard the door open and the sound of voices from people entering the hotel. Customers off the train looking for a warm meal and perhaps a warm bed, too. "I'll leave you to it, Lizbeth," I said with a slight tilt of my head in the direction of the newcomers and thought as I walked away that everything Mrs. Ericson said about Lizbeth was gospel. The girl was smart and she got along with people and she knew how to take care of herself. I didn't kid myself. It was Lizbeth Ericson who made the decision to work at the Bliss Hotel, not me. Which was fine. I seldom found fault with anyone, man or woman, who had a streak of independence, and young Miss Ericson had more than her share of that.

Despite it being declared a holiday more than twenty-five years earlier, setting aside the fourth Thursday in November for a national holiday still did not sit well with everyone. It was a Thursday, after all, a perfectly good weekday when stores could be open and American industry thriving. If there was a need for a holiday outside of Christmas, Easter, and the Fourth of July – and that fact was debatable all by itself – then the holiday should fall on a Sunday. Stores were closed anyway. But President Lincoln, God rest his soul, didn't see it that way, and so for these past years we have closed our shops on a Thursday and said our proper thank-yous, except for the hotel and restaurant, of course, which never closed, even when business was reduced to a trickle. Which it was that Thanksgiving Day because the railroad treated the holiday like a Sunday. With only one east-bound and one west-bound train for the day, a person didn't need more than two hands to count the passengers getting off at New Hope. I made the decision to schedule an early supper for the few hotel guests we had, then close the restaurant and send the workers home. For once, Chef didn't argue, but Darla gaped at me when I made the announcement and followed me down the hall to my office.

"As good a man as he is, I never knew Mr. Bliss to close the restaurant early for Thanksgiving Day," the girl told me.

"Mr. Bliss isn't here, Darla. He's across the ocean somewhere, likely in Paris, France, or some other place you and I'll never see, and that being the case, I've decided to close early." I gave a little emphasis to the word *I've* to be sure Darla understood who made the decisions in John Bliss's absence.

"Just like that?" Her tone disbelieving, she ignored my feeble attempt at showing authority and instead stared at me as if a horn had just sprouted out of the top of my head.

"Just like that," I said pleasantly, "and it hardly took me a minute. If President Lincoln thought it was important to have a holiday called Thanksgiving, who am I to say otherwise? Now hang up your apron and go home."

Darla shook her head at the sheer extravagance of the gesture but was gone in an instant, nevertheless. She was not, I judged, a young woman prone to looking gift horses in their mouths for any length of time.

When I entered the lobby, Ruth Carpenter turned from where she stood talking to Lizbeth to say to me, "There you are, Caroline. I was just asking for you."

"Is there something I can do for you?" I asked.

"I know it's short notice but Lizbeth was just telling me that the restaurant is closing sooner than usual and I hoped you'd join me and my family for an early supper. Nothing as fancy as you're used to from the restaurant. There's no way on earth my cooking could compare with that of a French chef, but you won't leave hungry and we're good company. You don't want to go home and sit in that big, unused kitchen of Sheba's. Not even Sheba enjoys that and it's her kitchen."

At Ruth's words, I realized she was right: Dredging through food left over from previous meals, heating it up on the stove, and then sitting down to a solitary meal in a dim kitchen suddenly held all the appeal of a winter cold.

"That's kind of you, Ruth, but Lizbeth should go and I'll take over the front desk while she's gone."

"Lizbeth is fine with keeping an eye on the hotel for the rest of the afternoon and then coming over later as she usually does to play with Alexander and tell me about her day. There's plenty of food. She won't go hungry."

When I still hesitated, Lizbeth said, "Really, Mrs. Moore. You go ahead. I've got a book called *The Prince and the Pauper* I can read to pass the time. Mr. Stenton loaned it to me. It's by Mark Twain and it's real good. Things are quiet enough, and if I need you, you're right across the street. You go along with Miss Ruth. I'll be fine. In fact, having quiet time on my own to read will be a real treat." She gave me a steady look. "I mean it. I don't get quiet time on my own very often." She was right and I understood that sometimes a young woman needed a spot of solitude.

That's how I found myself crossing the street to Hart's Boarding House half an hour later. Behind me I left a quiet hotel and an empty restaurant. New Hope seemed empty of everything except the cold November wind that whipped down Main Street. I felt the first hint of snow in that northwest wind, winter riding on its back and arriving earlier than anyone would wish. Well, no one I knew wished for winter's arrival, early or late, and the longer it took to get to New Hope the better as far as I was concerned.

What I recall most from that late-afternoon meal in the Carpenters' kitchen was the laughter. Laughter of any consequence in my own life – because hadn't my own kitchen once been as full of love and laughter and warmth as the Carpenters' home? As far as I trusted memory, I thought it had – stopped for me eight years earlier, when I awoke after the fire. At first, I was conscious only of the awful ache of my own burns, but it wasn't pain that made me so restless that the doctor had to strap me down on the bed to keep me still. It was instead the terrible but unnamed knowledge that I needed something very, very important and could not find it. My injuries and the laudanum I was given kept my thoughts hazy, almost dreamy, but later, calmer and aware that if I lay still the pain was less, the doctor decided he must tell me of Davey's and Jean's deaths in the hope that once I knew, I would accept my family's absence and allow myself to begin healing in both body and spirit. He was a good man and a good doctor. I owe him my life, I think, but I have yet to experience the kind of complete recovery he hoped for. All these years later, I've come to believe that it's not possible for anyone, man or woman, to fully heal from such a sudden and cruel loss, and I suppose believing this helps me see myself as less peculiar than I am, a woman who hears the crackle of flames where no fire burns but still not so different from anyone else.

Seen in the privacy of his own home, Si Carpenter, the head of New Hope's constabulary and a man of fierce and sometimes violent reputation, seemed like any other affectionate husband and father. He was a lean and wiry man with a ready smile and hair graying at the temples, who was not above holding a red-faced, crying baby so his wife could shift supper onto the table. Watching the man, I had to wonder if some of the stories told about him were myths that had grown up around commonplace happenings in the life of any officer of the law. People of the plains love their drama but have little of it in their lives, and I thought it was possible that Si Carpenter had become the hero of a few stories embellished with more spectacle than truth. But there was still the story of Emmett Wolf, New Hope's homegrown villain, and if even a small part of what I had read in the newspapers was true, perhaps there was nothing mythical about the marshal, at all. I hoped I wouldn't find out in person whether Carpenter was as deadly or as tough as his reputation claimed. If there was to be more drama in my life, I wanted it to be at my intent and from my own hand, without Silas Carpenter involved in it anywhere.

After supper, Silas wandered into the newly-added back parlor, his little son wrapped in his arms, and I helped Ruth with kitchen clean-up. She had made a half-hearted protest at my offer but seemed grateful when I put the kettle on to heat water and began to scrape plates until the water was hot enough for dish washing.

"I admit I'm tired," Ruth said in a low voice, drying the dishes as I set them on the strainer, "and I credit the new baby." At the look of surprise I gave her, she smiled. "I haven't mentioned it to Silas yet, so I'd appreciate your keeping it to yourself for a while, Caroline, but yes, I suspect there's a second baby going to show up about the same time the lilacs start to fade." We talked about newborns as we finished the supper dishes, how soft their skin was and how pink, how they took up all your time and didn't let you sleep and cried for reasons you could never figure out.

As I crossed the street to the hotel afterwards, I realized it was the first time since I'd lost my Jean that talking about babies hadn't left me feeling either empty or angry or lost. Progress of sorts, I supposed, and had the sudden suspicion that Ruth had so easily and innocently brought up the subject of babies to allow me to speak of my daughter without exposing myself to unwelcome sympathy or curiosity. How could Ruth Carpenter have known that my darling Jean was always alive in the privacy of my heart, but that I usually found it painful and upsetting to share the more tender memories of her with others? The kitchen conversation had allowed my baby to peek out and show herself among shared and unremarkable words common to new mothers everywhere, as painless a way as I had yet found to recall the feeling of a newborn baby in my arms without weeping at the memory. Maybe I gave Ruth Carpenter more credit than she deserved, but in my heart I doubted I was wrong about her. Ruth was a kind woman whose past held its own share of loss and grief and fear, so it wasn't such a stretch of imagination to believe she had known exactly what she was doing when she accepted my offer to help with the supper dishes.

After Lizbeth left for her warmed-over Thanksgiving meal at the Carpenters' and Kip was settled in for what would surely be a quiet night, I started for home. A cold, cloudy night sky greeted me, an expanse of black ice dotted with puffs of cotton batten.

"Mrs. Moore." Lucas Morgan's voice brought my attention back to earth.

"Deputy," I said. If he hadn't halted, I'd have run straight into him when I stepped from the hotel onto the boardwalk. "I believe you'll have a quiet night of it. "

"Let's hope you're right."

Morgan was broad in the chest and cat-footed, both good attributes for a man in charge of keeping a town safe and quiet through the night. The clouds didn't allow much moonlight, but I could tell he was smiling from the tone of his voice.

"Kip settled in, then, and Lizbeth home safe at the boarding house?" he asked, matching my pace as we walked together toward the jail.

"Yes to both." I thought the jail was his destination, but he didn't pause there, just kept walking beside me. "You don't have to trouble yourself to see me home, Deputy Morgan."

"Lucas is fine, Mrs. Moore. Nobody in New Hope stands much on ceremony."

"All right. You don't have to take the trouble to see me home, *Lucas*." We passed the jail and the undertaker's before I added, "I'm Caroline, by the way."

"It's no trouble, Caroline. I was going in your general direction, anyway. If you don't mind my saying, you seem to have settled into New Hope easy enough."

"New Hope made it easy for me," I said. "Good people, quiet town, and a peaceful business to run. Nothing like Ogallala."

"I suppose not. Ogallala has a rowdy reputation."

I laughed. “A reputation well deserved. New Hope seems safe and civilized by comparison.”

“It’s both those things, safe and civilized.” Morgan paused a moment. “Most of the time, anyway.”

“I’ve heard the Emmett Wolf story. He killed some young man, didn’t he?”

“It was before my time, but yes, Wolf killed a young man named Eddie Barts. A likeable fella, everyone says who knew him. He’s buried next to his mother in the church cemetery.”

As I knew only too well, being likeable and young was no protection against sudden death. I changed the subject.

“Speaking of young, how’s the new deputy coming on? What’s his name?”

“Clayton Kemp, and he’ll do fine.”

“He seems awfully young, but no doubt you’ll be glad to have a third person around. Has it always been just you and Marshal Carpenter?”

“No. We had a third man on the force, but he – died.” I caught the brief hesitation in Lucas’s voice.

“I’m sorry to hear that.”

“He was young, too, like Clay, but he didn’t want for courage. There are people alive today in this town who wouldn’t be here if it weren’t for him,” the words quiet but fervent. I had the idea that this was a subject Lucas Morgan did not often talk about.

“You sound like you admired him a great deal.”

“Yes.” We started down the alley that separated the telegraph and freight offices and Morgan surprised me by saying, “Lizbeth admired him, too. You wouldn’t know to look at her because she’s not one to talk about herself, but his death was a grief to her.”

By then we were at the front steps of the Bliss house with no time left for me to pursue what Lucas Morgan had just shared. Perhaps it was just as well. If this was something Lizbeth wanted me to know, she’d tell me in her own time. Or she wouldn't. I respected the privacy that grief sometimes demanded.

"I'm sorry," I said again and went up the steps to the front door. "There can be a cost to caring for people. An awful cost sometimes. Good night, Lucas. Thanks for the company."

"You're welcome, Caroline. My pleasure, and that's a fact."

I closed the door behind me, turned up the lamp I always left burning low on the hall table, and climbed the staircase to my room. *My room.* I considered the words and had to smile. This large, luxurious house wasn't my home and never would be, but for the time being I was happy to think of it that way. Today for the first time, I hadn't felt like a visitor paid to do a job, someone passing through New Hope on to the next place and the next job. Today for the first time, whether because of Ruth Carpenter's kindness or Lucas Morgan's trust, I felt that I fitted in and truly belonged in New Hope, Nebraska.

8

The following Saturday I looked up from where I sat behind the office desk and was astonished, simply astonished, to see Arthur Stenton standing in the doorway. He didn't look one bit uncomfortable or awkward as one might assume of a man who rarely sought out the company of other adults. Rather as if that doorway were a place he belonged and he had, in fact, stood there many times previously, which I knew wasn't true. But that was the measure of the man's public disposition: every situation of his making and under his control.

"Arthur," I said, taken aback, and then, "Is something wrong?" For some reason the question made him smile.

"Not that I know of." He removed his hat with one hand and brought the other hand forward. "I beg your pardon for appearing unannounced and no doubt interrupting your work, but I was in town and wanted to bring you something."

I stood and motioned to the chair facing me on the other side of the desk. "You're not interrupting me. Well, clearly you are but not from anything that will cause the ruin of Bliss House. Please, won't you have a seat?"

He entered the office but shook his head as he did so.

"No, I didn't come for a visit. I wanted only to share this book of Emerson's essays."

The schoolmaster was too polite to ask if I had made any headway with the author's poetry, and I volunteered, "I have enjoyed some of Mr. Emerson's poetry, Arthur."

"Only some."

"I'm afraid so, but there are a few that I have reread numerous times," I said and quoted, "'The wings of time are black and white / Pied with morning and with night / Mountain tall and ocean deep / Trembling balance duly keep.'"

"Yes, 'the feud of Want and Have.' That particular poem speaks to me, too." For a brief moment, I felt I understood Arthur Stenton perfectly and that he saw me with equal clarity, that we were two people of one mind. Only a brief moment, true, but startling and unexpected.

"I'm sorry," I said, grasping for conversation. "I should have returned the book."

Stenton shrugged and came far enough into the room to place the book he held onto the desk.

"I've been thinking that perhaps you're more a woman of essays than poetry so I wanted you to at least have the experience of reading some of Emerson's essays. This is his first volume, published some time ago now, but not out of date. In my mind, his value is more in the straightforward presentation of philosophy, and you may not agree with much of what he writes."

"No?"

"Emerson doesn't think along commonplace or traditional lines, Mrs. Moore, and I tend to regard much of his transcendental philosophy as claptrap, but there is still some fine writing in this book." His fingers resting lightly on the small volume stroked the book as one might pet a sleeping cat.

"Thank you," I said. "I appreciate your confidence in my mental abilities. I'll be sure to ask if I have questions about any of the essays." He raised his head from the book and met my glance with a straightforward look.

"You would be welcome to do so, of course, but I don't expect you will have any problem understanding Mr. Emerson's themes or intentions. You may not agree with them, as I said, but it won't be for lack of comprehension." I thought the man had just paid me a compliment but couldn't quite put my finger on what exactly it was and changed the subject instead of bothering to continue a conversation that was beginning to sound like a schoolhouse lecture.

"Ruby says Henry – how did she put it? – 'lights up like one of them new incandescent bulbs' whenever he talks about school now. It could be your teaching that's the cause of the boy's sudden brilliance, I suppose, but with no disrespect meant, I'm more inclined to think it's the new eyeglasses that are making the difference."

"No disrespect taken, Mrs. Moore" – then and there I vowed that before I left New Hope, the man would be calling me *Caroline* as if we'd been friends since our cradle days – "and you would be quite correct in your inclination. The eyeglasses were long overdue and have made an immediate difference in the quality of Henry's work." A brief silence followed his words before Arthur Stenton replaced his hat and said, "Good afternoon, Mrs. Moore."

"Good afternoon, Arthur." I tried to think of something more to add but was out of ideas and by the teacher's abrupt departure, he was equally out of time.

You're an unusual man to find in New Hope, Nebraska, I thought. Ralph Waldo Emerson and transcendentalism indeed! I'd read about Boston's transcendental school of movement in some local newspapers – most of them politely scornful in the way only no-nonsense Nebraskans can be – but still… I hefted the small book lightly from hand to hand. It was refreshing and flattering to be thought a woman capable of understanding the philosophical musings of a great writer like Mr. Emerson. Any number of men had complimented my eyes and my hair and my feminine form, but Arthur Stenton was the first man who had ever given any attention to my brain. That was the compliment I had sensed earlier. A novelty to it, but something else, something deeper, as well. Arthur Stenton's compliments were like white pearls on a cord. No dazzle to them, yet rare, lustrous, and in their own special way, priceless.

The first snow of the season fell on Les and Sally's wedding day. Sally's mother had not been able to get the two young people to wait until after the new year for their big day, young love being what it is, and after the vows were said and the service concluded, we all stepped outside the church to find big snowflakes floating softly from a low-hanging, gray sky. No one seemed to mind, least of all Les and Sally with their wide smiles and glowing faces, and I couldn't help but smile myself as I trudged back to the hotel. I vaguely recalled feeling a similar joyful wonder on my own wedding day, amazed that a good, handsome, spirited man like Davey Moore wanted to marry me, a woman with a dubious past and a history that might have caused a less generous man to question her motives for marrying someone recently come into wealth. But that wasn't Davey's nature and I loved him for it.

Still smiling at my own thoughts, I entered the hotel, shook the snow from my hat and shawl, and raised my eyes to find Mark Saylor, leaning with one arm casually on the check-in desk, watching me. He was smiling, too, and at the smile I couldn't help but think what a handsome man he was. I'm only human, after all. He straightened and came toward me, one hand extended.

"Mrs. Moore, what a pleasure to see you again! I believe the snow has put roses in your cheeks." He gave my hand a soft squeeze when I reached out to his and only released it when I shifted away from him toward the front desk and out of his reach.

"The first snow of the season does seem to have some magic in it, or so I've been told, anyway," I replied as I laid my shawl and hat on the counter, then turned back to face him. "I didn't expect to see you in New Hope until the February meeting. Are you on your way to see your father again?"

"Not this time, but I am meeting a man on his behalf to take a look at a herd that's for sale."

"A herd you're thinking about buying for the Anchor?" I asked, but he was kept from saying more by two people who came up wanting rooms for the night.

"I'll explain more at dinner later. That is, if you don't have other plans." A question at the end of his words.

I shook my head. "Not a one."

"Well, that's a pleasant surprise. You're always such a busy woman, Mrs. Moore, that I feared I would once again take second place to your hotel responsibilities," not said with any noticeable grievance in his tone, yet I still heard annoyance there. A man's pride can be a fragile thing sometimes.

We had moved to the far side of the hotel desk as Lizbeth greeted the newcomers in her usual calm and pleasant manner, explaining the amenities Bliss House offered, the available rooms, and the rates and rules. She was very good at putting people at ease.

"I can't deny that I have responsibilities, Mr. Saylor, but none of them will interfere with sharing a table with you this evening. Does seven work?"

He nodded. "I look forward to it." He nodded a second time, smiled directly into my eyes, walked over to where he had left his traveling bag at the foot of the stairs, and ascended to his room without another word.

If they were considering expanding the ranch and herd, they must be doing well, I thought as I walked down to the office, and that was something I wanted to find out more about. My husband and I had once been in the cattle business, and I knew how uncertain it could be, dependent on eastern markets and western weather. Did the Saylors plan to increase their holdings because of something they expected from the New Hope Beef Convention? Did they have some kind of private knowledge about the meeting's outcome that made them expect new markets for their beef? I didn't know Trenton Saylor, but I wouldn't put it past Mark. He was the kind of man who would enjoy moving people around to suit his own desires, not something I considered to be a bad trait in a man, but certainly interesting. I was curious enough about Mark Saylor and his expectations that even if the desk had been stacked with payroll records, shipping bills, and a month of invoices, I wouldn't have missed dinner with him for the world.

After I made a quick trip to the kitchen, counted the newly-laundered tablecloths just delivered, and took a casual stroll through the dining room with an eye for spots on either tableware or linens, I stopped by the front desk where Lizbeth was filling out her daily paperwork of customers coming and customers going. Between trains there was no line at the counter so it was a good time for putting the records in order. Lizbeth looked up when I appeared and set down her pencil.

"Was it very nice?" At my puzzled look, she added, "The wedding. I bet Sally looked like a princess."

"A princess all in blue," I agreed. "She had a little cuff of fur at the end of her sleeves and wore a cape over her shoulders that matched the color of the dress. Smart girl, really, because the church felt cold no matter how many people were squeezed into it."

"Sally may be Luther Winters' only child," Lizbeth said, "but he's a frugal man. Always has been. I imagine he had an eye on the expense and counted the firewood before the ceremony."

"Surely not," I said, laughing, but Lizbeth raised an

eyebrow.

"I've known the people of New Hope all my life, Mrs. Moore, and I've got a good understanding of their good points and their not-so-good points."

"And Luther's being thrifty is not so good?"

"I wouldn't say that necessarily, but it's his only daughter's wedding and in my mind a wedding is about as special as it gets for a girl. No expense should be spared, as long as the family can afford it, and I know Luther Winters can afford it. Still, that's just Lizbeth Ericson talking. I'm no expert in weddings, that's for sure."

I thought about the young man Lucas Morgan had told me about who'd been sweet on Lizbeth and had died too young, but I couldn't detect any grief or melancholy in her tone or words. She was a private girl, but I knew what grief sounded like, even hidden grief, and there was none in Lizbeth's voice. I was glad of it. She was too young to have to carry that burden, though God knows that death and loss aren't restricted to any particular age.

"Now when Miss Ruth got married to the marshal, it was all done in a heartbeat, it seemed. Miss Ruth's face was a sight – she'd had an accident, kind of, and there were little specks healing on both cheeks – but she was so happy, it seemed she shone brighter than the yellow dress she had on that day."

"On my wedding day I wore a dress the color of black raspberries with a little white lace collar," I said, "I wore gloves, too. Funny, I hadn't remembered about the gloves 'til just now."

Lizbeth sent me a shy glance. "Was it a happy day for you, Mrs. Moore?"

Oh, *happy*. How to tell this girl, hardly more than a child, about the way joy had caught in my throat at the sight of Davey standing so still and serious at the front of the church, about the way my heart raced when he reached for my hand, about the plain wonder of me marrying a man who loved me and thought I was a treasure and how the future stretched out in front of us. *Happy* was too simple, too easy a word for that day.

But because it was the only word I had, I smiled and said, "It surely was, Lizbeth. I think it was the first happy day I'd ever known in all my life." There was a quiet moment until I said, back to my usual tone, "I'll work in the office for a while, and then I plan to meet Mr. Saylor for dinner in the dining room. If you see Deb, ask her to set up the table in the southeast corner for us, will you, please?"

I thought she was tempted to make a remark about my request, but Lizbeth Ericson is a smart young woman with more discretion than a person would expect from a girl her age and she simply nodded and said, "Yes, ma'am."

My one concession to independence was not going home to change into something different, something prettier, for dinner, but then I had dressed for a wedding that day and wasn't wearing one of my plain work dresses. I examined my face and hair in the small mirror I kept in a desk drawer before leaving to find Mark Saylor. No ink mark on my cheek or hair flopping into my eyes as had been known to happen by the end of a long day. What I saw in the reflection of the glass was as good as it was going to get.

I came to dinner purposefully late – it never does to look too eager to a handsome man – and stood for a moment studying my dinner companion as he bent his head over the daily menu. Even seated and casual, Mark Saylor gave an impression of confidence and power. When he lifted his gaze and saw me approaching, he added charm to his other attributes. I thought he would be a man any willing woman would find easy to desire and wondered if, after all my years of being a widow, I was at last willing. I didn't think so, but perhaps time in Saylor's company would sway me otherwise. I was curious, though, about both his past and his present, and that made me willing enough for the time being.

He came around the table and positioned my chair for me to be seated, then returned to his own place.

"I trust you found your room satisfactory, Mr. Saylor." I placed my napkin on my lap and looked across the table at him. Saylor smiled.

"The first thing we should get out of the way is this habit you have of calling me Mr. Saylor. It's Mark. Surely by now you can find it in you to forget the formality."

"I make it a practice never to get overly familiar with customers," I replied, and when he opened his mouth to protest added, "but in your case I'll make an exception, Mark. As long as I'm Caroline."

"Caroline it is," and after another brief glance down at the menu, asked, "What do you recommend?"

"You really shouldn't miss the ham," I told him. "Sugar-cured and served with raisin sauce, sweet potatoes, and stewed tomatoes. It's one of the chef's specialties. You won't be disappointed."

He took my recommendation and I had the same. What choice did I have, after all? And I had told the truth: Monsieur Clermont did work wonders with any kind of pork.

Conversation was leisurely over the meal, this and that, the weather, President Garfield's tragic death of the previous year and President Arthur's hopes for another term, Thomas Edison's inventions, and the ongoing financial depression. The last topic brought the conversation to Saylor's personal life and history, which was where I had hoped it would wander.

"You've been in the cattle business eight years, then?" I asked. Saylor stopped as if to think, then nodded.

"That sounds right. I borrowed money to buy my first herd and a section of prime Colorado grazing land in '74. The last eight years haven't always been easy, but the place is on solid ground now and with any luck, the Anchor will continue to grow. This Beef Convention of yours could make a big difference to my future."

"It doesn't sound like you're waiting for February to grow. Didn't you say you and your father were considering buying another herd?"

"For the time being, I'm just doing what my father asked, but he and I both know that finding cattle isn't the problem, it's selling them. That's why the men coming together in February are so important. They own the beef markets in the East. If I can manage a deal with any of them, I won't have to go begging for appetites." I recognized from his tone how important it was to him to make the Anchor a success. "If things go right in February, I can buy out my father's share of the Anchor within a year. At the most."

That was the true heart of the matter, I realized. Mark Saylor desperately longed to prove to his father that he didn't need the older man in his life, didn't need his influence or guidance or advice, and especially didn't need his money.

Deb came to our table, wordlessly cleared off the used plates with her usual skill, and vanished back into the kitchen. The timely break allowed me to move the conversation to more humdrum matters.

"You'll want dessert," I said and at his inquiring look added in a voice lowered for theatrical effect, "Monsieur Clermont has a recipe for plum sherbet that's so special he's certain his rivals have tried to steal it. Keeps it locked up tight in the hotel safe."

Saylor laughed aloud at that – thinking I was teasing, I guessed, although I wasn't – and said, "I believe I need to taste something that prized."

"Yes," I agreed, "you do. You can trust me, Mark. I won't lead you astray with the menu."

He picked up his coffee cup but didn't drink from it,

simply held it before him with both hands and smiled across the table at me.

"Caroline, you have my full permission to lead me astray whenever and wherever you choose. I can't imagine a more enjoyable prospect," Saylor said with an expression that both invited and promised. Promised exactly what, I didn't know, but it was one more thing I was curious about.

After we finished the sherbet and took our last sips of coffee, Saylor asked, "I explained about it, didn't I?" He noticed my puzzled expression and lightly touched the glittering, anchor-shaped stick pin on his lapel. "You've been taken with it all evening, Caroline. I believe your attention dropped to the diamonds more often than you realized. I should be flattered, of course, since I had it custom made, but it can be humbling to a man to take second place to a bauble, though I know women love everything that glitters." His friendly smile took the reproach from his words, though not the arrogance.

Ignoring everything he said except the question, I answered, "Yes, you explained about the connection between Saylor and Anchor. I thought the design clever then and still do." I shrugged lightly. "If I seemed overly interested in it this evening, Mark, I beg your pardon. New Hope doesn't see a lot of fine jewelry, and the way the stones reflected the lamp light around us was remarkable. Almost blinding. I might have been a moth drawn to a flame."

My answer pleased him, as I had intended, and replaced the touch of scorn in his words with indulgence for what he now understood was perfectly reasonable, women appreciating trinkets the way they do. We sat talking until I finally stood and gestured toward the door that swung into the kitchen.

"The girls want to set the tables for the morning and go home," I said. "They're too kind to ask us to leave, but I can see them peeking through the crack."

Saylor stood, too. “Everything was wonderful, Caroline. Especially the company.” We walked into the lobby and I was surprised to see Kip behind the counter.

“Good evening, Kip. It’s early to see you here,” I said, glancing at the lobby clock.

“Lizbeth sent a message to ask if I could come in a little earlier than usual. Said she needed to go all the way home to her folks tonight and didn’t want to get caught by the snow.”

“Surely she didn’t head out to the farm by herself. How long ago did she leave?”

Kip shrugged. “An hour maybe. She wasn’t by herself, though. Lucas come in and said he’d take her out, said they had to leave right away, though, before the snow made the road worse. I don’t think Lizbeth wanted to bother him and they had a little discussion about it, but she’s a practical girl and it didn’t take her long to give up trying to tell Lucas not to bother. He can be as stubborn as her when he wants to. Anyway, Lizbeth was in good hands when she left.”

“I’m glad to hear it.” I *was* glad, surprised at the sudden spurt of worry I’d felt about Lizbeth at Kip’s first words. She was an easy girl to grow fond of. I supposed Ruth Carpenter and Lucas Morgan had discovered that the same as I.

When I turned to say good night to Mark, he asked, “Are you finished for the day, Caroline?” and at my nod, added, “Then I’ll see you home. This Lucas isn’t the only gentleman who knows how to keep a lady safe.”

“There’s no need, Mark. I’m staying at John and Sheba’s house and it’s just across Main Street.”

“No matter.” He put on the hat he’d been holding. “I recall you had a wrap of some kind when I first saw you. Shall I fetch it for you or –”

“No,” I said. “I left it in the office. I’ll be right back.” There was no use arguing with his tone and truth be told, with Lucas gone I didn’t mind the idea of Saylor’s company.

When we stepped outside, the falling snow had ceased, leaving behind a clean, white Main Street, a few store signs dusted with snow, and several upstairs windows glowing yellow behind curtains. A quiet, calming, innocent scene in a way. It was as if I'd never seen New Hope before, as if something magical had touched the little town. The effect of a first snowfall, I thought, but for an instant felt almost happy.

Everything seemed unnaturally quiet. A little snow had blown up onto the boardwalk but not enough to cause a hazard. Still, when Mark placed my hand in the crook of his arm, I didn't pull away. It was pleasant to be walking close to an attractive man on a darkly beautiful evening in a fairy-tale town. Down the street a figure stepped out of the jail and walked away from us toward the livery and the railway. Not Lucas Morgan, who would not be back from the Ericsons' place yet, so either the marshal himself or the new young deputy, Clayton Kemp. New Hope was never left unprotected. Too much to risk, too much to lose.

When we stepped out of the shadowy alley for the last steps up the short path toward the front porch, Mark stopped.

"That's quite the house." A cloud had shifted enough to let some moonlight through and the outline of the house showed dark against a sky briefly lit pale white. I was used to the large home by then but understood the surprise I heard in Saylor's voice. John and Sheba's house was everything New Hope was not: large, imposing, stately, dignified.

"It is, isn't it? I think John and Sheba are happy there. Sheba's a painter, as you may know, and much of the second floor is a working studio John built for her."

"True love, then, for John Bliss, is it?"

"Yes. For both of them, I think." My feet were cold and I was suddenly tired, tired from the day and just a little tired of Mark Saylor. I pulled him gently forward to the foot of the front steps that led up to the porch. "Thank you for the escort, Mark. Are you out on the 7:05 in the morning?"

"Yes."

"Well, I wish your trip every success. I hope the herd is what you're looking for."

"As do I." He paused. "You sound like you understand ranching, Caroline. I don't mean to pry, but did you and your husband ranch?"

"He was more a miner," I said. "He partnered with John Bliss and they struck silver in Virginia City in '71."

"So that's where Bliss got the money to set up everything he has here." I guessed Saylor was curious about Davey, about what happened to my husband's share of the silver mine, and wondering if I wasn't the poor working widow I seemed, but I had no intention of continuing the conversation. When he placed a foot on the bottom step, I tugged him back with gentle pressure and removed my hand from his arm.

"Good night, Mark. Thank you for the company. I'm home now and perfectly safe, and you have an early start in the morning. You should get back."

Without a word, he leaned forward and kissed me squarely and firmly on the mouth, something I hadn't expected. I took it firmly in stride but didn't return the kiss. It wouldn't do to encourage his attentions any further. Not yet, anyway.

"Good night, Caroline." He said nothing about the kiss. It might not have happened, and the moon had withdrawn behind clouds again making it too dark for me to gauge his expression. "I hope to see you on my way back to Denver. It'll most likely be my final visit of the year before the Beef Convention."

I was conscious of his gaze on me as I mounted the steps to the porch. With one hand I opened the front door, then turned slightly to raise the other hand in a small wave of farewell that he probably couldn't see. Once inside, I closed the front door so firmly behind me that the click of the latch sounded as sharp as a gunshot. I slipped out of my wet shoes, picked up the low-burning lamp from the entry table, and padded upstairs to my room. Out of nowhere, I thought, this is Les and Sally's first night together as husband and wife and couldn't help but smile at the memory of my own wedding night. Davey and I had burned bright most of that night and our Jean had been the result. Tears would come later, of course, a river of them, but for all the grief that followed, how could I do anything but smile just then, thinking about Les and Sally and remembering the pleasure and the joy of my first night as Davey Moore's wife?

9

When I saw Lizbeth at the hotel the next day, she at first seemed her usual self: quiet, controlled, and pleasant, but after a second, closer look at her face, I said, "I was worried when I heard you left to make a trip out to the farm yesterday, Lizbeth. You didn't say anything about that when we were talking earlier in the day." Something about her face looked drawn and tired, a far cry from the Lizbeth who usually greeted me in the morning with fair, flushed cheeks and bright eyes.

"I didn't know then, Mrs. Moore. My ma had sent a message by one of the neighbors, but the snow slowed him down."

"What's happened?"

She hesitated before giving me a quiet answer. "My brother Charlie and my pa got into an awful ruckus. They don't get along even on their best days. Pa was drinking and Charlie just got sick of it, I guess. He said some terrible things to Pa and drunk or sober, Pa won't stand for any sass from anybody. They got into it something awful."

"What did your mother expect you to do about it?"

"Oh, I'm the peacemaker in the family," Lizbeth replied with a sigh. "Always have been. After the fight, Pa fell asleep like he always does when he drinks, but Charlie was still raging and bound to leave. Ma couldn't talk him out of it. The best she could get from him was that he'd wait long enough to say goodbye to me. We're close, Charlie and me. He's next to me in age." She paused. "But he's still only fifteen, Mrs. Moore. Too young to be on his own."

I didn't tell her that I left home at fifteen, that being on your own was a lot harder for a girl than a boy, and if I lived through the experience, her Charlie probably would, too. It was all true, but I wouldn't wish on young Charlie any of the hardships I'd had to tolerate and besides, the idea of Charlie leaving home was clearly a grief to Lizbeth and probably to her mother, too, while I doubted anyone gave much of a thought to my absence except to grumble over having to take on my chores.

"You're a good sister, Lizbeth. Did your brother listen to you?"

She nodded. "Everybody in the family usually listens to me."

"Even your father?"

She nodded again. "He isn't a bad man. He's never raised a hand to Ma or me. Never threatened it even once. But nothing he's put his hand to has gone right for him in his life, and he's tired. Charlie tries Pa's patience sometimes. They're too much alike is the trouble, both stubborn and thick-skinned, and they don't get on. They never have."

"Did you manage to convince Charlie not to run away?"

"Yes, ma'am. He said he'd wait until after Christmas 'cause he knows him being gone at Christmas would break Ma's heart."

"You know there'll come a time when for all your peace-making skills you won't be able to keep Charlie at home, don't you?" I asked. "Boys grow up and they want to see something of the world."

Lizbeth wanted to disagree, but after a long look at my

face, she gave a small smile. "I expect you're right, but I like things done my way and on my timetable."

"So I've noticed," I said but returned her smile with one of my own. "I expect Ruth Carpenter is the person you go to for advice, but if there's anything I can help you with, you just need to ask."

"I love Miss Ruth as much as my own mother, maybe more, but she thinks the best of everybody almost all the time, and sometimes a person's got to think about the worst that can happen if she wants to get out ahead of a situation. From what I've seen, that's something you're good at, so thank you for your kind offer. I might show up in your doorway sooner than you expect."

Later in the morning as I busied myself with the daily and constant activities of managing the Bliss House Hotel and Restaurant, I found Lizbeth's observations running through my mind at odd moments. She was right about needing to plan for the worst. Right, too, that my regular practice was to do just that. It was how I'd made my way in the world and how I'd gotten ahead. If I do this or that, what's the worst that could happen, I'd ask myself, and then I'd move forward – or not – according to the answer. Fancy Lizbeth, at least ten years younger and living her whole life in the same small town, understanding me as well as she did. One smart girl, that Lizbeth Ericson, and I would be wise to keep that in mind.

By mid-afternoon, the snow from the previous day had disappeared under a December sun so warm it might have been September. Leaving the bank, I crossed the path of young Jem Fenway and Frederick Lincoln as they made their way home from school. Never really a *straightforward* way home, as I had noticed on other days. They were two young boys, after all, and I imagined adventure beckoned them to places unnoticed by those of us who were all grown up.

"You're looking a little down in the mouth," I said.

"Have you lost something?"

"No, ma'am," said Frederick but Jem disagreed.

"Sort of. It's the snow. Frederick and me were ready for some fort building after school but–" he flung out his arms as if I might not have noticed otherwise "–it's all gone." Jem was Sheba Bliss's nephew and despite the fact that his hair was as dark as Sheba's was red, for just a moment I saw his aunt reflected in the boy's expressive face and dramatic gesture.

"I guarantee that it won't be long before you have enough snow for a dozen forts. This isn't your first winter in New Hope, is it?" We started down the boardwalk, the boys skipping slightly ahead of me, half-turning now and then to look back at me and keep me in the conversation.

"No, ma'am!" The words were spoken in unison.

"Frederick was here first," Jem explained. "Wasn't it two years ago now that you and your family moved here, Frederick?" Frederick, whose father owned the meat market that stood directly across from the hotel, nodded. He was a dark-skinned boy with intelligent eyes and a shy but beautiful smile. "And my mama and I moved to New Hope last year so this is my second winter." There was pride in the way he said *second.*

"Then you know what I'm talking about," I said.

Jem stopped at the door of the Gooseneck Hotel and Billiards Parlor, where his mother, Sheba's sister, Dee, lived with her husband Bert Gruber.

"I got chores to do," Jem said without any resentment in his tone, just stating a plain fact. "See you tomorrow, Frederick. Good afternoon, Mrs. Moore. It was a pleasure talking to you." Good manners came easily to him, I thought as he went inside. Proper raising there, for all the unsettled history in the boy's past that I had pieced together from some of Ruth's remarks. Despite – maybe because of – seeing the worst of some people, it was likely Jem Fenway would grow up to be the best of men.

Frederick and I walked together and stopped at the door of the meat market long enough to allow a customer to exit. When I said, "I'd like to talk to your father a moment, Frederick," he backed up and waited for me to enter the store ahead of him. Proper raising there, too. Isaac Lincoln, busy behind the meat counter, looked up when his son and I entered.

"Afternoon, Mrs. Moore."

"Good afternoon, Mr. Lincoln."

He wiped his hands on his apron. "Frederick, your mother has need of you in the kitchen." Then, to me, "Anything special I can help you with, Mrs. Moore?"

"Chef Clermont has trout almondine on the menu next week," I explained, "and just this morning I placed an order for Montana trout, the finest trout in the nation – according to Chef, anyway. I was hoping you'd have space in that grand icebox of yours to hold the fish when it arrives until Chef gets to it. We can find the space if we have to, I suppose, but the restaurant's icebox is smaller than yours to start with and it's always so crammed with all the other things we're trying to keep fresh. We really appreciated your keeping our salmon for us last month. Of course, I ordered extra trout for you in case you might want to run a special for the good citizens of New Hope, compliments of Bliss House as a gesture of thanks for your being so accommodating."

Isaac Lincoln was a man with a face that had known grief and hard work and the same dark, intelligent eyes as his son.

"That can be arranged, yes, ma'am, and I appreciate the offer of the extra trout. Ain't seen good trout in New Hope in some time. I don't mind paying my share, either."

"No, no, no," I replied, shaking my head for emphasis. "That would never do. Believe me, John Bliss would have my head on a platter if I did anything to change the arrangement you and he have worked out." I paused. "The two of you are good friends, I think. He speaks very highly of you."

"We are friends, that's true. Guess we both believe New Hope's done good by us." This time he paused. "I heard about your helping young Henry Strunk get them new eyeglasses of his. That was decent of you. Frederick says they made a world of difference to the way Henry reads in school now." For some reason, Mr. Lincoln's words made me self-conscious.

"It was more Mr. Stenton's doing than mine," I said quickly.

"Arthur Stenton is one of the finest men I know, but it wasn't him that Ruby said made a miracle happen for Henry. *Mrs. Moore* is the one Ruby gave credit to." The market's door opened behind me and Isaac raised a hand to the newcomer as he finished speaking to me. "Well, you let me know when that trout arrives, and I'll make room for it."

When the shopkeeper turned to face the waiting customer, I murmured a good afternoon and slipped outside. This small town, this New Hope, still had the power to surprise me. Clearly, I hadn't fully understood that its citizens would know about and talk about anything and everything, no matter how small or how private, that took place in their community. It wasn't nosiness on their part, not really. I realized with a little shock that because I'd been caught up in my own life and loss and in all the complications of grief for years, for *too* many years maybe, I had forgotten how ordinary people lived, how they found comfort in the humdrum of daily life and were curious about even the commonplace. It was another endearing quality of life in New Hope, Nebraska – one of several, truth be told – that I hadn't recognized or considered or expected. Until today.

Our good weather held another week, a fact that Darla remarked on in passing one morning as she hurried toward the kitchen for final instructions. Chef Clermont insisted on giving daily direction to the girls who waited tables and had an intimidating frown for anyone who dared be tardy for the morning ritual. Since I'd been on the receiving end of his frown a time or two, I understood Darla's rush and nearly missed her quick words.

"Morning, Mrs. Moore. It don't feel quite right to start planning for the big Christmas dinner Mr. Bliss holds every year, does it, not when it feels like spring outside?"

Darla was tying on her apron with a shoulder pressed to the swinging door that led into the kitchen when I said her name.

She stopped long enough to say, "Yes, ma'am?"

"You go on," I told her, "so you don't keep the great man waiting, but as soon as you're done, come see me in the office, please." She nodded and disappeared behind the door.

When she reappeared in the office twenty minutes later, I continued the conversation as if we hadn't been interrupted.

"Tell me more about Mr. Bliss's Christmas dinner. Is it here at the hotel? It's the first I've heard of it."

"He must've forgotten in the excitement of planning his and Miss Sheba's trip, then, because Mr. Bliss's been putting out a Christmas spread for them that don't have a family or a place to go before he ever got married. There's a number of folks that count on it."

"Such as?"

"Let's see, last year I recollect seeing Old Cap Sherman and Mr. Sellers and Benny and Mr. Tull, and the Lowe brothers, not to mention the few guests that got off the train that day. There's only one train east and one train west on Christmas Day and most folks are just passing through on the way to their own families, but if someone takes a room at the hotel for Christmas night, they're invited, too."

"A dozen or so people, then, and the Chef doesn't mind

working on Christmas Day?" Darla grinned at that, sat down in the chair across from the desk, and leaned towards me.

"Well, that gets interesting, Mrs. Moore, because Chef could always have Klaus take over the meal – he's the apprentice chef, after all – but that doesn't happen. Instead, Mrs. Liggett from the Nebraska Café shuts her place up tight and comes to help Monsieur Clermont get the meal ready." I knew I was staring at the girl but couldn't help myself.

"Surely not in the hotel kitchen, Darla? Not in Chef Clermont's kingdom? He barely lets me cross the threshold. I can't see him letting anyone else touch a thing in it."

Last year," Darla said, enjoying the tale, "Mrs. Liggett had on her best dress and Chef wore a tie."

"To cook in the kitchen?"

"Oh, yes, ma'am, and I'd swear they were both enjoying having the other person around, kitchen or no kitchen."

I sat back in my chair and exhaled quietly. The twin ideas of a free Christmas dinner for all and sundry and a romance going on for Chef Clermont at the same time nearly took my breath away. It was those kinds of unexpected tidbits that gave life its spark, and I grinned back at Darla.

"That is very interesting, Darla. Do I need to arrange table or clean-up workers?"

"That's already taken care of, Mrs. Moore. Us girls work it out among ourselves. Mrs. Pikert's a widow and she brings along her children. She'll help serve, then sit down with the little ones for a meal and stay after to help with dishes, too. It makes a long day for her but she never seems to mind. Susie lives with her aunt and uncle, but they don't get along very well so she's more than willing to help with the tables on Christmas. It's like that. Anyone who helps out gets to eat a fine meal and gets paid for the time, besides, so there's always somebody willing to be here."

"Will you be here?" I asked.

"No. My folks count on me staying home that day. Ma's no Chef Clermont but she sets a good table and she's partial to having her family around her at Christmas." Although I'd never met the woman, I liked Mrs. Jones the better for knowing that about her. Darla stood. "I got to go, and I'm sorry about you hearing about all this so sudden, but you don't have to worry. At Bliss House, Christmas dinner kind of takes care of itself."

Chef Clermont echoed Darla's words when I asked him about his Christmas Day menu. "You do not have to involve yourself, Madame Moore. I, Emil Clermont, will make sure all goes smoothly," conceding as an afterthought, "and you, of course, a woman on her own, may wish to join us. The meal will be perfect, I assure you."

"I understand the company is quite pleasant, as well. Young Lonnie Markman. Mr. Tull. Russ and Mitch Lowe. Mrs. Liggett." It was definitely not my imagination that his face brightened at the woman's name.

"Yes. Yes. The company. The menu. The conversation. All will be flawless under my direction."

"I have no doubt of it, Monsieur. It is a gracious gesture on your part, that a man of your distinguished talents would sacrifice his own time for the good of others. I salute you."

I could not have kept a straight face if I'd said anything that flowery to another person in all of New Hope, but Monsieur Clermont took it as his due with a stiff bow and a serious nod in return before saying, "And now, Madame, I have work to do." Dismissed from the great man's presence, I left the kitchen and made my way through the dining room that had begun to fill with luncheon customers. I got as far as the lobby and turned back to snare Darla by the arm for a quick question.

"Does Mr. Stenton show up for the Bliss House

Christmas meal?" I asked.

Darla, in a hurry, paused long enough to say, "No, not that I recall. He's one to keep himself to himself. A good man but not one for social gatherings is how most people see him," before she moved in the direction of a table of newly-seated diners.

After the spring-like temperatures, the weather turned, just like that. Sunny one day and greeted the next morning by a heavy gray sky that spit pellets of ice as sharp as glass. Ah, Nebraska. A light snow fell every day the week before Christmas, and because the sun seemed to have fled, the temperatures dropped and layers of snow accumulated. Which no doubt delighted the young friends Jem and Frederick, finally able to practice their fort-building skills, but did not delight those of us who had no interest in building forts, whether made of snow or not. That group included every adult in New Hope. Just because we were familiar with a Nebraska winter didn't mean we had to like it. Even Ruth, usually the most cheerful of women, couldn't keep a sigh from her voice when commenting on the weather.

"I'm just worried the weather will keep us from visiting my sister for Christmas," she explained as she pulled back the curtain from one of the front windows in the boarding house lobby and peered outside.

"I didn't know you had plans to travel," I said. "What about Hart's?"

"I've just got the one boarder for a while, Mr. Jessup, the bank clerk, and he'll be fine on his own for a few days. I'll put out a sign that we're closed to new boarders until after the new year. It's not the boarding house that's kept me from making a trip to see my sister." At my questioning look, Ruth's voice got a little heated.

"It took some serious effort on my part to convince Silas that New Hope can spare him for a day or so, and thank the good Lord, he finally agreed. My sister Vera Ann lives in

Omaha with her family, and it's time they met my husband. Time he met them, too. My oldest niece is fourteen, almost grown, and I've hardly spoken a dozen words to her in my life, less even for her younger sisters. I want Alex to know his Aunt Vera Ann and his Uncle Milo and his cousins, not that he'll remember them at this point, but that's not the point, is it? Families should do their best to stay close."

Then in a quieter voice and more for her own convincing than mine, she said, "We won't be gone but a few days, and there's no reason Lucas and Clayton can't keep watch on New Hope while we're in Omaha. The town always slows down Christmas week because the railroad slows down." She heard the doubt in her voice the same as I did and shook her head, laughing a little. "Listen to me, having second thoughts. I really do believe everything I told you, Caroline, but living with a lawman makes it harder than it used to be to always believe the best about things."

"Lizbeth and I talked about that a while ago," I said thoughtfully. "She said that sometimes a person's got to think about the worst that can happen if she hopes to get ahead of a situation."

"Yes, well, that's Silas through and through, and Lizbeth's got that same hard-headed streak in her. Is that how you look at life?"

I nodded. "I've had to make my way in the world, Ruth, and taking time to consider the worst that can happen before making a decision has helped me more than once."

Ruth smiled at that, a kind woman who was exactly as Lizbeth described: a person that naturally thought the best of everybody, who despite being once widowed somehow still expected matters to turn out just fine, a woman it was a pleasure to be around.

"Thinking that way doesn't come naturally to me, Caroline. Never has." I pulled my jacket tighter around me and reached for the doorknob with one hand while holding up a small wrapped towel in the other.

"Thank you for the cookies. They'll be just the thing with a cup of hot tea when I get home tonight. And, Ruth," I sent her a quick smile, "don't stop being who you are. Not for anything. If you didn't point out the bright side of life to the rest of us, we'd be stumbling around in the dark most of the time."

It wasn't that I didn't get along with other women or that I hadn't worked side-by-side with women in my past years because I did and I had, but I'd never really enjoyed a close friendship with a woman before. Like Arthur Stenton, I was a person who kept herself to herself, not very trusting of either women or men, but while I couldn't yet say that Ruth Carpenter and I shared a close friendship, I thought there was a good chance we were headed in that direction. Oddly enough, the thought made me a little sad, wondering how many good friendships I'd missed out on in the past. It was beginning to dawn on me that part of the measure of a person's life might be found in the number of people she could call *friend*.

The Carpenters left for Omaha on the Friday before Christmas. I saw them through a front window of the hotel and stepped outside to wave to Ruth as she passed on the other side of the street. They had the look of a typical little family about them, Si Carpenter carrying a large traveling bag and Alexander so bundled up in Ruth's arms that she looked like she was carrying nothing but a thick roll of blankets. Was there really a baby in there somewhere?

"Have a good time!" I called and was rewarded with smiles from both Si and Ruth, though they didn't slow their pace. Of course, they'd have a good time and, of course, New Hope would be fine without its marshal for a few days. Still, there was something unsettling and almost sad about having him gone, about having them both gone. Back inside the hotel lobby, I caught Lizbeth's eye where she stood behind the check-in counter. The girl gave me her usual pretty smile, but the look on her face told me that if I were to speak my thoughts about Ruth and Silas Carpenter's absence out loud, she would nod in understanding and complete agreement.

10

Snow started to fall the morning of Christmas Eve. Not a snowfall heavy enough to interrupt people's plans or keep them from traveling to see the children act out the Bethlehem Christmas story at the church that evening, but a dusting of constant snow that reminded me of sugar being sprinkled on gingerbread.

Sometime during the morning, I said, "If you need to leave early today, Lizbeth, you know you can. I don't like to think of you out on the road when it's dark and snowy."

"Thank you, but the family's coming in for church, and I'll go home with them after that. Charlie'll bring me back in the morning, and then I can stay over at Hart's, even if they're gone. I won't miss any work."

"But if you need to," I insisted, "it's all right. I'm able to watch the desk."

"Thank you," Lizbeth said again with a firmer tone as she raised her face from examining the check-in book to meet my gaze, "but I won't need to miss any work, Mrs. Moore. You can always count on me. I'm not one to shirk or take advantage."

What argument could I raise to that, really, without sounding like I thought she was indeed a shirker, so I returned a simple, "All right. Thank you," because I'm not one to shirk either, and I had learned some time ago that it was best not to pursue a topic with Lizbeth Ericson when she had that particular tone in her voice.

Because the Union Pacific Railway was central to life in New Hope, nearly every activity of any importance to the town was planned around the train schedule, and that meant that the Christmas Eve pageant wouldn't start until early evening. As it turned out, the service could have begun earlier since the 7:30 westbound didn't load or unload a single passenger at the New Hope platform that day, but there was no way of knowing that in advance. And the children were in no mood for an early bedtime that night, anyway. On the night before Christmas, what sensible child is?

So at eight o'clock on a dark, cold, and slightly snowy Christmas Eve, the population of New Hope, Nebraska, and its surrounding area squeezed themselves into the small church that sat in divine dignity east of town. There wasn't enough pew space for everyone, but it seemed that was expected because the men of the congregation had brought in additional benches and lined them up along the sides and the back of the church before the first people started to arrive.

It was my first time attending a small town Christmas Eve service, and it was quite an experience, somehow exactly what I expected and yet more than I expected. Children dressed up as shepherds and wise men and angels and Mary and Joseph and a variety of animals. Jem Fenway took his part as head shepherd very seriously, raising his shepherd's crook and shouting, "To Bethlehem!" the way General Sherman might have roused his troops to storm Atlanta. As one of the Wise Men, Frederick Lincoln wore a paper crown with the dignity of a judge. For some reason, when Frederick knelt in front of the manger and the baby Jesus – a doll donated proudly by one of the little girls – I felt unexpectedly moved. I don't know why exactly, only he was so serious as he approached the makeshift manger and so respectful that for a moment it wasn't a doll lying in the hay at all but something more real and much more important.

After the little play, there was singing and a prayer by the minister, then more singing and at the end all the children received two pieces of wrapped saltwater taffy and an orange. (God bless the person who arranged to have all those oranges ready in the middle of a cold December night in Nebraska; I never did find out who it was.) Mothers had to nudge children to say a proper thank-you because naturally the children of New Hope found oranges and saltwater taffy to be more fascinating than good manners. Truth be told, I felt the same as they did. If there were two items further removed from the plains of Nebraska in December than saltwater taffy and oranges, I couldn't think what they'd be. The Union Pacific Railway was bringing the world to New Hope in more ways than one.

When the evening's festivity finally ended and talk died down, parents gathered up their children and everyone trooped out of the church, all of us, as far as I could tell, satisfied that we had given proper tribute to the special occasion.

Once outside the church, I tightened my woolen scarf around my neck, said Merry Christmas to anyone I passed, and hurried to catch up with the familiar figure of Arthur Stenton, who strode purposefully ahead of me in the direction of Main Street.

When I called his name the first time, he didn't pause, probably because he didn't hear me over the chatter of the people around us, but when I called his name a second time, he stopped long enough to look behind him. It gave me the time I needed to catch up. When he at last made out who it was that had called to him, he removed his hat and stood still, waiting for me to reach him.

"Merry Christmas, Arthur." I was panting somewhat from hurrying and because I thought the words might have been too choppy to be understood, I said, "Merry Christmas, Arthur," again and more firmly.

"Merry Christmas to you, Mrs. Moore." At first, the moonlight made his face look more sober than usual, shadowed and almost secretive, but then he smiled and the beauty of the smile, something I had rarely seen on his face, made me suddenly breathless again, though not from hurrying in the cold night air. It was some other reason that briefly took my breath away.

"Did you enjoy the service, Mrs. Moore?" he asked.

"It was–" I paused to choose the right word "–enjoyable. I thought it was enjoyable."

"Not to mention entertaining," his tone perfectly innocent but tinged with a touch of wry humor.

"Well, that, too, of course. There was that moment when the donkey suddenly started crying and tumbled off the stage in his rush to find his mother."

"And when the star fell out of the sky and landed right in the middle of the flock of sheep."

"And when Mary held the Baby Jesus upside down."

"And the head shepherd stomping into the stable as if he were stepping on poisonous spiders."

That last picture Arthur drew of young Jem Fenway so stalwart and determined to find the newborn baby made me chuckle.

"You're right, Arthur. It was definitely entertaining as well as enjoyable." For a moment I felt so in charity with the man that I might have known him for a lifetime instead of only a few weeks. After a slight pause, I went on, "If you haven't made plans for Christmas dinner, I wanted to remind you that Chef Clermont has a fine menu planned in the hotel's dining room tomorrow. I only recently found out about the Bliss House Christmas tradition or I'd have said something to you earlier." When Arthur remained silent, I pressed, “Do you have plans for Christmas dinner tomorrow, Arthur? Special plans, I mean, in honor of the occasion.”

“No.”

“Good. It’s settled then. Twelve o’clock sharp. If you come late, you risk the wrath of Monsieur Clermont so plan accordingly.”

“I don’t make it a habit to accept charity, Mrs. Moore,” his earlier smile gone, replaced by the composed and formal tone I was used to.

“No doubt that’s true, but John Bliss actually pays people to serve this dinner, and they look forward to the extra money they’ll get for working so you should think of the meal as Christmas charity for other people, not for yourself if that will make you feel better. You have to eat, after all, Arthur, and even Mr. Emerson would approve. Didn’t he say, ‘Beneath the calm, within the light / A hid, unruly appetite’?” Whatever Arthur Stenton expected to hear, it wasn’t a quote by his favorite author.

“He did.”

“There it is, then. Approval from on high.” I couldn’t help but laugh as I picked up my skirts. “I’m going to count on seeing you tomorrow. You as good as promised. Twelve o’clock and don’t be late because Monsieur Clermont is a stickler for timeliness.” Arthur opened his mouth, prepared to dispute that he had promised anything, but I went on without giving him a chance to get in a word. “Now, though, I have to stop by the hotel briefly and then I long to sit in front of the fire in the Blisses’ parlor with a cup of hot tea.” I looked around us. “While we were talking, it appears everyone else disappeared into their warm homes. Will you escort me to the end of the alley?” The well-born son of a judge refuse to accompany a solitary widow on a dark night? Not a chance of that, I was sure.

“Of course.” I thought I caught a faint reluctance in his voice, but when we reached the end of the alley, he turned with me, stepped up onto the boardwalk and continued by my side toward the hotel until I finally halted.

"You don't have to come any further, Arthur. I'll be fine. You can see the light from the front windows of the hotel from here." His limp had become more pronounced as we walked and I felt a little guilty. Even after he retraced his steps and crossed Main Street, he would have to trek down the alley on the other side and over the hilly area that led to the schoolhouse, and then walk beyond the school yard to reach his little house. All in the cold and the dark and over ground that was slick with light snow. It wasn't guilt I felt, I realized with a mental start, but worry. I was *worried* about Arthur Stenton, as if I had some kind of ownership in him, as if I would mind if something happened to him. Obviously Ruth Carpenter wasn't the only person I had come to think of as a friend during my first weeks in New Hope.

In a natural gesture, Arthur Stenton held out his arm toward me. "Come along, Mrs. Moore."

Was that humor in his tone again, warmth, even? It didn't seem credible, but I liked the sound of whatever I heard and decided not to insist on sending the man away. Instead, I tucked my hand under his arm, and we walked together to the hotel. Lizbeth had set up a small nativity set under a lamp on one of the lobby tables and that small display along with the dim lights and warmth of the lobby made the place seem cozy and welcoming.

"Everything looks quiet," Arthur Stenton said from where he stood just inside the doorway.

"There's hardly anyone booked in tonight," I replied, "and Kip will have taken care of all the necessary details. I just feel better if I check on the boy – he sleeps in a back room next to the office – and make sure everything's in order before I go home."

"I can wait." Well, I thought, perhaps that hadn't been reluctance I'd heard in his voice.

"No, that's not necessary, but thank you. I'll spend a little while here and then Lucas Morgan usually makes it a point to pass by just at the right time to be sure I get home safe and sound."

Arthur gave a quick nod. "Ah. I see." His abrupt words made me think he had read more into my explanation than I intended, but there was no way to clarify, no time either, because he had already opened the door to depart.

"Arthur."

A half-turn on his part. "Yes?"

"Thank you. And merry Christmas."

"Merry Christmas to you, Mrs. Moore." He gave a brief nod and a briefer smile before he stepped outside and pulled the door shut firmly after him. For a moment, a wild and unreasonable moment, I wanted to call him back, but I gave a brief shrug to settle my feelings and headed toward the office. I'm not an especially sentimental woman, but it was Christmas Eve and it was company I supposed I wanted. Not Arthur Stenton necessarily but company of some sort.

As if in answer to my thoughts, when I turned up the lamp in the office, Gypsy raised her head from where she curled comfortably on top of the desk and blinked both golden eyes at me. How the cat found her way into and out of rooms with closed doors continued to baffle all of us, but she did it without effort and shame. We stared at each other a long moment until she stood on all fours and arched her back into a slow stretch.

"I beg your pardon," I said. "Did I wake you?"

As if considering an answer, Gypsy tilted her head to one side, never taking her gaze from me, blinked again slowly, and then once more curled herself into a tight spiral.

That settles it, I thought, taking the cat's choice of lying right on top of the accounts book as a sign from heaven, there's nothing to be done here and turned the lamp back down.

Kip woke when I pushed open the door to his little room and raised his head from the cot where he slept.

"Trouble, ma'am?"

"No," I said. "Everything's peaceful and like to stay that way. It's Christmas Eve, after all, and we've only got the three guests and they'll be out on the morning eastbound. I'll be here early so you can go straight home to be with your family. Go back to sleep." He'd taught himself to wake quickly in case he was needed in the night but with that had come the skill of easy sleep, back to his dreams before my shadow disappeared from the hallway. One of the benefits of youth and a mind still free of troubling memories.

After a final look at the hotel lobby, I stepped outside and looked both ways along Main Street. A few lights still burned in upstairs windows, people decorating their trees, maybe, or raising a final glass of hot cider before heading for bed, but for the most part the shops and the rooms over the shops where many of the owners resided were dark. Everyone tucked in. I looked up at the sound of footsteps on the boardwalk. Lucas Morgan approaching on his usual route back to the jail, checking that all was quiet, that everyone was safe, that the town could sleep in peace – could sleep in heavenly peace on this night especially. There was comfort in the knowledge. Waiting until Lucas reached me, I turned toward home and he fell into step beside me. We had made the short walk often enough that there was no need for a greeting. Across Main Street and down the alley, sometimes talking, sometimes not. That night it was *not*. I knew where my thoughts were and had a fair guess about his, though I'd never have presumed to share my ideas aloud.

Looking down at the deputy from the front porch of the Blisses' house, it was too dark to make out the features of his face. I saw him only as a shadowy but still substantial figure, reassuring despite being faceless.

"Thank you, Lucas. Merry Christmas."

"My pleasure, Caroline. Merry Christmas to you."

Once inside, I turned up the lamp on the hallway table, hung up my coat and scarf, and went into the kitchen to put on the kettle. Later still, sitting on the parlor loveseat with an afghan across my lap, a mug of tea clasped in both hands, and my feet tucked under me, I allowed my memories free play, let them tumble about in my mind: faces and voices, snippets of songs, laughter, the warmth of Davey sleeping close beside me, Jean nuzzling at my breast, and expected to feel the usual heartbreak and anger that remembering the past brought. But not that night. That night the memories were the same but somehow I had changed. No crushing sense of loss. No tears. No furious fire crackling through my body. Nothing but a bone-deep melancholy.

Oh, I thought, sitting bolt upright with a kind of panic, what's happened to me? I loved my husband and I loved my daughter and I still missed them, but the missing was different now. Softer, and peaceful in its way. Something had altered, something in me, and though I didn't know when or how it happened, I knew with certainty what had brought about the change. It was all New Hope's doing. The town had worked its way into my heart without being invited and filed down the rough edges of my grief with its disciplined goodness. A woman of ordinary emotions would be grateful for the peace, but however I seemed on the outside, I hadn't been ordinary inside, in my heart of hearts, for eight long years. Over time I had grown comfortable living with the fires of grief and resentment, their presence a reminder that I had a purpose and a plan, but if those fires cooled and dimmed, what would be left? What would I have for company then? Through all the past years, one thing had kept me moving forward, from Denver and on to Ogallala and here to New Hope, too. One thing.

And if I wasn't careful, this common little town would rob me of the one, the only, satisfaction I could still look forward to.

Well, things always look different at night, I told myself, resolved to reclaim what felt familiar and safe. New Hope is just one of many small towns that all look the same spread across the whole state of Nebraska, and New Hope's citizens are nothing different from the citizens in any of those Nebraska towns, nothing different from any Colorado or Kansas town, either, for that matter. I'd passed through my share of those kinds of places and they had all seemed the same, same people, same streets, same stores, churches, and schoolhouses. Every one of them just New Hope with a different name. Besides, it was Christmas Eve, and everyone knew important matters couldn't be examined properly on Christmas Eve. I could be convincing when I put my mind to it and began to feel better. Nothing had changed, not really. Not all that much. Not enough to worry about. There was still satisfaction to be had if I kept my head.

I stood, made sure the hearth fire was safely dying, and trudged upstairs to bed. Things will look different in the morning, I said aloud as I got ready for bed, but I lay awake a while before sleep came thinking about what had happened in the past and how it marked both my present and my future, how it had marked me as a woman. What kind of woman would I be today if the fire in Wyoming had never happened? It was a different kind of grief to realize that was something I would never know.

I wouldn't have believed it if I hadn't seen it with my own eyes, but the first moment Monsieur Clermont spoke to Ezzie Liggett as they worked together in the Bliss Restaurant kitchen, I knew the rumors about them were true. I didn't know Ezzie very well but I certainly knew our resident chef, and in all the weeks I had worked with him, he had never once shown an ounce of tolerant charity toward anyone including, maybe especially, me. And here he was, chatting with Ezzie in her apron-covered pretty green dress at the huge kitchen worktable as she stood vigorously mashing a big bowl of potatoes and he stirred spoons of butter into a large roasting pan filled with corn. A perky black bow tie peeked over the top of his white kitchen smock. Steam rose from the potatoes, the corn, and in a less obvious but just as real way from the pair absorbed in their conversation. Ezzie ran the Nebraska Café with its more common but popular local specialties and Emil Clermont was a famous chef, but it was clear that each was as interested in the other as they were in the food they were preparing. For two people who made their livings from food, that could only mean true love. I smiled at the sight and thought that one day family meals in their home would be something to experience. As if aware of being observed, both Ezzie and Emil looked up at the same time and eyed me where I stood in the doorway. She smiled, he didn't, and neither of them looked as if they wanted or needed company in the kitchen.

"Merry Christmas," I said, then made a quick pivot and exited. The restaurant's kitchen was foreign ground to me during normal times and even more so at that moment. Far be it from me to get in the way of true love, in whatever room I found it.

Everything was ready for the Bliss House Christmas dinner at exactly twelve o'clock, tables set, plates stacked, the smells of ham and turkey and the rest of the trimmings drifting into the dining room from the kitchen. It was a tribute to Chef Clermont's widespread reputation for correctness that not a soul appeared under the connecting arch from the hotel lobby or in the restaurant's doorway even one minute before the hour. But exactly at noon people emerged, all of them men. The Lowe brothers led the way into the dining room, followed by old Cap Sherman, Harold Sellers, Benny Tidwell, Con Tull, and the junior deputy Clayton Kemp, a parade of bachelors, each man regardless of age neat as a pin, dressed in a fresh shirt, his hair combed and not a shadow of stubble on cheek or chin, even Cap, whose rumpled appearance always made me think he'd just pulled himself out of bed after a wild night on the town. A few more men from outlying farms who had come into town for the Christmas morning church service brought cold air into the dining room with them when they entered from the outside.

The single eastbound train had pulled in early, picked up the three people who had stayed overnight in the hotel Christmas Eve, and departed without leaving anyone behind. With regular schedules resuming tomorrow, I figured we'd have a few paying guests off the late westbound train Christmas night, people happy to resume their trip the next morning after sleeping in a comfortable bed for the night, but the hotel was still as empty as it would ever be. John Bliss hadn't warned me that a lack of paying guests was normal for this one day a year, and I might have been concerned about the loss of revenue – keeping that from happening was one of the reasons I was brought in, after all – if the restaurant workers hadn't made all the arrangements in advance without any input from me. That's the way it happened, though, so if the help at Bliss House saw an empty hotel and a free restaurant meal as run-of-the-mill, I wasn't about to worry. John Bliss could afford an empty establishment a day or two a year, anyway. He had started out with the proceeds from half of a very profitable silver mine and turned his share into New Hope gold. Alchemy for sure. Davey had tried for a similar result with his half of the silver mine but despite a promising start, it didn't end up gold for him – anything but, in fact – though it wasn't for lack of hard work and trying. Something or better, someone, had stolen my husband's silver dreams. Like John's, Davey's plans might have turned into gold, too, but now I would never know.

Mrs. Pikert's two children sat wide-eyed and quiet on the floor in a corner of the kitchen while their mother worked serving the guests: a sturdy boy with curly red hair and a little girl with red pigtails, both noses sprinkled generously with freckles. They watched Chef Clermont nervously, and I guessed their mother had given them strict instructions not to get in the great man's way. But Monsieur Clermont, softened by the day and even more so by the presence of Ezzie Liggett in his kitchen, gave each child an apple and told them in the kindest tone he could muster that it would not be long before they would sit down for their own Christmas meal. I'm not sure the children believed him – I think their mother must have been very firm in her warning – but I appreciated the chef's attempt at kindness. He was a commanding man who didn't hesitate to raise his voice and point fingers when he wasn't happy with something or someone in his kitchen. That unhappiness had been directed at me a time or two so I knew that for the young or timid, Emil Clermont in a temper could be a frightful sight. I also recognized, however, that the man wasn't unkind on purpose and that he was more excitable than bullying. When he bent toward the children with apples in his hand and a twinkle in his eye that afternoon, Ezzie Liggett met my surprised gaze with a smile. I know my way around this kitchen, her amused glance said, and around this cook, as well.

Arthur Stenton came late, but he came, which pleased me more than I cared to admit. He stepped into the dining room and from where I stood in the connecting doorway, I thought I spied – for the briefest moment – a flash of discomfort in the man's expression. The idea of the proud, serious man feeling awkward and out of place made me – also for the briefest moment – feel guilty, as if I had somehow forced him into doing something he found disagreeable, a boy made to eat his vegetables or wash behind his ears. But that mental picture almost made me giggle and the moment passed.

"Welcome, Arthur," I said, going up to him. "I thought for a while you weren't coming."

"How could I not – since I as good as promised?" He gave me a slight smile.

"So you do listen to me?" I laughed. "Whoever would have guessed? Give me your hat and coat, and I'll hang them for you. And take a seat. Susie will have your meal to you practically before you sit down."

He sat at a table by himself, I noticed, but the other men in the room raised their glances from their plates long enough either to raise a hand or say a word by way of greeting. The high regard in which the schoolteacher was held showed in their words and gestures. Something had happened in New Hope last year, something serious, that Arthur Stenton had played a part in. People didn't talk about whatever it was, even Ruth grew quiet at the memory, but whatever the details, people showed their approval of Arthur's behavior with their unspoken respect and quiet admiration. I felt both in the hotel dining room that Christmas Day.

I had been right to praise Susie's prompt service. Steam already rose from Arthur's coffee cup when I returned to the dining room, and I caught just a glimpse of Susie's back as she disappeared into the kitchen. A plate of Christmas dinner would appear next. Like all the girls that worked in the Bliss House restaurant, the girl was a wonder on her feet.

Lucas Morgan was the only person I could think of who might have shown up but didn't. Maybe he'd accepted a generous Christmas invitation from one of New Hope's families, but with Clayton sitting there in his best duds, staring at his apple pie like he'd just fallen in love with it, I thought it more likely that Lucas was on his usual tour of the town, making sure all was in order and everyone was safe. I knew from our nighttime walks to the front steps of the Blisses' big house that Lucas Morgan was a man who believed in duty. Once he'd even mentioned in passing that for him the measure of a man was in doing his duty, his voice grave and flat when he said it. At the time, the grim words and tone had made me wonder briefly about Morgan's past, but those kinds of questions weren't asked. We all had pasts we kept to ourselves, pasts that people didn't need to know about, and questions would be seen as meddling. In a small town like New Hope, it was pretending to mind your own business even if you weren't that kept things moving along as smoothly as they did.

My business or not, I couldn't help but wonder about Arthur Stenton's past. He sat at his table almost too straight-backed, a man unused to bending, with a manner about him that was always courteous and proper, but distant, too. He seemed surrounded by a wall of his own making, and yet grown men admired him and children respected him. What did he need that wall for? Who was he trying to keep out? My impression was that Arthur was a man with little time for and experience with women. Curious that. There was nothing out of the ordinary about the man, but his hazel gaze was direct and clear and he had the kind of hair a man wouldn't lose with age, thick and dark and no gray showing yet. He looked lean and strong in the arms and shoulders with a form that wouldn't run to fat no matter how old he got, a solid citizen who was intelligent, gainfully employed, and respected. Other than his noticeable limp, he didn't display any obvious flaws of body, mind, or character. If I put him up against all the men of New Hope and threw in Ogallala as well, the schoolteacher would fall somewhere in the middle of the crowd of males that came to mind. Then I remembered his smile, a beautiful thing that lit up an otherwise grave face, turning him into another man entirely, and decided that if I threw his quiet humor into the mix, Arthur Stenton would rise straight to the top of the heap. In my opinion, anyway.

As if sensing my study, Arthur looked up from the table and over at me, letting his serious gaze rest on my face as I examined him. I felt myself blushing in a way I hadn't done in years and was glad when Susie came out of the kitchen and hurried toward Arthur with a plate of hot food. That would occupy the man for a while and give my cheeks time to cool down. I'm a woman familiar with men and used to observing them to see which ones were sober, which ones would cause trouble, and which ones had cash in their pockets, but being caught in an unguarded moment studying Arthur Stenton had momentarily flustered me.

The men who had a distance to travel before they were home took their last bites of pie and sips of coffee, stood, stretched, murmured a word to me in passing, found their coats, and paraded out of the dining room in much the same manner they'd arrived. The New Hope regulars stayed behind longer, taking more time with their meals and with their conversations. Mrs. Pikert brought her children out from the kitchen and seated them at a table in the corner, gave each of them a quick kiss on the cheek when she thought no one was looking, and proceeded to fill the table with plates of food. Emil Clermont followed Ezzie Liggett into the dining room, pulled out a chair for her with a gallant flourish, went back to the kitchen, and returned with plates of food for them both.

Susie, the last person besides me still on her feet, poured fresh coffee for everyone who remained, then came to me and asked, "Won't you sit down and have something yourself, Mrs. Moore? I'm happy to bring you a hot plate."

"Thank you, Susie, that's a kind offer, but I can find my own way. You get something for yourself and sit down a while. You've been on your feet all afternoon. I won't forget to tell Mr. Bliss how hard you worked today and what a good job you did." Susie smiled her appreciation.

It took me only a moment to place two pieces of pie on two plates, grab an empty cup and a pot of coffee, and make my way to the table where Arthur Stenton sat finishing his first piece of pie. He looked up as I approached.

I refilled the cup next to his plate and put down the coffee pot before asking, "May I join you for a little while, Arthur?" A bold request to a man who guarded his privacy so carefully, but he'd been raised with the manners of a gentleman, and I thought his conscience wouldn't allow an outright no. To my surprise, it didn't appear that the word *no* ever crossed his mind. Instead, in the formal way I'd come to expect from the man, he laid his napkin on the table and stood.

"It would be my pleasure," he said and came around to pull back a chair. "Please."

"Thank you." I sat down and reached for the coffee pot. "I hope you enjoyed your Christmas dinner."

"I did." A short silence followed before I pushed one of the pieces of pie in his direction.

"I know you had the apple," I said, "but this is the chef's dried pear pie. He had it out in case we ran out of apple. We didn't but I took the bull by the horns and cut us each a piece anyway. It's worth the scold I'll get for interfering in the kitchen."

Arthur looked over to the table where Emil and Lizzie sat making lively conversation, enjoying each other's company.

"Your chef doesn't look especially intimidating."

"Not now," I said, following his gaze, "but while the man has no bite in him at the moment, he can give an awful bark when he has a mind to." I smiled to take the bite and the bark out of my own words. "It's Christmas, though, so I believe he'll mind his manners."

Arthur and I made easy conversation about commonplace things – the weather, the school, the town of New Hope – and when not talking sat in companionable quiet over pie and coffee. I hadn't enjoyed such an agreeable Christmas in many years.

At last, our plates empty of pie and the last of the coffee poured, I looked around the dining room, now empty of people except for Mrs. Pikert moving from table to table to shake cloths and straighten chairs. Tomorrow it would be trains and meals and business as usual.

"I should help tidy the dining room," I said, "so Mrs. Pikert can take her children home before it gets dark." Arthur and I stood at the same time. "Thank you for the company, Arthur."

"It was my pleasure, Caroline, completely my pleasure." I was proud that I didn't even blink at the sound of my Christian name, just smiled and turned to fetch his coat and hat. From the look on his face, I doubted Arthur realized that he'd slipped into such a familiarity.

Hat and coat on, he stopped at the door long enough to say, "Please give my compliments to the chef. Tell him I haven't tasted anything better in any Boston restaurant."

"I'll tell him," I said, "but he won't be surprised at your compliment. In fact, he'll probably feel slighted that you didn't add in Philadelphia and New York. Monsieur Clermont is a very confident cook." Arthur laughed at that and adjusted his hat.

"No doubt it's true about Philadelphia and New York, too, only I haven't eaten there so I can't say for sure. I wouldn't want the man to think I was making something up." Arthur's dry tone made me laugh, as well.

Later in the day, everything quiet at the hotel and the restaurant, everything quiet in New Hope, too, I pulled on my coat, tied a scarf around my head, and stepped outside. The jail was lit, but when I stopped there with a plate of Christmas dinner for Lucas, the place was empty. Lucas making his rounds no doubt. He deserved more than a platter of cooling leftovers left on the desktop, but it was all I had to offer. I walked through the dark alley and sighed when I pushed open the front door of the big house.

"Home," I murmured aloud as I turned up the hall lamp, but the word jarred me to a sudden stop, one hand still on the lamp. Home. For all my years in Ogallala, I had never once called that town home, and I'd stayed there a long while, certainly longer than in this little community. Why should New Hope be different from other places I'd lived? I couldn't say for sure – something to do with the people and the feel of the town, I supposed – but different it certainly was. For better or worse, New Hope, Nebraska, was as close to home as I'd been in a very long time.

11

The new year brought frigid temperatures, the first of many meetings of the Beef Convention's planning members, and an unexpected visit from Mark Saylor. I recognized Saylor immediately, even with his back to me and his head bent over the sign-in book on the front desk. Lizbeth was speaking to him as he did so. It was Mark's companion, a large, dark-haired man, who first caught sight of me where I stood in the arched doorway. He straightened from a casual stance and stared at me longer than was comfortable before finally looking away. I didn't see him speak a word to Mark.

Lizbeth looked over Mark's shoulder directly at me – I thought for a moment she might be trying to send me some kind of message but was too far away for me to read her expression – just as he straightened. Mark caught enough of the glance to make a half turn to see what had Lizbeth's attention, and when he saw me, took several steps in my direction. I met him part of the way.

"Mark," I said, "what a surprise! I didn't think we'd have the pleasure of your company until the big meeting next month." I put out a hand in greeting, which he took in both of his.

"As if I could stay away that long," he said. When it seemed he didn't plan to release my hand anytime soon, I withdrew it gently. "You draw me like iron filings to a magnet, Caroline. I just couldn't keep away." He looked in high spirits, which made him especially engaging on an otherwise gray, cold day, so briefly irresistible that I couldn't help but meet his eyes and smile in return.

"Lovely words, Mark, but I'd guess it was business that brought you through New Hope. You must have just stepped off the 11:15. Are you headed for St. Jo?"

"Not St. Jo, no. New Hope is as far east as I'm traveling. And while I admit I did make the trip for business reasons, I could have conducted that business any place along the line that had a good bank. You're the reason I picked New Hope, Caroline. Surely you know by now that I like being around you." My slight smile must have hinted that I was more interested in his business reasons than in his compliments because he went on, "Tomorrow morning I'm meeting a man from Yankton off the first eastbound train, and if what he's got with him looks as good as Ray says, I'll be able to take possession of twenty-two hundred pounds of the most beautiful Angus beef you've ever seen right on the spot." It took me a moment to understand what he was talking about.

"Ah," I said finally. "You bought a bull to expand the herd, didn't you? That's a serious investment, Mark, and a big step. A man once told me that a good breeder is worth its weight in gold and costs that much, too." It was Davey who told me that, but Mark Saylor didn't need to know that detail.

"The man was right," Mark agreed, "but Ray says–"

"Ray?"

"Ray Summerton." Mark turned, nodded toward the man still standing by the lobby front desk, and raised his voice enough to call, "Ray, come over here. There's someone I want you to meet."

Summerton walked with the slight bow-legged list of a man who'd spent more of his time in the saddle than on the ground. Up close, he was taller than Mark Saylor with graying hair in need of a cut, long sideburns, a generous mustache over prominent teeth, and rough cheek stubble on skin as weathered as leather. His eyes were the most memorable thing about him because unlike the rest of him, which looked shabby and worn, his dark eyes were so alert they seemed to be always moving. Nothing would ever get by a man with that kind of sharp, sly look. I'd met men like Ray Summerton before, men easy to underestimate and risky, too, because they always knew what was in their own best interests and made sure that's how things turned out. Whatever it took. I was certain as I watched him cross the lobby toward us that for all the distance between us, Ray Summerton had still known the moment Mark Saylor spoke his name and had watched my reaction to it with interest.

When Mark introduced us, Summerton said, "Pleased to meet you, Mrs. Moore," in a questioning way, making it seem like he thought we might have met before but he wasn't quite sure. I was sure, though. I didn't forget the Ray Summertons of the world. As deceptively easy going as they might appear, they could be dangerous if a person misjudged them at the wrong time or for the wrong reason. Ray Summerton was new to me but the character of the man himself wasn't.

After some polite chitchat, Mark said, "Nobody's got a better eye for beef on the hoof than Ray. Once I had my first herd, I needed someone to get the Anchor brand on every head, then figure out how and where to winter the herd. Ray coming along when he did was good timing for me. We made it through that first winter without losing a single head, not a one, and those heifers? They were the best breeders I ever saw. Every head sold for top dollar and things just got better from there."

I murmured, "That was lucky for you. Lucky for you,

too, Mr. Summerton."

"I don't hold much store with luck," Summerton replied. His gaze had been on Mark's face and for a moment, I would have sworn he was having a laugh at Mark's expense, but when he turned to me, I thought I must have been wrong. There was nothing out of the ordinary in Mark's words that would cause him to be mocked. "My pa always told me a man who keeps his eyes open makes his own luck," then concluded with, "but I guess if anything in my life's been lucky, it would be my being at the Poudre River the same time Saylor was bringing his herd south into Colorado."

"South?" I asked, looking at Mark. "So you bought them up in Wyoming Territory?"

"There was a man selling out up toward the Laramie mountains, said he was going back East where life was civilized," Mark laughed at the word, "and he sold me the whole herd. Lock, stock, and barrel, just like that. Best deal I ever made in my life. I hired three men, but they turned out to be worthless. Got as far as the Poudre before they disappeared, and there I was with a herd of cattle on my hands and no help to move them along." He gave Summerton a friendly slap on the back. "No matter what Ray says, his coming along when he did was pure luck. I couldn't have managed without him. He found us a couple of Mexican drovers to get us as far as the Anchor, not much English but hard workers. After that, we were busy getting settled, branding night and day, then moving the herd onto good grazing land."

"It sounds like a match made in heaven," I said lightly, but looking at the two men side-by-side, I thought that heaven had very little to do with their working together. The only true thing I'd heard Summerton say so far was that he believed a man made his own luck, so if he was working for Mark Saylor, it was because that's where he wanted to be and what he wanted to do. He was a man who probably knew even more about people than he knew about livestock, a man who had no problem hoarding secrets until he needed to use them, always to his own advantage.

Apparently tired of the memories, Summerton looked around the hotel and said, "This place looks a little fancy for the likes of me. What's the town got to offer a man with a thirst?"

"The Music Hall's open right next door," I answered, "and Tull's Beer Garden is a few storefronts south and down the alley. You'll find what you're looking for at either place."

To Saylor, Summerton said, "I'll see you later, boss," and without waiting for Mark to speak, crossed the hotel lobby in the direction of the door.

"Ray's a little rough around the edges," Mark said, "but he came back from Yankton singing the praises of this bull, and I trust the man's judgment better than I trust my own when it comes to recognizing prime beef." Mark laid a hand lightly on my forearm and purposefully changed the subject. "You're looking lovely, as usual, Caroline. Will you give me time to get my coat off and take my bag up to my room and then join me in the dining room?"

"I don't sit down much during the workday, Mark. Not for luncheon, anyway. I thought you knew that."

"Supper, then. A person's got to eat, after all and I'd enjoy the company. I always enjoy your company, Caroline, and maybe I'm mistaken, but I'd have said you enjoy mine, too." Men seldom catch anything when they fish for compliments from me and this time was no different.

"Supper would be nice," I said, "and you're in luck because Chef has some trout to use up so his pan-fried trout is on the evening menu. You won't be disappointed."

Mark raised one of my hands to his lips, said, "Nothing could disappoint me if you're sitting across the table from me," and dropped a light kiss on my fingers. He was practiced at being charming, but it didn't always work to his advantage.

"Supper it is," I said. "I'll watch for you in the dining room. Did Lizbeth get you all booked in?" Mark found himself following me as I walked to the hotel desk and waited to speak until we both stood where Lizbeth was checking in a well-dressed couple.

"She did." To his credit, he had remembered my question despite our conversation being interrupted.

"Good. Then I'll leave you to your business and plan to see you later. Will Mr. Summerton be joining us?"

"God, no. The idea of Ray Summerton sitting down in a fine restaurant with linen napkins and delicate china and then making polite conversation over dinner would make anyone who knows the man laugh out loud. He's a lot of things, Ray is, but well-bred isn't one of them. No, it'll just be the two of us, Caroline. I hope you're not disappointed." This time I allowed the man a tiny nibble on his line.

"No more than you will be with the trout, Mark," I said and let him make of that what he chose.

I watched him ascend the stairs behind the couple who'd just arrived and turned back to find Lizbeth watching me with an equally attentive gaze.

"Mr. Saylor carries himself well, doesn't he, Mrs. Moore?" Lizbeth asked.

"He does."

"He's a handsome man, too, always so well turned out."

"He is that," I agreed.

"Hmmm." The girl responded with a thoughtful but wordless sound, as if reflecting on an especially serious matter and then added, "I don't know Mr. Saylor but what I do know I like well enough. Not that other man, though, not the one that came in with him today."

"Ray Summerton, you mean."

Lizbeth glanced down at the scrawled signatures in the check-in book and nodded. "Yes, that one. I don't mind telling you that I wouldn't trust him any farther than I could throw him. If you know what I mean."

"I know exactly what you mean, and I don't disagree. You mind yourself when you're around Mr. Summerton, Lizbeth."

Lizbeth returned my glance with a clear-eyed look of her own. "You do the same, Mrs. Moore. The moment Mr. Saylor asked for you by name and they both turned and saw you, that other one couldn't take his eyes off you. It was a funny look. Not admiring, just funny. Made me uneasy."

"He made me a little uneasy, too," I admitted. "I always think his kind know more than they should and never in a good way, but he's leaving in the morning and we can both watch our step until then." I might have talked longer with Lizbeth about Ray Summerton except Marshal Carpenter, better known as Ruth Carpenter's husband, interrupted the conversation. He came up beside me, bringing some January cold in with him, and placed a sizeable paper leaflet on the counter in front of Lizbeth.

"I almost forgot to give you this, Lizbeth." As she picked it up for a look, Silas turned to me with a greeting.

"Afternoon, Mrs. Moore."

"Good afternoon to you, Marshal. Are you used to being on your own yet?"

Si had returned from the Christmas visit to Ruth's sister in Omaha without his wife, who had decided to tack on an additional week to her stay. Another whole week was too long for Silas Carpenter to be away from his constabulary duties in New Hope, though, and he had come home without his wife and son. Carpenter was a man who took his community responsibilities seriously, but I guessed that he felt the separation from his family equally as seriously.

"I lived on my own a long time, but I guess the last four years made me forget what it was like."

"The difference between sunshine and shadow," I said, and the marshal smiled a little.

"True enough, but I expect the sun'll be back out in a couple of days, so until then I guess I'll just have to keep stumbling along in the dark." The man surprised me sometimes with a kind of sly, dry humor. To Lizbeth, Si said, "Ruth sent that for you to look at. Said she'll talk to you about it when she's back home."

"Thank you," Lizbeth said but her attention was already more on the flyer in her hand than the man standing in front of her, and she gave him only a half-hearted goodbye.

"Must be important," I said to Si, nodding toward the paper in Lizbeth's hands.

"My wife said it was, and I've learned over time that when Ruth says something's important, it always is. She knows important when she sees it." So do you, I thought, which is why you miss your wife like blue blazes and can't wait for her to get home, no matter how offhand you try to sound about her being away. Silas and I smiled at each other. Then he gave a single nod that took in both Lizbeth and me and left.

I didn't say anything more to Lizbeth because she had gone back to studying the flyer Si had brought her and any comment I'd have made would have gone unnoticed. Whatever was on that handout had Lizbeth's complete attention.

Over supper that night, Mark couldn't stop talking about the bull he planned to buy in the morning, how it was the step he needed to take to expand the Anchor brand, and how this particular bull, strong and healthy and from excellent breeding stock, would make his beef more attractive to eastern appetites.

"It was quite a bidding war," Mark said, "because I wasn't the only man interested in the beast, but in the end, I won. I was determined to have it."

"Do you always get what you're determined to have?" I asked. At my question he stilled, set down his coffee cup, leaned forward across the dining table, and stared right into my eyes.

"Yes," Mark said in a low voice, unsmiling, intent, "always. When I see something I want, something I need, I don't stop until I have it. Whatever it takes. It's something you should know about me, Caroline. I always get what I'm determined to have."

I believed every word he said and was momentarily spellbound, seeing something in the man that took my breath away. Then suddenly the spell was broken.

"What if what you want belongs to someone else?" I asked innocently.

"Everything's for sale, and everybody has a price," Mark said, "and I have a talent for figuring out the price of things. I'm a patient man, besides, so if I have to I can wait for what I want. In fact, I've found that waiting makes winning feel better."

I tucked everything he said away in my mind to think about later because watching him as he spoke, I was beginning to believe that I needed to rethink my opinion of the man. Charming. Good-looking. Easy with women. Used to a comfortable life. All those things were true, yes, but before tonight I had thought Mark Saylor was more a rebellious son than anything else, certainly not a dangerous or an especially powerful man. Those were qualities I hadn't appreciated in him before, qualities I now believed it would be a serious mistake to ignore.

After our supper together, I refused his offer of a walk home, explaining that I needed to spend time with Monsieur Clermont before the chef left for the day and then clear a few papers from my desk before I could do the same. Both were lies. By the time Mark and I rose from the table, only dishwashers would be working in the kitchen, and there wasn't a single task waiting in the office that couldn't be done tomorrow. The truth of it was that I was done with Mark Saylor for the day, and for the night, too. I appreciate confidence in a man – my Davey had had his share of it and I had loved him for it – but Saylor's words had hinted at more than confidence, at something less attractive, and I needed time away from the man to decide what lay at his core. It was important to me to learn and understand as much as I could about Mark Saylor.

By that time of the evening, the girls were shaking out table linens and overturning clean cups onto saucers to be ready for the breakfast customers. John Bliss was a man who knew how to turn a profit even as he traveled the European continent with his beloved wife, a man smart enough to set up a routine to keep his business one step ahead of his customers. Davey Moore, John's partner in the silver mine that made them both rich and as close as a brother, lay in the grave. Two men equal in everything that mattered, yet today one was rich and happy and the other wasn't either of those things. Not anymore. How did a person make sense of the way things turned out in this world?

Mark said my name, bringing me back to the present. Transfixed again, I thought, and smiled at him to show I was paying attention.

"I'm sorry," I said. "The light from the wall lamps made the diamonds in your tie pin sparkle, and I was spellbound for a moment."

He came around the table to my side, whispered, "As I was all evening looking across at you," against my cheek, and took my hand in his. We walked together into the bright hotel lobby where Kip had just arrived and was hanging his coat and hat on the wall hooks. Lizbeth was nowhere in sight, already off to the boarding house for the night, probably taking that precious paper from Si Carpenter with her. She hadn't volunteered its contents and I hadn't asked, but I wasn't above snooping around the desk in her absence, just in case she'd left it behind. I'm as curious as the next woman.

"Good luck with your purchase tomorrow," I told Mark.

"Will you head home as soon as the business is done?" I didn't know if I was disappointed or relieved by the idea.

"Once Ray gives the okay, I'll have to make a trip to the bank, but when the papers are signed and money changes hands, Ray and me and the bull will be on the next train west. I don't want to get held up by the weather this time of year."

"It's cold, but there's no snow in the air."

"Not yet, but the right combination of snow and wind blowing across the plains can cause drifts high enough to bring the Union Pacific to a full stop. I want my boy safe and warm where I can keep an eye on him. I've got plans for him."

"I can see that," I said and retrieved my hand. "Good night, Mark."

"I'd still be pleased to be sure you get home safe."

I could tell he remembered the last time and the kiss and that he wanted that again, hoped for more, in fact. He may be able to find his way around a woman easily enough, but he understood very little about me. I wanted to keep it that way.

"Thank you, but it's not necessary, and you have an early morning. The first train is always on time, and Abner Talamine will be behind his desk at the bank by eight o'clock sharp. You should be able to transact your business, transfer your cargo, and be on the afternoon train with time to spare."

"That sounds about right," but his tone was miffed, like a boy deprived of a promised treat.

I kissed him lightly on the cheek, a gesture that took him off guard, and said, "It was a pleasant surprise to see you today, Mark." Then I turned away without giving him time for a response and went back into the now-dim dining room toward the kitchen. Henry Strunk was wiping dry the last of the pots when I entered.

"Is everything in order, Henry?"

"Yes, ma'am." Looking at him, I couldn't recall what the boy had looked like before wearing glasses. They had become as much a part of his features as his eyebrows and pug nose.

"Did you learn anything new from Mr. Stenton in school today?" Henry's eyes brightened at the question as if he'd been waiting for someone, anyone, to ask.

"Mr. Stenton told us that Mr. Edison – you know, Mr. Thomas Edison, the inventor? – built a power factory in New York City that makes light. It makes light, Mrs. Moore, something called electrical light! Mr. Stenton said the factory had so much power it was able to light up a whole square mile at the same time. Can you picture what that must've looked like? I'd give anything to see it!" I had read about the new incandescent bulb, but clearly the boy didn't need help from electrical power when just the idea of a new invention could make his eyes shine. Henry Strunk was lit from within by his own imagination.

"There's no reason why you shouldn't see it someday, Henry. I read that in another twenty years or so electrical power will be so commonplace we'll all take it for granted."

"That's exactly what Mr. Stenton said."

I felt more pleased than Henry's remark deserved, but I admired Arthur's learning and to have echoed his words was a compliment of sorts.

"Then it must be so." I looked around the kitchen. "It looks like everything's in place, Henry. Go home. I'll dim the lamps. Your mother'll worry if you're out too late."

Then I went to get my coat and scarf from the office, said good night to Kip, and stepped outside into the dark, still, frigid, Nebraska night. Winter made New Hope turn in on itself, all its inhabitants safe, snug, and warm behind sturdy walls. Windows and doors pulled shut and tight to keep winter out. The sky looked so heavy and low that I thought if I reached up my hand I could pull down a cloud.

The air felt damp with snow just waiting to fall.

I stopped at the jail, but it was dark and empty with no sight or sound of Lucas Morgan anywhere so I lifted my scarf over my head for warmth and crossed the empty street, taking the steps up onto the boardwalk and passing the darkened stores run by the Lowe brothers. The neighboring establishment, the Feed and Grain Store, was dark, too, but I could see lights in the rooms on the second floor where Norm and Gladys Janco lived with their children. It wasn't a very big place for five people, but on a cold night being snuggled together with the people you loved had a way of keeping all kinds of fires kindled. Good fires.

When I stepped down from the boardwalk and turned into the dark alley, I knew someone waited there before he made a sound or stepped into my path. Ever since the fire that killed my family, I had somehow developed a sense that warned of danger, even danger hidden by darkness and lies. Not worth what I lost that dreadful night eight years ago but still a valuable gift.

"Mrs. Moore." Because the alley was dark and shadowy, I couldn't make out the man's features, but I didn't need light to recognize the voice.

"Mr. Summerton. Do you make it a habit to accost women in the dark?" With some men it was better to go on the attack, better not to show fear. I might have imagined it, but he seemed to back up a step at my words.

"Sorry if I scared you."

"What do you want, Mr. Summerton, that couldn't have been handled in the light of day or in a place more public than a side alley?" Keeping at him so he couldn't tell he was right, that he did scare me.

"I stopped into the hotel but the boy at the desk said you were in the kitchen, and the kid in the kitchen didn't know where you were." Summerton must have hurried to get to the alley ahead of me where he guessed he'd find me alone and private.

"Well, you've tracked me down now. What do you want?"

"Just wondering if we've met before."

I stared at him and wished I had a clearer view of his expression. The question was the last thing I expected him to say. What was he playing at, I wondered, followed quickly by, *Should* I know him? *Did* I?

"Not to my recollection," I replied, which was as true as it went. "I spent the last few years running Ogallala House and before that I worked at a restaurant along the railway in Denver. "

"No, not Ogallala. Not Denver, either." He paused. "Wyoming Territory maybe. You ever spent time there?"

"Yes," I said. Unless we had met all those years ago when Davey and I were first putting down roots along the South Fork River, how would he know? Yet I was sure I'd never met Ray Summerton before. "How long ago since you were there?" I asked, more curious than afraid now. A little excited, too, feeling I might be on the edge of something very important.

"Nine years ago or so. Good cattle country up there. I hired on with an outfit outside Fort Laramie. Stayed a year. Maybe I saw you at the Fort."

"No," I said. "We were farther north. Close to the old Fort Caspar. We never got down to Fort Laramie."

"You and your husband, you mean."

I was a widow, after all. Why shouldn't he guess I was talking about what my husband and I did? Setting aside my feeling of unease, I prodded him along toward the point of this meeting and the reason he was talking to me in a dark alley.

"Yes. We ranched for a while." I made a point of pulling my scarf more tightly around my neck. "Good night, Mr. Summerton. It's too cold to be standing out here passing the time." I took a step or two forward, but he didn't move out of the way or back up.

"Your brand was something with a J, wasn't it? A double J on the bottom maybe?"

"Yes," I said again, unwilling to give more details.

"I heard something about your place then. A bad business all around. Talk was that nobody made it out alive." I remained silent, wishing there was more light so I could see those sharp, ever-watchful eyes of his and try to make sense of the man's message. With a man like Ray Summerton, there were the words and always something behind the words, too.

"That's the thing about gossip," I said. "You can't count on it to get all the facts straight."

"Your husband was a miner, folks said," Summerton ignored my comment. "Heard he made his money in silver so maybe he didn't know as much about running cattle as he should've."

"And maybe it's none of your business," I retorted, the man's words too close to the truth for comfort. "What is it you want me to know, Mr. Summerton? Can you get to the point, please? I'm cold and tired."

"It's a damned shame what happened, Mrs. Moore, you losing your husband and your herd the way you did, but I heard you still lay claim to the land. That's good land and pretty country up there along the South Fork. With your husband making a fortune in silver, I'm surprised you have to work like this. You must have plenty to live on without having to keep an eye on somebody else's business."

"Why should the money I have in my bank account mean anything to you, Mr. Summerton? I guarantee none of it's coming your way."

"Well, that's the thing, Mrs. Moore, that's the very thing I wanted to talk to you about. Last I heard, ain't nobody been held responsible for what happened to you and your husband, and that seems a real pity to me. I might be able to help you get justice done, if you're interested enough, that is. A man who travels around like I do sees and hears some interesting things."

"But you don't deal in facts," I said coldly. "You're a man who listens to gossip and gossip doesn't help me."

"Sure, I listen to gossip, but it's facts I hold on to. A man never knows when some of those facts will come in handy."

"What exactly are you talking about? Are you claiming you know something about what happened to the Rocking J eight years ago? If you are, you should take what you know straight to the law."

"Maybe I will, with a little persuading."

"Persuading meaning money."

"Everything has a price, ma'am," his words echoing what Mark Saylor had told me earlier in the evening, "and I guarantee you'd like to know what I know."

Both of us heard the quick footsteps on the boardwalk before someone rounded the corner into the alley, someone who didn't bother with the wooden steps but instead jumped lightly down onto the packed earth with a muffled thud.

"Everything all right here, Caroline?" Lucas Morgan, I thought, torn between relief and frustration. I may not trust Ray Summerton, but he was right about one thing: I *would* like to know what he knew. That wouldn't happen now, not with Lucas present.

"Yes. Mr. Summerton was making conversation is all."

"Funny place to do it. Funny time, too." Lucas walked up beside me and then took a step in front of me, putting himself between me and the other man and directly in Summerton's path. Both figures looked similar, even in the darkness, but I wouldn't have bet against the deputy if push came to shove. Which it didn't, thank God.

Summerton ignored Lucas and said to me, "It was a pleasure talking with you, Mrs. Moore. If there's ever anything I can help you with, you be sure to let me know.

I'm leaving in the morning, but maybe you'll think of something by February. Mr. Saylor says we're coming back to New Hope for some big meeting then, and I bet you and I could find time to talk then," taking two sidesteps past where Lucas and I stood as he spoke the last few words. His feet crunched against the cold dirt, and Lucas and I both turned to watch Summerton's figure disappear into the darkness.

"What was that all about?" Lucas asked.

"What *was* that all about, I asked myself with an edge of excitement but aloud answered, "It seems he thought he knew me, knew *us*, I mean, my husband and me, when we lived in Wyoming Territory."

"Did he intend harm?" The question sounded innocent, but if I said yes, I had no doubt where Lucas would head as soon as he'd seen me safely onto the front porch of the Blisses' house.

"No," I said, "I don't believe he did. He was sober as a judge but curious." Lucas might have pursued the matter, but I placed a hand on his coat sleeve. "I appreciate your coming along, Lucas, I do, but I've had enough conversation, and it's blasted cold, in case you didn't notice. If it makes you feel better, you can stand there and watch until I close the front door behind me. No harm was done."

"All right," not a man to waste time when he knew the argument was lost and probably just as cold as I was, besides.

Once up on the porch, I gave a broad wave of my arm in Lucas's direction and made sure to shut the door harder than usual so he could hear when I was safely inside. Settled in later, bundled up in a heavy shawl and clutching a cup of steaming tea, I sat close to the kitchen stove and mulled that whole unexpected exchange with Ray Summerton in the alley from start to finish. Doing so naturally led to earlier in the evening: how Mark Saylor's words had made me see him through different eyes, and how the diamonds of the small pin he always wore, a pin in the unique form of an anchor for the special brand he'd created to mark his stock, had glittered in the light. I sat there with my hands laced around the cup, deep in thought, until the tea – and the stove – cooled. Finally, feeling a tiny ember of an emotion I'd thought was extinguished long ago begin to flicker somewhere in the region of my heart, I went upstairs to bed, smiling at the idea that this little Nebraska town couldn't have had a more fitting name.

12

Snow fell during the night, and it was a serious snow, big flakes that fell fast and heavy and thick. Fortunately, there wasn't a wind, but even the alley, which was sometimes spared inches because of the buildings on each side, already had enough snow to reach the hem of my skirts. I picked my way up the steps to the post office to leave some coins and an addressed envelope on the counter along with a note to Lonnie asking him to be sure my letter went out in the next mail bag. When I was outside again, I looked across the alley where Gladys Janco stood doing her best to sweep the opposite set of steps clean. She looked up and smiled when I appeared.

"Good morning, Mrs. Moore. Watch your step over there. It's a little slick. I've told Norm more than once that we need a railing up both sides of these steps, but the only time he takes me serious is when it's snowing. I'll get to it as soon as the snow stops, he says, but I'm still waiting." Gladys Janco, a short, stout, jolly woman whose age I couldn't guess, gave a loud laugh that was part snort and said, "That's husbands for you. Always have a better idea stuck in their heads, but if something needs doing today and not tomorrow, it'll end up being his better half that gets it done."

I agreed with a laugh, carefully descended, crossed the alley, ascended her well-swept wooden steps, and kept walking south along the boardwalk, past the leather goods stores and the City Meat Market until I couldn't put off crossing the street any longer. The few wagon tracks from early morning traffic were almost filled in by new snow. Ruby had warned me about the snow over coffee and biscuits that morning so I knew to wear my high-top leather shoes, but by the time I entered the hotel lobby I felt damp and bedraggled. Lizbeth, already in place behind the front desk, looked up when she heard the door.

"Isn't it pretty out there?" she asked.

Youth, I thought as I shook out my scarf, might find snow pretty, but age and experience never did. I made some kind of halfhearted yet agreeable reply because it was too early in the day to be cranky, but Lizbeth must have heard what I didn't say because she gave a little grin. The kind of grin a young person gives when she feels just a tiny bit sorry for someone who seems to have grown too old to appreciate all the adventure life has to offer. Not disrespectful, not Lizbeth, but slightly superior. In a kind way, of course. I bridled a bit at the idea but supposed that the decade between our ages and the high-collared, dark dresses I usually wore probably did make me seem closer to her mother's age than to hers.

"Don't worry, though. When Tillie came in this morning, she said her pa told her the snow won't last," Lizbeth added, still feeling sorry for my advanced years, I guess, and doing her youthful best to encourage me to buck up.

"Is that the news from his big toe?" Tillie's father, Eb Fry, had a big toe with the miraculous ability to predict the weather. My question made Lizbeth giggle.

"Yes, ma'am, it is. Tillie says her pa told her there'd be sunshine before she got back home today."

I glanced over at one of the lobby windows where the snow outside nearly made it look like there were two curtains covering the glass, both white but one made of fine muslin and the other of snowflakes.

"I wouldn't dare doubt Eb Fry's toe, Lizbeth, but that's hard to believe." I carried my slightly soggy scarf with me and draped it along with my coat over an office chair I placed close to the little stove that did its best to keep the room warm.

Gypsy, curled nose to tail in her basket by the stove, opened one eye to follow me when I went to sit behind the desk, and then immediately went back to her relaxed sleep, getting her strength back for another day of mouse chasing and cream lapping. Like Gypsy, I had work waiting, too. Menus to be reviewed and the receipts ledger to be balanced, needed items to be checked off one list and other items to be put on another, payroll to approve and a bank statement to balance. Some days it seemed the paperwork needed to keep an enterprise moving forward went on forever, but I usually took it in stride as part of the job. Usually. Not that morning, though. That morning I couldn't get yesterday's events off my mind. Just before lunch, when I looked up to see Mark Saylor standing in the doorway, it was as if I'd conjured him from my thoughts. He'd been on my mind most of the morning.

There was something about the way he stood there, poised on the balls of his feet as if ready for action, that made me say, "I don't need to ask. You have the look of a man pleased with the world. Ray Summerton must have been right about the bull." Mark came into the room as I stood and went forward to greet him.

"He's as pretty a thing as you'll ever see, Caroline." I heard the restrained excitement in his voice. "Do you have time to come take a look?"

I replied as I reached for my still damp coat and scarf, "Of course. I'd love to take a look." More enthusiasm than honesty in my answer, but Mark grinned with pleasure and excitement at my words. The boyish look he wore just then was more attractive than any of his other poses – sophisticated charmer; prosperous businessman; defiant son – and I grinned in return. Most men thrived on attention, and on this occasion I didn't mind giving Mark Saylor his due.

The bull was a Red Angus, not the more common black that was so admired, but still magnificent in its power and breadth. All meat. All muscle. The seller from Dakota Territory and Ray Summerton stood close together conferring on the best way to move the beast from the pen outside the livery where it had been earlier that morning and back into the livestock car of the recently-arrived westbound train.

The men had plenty of time for discussion because that particular westbound train had a long layover in New Hope. The Union Pacific maintained a complicated schedule that changed often because it had to. In those days, railroads were as common as cornfields, new lines begun, old lines renamed, familiar lines consolidating under a single name. Somebody in a fancy Union Pacific office somewhere had to make sense of it all and juggle connections for the Atchison, Topeka, and Santa Fe Railroad, the New York, Lake Erie and Western line, and the Northern Pacific Railway, but a change of schedules or owners never troubled New Hope as long as the trains kept coming and going. The town's population of flexible merchants knew they owed their wellbeing to the railroad, whatever its schedule and whatever its name happened to be at the time.

Watching from a distance, it was clear that Mark's purchase was a spirited creature with a mind of its own, resistant, even defiant, to being driven, but with help from a third man, it was finally prodded forward up onto an enclosed ramp, onto a small platform, and then down the other side of the ramp directly into the train car where a fourth man waited. A brave man, that one, I thought, inside a small space with a ton of bold but confused beef snorting and stomping its disapproval.

By then, Summerton had vaulted the fence and was inside the train car, too. Despite the weather, there were a few others, men from the train and from the town, standing back and observing the same as Mark and I were. They stood stamping their feet against the cold and talking among themselves, interested in the bull's coming and going and as fascinated as I was by how easily Summerton controlled the big animal, using a mix of force and commanding speech that wouldn't tolerate argument from either man or beast. Summerton seemed to me to be strangely and maybe foolishly fearless, since he wasn't especially brawny, but because he was a man who didn't miss much in his surroundings and would always make sure he had the upper hand, I suppose he considered himself unbeatable in a way. Thinking like that would get him into trouble but not that day. I wouldn't have believed it possible, but watching the man through the open side doors of the railway car, I had to admit that he understood cattle and especially this bull, keeping one step ahead of it and handling the creature as fearlessly and confidently as he might have wrangled a calf. He put on an impressive show for all of us standing there and seemed to be enjoying himself in the process.

"We've worked together a while now," Mark said, watching with the same admiration as the rest of us, "and there's no man I've ever met with the savvy of Ray Summerton. You wouldn't guess to look at him that he knows as much as he does. He took over that herd I brought from Wyoming like it was his own. Made sure we didn't lose a single head that winter. We think alike, him and me. He gets things done."

"I had that same thought about him," I said, "that he gets things done, I mean." I paused and turned to face Mark.

"When he and I talked, I admit I wondered a time or two if he thought he was the boss."

An odd expression flitted across Mark's face and was gone so quickly I might have imagined it: a touch of something like fear mixed with resentment, followed closely by a hard determination that turned his pale eyes a darker shade of blue.

"I'm the boss, Caroline. Make no mistake about it. If Ray's getting that mixed up, I'll have to set him straight." He looked at me, his expression still cold. "When did you have a chance to talk with him? You were on your way home when I talked to you last."

"I saw Mr. Summerton on my way home, as a matter of fact. He stopped to pass the time. It seems he thought we might have met when he was working in Wyoming, before he hired on with you."

"I don't recall you ever telling me you spent time in Wyoming." There was surprise and a touch of suspicion in his voice.

"No? Well, it was a long time ago and there's not much to say about it so I guess it never came up in any of our conversations. Anyway, it turned out that Mr. Summerton was mistaken. We'd never met before, not in Wyoming or anyplace else."

Mark Saylor stared at me like he was trying to get a handle on something that was more complicated than he'd expected. Once more I had the uneasy feeling that I had overlooked or underestimated something very important in the man.

"You would be hard to forget, Caroline," Mark gave a little laugh, the hard expression now one of admiration, "especially for a man like Ray, who as far as I can tell never forgets a thing. I think he just wanted to make your acquaintance, and I can't hold that against him. You're the kind of woman a man enjoys looking at. Ray was just trying his luck."

"I heard him say he doesn't believe in luck."

"He does when it suits him. He'd believe the sky was green if it suited him at the time."

"It's a good thing you understand each other, then. Otherwise, there might come a time when what you say doesn't suit him and he'll just make his own decision, no matter what you want him to do."

"I make the decisions," the clipped words said in quick response to my comment, "not Ray. He's not a fool. He knows who's boss. Do you?" Challenge in the question.

"From what I've seen, you're the man with the ideas, Mark, the man with the plans. It's you who makes things happen and gets things done." My words took all the irritation and suspicion from Mark's face and voice.

"Exactly. That's exactly right, Caroline. I knew you were the kind of woman to understand." He took a step closer so that I could smell the lightly scented oil he used on his hair and mustache. "A man could get used to having a woman like you around. A beauty true enough, but a woman with more to offer a man than that. I like the way you think almost as much as I like the way you look," adding in a low voice, "I wish you were coming with me. That would make everything as close to perfect as a man could expect."

I resisted the impulse to back up a step and instead laughed off the comment. "John Bliss wouldn't agree with you."

"To hell with John Bliss. You don't owe him anything, and I can give you more than he ever could. I promise you I could. Come with me, Caroline. I swear you won't regret it. A woman like you shouldn't be alone, shouldn't be without a man in her life. I can give you anything you want and maybe some things you don't even know you want. Not yet, anyway."

I studied him. Did he really expect that I'd leave everything behind and hop on board the train with him at the drop of a hat, that I'd betray John's trust and leave Bliss House adrift? How little he understood me if that was the case!

"I'll see you next month, Mark, and we can talk about it then. Go on now. I'll send you some sandwiches on the house so you don't need to go hungry while you keep an eye on your new purchase. You know that's what you want to do. And you should check with Ray to make sure he's got it all tied up tight and doesn't need anything."

The side doors of the train car had been shut a while ago and with that, the men who had been standing and watching with us in the cold figured out the show was over and went in search of warmth. One of the engine men, intent on making sure everything was in order and all the doors were firmly closed, paced along the side of the train headed toward the end car and away from where we stood. Mark and I were alone at the side of the tracks.

Without warning he pulled me into his arms and kissed me hard, lifted his head to stare at me with the look I'd seen earlier, that hard determination to be the boss and have things go his way, and then he kissed me again, holding me so tightly against him I couldn't have escaped without causing a spectacle. Or more of a spectacle, since being grabbed and then kissed in public was showy enough. The heat of Mark's breath warmed my cold lips and flushed my cheeks, but there was nothing tender in the kiss, nothing lover-like. My lips felt bruised, and more than once that afternoon I had to stop myself from scrubbing my hand across my mouth.

"Next month then," Mark muttered at last and let me go so abruptly I needed a stumbling step to catch my balance. Without a backward glance he took off at a fast walk along the tracks, kicking up snow as he went, then hopped onto the station platform and up into the first car he came to. I took a long steady breath and turned away from the empty stock pen to retrace my steps back to Bliss House. I didn't give a backward glance, either. As Eb Fry's toe had predicted, the snow had stopped a while ago and unexpectedly bright sunlight streaked through the clouds. Mark might have had time for a noon dinner at the restaurant, but for all his passionate words and rough kisses, it was the bull on his mind just then, not me, and that suited me fine.

Davey had been the same when he bought our first herd, just as excited and full of the future as Mark Saylor. Maybe he hadn't known a lot about ranching, but with advice from a friend we'd met along the way, the cattle my husband invested in had been the finest stock money could buy, every head healthy and strong, much as Mark had described his first herd. Davey's plan was to pay for the use of a neighbor's bull to seed our heifers until we bred the bull that would be the father and the future of the Rocking J, the ranch of Davey's dreams, the home of mine. My husband was sure he'd recognize the bull that would be our future the moment it was born, believed everything would happen exactly as he imagined, exactly as he wanted, but although he was a man of hard work and high hopes, nothing turned out as he expected. Because there were some things a person just couldn't plan for.

Back at the hotel, the dining room was full of customers with more arriving as I watched from the doorway. The girls were busy at the tables. They'd been trained by John Bliss to be pleasant and efficient and they didn't miss a step, every one of them neat and smiling and knowing exactly how to make a person feel welcome. Mr. Harvey's girls could take lessons from ours, I thought with pride and slipped quietly through the busy dining room into the kitchen. I knew the chef didn't welcome visitors during the busiest hours, well, didn't welcome visitors in his kitchen period, but I couldn't help myself. Watching Chef Clermont manage everything and everybody required to serve a room filled with hungry travelers who needed to be fed within a very limited time was a lot like watching Ray Summerton handle that bull. Each man the boss of his own territory.

I took a quick look around the bustling kitchen and rested my gaze on something hanging from a hook on the back wall: a rough piece of burlap pulled up into the shape of a bag and cinched with a drawstring of heavy twine. I had seen it before, but usually at the end of the day and usually empty, not weighted down like the bag looked then. I slipped into the kitchen as careful as a midnight thief entering a house, retrieved the bag from its hook, and peeked inside. Not a lot there, just something tied up with brown paper and string and two loose cookies, but I knew it was Henry's lunch bag and that it should be at school where Henry was, not hanging in a corner of the Bliss House kitchen. A growing boy needed his lunch.

Taking the bag with me, I retraced my steps back to the front desk and reached for my coat and scarf. The snow had stopped and the sun was out and no one needed me just then. Lizbeth had the hotel well in hand and Monsieur Clermont ruled the dining room, the woman who cleaned the hotel rooms had already finished and left for the day, Ruby had delivered and stacked the clean linens, and whatever papers waited on the office desk could wait a while longer. I needed a walk, a brisk, arm-swinging walk, to banish the memory of Mark Saylor's unexpected kiss, which had left a bad taste in my mouth and in my memory.

When I reached the bench at the top of the hill that hid the schoolhouse from view, I saw it must be recess. Children in their coats and hats and gloves played outside, looking as delighted as Lizbeth had been with the snow. I picked out Henry, even from the distance, and decided he didn't look woebegone for lack of lunch, didn't even look hungry. Like the other older boys, he was too busy chucking snowballs around. As I got closer, I saw with approval that he wasn't wearing his glasses, which might throw his aim off but would spare any damage to the spectacles. Henry was a smart boy, after all, with plans to visit Mr. Edison's power factory in New York City one day. For that to happen, he knew he needed to be able to read and study and learn and doing that depended on his glasses staying in one piece. That was how Henry Strunk thought things through.

I plodded down the hill, waved at Jem and Frederick in the distance, passed one group of younger children stomping out a circle in the snow for a game of *Cut the Pie* and another group assembling a snowman, and pulled open the schoolhouse door. Inside it was surprisingly warm considering there was just the one pot-bellied stove, but it was a big stove and there'd be a lot of bodies crowded into the room, besides, adding their own warmth. The place smelled of children and wet wool and burning coal, but I didn't find it unpleasant. Just the opposite, in fact. The room had the look and feel and yes, the smell of a house full of children, something I would never criticize or begrudge, something at one time I had hoped to have myself.

Arthur looked up from where he sat behind his desk, no doubt expecting to see a child and unable to hide his surprise at seeing me. I pulled the door shut, dropped my scarf from my hair onto my shoulders, and stood at the back of the schoolroom, holding up Henry's lunch bag like it was a rabbit I'd bagged for supper.

"Henry forgot his lunch at the restaurant," I explained. "Is it too late for him to eat it?"

"He's not here right now." Arthur had stood up when he saw me, but he hadn't come out from behind the desk. It wasn't sensible to think so, but it almost seemed that he was keeping the desk as a kind of wall between us. A silly idea because there'd be no reason for him to do that, but I couldn't help the thought.

"I can see that, Arthur. Henry is outside with the rest of

the children doing what children do when there's good packing snow, but children study better with full bellies and I know Henry wants to learn as much about electricity as he can. If I can pry him away from his snowball war, will he have time to eat his lunch?"

"I keep extra bread and preserves in my desk for any students who don't have a lunch, Mrs. Moore. Henry's already had something to eat."

Mrs. Moore again. I thought I had made progress with the man but with Arthur Stenton it seemed to be two steps forward and three steps back. For an educated gentleman, he knew little enough about getting along with grown-up people, and with grown-up women in particular. He must have missed that lesson completely.

"But I'll have him come in and eat the lunch you brought, if that's what you want. It was kind of you to bring it out to him. Just leave the sack on my desk, and I'll take care of it. No doubt you have to get back to your work at Bliss House." He sent me a serious look. "Our schoolroom isn't as warm as you're used to, and I wouldn't want you to catch a chill."

I knew he meant the words kindly, but there was something in his tone that made me feel like an old woman so decrepit and feeble she needed a cane and a mustard plaster slapped on her chest to survive. Did I seem as old as Methuselah to Lizbeth Ericson and Arthur Stenton both? Did my refusal to accept Mark's passionate but abrupt invitation to leave with him mean that I was now afraid of adventure and fearful of risk? Me? Caroline Temperance Moore, a woman who'd fallen in love practically overnight and left everything behind to make a new future with a man she knew nothing about except that she wasn't going to let him out of her sight? Years may have passed and times may have changed, but I hadn't changed, not that much, anyway.

Aloud I retorted, "I've never caught a chill in my life.

Not once. Not ever. And I am not about to start now." The very idea made me laugh, considering how often I dreamed of fire and felt its flame against my skin no matter how cold and dark the room was around me.

"Nevertheless," Arthur ignored my firm protest, walked down the center aisle between the desks, pulling on his long coat as he did so, stepped past me, and reached for the door, "you should warm yourself by the stove a moment and then get back to town. Surely you realize we're not equipped with radiators out here."

The man was simply stating a fact, one so obvious and basic that only a simpleton could miss it. Did he think me not only old and infirm but simple-minded, as well? Caroline, I warned myself, you are being altogether too sensitive, which was probably true, but by then it was too late to do anything about the restless feeling of aggravation that was making my heart pump faster.

I didn't bother to answer Arthur's question, and instead of taking his advice to warm up by the stove followed him outside into the snowy, sunlit schoolyard. He walked through the playing children over to where the bigger boys were running around with their snowballs ready to be thrown, and when he called Henry's name, not just Henry but all the boys came to a stop and stared at their loaded hands with sudden alarm. Had something happened? Were they in trouble? What if, heaven forbid, a misguided snowball had somehow offended the dignity of Mr. Arthur Stenton? I could tell from the boys' expressions that the awful idea had crossed their minds, though they had no idea where and when it might have happened. What crossed my mind was: heaven forbid that the man was human!

That was the thought that made me reach down with my gloved hands, scoop up a handful of fresh snow, pack it into the perfect ball, take aim at the center of Arthur Stenton's back, and let loose. The snow splatted against Arthur's coat but didn't do any serious damage. I didn't have much throwing strength, and the sun hadn't had time to melt the snow into a heavier weapon. Still, from the reaction of the children, a person might have thought I had unloaded a shotgun into the man. As the word spread among the children, even those who hadn't seen the shameful deed stopped their play and turned to stare, either at me, the cowardly culprit, or at their teacher, who was sure to have some kind of reaction worth seeing. No doubt by the end of the day everyone in New Hope would know that Mrs. Moore hit Mr. Stenton with a snowball. Let them make of it what they want, I thought, and waited to see what Arthur would do. Dignity was all well and good, but sometimes a snowball was well and good, too.

Arthur turned slowly until he faced me, and it took him a moment to figure out that the person most likely to be his attacker would be the person shaking snow from her gloves and directing a challenging stare straight at him. That narrowed down the guilty party to just one person. Me.

To this day, I truly believe that at first Arthur Stenton simply didn't believe, or couldn't believe, that I would do anything so impolite and undignified – undignified for him and me both – as hit him with a snowball in front of his students. The idea would never have crossed his mind, for sure.

"I beg your pardon," I said, "I was aiming for Henry." When Arthur didn't respond, I added, "I apologize for my poor aim." When the schoolteacher still stared in mute disbelief, I turned to retrace my steps toward New Hope, expecting to hear the children resume their play behind me. But ten steps forward, I felt, not heard, the gentle thud of a snowball land right between my shoulder blades. The feel of it brought a grin to my face even before I turned to see Mr. Arthur Stenton, stern schoolmaster and serious man, dusting snow from his hands. From where I stood, he looked completely unaware of the fact that he was surrounded by gaping children who would carry this lunchtime tale to everyone within shouting distance as soon as they were set free from school. It was a story perfect for a cold winter's night, after all, when people had little enough otherwise to occupy their time and their thoughts. The tale of Mr. Stenton and the Snowball was sure to get retold as long as winter held people indoors and there was someone to listen. Arthur had to understand that even better than I did, but he didn't seem to care one bit.

Instead, he took a few steps closer and said, loud enough for everyone to hear, "I beg your pardon. I was aiming for the bench." Pause. "I apologize for my poor aim." Then Arthur turned back toward the children and called, "Bertie, go ring the bell. It's time to line up. Recess is over."

Whether Henry had the opportunity to eat the lunch I delivered I never knew. Later in the day the boy made it a point to find me and thank me for taking the time to bring it out to him, but in a contrary way, I felt I should be thanking Henry for forgetting his lunch in the first place. For such a slight thing, an insignificant thing really, just a snowball thrown and another one returned, the memory of the incident on the playground stayed with me for days afterward. Twice that day I had given the gossips something to talk about, but it was Arthur Stenton's snowball and not Mark Saylor's kiss that lightened my mood and made me smile for no reason.

13

The day Ruth arrived home – or almost didn't arrive home – was the day January really made itself felt. Snow started to fall thick and constant from mid-morning on and in the afternoon steady gusts of wind took the snow and blew it into drifts high and deep enough to block town alleys and country roads. Unless a person had experienced how suddenly a snowstorm could arrive on the plains of Nebraska, how you could start the day out calm and then just like that find yourself in the middle of a blizzard, it would be almost impossible to believe it could happen that way. But the wind and the snow and the slowly dropping temperatures that morning were proof of the fact.

Lizbeth had said Ruth was expected to arrive on the mid-afternoon train, and when the scheduled time came and went with no announcing train whistle, the girl came out from behind the lobby counter to pull back a curtain and look outside. As she did so, Lucas Morgan stepped through the front door into the lobby, letting in a little snow with a lot of wind. He stopped just inside, stomped his boots, and used his hat to brush off the snow sticking to his heavy coat.

Lizbeth let the curtain drop and turned toward the

deputy. "Any sign of it?"

"No." They were both talking about the train.

"And no word either?" I asked from the foot of the staircase. I had descended from the second floor just in time to see Lizbeth go to the window.

"No."

"Are the lines down, do you think?" I asked.

Lonnie says not," Lucas told me, "but it could be just a matter of time for that."

"The marshal must be fit to be tied." Lizbeth frowned as she spoke and walked back to the front desk.

"He's not a man to give much away, but that's about right. Si's been wearing a path through the snow between the telegraph office and the ticket office looking for news most of the day."

"They've never been apart very often or very long," Lizbeth observed. "The longest was fall of last year when you and him went after those bank robbers. You remember."

"I do."

A quiet followed, filled with something unsaid but understood between Lizbeth and Lucas before Lizbeth continued, "So it's only natural Silas would be worried about his wife and son, worried they're caught in a snowstorm on a train out in the middle of nowhere and he can't get to them. He'd walk through fire for Miss Ruth." The girl sent me a quick, worried glance right after she spoke, wondering if her words about fire bothered me, which meant she knew something of my past even if I'd never discussed it with her. That was New Hope.

I ignored her words and her glance so she'd know she hadn't offended and said, "Even if the train gets held up by the snow, the passengers should be fine as long as they stay inside the car and wait out the storm. And Ruth isn't a woman to panic. The marshal knows all that."

"I stopped by to ask you both not to take your usual

walks home tonight," Lucas said. "You should stay at the hotel until the snow stops, and we can dig out the street and the alleys. Will you do that?" He spoke to both of us but he looked at Lizbeth.

"Yes." I answered for Lizbeth, too. "Lizbeth and I'll find room, Lucas. We'll be fine."

"Good." He replaced his hat and gave it a hard pull to keep it in place against the elements. "I got some other places I need to check."

"What about the school?" I asked suddenly. "What about the children?"

"Mr. Stenton sent the students from town home this morning already and the children that come in from the country are staying with them here in New Hope. He's got it all arranged and it always works out. Everybody knows they can count on Mr. Stenton to keep his students safe."

"Like he did last year." Lizbeth repeated her earlier words softly and said to Lucas, "You remember."

"Does he stay out there all by himself then?" I interrupted her recollection without apology. "Is that safe?"

"It's safe enough," Lucas told me. "He's got a snug little place and in winter I've never known him not to be prepared with enough wood and food and water to stay warm and healthy. Arthur Stenton's not a boy fresh to Nebraska, Caroline. He's had seven years to get used to the winters we have."

All true enough, I thought after Lucas left, but that didn't mean I liked the idea of Arthur Stenton on his own in the middle of a blizzard, not that it was any of my business or that he needed my approval to do whatever it was he wanted to do. But I still didn't have to like it.

The overdue train pulled into New Hope two hours late. Fortunately, the telegraph lines held, and we were able to get word from the railroad's central office that all trains west of the Missouri River were running late because of drifts on the tracks and were to stay put at their next station until further notice. The news meant that New Hope would be filled with travelers for the night that no one had anticipated, but the advanced warning gave us time to have extra rooms ready, and not just the Bliss Hotel but Bert Gruber's Gooseneck Hotel, too, and the two modest rooms over his Beer Garden that Con Tull sometimes let out.

Lizbeth stepped back inside from under the hotel overhang where she had gone as soon as we heard the long whistle of the arriving train.

"I believe the snow's stopped," she announced, smoothing down her hair and removing her shawl, "but not the wind. It's still fierce as ever. I saw Miss Ruth across the street on her way home, her and the baby and the marshal holding onto her arm so tight you'd think he feared the wind would blow her away. I saw a number of folks on the way to the Gooseneck and some coming our way, too. Knowing Miss Ruth, she'll open up the boarding house if needs be though she only just got home herself."

Lizbeth was hardly back behind the front desk when several people trooped into the hotel, seeking warmth and food and rooms for the night, all of which it was our pleasure and our business to provide. I was helping out where I was needed when the front door opened again. The winter wind that snuck in ruffled the curtains and got as far as the front desk, stirring some of the papers lying there, but it wasn't the wind that made me cold. It was seeing Ruby Strunk standing just inside the doorway with a look on her face I couldn't quite interpret except to know that something was wrong. Lizbeth as usual had everything in order and I excused myself to approach Ruby.

"What is it?" I asked.

"I'm looking for Henry. He was headed this way when I saw him last."

"It was only Bertie back there when I last looked," I said, but Ruby was already ahead of me, making her way into the dining room on her way to the kitchen in the back.

I followed.

The kitchen was like a beehive, Chef Clermont and his helper, young Fenstermeier, busy at the stoves and the girls in and out with supper plates to be collected and delivered to hungry customers waiting in the dining room. Amid all the hubbub, Henry was nowhere to be seen.

Pulling Ruby to the side and out of the way, I repeated my earlier question. "What is it? What's wrong?"

The color the winter wind had stirred in Ruby's face had disappeared. She looked pale and worried and all of her age.

"Henry come right back from school this morning. Mr. Stenton had sent everybody home right away on account of the storm getting worse so I put the boy to work, but when he got done with the chores I give him, he went looking for his eyeglasses and he couldn't find them. Not anywhere. Oh, he was fit to be tied – you know how he is about them eyeglasses of his – and worse was he couldn't remember exactly where he might've left them. He remembered that he had them washing dishes before school so he was thinking that maybe they dropped out of his pocket here in the kitchen. I told him to let it be until the storm passed, that them spectacles weren't going anywhere, but he couldn't rest. He told me he needed to be sure and he was gonna go check in the kitchen. It's just across the street a ways and anyway, I couldn't keep him from going. Boy's got his pa's stubborn streak." Ruby took a deep breath from the story she had just rushed through and finished, "But he ain't here, is he? And I don't know where else he could be, not in this weather." The two of us stood still, Ruby with her eyes fixed on my face and me trying to imagine how skinny Henry Strunk could possibly have disappeared in the middle of a snowstorm.

I put a hand to Ruby's arm. "Let me find out if he was here," and went from person to person in the kitchen, braving the chef's displeasure and slowing down the service without apology. I finally got the answer I wanted, or didn't want more to the point, from Deb.

"Yes, ma'am, Henry was here maybe an hour or so ago – no, it must've been longer than that because it was before the supper rush started so before the train got in, I guess."

I took a breath for patience before asking, "He didn't stay to work, though, did he, Deb? Not then." There were dirty dishes still stacked and waiting.

"No, ma'am. He was looking for his eyeglasses is what he told me, said he'd had them in the kitchen this morning but that he couldn't find them now and asked if I'd seen them. I told him no and that I knew for sure they weren't in the kitchen anywhere on account of me having to do double duty for Mrs. Pikert, who couldn't make it in 'cause of the snow. Chef asked me to do her job and make sure everything was in order for supper. Which I did, so if there were eyeglasses sitting anywhere, I would've seen them, and there weren't."

"What did Henry say to that?"

"He said–" Deb stopped and her eyes widened. "He said he must've dropped them at school, then, that maybe they fell out of his coat pocket when he took off his coat and shook off the snow before he hung it up. He said Mr. Stenton had everybody go right back home and he never thought to check his pockets 'til later and the glasses weren't there." Deb paused. "But he wouldn't have tried to go out to the schoolhouse in this weather, would he, Mrs. Moore?"

"I hope not, Deb," I said, but in my heart I thought that was exactly what Henry Strunk, a boy so careful about his eyeglasses that he wouldn't wear them when he played outside, would do.

I watched Ruby's expression turn to fear when I returned to the corner where she waited and passed on Deb's information. Ruby knew her son better than I did, and it was clear that she believed Henry would make a trip back to the schoolhouse in the middle of a snowstorm without a second thought if his beloved spectacles were at stake.

"We'd better let someone know," I said and the two of us hurried back through the dining room into the lobby where I went to fetch my coat and scarf. At the last minute, I was spared having to brave the frigid wind and blowing snow to find either the marshal or one of his deputies because Lucas Morgan stomped into the hotel just as I was sliding into my coat.

Lucas eyed me and my coat with suspicion. "I thought we agreed you'd stay at the hotel tonight."

"We did," I said and with Ruby coming up behind me went on to tell him about our concern for Henry. "I don't know of anyone who's seen him after he was here in the kitchen," I concluded, "and that's a concern, Lucas. A real concern."

Turning to Ruby, Lucas asked, "Are you sure he hasn't showed up at home, Ruby?" The question gave the woman pause.

"Well, he wasn't there when I left." Her usual down-to-earth tone was tinged with worry and her voice held a slight quaver. My heart went out to her.

"Then you should get back home in case he turned up there while you were away," Lucas told her. "I just came from your direction. Stay up on the boardwalk until you cross the street and steer clear of the drifts. The wind's piled the snow up at least three feet deep on one side of the alley, but you'll get home safe enough if you stick to the sidewalls. You wait there, Ruby, and I'll get the boy back to you as soon as we find him. And don't you go out again. We don't need to be searching for two Strunks."

Ruby gave a quick, firm nod, and when she would have left wearing the lightweight shawl she'd come in, I put my coat over top of it and wrapped her head in my scarf. "They'll find him," I said as I tied the scarf in a knot under her chin. "He'll be fine. You'll see." Ruby gave another mute nod, but I didn't think she believed me. Instead, she had the look of a woman preparing herself for some very bad news.

"You be careful, too," I said sternly to Lucas as soon as Ruby was gone. "Even an officer of the law can get lost in the snow or have his nose freeze off."

"I'll let Si know I'm headed out, and I'll take enough rope to tie to the end rail by the newspaper office and get me out as far as the bench. It's downhill then, and I'll be all right. The rope'll guide me and as long as I don't let go I'll be able to move around a little and keep an eye out for Henry."

Or Henry's body, I thought, buried under drifting snow and cold as ice, but I didn't say that. Instead, I repeated, "Just the same, you be careful."

"I've done this before, Caroline, up in Dakota Territory looking for a woman who went winter-crazy. Left her family to home and went running outside into the worst blizzard of the year."

"Did you find her?"

"We did, yes."

"A good ending, then."

"We found her, but it was too late. I don't intend to let that happen here."

After he left, I turned to find that Lizbeth had been watching Lucas and me. She can be still in a way that tells you she hasn't missed a single thing that's been going on, and she was still just then. I couldn't read her expression.

"He'll be all right," I assured the girl, in case it was worry I saw on her face, whether for Henry or Lucas I couldn't tell.

"I know," Lizbeth said, then, "The hotel's as full as I've ever known it to be. Is it fitting, do you think, to charge them full price for something they couldn't help? It isn't like they wanted to stay overnight in New Hope."

A conscience that prickly must be awfully uncomfortable sometimes, I thought, and replied, "They could have stayed over at the Gooseneck or even stayed on the train, for that matter, so you charge them full price and do it without any apology."

She must have caught something of a scold in my voice because she tried to explain. "I only meant that Mr. Bliss has been known to–"

"Mr. Bliss isn't here, Lizbeth. You collect full price from every one of our guests, and I'll give you two bits if a single one of them complains about it. Deal?"

She smiled at that, back to her usual self and her odd mood past. "Yes, ma'am. Deal." The next day, when the rails were finally cleared and all our unexpected customers had resumed their travels, I was gratified but not surprised that I didn't lose a single cent to Lizbeth. If there's one thing I've learned through the years, it's that people like their comforts and they're always willing to pay for them.

But that was the next day, when the storm was over and the streets cleared and Henry Strunk had been returned to his mother safe and sound.

The afternoon of the storm, however, wasn't so lighthearted, not as I pictured a skinny boy stumbling into the snow or falling into a drift, unable to rise, and slowly falling into that lazy, deep sleep I'd always heard led to a freezing death. As people wandered in and out from the lobby to the dining room, from the dining room back into the lobby, and eventually up the stairs to their rooms, I did the same: paced and wandered. A word or two of nonsense to Lizbeth as she stood at the counter, followed by a glance through a lobby window into the darkening late afternoon, a meander into the kitchen, followed by another glance and another window and another unimportant remark to Lizbeth. That was how I spent the time until every last bit of my patience had vanished.

"Can I borrow your coat, Lizbeth?" I finally asked. "I

loaned mine to Ruby."

"You don't need to go out, Mrs. Moore. Lucas said he'd bring word as soon as he knew anything."

"I should be there with Ruby," I said. "in case – well, in case she needs me. She's alone like I am and might need a shoulder to lean on." I doubted Ruby Strunk ever needed a shoulder to lean on, but I wanted to be with her just in case there was a first time.

Foolishly bare-headed and bundled in Lizbeth's too small coat, I stepped out into the cold air of a January evening, took a breath of air so frigid I felt its cold all the way down to my lungs, and slogged my way past a bright Music Hall and a dark Meeting Hall down into the vacant street, through drifts of snow that when seen in the daylight would resemble waves on the ocean, and into the side alley. Then I followed Lucas's earlier advice to Ruby and stuck to the alley sidewalls.

Just ahead of me was Ruby's modest house and outlined against the light from her open front door I could make out the figures of three men. Just coming? Just going? I couldn't tell.

With a last burst of strength I propelled myself forward, plowed through a final snow drift, pulled myself up onto Ruby's small porch, and grabbed hold of the first arm I could reach, which happened to belong to Arthur Stenton.

"Caroline! Good lord! What are you thinking to be out on a night like this?!" It was the first time I'd heard the man sound anything but collected and calm so my sudden appearance must have truly shocked him. Arthur placed one hand over mine where it clutched his arm and with the other hand pushed me through the doorway into Ruby's crowded front room where Lucas stood next to another man. The Strunk children stood pressed together against the far wall, all of them, even the littlest ones who were twins, solemn and quiet and trying to take up as little space as they could. I doubt even one more person could have squeezed into that room. At first, I couldn't respond to Arthur's question or Lucas's nod, couldn't speak even a syllable because of the feeling of relief that washed through me, as if I'd just swallowed a cup of hot tea. Wrapped into what must have been every single blanket in Ruby's house and lying flat on a straw-filled mattress next to the old stove that crackled with flames lay Henry Strunk. All his freckles stood out against skin that looked the same color as the snow and despite the blankets he still shivered, but he was alive and just then that was all that mattered.

Ruby bustled toward me and repeated her version of Arthur's words. "Caroline! Look at you! Nothing on your head and your skirts soaked! What were you thinking?!"

"I wasn't, I guess." Then, after a pause and in a lower voice, I asked, "Is he all right, Ruby? Will he be all right?"

"Doc Danford says I should keep him warm through the night and watch his hands and feet for darkening, but he doesn't think there'll be any lasting damage. They found him in time, I reckon, but time will tell." Despite her foreboding words at the end, the woman didn't seem worried. That might come later if Henry ended up losing any fingers or toes, but at that moment Ruby Strunk was alight with relief.

Tom Danford, the third man of the trio whose figures I'd seen outlined against the light, had been ready to depart when I had appeared like a ghost out of the darkness, his coat and hat and gloves already pulled on and fastened.

"I'm so glad," I said to Ruby and to the doctor asked, "Is there anything special Henry needs? Would it be better if he was at the hotel, do you think?"

Danford was tall, slightly stooped, balding, and bespectacled, a good man considered a pillar of New Hope's community for at least the past fifteen years. Like Arthur Stenton, I'd never heard one word of criticism about Tom Danford.

"He'll be fine right here, Mrs. Moore. His mother knows

what to watch for and I'm just across the street if she needs me. I predict the boy'll be fine, but like Ruby said, time will tell," Doctor Danford made Ruby's earlier words sound more cheerful. He spoke a calm good night to the room in general and slipped out the door, trying carefully to keep the cold air outside where it belonged.

"I'll be going, too," Lucas Morgan said and looking down at Henry added, "You're a lucky young man. Your ma can always replace your eyeglasses, Henry, but she can't replace you. You remember that," his tone as stern as the tone Arthur Stenton used in the classroom.

"Yes, sir." Henry's voice was fainter than usual but still firm. "I will. I promise. And thank you for coming in search of me. It was awful good of you."

"Maybe I was the one who started the search, but it was Mr. Stenton here who found you. It's him you should be thanking." To me, Lucas said, "Should I walk you back to the hotel, Caroline?" I took a quick, sidelong look at Arthur and shook my head.

"No, Lucas, thank you. Arthur can see me back," adding quickly so Arthur couldn't get a word of dispute in, "You need to let Silas know right away that the lost is found. I think I saw him pass the hotel window on his way to the jail, and if you wait too long, he'll be getting a search party together to look for you."

Lucas nodded and reached for the door. When Ruby started to speak, he turned and made a dismissing motion with his hand in her direction.

"You already said your piece before, Ruby, and you're welcome. Part of my job is keeping New Hope's youngsters safe, and I'm glad we got to your boy in time." Lucas's exit left just Arthur and me facing Ruby in the little front room.

"What can I do for you?" I asked her. "Is there anything you need? How about if I send some extra blankets over? Or something from the kitchen? Do you have enough wood for the stove?"

"Thank you, Caroline, but we got everything we need. I kept myself busy waiting for word by cooking so there's a pot of soup and fresh bread in the kitchen. Joe Chandler brought over extra wood last night, and we'll manage to keep each other warm enough."

I looked at the six young faces staring at me from the back corners of the room and had to smile. "If you don't, it won't be for want of enough bodies in bed."

"I'll see you in the morning, then," the woman said. "I got fresh biscuits to offer."

"You stay home tomorrow. Lucas made me promise to sleep over at the hotel tonight to give the men time to shovel out the alley so the big house'll be empty first thing in the morning." She frowned at the news, a woman bound by her duty, and I said quickly, "Arthur, the hotel is bursting at the seams. We don't have a room to spare, and I've got to get back. You'll see me home, won't you?"

"Here," Ruby said, grabbing my coat off a hook, "you'd best take this back now and thank you for it. That coat you come in would fit a girl right enough, I suppose, but it wasn't made for a full-grown woman's curves." I slipped my coat on over Lizbeth's coat without comment. To Arthur, Ruby said, "Henry and me are obliged to you, Mr. Stenton."

I felt a moment of pity for poor Arthur, caught between my invitation and Ruby Strunk's gratitude, uncomfortable with both and no doubt wishing he was back in the privacy of his own house with no woman anywhere in sight.

To move the conversation along, I took hold of the man's arm and turned him, not as gently as I probably should have, toward the door and said, "Good night, Henry, children. Ruby, you send Olive over to the hotel in the morning if there's anything you need." I allowed myself a smile. "I'm awfully glad things turned out the way they did."

By then, Arthur had the door open and both of us stepped out into the frigid night, where the wind at our backs pushed us along with enough strength to make me lose my footing in the snow. Arthur, no doubt tired from traipsing through the snow looking for Henry and with a weak leg of his own, caught me firmly by one arm and stepped in front of me to grab the other, as much for his own balance, I suspected, as mine. That close and with the dim light thrown back by the moon off the snow, I was able to take in the man's face with startling clarity, dark brows over steady, thoughtful eyes, a straight nose, and surprisingly full lips – why had I never noticed *that* before? For a wild moment I wished the wind and snow and freezing temperatures to the devil and considered placing both hands to the back of his neck and pulling that mouth down to mine. What would Mr. Arthur Stenton, scholar and gentleman, do then? Had he ever been alone with a woman in his life or been kissed by any woman other than his mother? I was strongly tempted to find out, for one brief moment as drawn to the composed and serious man standing before me as I had once been drawn to my open and passionate husband. Two men as opposite as men could be, and yet...

What I might have done and how Arthur might have reacted remained a mystery, however, because another gust of wind blew down the alley and suddenly my common sense took over. Arthur's, too, because for just a second I would have sworn his eyes had lingered on my lips with the same hunger I had been feeling, but we were both too practical and too cold, for that matter, to be thinking about kissing in a dark alley with the temperatures still falling and the wind still rising. If we had nothing else in common, Arthur Stenton and I were both cursed with a practical nature. More's the pity.

14

Once back at Bliss House, I called from the front door to Lizbeth, "Did you hear? Henry's home safe," and turned to Arthur. "I don't know about you, but I could use a cup of something hot. I'll join you in the dining room in a minute. I want to hear how you found Henry."

Arthur gave me a quizzical look, not used to being bossed around, and then seemed to decide that it was in his best interest to do as he was told. From the little I knew of the man, I thought doing what he was told did not come naturally to him, that he was one to take time to weigh all the sides of a matter and decide on his own what made the most sense. But he looked cold and disheveled by the wind with his face showing lines of fatigue and his limp more noticeable than usual, so I supposed that searching for Henry Strunk might have honed down some of Arthur's independent edges.

The dining room was empty of people, tables readied for breakfast, and the wall lamps turned down. It was the same for the kitchen, and I had to give myself a stern reminder when I crossed the threshold that I had every right to be there and did not need anyone's permission to light the stove and put on a kettle or dig around for the tea canister.

The place might be the chef's kingdom to rule in the daytime, but the chef wasn't there just then, I was, and hadn't John Bliss put me in charge? Fine words, of course, and true, but even as I carried the tray with two china cups and a pot of steaming tea out to the table where Arthur waited, I was already planning the words I'd use to explain to Emil Clermont my nighttime presence in his kitchen.

For a while neither Arthur nor I spoke. I poured the tea, and he spooned sugar into his while I uncovered the plate of molasses cookies I'd discovered during my kitchen invasion. Finally, all my fussing finished, I took a sip of tea, briefly closed my eyes and sighed at the bliss of it.

When I looked up, Arthur was watching me, not smiling and with a sober look in his eyes that made me say quickly, "What's the matter? You don't have the look of a man that just saved a boy's life."

He was a solitary man used to keeping his own counsel, and I wouldn't have been at all surprised if he had dismissed or even ignored my observation. That he didn't make a curt reply told me something weighed on his mind, something troubling enough that he would share whatever it was with me, which both pleased and humbled me. I didn't know exactly when or how it happened; I only knew that Arthur Stenton's trust and approval were important to me, more important than I had realized until that moment.

"I knew Henry had left his eyeglasses behind at school." Arthur's tone was flat. "I saw them where they'd fallen and I knew how important they were to the boy. I could have done something then. I should have. The weather wasn't so bad that I couldn't have brought them into town to give to him. But I–" Arthur shook his head. "I didn't want to be bothered to get out in the snow and hike into New Hope, so I set the glasses off to the side and told myself they could wait until the storm passed. But I knew they couldn't. I knew they were more valuable than gold to Henry and that he'd never rest until he had them back in his pocket."

Arthur took a deep breath. "I failed that boy, Caroline, and he could have died because of it."

Arthur's confession so surprised me that at first I truly couldn't believe he was serious. It was the bleak look on his face that convinced me. The lips I'd found so shockingly attractive only an hour ago were pressed thin, nothing tempting about them now. The lines of his face had deepened. His expression was sober and almost bitter, the look of a man so disappointed in himself that he seemed suddenly twice his age. There was no doubt in my mind that Arthur sincerely blamed himself for what happened to Henry, just as there was no doubt in my mind that the man was being completely ridiculous.

He didn't expect sympathy from me – I thought him a man who would view sympathy as a weakness – but I believe he did expect something from me, maybe that I would be as disappointed in him as he was in himself. Maybe that I shared the same impossibly high principles that he held. But I didn't. God forbid. Making it from one day to the next was difficult enough without trying to follow a set of invisible and unbearable rules. Poor man, I thought, where did that come from?

For a second time that evening I felt a wave of deep emotion for Arthur Stenton and wanted to say something tender and comforting, but since I was sure he would have recoiled from anything of that nature, I said instead, "Good heavens, Arthur, I know you're important to your students, but not *that* important. You're their teacher, not their father." Whatever the man expected to hear from me, I could tell it wasn't that. Leaning forward, I placed a hand over one of his, looked directly into his eyes, and said with conviction, "You're a good teacher, Arthur, and I have no doubt a good man, too, but you're taking too much credit for yourself. You're not responsible for your students' foolish actions any more than for their worthy ones. You put information in front of them, but what they do with it is up to them, to them and their parents. We're all the same, Arthur, and you're as human as the rest of us. We do the best we can, that's all. What else is there? We do the best we can at the time, and that's what you did when you found Henry's glasses."

I doubt that in all his adult life anyone had ever spoken to Arthur Stenton as I just had. He was a man admired in New Hope, honored, and rightfully so. People said his name with deep respect. But he was a man, all the same, and I didn't want him to go through the rest of his life expecting more of himself than any man could possibly give. Carrying that kind of burden could suck the joy right out of life. Years ago I had seen exactly that in John Bliss as he carried with him the final memories he had of my husband, two men once so close but separated first by harsh words and rash judgment, then by distance and time, and finally by Davey's sudden death. Things could never be made right, and John had been weighed down with the burden of his past mistakes. If Sheba hadn't come into his life, made him see things differently, and given him back his joy, he'd be a different man than he was today. I wanted to spare Arthur that same burden if I could.

The only thing I had ever imagined that John Bliss and Arthur Stenton – from the outside two very different men – had in common was the town they lived in. I could have made a list of their differences a mile long, believing I hadn't missed a thing about either of them. And I'd have been wrong. For a woman who prided herself on understanding men, it was humbling to realize that Arthur wasn't the only person sitting at the table who had things to learn. The restaurant's meals for tomorrow were already in place and humble pie hadn't been mentioned, but whether it was on the menu or not, I had just been served a big slice of it.

I had time to consider all this because Arthur hadn't replied with a single word. He hadn't yanked his hand away from mine, either, which was a promising sign that he wasn't outraged by an opinion he hadn't requested. He was just very quiet, still looking back at me but not really seeing me. The man was mulling my words, I realized, and felt pride at the knowledge. I was taught early reading and sums as a little girl by my grandmother, who had learned the same from hers, and after she passed and I left home, I picked up all kinds of knowledge through the years, kept reading on my own from newspapers and the Bible and any discarded book I found along the way, and grew up to be smart in a lot of ways that aren't taught in books. But I never went to school, and here was Arthur Stenton, an educated man whose grandfather had been a judge, acting as if my words were important and had value for him.

Pulling my hand away and sitting back further in my chair, I said, "I didn't mean to presume, Arthur. I was speaking to you as a friend." My words brought him back to the present.

"I know. Thank you." That and a small smile were his only reaction.

When I figured out that was all he was going to say, I asked, "Did Lucas say it was you that finally found Henry?"

"Just luck. Morgan made it to my house west of the school and he said we should split up the search. He started back to town to get some help and went north around the schoolhouse. I went the other way, and that's where I saw Henry, all curled up at the corner of the school, covered by a little snow but not bad. It wasn't dark yet. Back at his mother's, he told us he got confused about where he was, that he got tired and decided he'd just sleep a while."

The words made me catch my breath with their innocence. That was how people could so easily be lulled to their deaths in a snowstorm. Close your eyes for just a little while, the cold says. You'll feel better. Rest here, the snow says, and I'll keep you warm. Anyone who spent a winter on the plains had heard the stories and knew the dangers.

"I picked the boy up," Arthur said, "and tried to follow Morgan's footprints until I reached the end of the alley where he'd managed to clear away some of the snow. I could see the lights from Con Tull's place up ahead because the snow had stopped and the alley blocked a lot of the wind, so I knew where I was then." Arthur had managed to make his part of the rescue sound unexciting and humdrum, but I knew it had been anything but. He was smaller in stature than the deputy so stepping into the tracks Lucas had made going up the hill by the schoolhouse and then coming back down, and all the while carrying an unconscious Henry in his arms, must have made it an exhausting trip. His poor leg. No wonder he looked drained.

After another silence, Arthur pushed himself away from the table and stood. "I should get home now." Following him into the lobby, I couldn't help but notice that his limp was more pronounced than usual.

"Of course, you're not going home this late and in the cold! I won't hear of it!" I told him, my tone too sharp. Fighting words for a man not used to having a woman tell him what to do.

At my words, he stopped, straightened his shoulders, turned, and eyed me, raising one brow in the way he had that made a person think she had just questioned all the laws of science. I wouldn't have been surprised if he'd made a cutting reply, something that told me to mind my own business, and in all honesty, I might have deserved it. Most of the time, I'm practiced at tempering my opinions to get what I want, but that hadn't been one of them. To his credit, however, and proving himself to be a better man than I, Arthur's reply was both mild and reasonable.

"Well, I can't stay here, Caroline."

"Why not?"

"Because you said there wasn't a room to spare." He was right, damn the man for remembering. "Didn't you?" And for rubbing it in, too.

I ignored his question and said, "We'll figure something out."

Lizbeth, following the conversation unashamedly from where she sat in the lobby, rose.

"Mrs. Moore, what if you and I share that room we set aside and let Mr. Stenton sleep on the cot that Kip usually uses? Kip's not going to make it in tonight, but I fired up the stove in there just in case." I could have hugged the girl.

"A perfectly sensible idea, Lizbeth. Will you please show Mr. Stenton where he'll sleep?"

"I'd be happy to." She and I exchanged satisfied smiles.

Arthur Stenton, a man of uncommon intelligence, recognized defeat. He gave a barely noticeable nod of surrender, a quiet thank you, and followed Lizbeth down the hallway to the small back room where Kip spent his nights.

"Are you sure he'll be warm enough?" I asked Lizbeth when she reappeared. "Maybe we should get him more blankets or–" Lizbeth laid a hand on my arm.

"Mrs. Moore, the man was asleep practically before I left the room. He'll be fine."

"Yes. All right." I realized suddenly that I felt as exhausted as Arthur Stenton had looked. The restaurant was dark and the hotel so quiet all I could hear was the rattle of the snow the wind threw against the lobby window glass. "Go to bed, Lizbeth, and get some sleep. I doubt the trains will be running on schedule first thing in the morning, but I know the U.P. won't waste any time getting itself back to normal. We'll have a busy early morning."

"But you're coming, too, aren't you?" At her words, I felt a rush of affection for the girl. It had been a long time since anyone had worried about me, and there was no doubting her heartfelt concern.

"I am, for sure. I just want to take one more look around and be sure everything's in order. I'll be there before you have time to turn back the covers," which was almost true. I was upstairs in a short time and pushing open the door of the one room we couldn't let to guests until its new rugs, wallpaper, and curtains arrived, the original furnishings ruined by a dragged-out disagreement between two brothers staying in the room the previous month. The cost went on their bill, of course, and they didn't argue the fact. No doubt they were glad to see the last of a stern Si Carpenter, Bliss House, and New Hope.

From her breathing, I could tell when Lizbeth, curled onto her side next to me, fell asleep, but for me sleep didn't come as easily or as quickly. There was too much to remember from the day. It was good to know Ruth was home in the flesh – Was that just a few hours earlier? It seemed like days ago – and I looked forward to hearing about her visit to her sister. There was young Henry, too, bundled and safe at home when it could have been a story with a whole different ending. And that brought me to Arthur Stenton, a man difficult to read but beset by his own devils like everybody else on the planet. Just before falling asleep, I decided to make it my business to get to know the man better. Counting all the times he'd called me by my first name that night worked faster than counting sheep, and I quickly fell asleep.

Lizbeth was already up and dressed when I awoke. She squinted in concentration as she pinned her plaits so the braids resembled a crown sitting atop her head. A shaft of dim light found its way between the window curtains and briefly made the girl's fair hair gleam golden yellow, even more crown-like.

She caught my gaze on her and said, "It's early yet, but I thought I'd go down and make sure I've got all the guests' names and room numbers straight before they start wanting to check out. Maybe I can make a quick trip down to the depot, too, and see if there's any word about getting the line back on schedule. People will appreciate knowing what to expect for the day. I know I would." That was Lizbeth, always thinking ahead and usually thinking of others ahead of herself. To counter any objection I might make, she added, "The wind's died down and it's not snowing, and my guess is there's already an effort being made to clear the street. It'll be safe enough for me to go down to the station. I promise not to fall in a snowbank."

I swung my legs over the edge of the bed, shivering in the cold room, and reached for my dress from the back of the chair where I'd draped it the night before.

"You do whatever you feel is best, Lizbeth. I should make sure we've got somebody helping in the kitchen. I can wait tables as good as the next girl, but I'd rather not."

I knew we'd have a chef in the kitchen, no matter what the weather was because Monsieur Clermont lived in rooms upstairs at the rear of the Bliss Music Hall, which was right next door. He never complained that the noise from below bothered him, and since the Music Hall and the Bliss Restaurant shared a connecting covered back porch, it took no effort for the chef to step out the back door of one place and enter the back door of the other. Except for cooking, he was a man who liked to keep things as simple as possible.

As far as I could tell on my way downstairs, there was nothing to indicate we had guests up and active, but I knew the quiet wouldn't last long. Hungry people would start gathering in the dining room. People impatient to be on their way would be checking at the front desk to get word on train status. It would be a long, busy, and profitable morning.

Lizbeth and I were up early but not early enough to catch Arthur before he left. It must have still been dark outside when he woke, folded the blankets neatly at the foot of the cot where he'd spent the night, and made his way home. At least I hoped he found his way home, but the man was an adult, after all, and able to make his own decisions and if he thought stomping his way through waist-high drifts of snow before sun-up and without a warm breakfast in his stomach was something he needed to do, then who was I to argue? Thinking about my words from the night before, how I'd taken it upon myself to give him advice about life – me, of all people, as if I was some kind of expert! – I could understand why the poor man might want to get back to the safe solitude of his own house as quickly as possible. It was my experience that all men needed to be managed by a woman from time to time, but that none of them appreciated having it pointed out to them when such a circumstance occurred. I remembered falling asleep over the decision to get closer to Arthur Stenton and get to know him better. Now the thought of doing so seemed, if not outlandish, certainly easier said than done, an idea that had made sense, as many ideas did, when a person was in a state of drowsy warmth but didn't seem nearly as attractive or possible in the clear light of day. Especially the light of that particular day, which ended up being even busier than expected. From the first guest to make his way downstairs to the first train to leave the station on time, I didn't have a moment to spend musing on the likes of Arthur Stenton.

When the afternoon train that had arrived hours late the previous day left at its regularly scheduled time, we realized that life would get back to normal. That had been questionable for a while. Too many people with time on their hands wandering in and out of the lobby, asking us for information we didn't have, and full of advice for the Union Pacific Railway – most of the advice uncharitable – sometimes made the morning difficult. Lizbeth shines in that kind of situation, though, always pleasant and patient, smiling and sympathetic, and that day she did her best to manage everyone's displeasure. It's amazing how attentive interest from a pretty young girl can soothe even the most irritated man. Magical, really. I've seen it done before, but what was so special about Lizbeth was that she wasn't pretending; she truly cared if someone was bothered or inconvenienced or anxious. That day the girl was worth her weight in gold.

At the end of the day, when most of the travelers were back on their way and New Hope's Main Street was once more passable, I went over to the front desk. Lizbeth was transferring the count of guests to the ledger where we kept that kind of information, and I waited until she finished the count before I spoke.

"Thank you, Lizbeth. I don't know how you manage to keep your patience like you do, but I know I couldn't have handled all the coming and going in the hotel without you. John Bliss would be wise to do whatever it takes to keep you behind the desk for a good long time." The girl's cheeks flushed pink with pleasure at the compliment even as she shook her head.

"That's kind of you to say, Mrs. Moore, but I don't expect I'll be here next year at this time."

"Why would you say that?" Her words caught me by surprise.

Lizbeth reached under the counter, brought out a folded paper, and smoothed it open. Then, turning it so I could read the words right-side-up, she said, "I'm going away to school, Mrs. Moore. I've made up my mind. I'm going right here to Brownell Hall in Omaha." She jabbed a forceful finger at the paper before me. "My pa says I'm dreaming, that nobody in our whole family, let alone a girl, has ever got past the sixth grade. Well, I plan to change that."

"What does your mother say?" I asked.

"Not much. Ma doesn't ever say much, but she hasn't said no, and even if she did–" Lizbeth's voice trailed off and then resumed, "–even if she did, I believe I'd go anyway. Mr. Stenton's been awful good to me, sharing his books and working on my composition, and last year he gave me a geography book that he ordered all the way from Boston. Just gave it to me, Mrs. Moore. It was full of pictures and maps and I saw how big the world was and I knew I wanted to learn everything about it. Mr. Stenton's opened a door for me, but I'm the one who's got to walk through it."

I looked down at the flyer. "And you think this Brownell Hall is the place to do that for you?"

"I do. Miss Ruth said her sister told her in a letter that her oldest girl started there this fall – her name's Mary – and Mary can't say enough good things about it. There's classes on history and books and art and music and mathematics. I want to learn about those things, Mrs. Moore."

"I can see that," I said. Lizbeth's clear eyes sparked fire from the thought of going to school. "Education is a fine thing, and if that's what you want, then that's what you should do, but I wonder if you've thought about what you'll do when you graduate because education or not, being a woman can hamper your dreams."

"I have some ideas about that, but for me, it's first things first. I've got to send in my application, and then I've got to get accepted as a student. They want you to be a member of the Episcopal Church, and I'm not, but Miss Ruth's sister Vera Ann is and she said she'd put in a word for me." Lizbeth paused for breath and repeated, "First things first, Mrs. Moore."

I looked down at the paper again. Brownell Hall, I read, was instituted to "promote the growth of a higher life in women." The words carried a noble ring, and I could see why Lizbeth was so fervent about the idea of attending Brownell Hall. I folded the paper and gently pushed it back toward her.

"It sounds wonderful, Lizbeth, and just the thing for you. If there's anything I can do to help, you just have to ask. I know Reverend Shulte isn't a minister of the Episcopal Church, but he's a respected preacher and a man of God, so maybe if he wrote a letter to the school officials on your behalf that would mean something to them. I just read on that paper that Brownell Hall's goal is to build a young woman's character, and I know Reverend Shulte will say good things about your character."

"Not too good, though," Lizbeth said thoughtfully. She seemed to give my final words serious reflection because she added, "Maybe he should say I have a *promising* character, so the school will know there's still a lot of work to be done on mine and they'll have plenty to keep them busy for a while." That was Lizbeth, planning, thinking ahead, figuring out how to make things turn out the way she wanted. She had a gift for it. But then she looked over at me and grinned, and I realized she'd been teasing a bit, and that was Lizbeth, too. The girl had more sides to her than a pair of gambling dice.

15

Once the railroad was back to normal, so was New Hope. That's how closely the two were connected. As long as the trains ran, stores needed to be open for business so men with shovels pushed snow to the side to make Main Street passable and merchants brushed their boardwalk steps and overhangs clear. Business as usual returned with hardly a hint that it had ever been interrupted.

My life returned to normal, as well. Ruby once more set out my breakfast in the Blisses' kitchen, mentioning in her straightforward way that it looked like Henry would "keep all his fingers and toes" and then never referring to the incident again. Life went on. Kip returned to night duty at the hotel and the cleaning and table girls picked up their schedules like they'd never been interrupted. The citizens of New Hope, Nebraska, thrived on order and decorum and without making a big show of it went out of their way to maintain both in their establishments and in their day-to-day lives.

If it hadn't been for Arthur Stenton, I could have done the same, but I was thrown off balance at unexpected times when I recalled the unlikely, brief, and very hot flare of attraction I'd felt for the man as we faced each other in a dark alley on a freezing night. That was an unsettling memory that didn't fade and I couldn't erase. Or I remembered the quick tug of pity that had made me long to smooth out the bitter lines of his face and assure him that he was a good human being, better than most, in fact, and that doing the best you can under difficult circumstances should be enough to prove that. It wasn't motherliness I felt toward him, anything but. It was more like a rush of protective tenderness that I didn't know how to explain. He was stronger and smarter than I was, educated, important, a man in a world made for men, so why I thought he might need or even want any shelter I had to offer didn't make sense. An uncomfortable feeling of being pushed toward something I didn't welcome or understand was new to me and worrisome, too, because if I wasn't careful, all the plans I had so painstakingly laid out for myself would be upended, and after all the years it had taken me to make it to this particular place in my life, that would be a special failure all my own. For the time being, it was to my benefit to keep a comfortable distance away from Arthur Stenton, a resolution that should be easy enough to keep because the schoolhouse was so far away that it was entirely out of my sight. Winter wasn't a time for many social diversions, either, but even if the Merchants' Association scheduled a community activity now and then to break the season's boredom, there was no reason that should involve me. Arthur had no reason to attend the Beef Convention committee meetings, the number and length of which were increasing as the gathering date got closer, and the only regular social contact I had was with Ruth when I dropped by the boarding house once in a while to chat with her. Day in and day out, I wore a steady, regular path between the hotel and the big Bliss house at the end of the alley, and there wasn't a single reason I could think of that my path should cross Arthur's. As far as intentions went, mine were solid and sensible. There turned out to be only one fly in my well-planned ointment, and it came from the man himself.

The year 1883 would end up being a year of contrasts for me, endings and beginnings, failure and success, loss and gain, but for all that happened that year, the moment that first comes to mind when I recall all its unexpected events is that January Saturday when I looked up from the desk in the hotel office and saw Arthur Stenton standing in the doorway. It hasn't happened to me often in my life, but at the sight of the man I was completely speechless. If George Young had been there at that moment to flash his camera, I believe the ensuing photograph would have shown me staring forward with my mouth hanging open. Hardly a becoming pose but I can be honest to a fault when I choose to be and that's exactly how I'm sure I looked at that moment. I was so taken aback I had to swallow twice before I could get a word out.

"Arthur," I finally managed to say, "what are you doing here?"

"Good afternoon to you, too, Caroline." A part of my mind noted with relief that he had used my Christian name with ease so at least I wouldn't have to fight that battle again. "I was in town to get a few things at the grocery store, and I thought I'd take a moment to say hello, but it looks like I'm interrupting your work." Now that the shock had worn off and my breath had returned to normal, I was able to smile.

"You are, but–" I spoke quickly because I wouldn't put it past the man to feel that my words required him to depart as quickly as he had appeared, "–I'm ready for an interruption. I usually wrestle with the account books on Saturday afternoon and today they're winning." I closed the ledger. "Come in and sit down. You'll have to move Gypsy, I'm afraid, but she won't hold it against you." At the sound of her name, the cat lifted her head and sent me a long, lazy look from the chair where she slept, then, satisfied that she was still in charge, once more rested her cheek on her curled paws and closed her eyes.

"She kept my feet warm most of the night I slept in your back room so I won't disturb her. That wouldn't be right." Arthur took two steps into the room. "I can't stay, anyway. I just came by to see what I owe for the accommodations last week."

"You'll have to take that up with John Bliss when he gets back," I answered. Arthur Stenton might have several qualities I would find surprising, but his pride wasn't one of them, and I had expected something like this. "When Kip's at the night desk, he sleeps back there so we don't let the room out. I have no idea what John would think was a fair charge. You'll need to wait and ask him."

"I can do that," he said and didn't pursue the subject further, which surprised me enough to make me wonder if he had been serious about the request to start with. But Arthur Stenton was a serious man, and why else would he have brought it up?

After a pause that went on too long, I asked, "Arthur, is everything all right? You're not here about Henry, are you, because he looks to be back to his usual self. Is there something about the schoolhouse I can help you with?"

"No." Another pause that made me sit forward in my chair and study Arthur's face with curious care. Did he look uncomfortable? Was that what I saw in his expression? And was that even possible for the dignified and disciplined Arthur Stenton?

"You may have seen the poster about the Lyceum to be held at the Meeting Hall this Friday," his words really a question.

"I don't think so. I don't recall seeing it."

"There's one posted right outside the front door of the restaurant."

"I'm clear-headed enough to know what I have and haven't seen, Arthur, and if there are a hundred posters lined up outside the restaurant door, I still haven't seen a single one of them." Deciding he deserved further explanation, I added, "I always come in through the hotel lobby."

Whatever discomfort I thought I had glimpsed on his face was replaced with a glimmer of humor, one that had surprised me at other times and usually left me puzzling out what the man found amusing.

"That explains it then. You'll have to trust what I say, Caroline. Mr. Peregrine Alice is a noted man of the stage in these parts, and he's scheduled to perform several of Mr. Shakespeare's most famous soliloquies in New Hope on Friday evening."

"I've heard of William Shakespeare, but I have no idea what a soliloquy is." The word was brand new to me and there was no way to hide that from Arthur. He wasn't a man to miss much so it was better to confess my ignorance and get it over with. "Did I say it right?" Another flicker of good humor crossed his face along with a barely noticeable twitch at the corners of his mouth.

"Yes. A soliloquy is a discourse by a person who is talking to himself. It's used by a playwright to let the audience in on how a character thinks or feels about something, and William Shakespeare is considered to be a master of the practice."

"Thank you."

"You're welcome. I believe you'd enjoy hearing Mr. Alice, and if you don't already have an escort, I wondered if you'd accompany me to the performance."

I stared at him, taken completely off guard. That Arthur Stenton was asking to spend time in my company was a wonder! Now it's true that I had recently put a lot of time into planning how to keep my distance from this man I found unexpectedly interesting and that the distance was necessary if I hoped to complete the task that had brought me to New Hope in the first place. But at that moment, I never gave any of that a thought.

Instead, as green and eager as a girl sixteen and unkissed – neither of which was true for me – I said, "That sounds very pleasant, Arthur, though you realize tongues will wag. This is New Hope, not Boston or New York, so our going anywhere together will be remarked upon."

"As was the snowball."

I couldn't help but laugh out loud at both the words and the memory. "Was it? I didn't know."

"Hmm," the kind of sound I imagined a teacher would make if you hadn't answered properly. "Then you don't know New Hope as well as you think you do."

"No doubt you're right, Arthur."

His turn to laugh this time. "Your tone often means exactly the opposite of your words." I only smiled. "You're staying at the Blisses' home, I understand." I nodded, still mute. "Then I'll knock on the front door about half past seven on Friday, if that meets your approval."

"And if we don't have another blizzard. I'm not prepared for another alley walk in the middle of a snowstorm," I said and met his gaze. For just a second, I knew he was remembering the same moment I was, how he had steadied me, how I had felt the warmth of his hands on my shoulders through the layers of coat and dress, how I had felt a sudden blaze of emotion at his nearness burn its way up into my chest, and how I had seen that same emotion reflected on his face. Not just in my imagination, then, I thought, and was a little surprised. I've known my share of men and can recognize signs of interest, carnal or otherwise, but I had considered Arthur Stenton to be different from the men I was used to. He *was* different, of course, different in a number of ways, but from the look in his eyes when his gaze had lingered on my lips, it was clear that he still held a few things in common with all his sex.

That same afternoon, I crossed the street to the boarding house. Whenever I felt restless or talkative, both of which recently seemed to take place more often than I was used to, I ended up in Ruth Carpenter's kitchen. She can be both entertaining – her stories of the time she'd spent in Omaha with her sister were an example of that – and calming, though usually not at the same time.

Earlier in the week, when I had told Ruth how serious Lizbeth was about going to Brownell Hall outside Omaha, my friend put down what she was working on and sat with her hands folded and still in her lap. There was nothing entertaining about Ruth Carpenter that afternoon.

"Do you think I've made a mistake getting Lizbeth's hopes up, Caroline?" Ruth asked. I could tell the idea concerned her a great deal.

"No. Lizbeth Ericson is a girl full of hope," I answered, "and if Brownell doesn't work out for her, she'll find something else. It's been my experience that a person who wants an adventure generally finds it. But Lizbeth said your sister has a connection to some of the people in charge of Brownell."

"She does. Vera Ann goes to the Episcopal church there, and she knows the bishop's wife, and her oldest girl, my niece Mary, was already accepted at the school. A good word from Vera Ann might help, of course, but that doesn't guarantee a place for Lizbeth."

I mentioned my suggestion that New Hope's Reverend Shulte send a letter of recommendation for Lizbeth to the school. "He's a man of the cloth, isn't he, even if he isn't from the same church?" I asked. "I have to believe a letter from him would be of some help to Lizbeth." Ruth brightened at the idea.

"I think that's a fine idea, Caroline. I'm going to ask Pastor Shulte myself. I don't know if I ever said, but he was a great help to me when my first husband died. I wasn't myself for a long time after Duncan's death, but when Pastor Shulte came to New Hope, he helped me see things differently." Ruth paused and her voice softened. "I hope you had someone to talk to, Caroline, during your hard times. No one should go through something like that alone."

I didn't respond, but shrugged and stood. "I have to get back to the hotel," was all I said. I couldn't talk to Ruth about Davey and Jean. There were things about their deaths that I needed to keep to myself, and Ruth was too good a listener. If I wasn't careful, I'd end up spilling the whole story out to her, and doing so would be unwise, Ruth being who she was. Such a sympathetic listener, and the town marshal's wife, besides.

That Saturday, not quite over the surprise of Arthur Stenton asking permission to take me anywhere, let alone to an activity at which most of New Hope would be present, I asked Ruth, "Are you going to the Lyceum on Friday?" She nodded without interrupting the mending she was working on.

"I'll have to take Alex so we'll sit in the back, but Silas and I don't want to miss it. We've heard Mr. Alice perform before, and he has a wonderful voice. Peregrine Alice is a particular friend of Dee Gruber. You know Dee used to perform on the stage herself, don't you?"

"I knew her in my Ogallala days," I answered, "but she went by the name of Florence Delarose then. We were on speaking terms but more friendly than friends. Sheba came to Ogallala looking for her, and that's how I met Sheba. But her sister disappeared one night, and I never heard where she ended up until I saw her here in New Hope. It took me a while to place her, but when I saw her with Sheba on the train platform, it all came back to me."

"Dee was running away from all sorts of things back in those days, mostly from bad people and bad memories."

"And she ended up in New Hope, Nebraska, married to Bert Gruber!" Her sister might live here, but the idea of the woman I knew as Florence Delarose settling into a quiet life in New Hope, Nebraska, with short and balding Bert

Gruber seemed far-fetched to me.

"It's not as strange as you make it sound, Caroline. That man loved Dee through all her hard times. Why wouldn't she love him back? I know from my own life how hard it is to resist a man who thinks you hung the moon."

Did Arthur Stenton think *I* hung the moon? I sincerely doubted it and couldn't decide if I was relieved or disappointed.

"Do you want to come to the Lyceum with Silas and me? You know you're welcome, and we'd enjoy your company."

"Thank you, but no, I already have a –" Ruth caught my hesitation. How exactly should I describe Arthur Stenton? *Friend*? Was *companion* better? Or *escort*? Ruth sent me a curious look, and I settled for *escort*.

"I already have an escort," I said and watched her expression as I explained, "Mr. Stenton has kindly offered to accompany me."

Ruth Carpenter has a face that shows her feelings the way a mirror shows her reflection and try as she might, she couldn't hide her surprise. Surprise and something else that was harder to figure. Something more than being pleased, I thought, something more like satisfaction: the way a person feels when she beats the odds and gets something right that everyone else got wrong.

"Lucky you," Ruth said. "because there won't be a person there who knows more about the plays of William Shakespeare than Arthur Stenton. My first husband was from England so he knew a lot of Shakespeare's speeches by heart and could recite them at the drop of a hat, but this is the truth, Caroline–" Looking a little shamefaced, Ruth stopped what she was working on long enough to admit, "There were more times than not that I had to ask Duncan what in the world Mr. Shakespeare was talking about. Poor man." I didn't ask whether she meant her husband or William Shakespeare. "And you'll have Mr. Stenton right there to ask." Then, because she thought I might hear her last words as an insult, Ruth said quickly, "No offense meant, Caroline. I know you're an intelligent woman who doesn't need a man to explain things to her."

I had to laugh. "No offense taken. Arthur said that this Mr. Alice was going to perform some of Shakespeare's soliloquies," pronouncing the word as if I used it every day instead of hearing it for the first time that afternoon, "and I had to ask what a soliloquy was. Turns out it's a special kind of speech, but for all I knew, it was some kind of dance, like that French can-can, which is not the kind of entertainment New Hope would appreciate." Ruth and I were both laughing by then.

"I've heard about it and I should say not," she agreed. "I'm sure you'll have an enjoyable evening, Caroline. Winter can seem awfully dark and long if you don't make time to spend with friends."

We talked a while longer before I wrapped up in my coat and scarf and trekked back to Bliss House. I had never been a woman who spent much time with friends, I thought. Except for that short, happy time with Davey Moore, I was more solitary than not, busy making a living and later, making plans. Now I couldn't help but wonder what I'd missed along the way, *who* I'd missed, and was sad to realize I'd never know.

Having never attended a lyceum before, I wasn't sure how to dress for it, but while the day was dry and sunny, it was also bitterly cold and I let the weather make my decision. I didn't have a great deal of choice, but it wasn't a sacrifice that my warmest dress, made of lightly-woven wool the color of sunflowers with cuffs and collar embroidered in delicate, dark-red flowers, fit both the occasion and the temperature.

Looking back, I can't remember what I expected from the evening or from Arthur Stenton, but I know it ended up being much more pleasant than I imagined. Arthur was pleasant, considerate but not in an overbearing way, and easy in his manners. Neither of us felt the need to talk for the sake of talking so there were times of silence as we walked down the alley toward the Meeting Hall, but it was a comfortable silence. He extended an arm when we reached the end of the alley to offer me support as I ascended the steps to the boardwalk, and I never bothered to let go afterwards. There were other people walking in the same direction – in fact, I can't recall a single person of my acquaintance who wasn't at the Lyceum that evening – but except for head nods and murmured greetings, it was as if my being on the arm of Arthur Stenton at a social occasion was no surprise to anyone. And maybe it wasn't. The last time New Hope had been surprised was a few years ago during the Emmet Wolf trouble. After that, Ruth said, people decided to keep track of their neighbors. In a good way, of course, without being meddling or nosy, and from their lack of surprise at the sight of Arthur Stenton first hanging up my cape and then settling himself next to me in the audience, they must have kept to their resolution because I didn't see a flicker of surprise anywhere in the hall.

"I thought us being here together might be under discussion more than it is," I whispered to Arthur.

He turned and smiled, reminding me what a nice smile he had when he chose to act more man than schoolmaster, and whispered back, "The effect of the snowball continues to make itself felt," which made me giggle, but not even that sound turned any heads in our direction. Apparently the good citizens of New Hope knew the rules of politeness and followed them, no matter what.

Perry Alice, when he came on stage, gave a small bow and introduced himself to the audience. He was a handsome man, but it was his voice that grabbed hold of a person's attention and wouldn't let go. It was deep and seemed to reach the far corners of the hall, though he didn't seem to be speaking unnaturally loudly. And what emotion that voice held! How it could throb with fury or whimper with grief! From the first words of the first speech, I was enthralled. Virginia City had had its share of theatricals, but the miners preferred pretty singers in flounced skirts, even if the girls couldn't carry a tune. I'd been a decade younger then, and my memory of those early days in Virginia City could be spotty, but I was certain I'd never in all my life heard anything like Peregrine Alice reciting the famous speeches of Shakespeare.

Walking home afterwards, my hand once more tucked comfortably under Arthur's arm, I asked, "When Prince Hamlet talked about taking up arms against his sea of troubles and being able to end them by opposing them – it was something like that – was he talking about taking his own life, Arthur? Is that what he was arguing with himself about?"

"Yes. He calls death a sleep, like the Bible does sometimes, and then says he believes death would end the heartache life holds."

"'A consummation devoutly to be wished.' Isn't that how he put it?" We had started out walking among several other people on their way home, but by the time we reached the alley that led back to the Blisses' house, it was just the two of us.

"That's what he thought at first," Arthur agreed, stepping down to the ground from the boardwalk and then reaching for my hand to steady me as I joined him on the snow-packed ground, "but he wasn't completely convinced."

"Because he worried he'd still dream," I said, "even if he was dead, and I guess he thought they might be bad dreams."

"The idea certainly gave him pause."

"How does the story end?"

"Oh, just about everybody dies. One way or another.

There's a reason *Hamlet*'s known as a famous tragedy." Arthur gave the last word a slight emphasis. Ahead of us, the big house was outlined against a backdrop of bright moonshine.

"I'm not surprised. I can't argue that the prince was smart enough and had a way with words, but he seemed awfully mopey to me. That would get tedious after a while."

Arthur laughed but didn't speak as we climbed the porch steps and stopped at the front door.

"Come in for tea, won't you?" I invited. It wasn't courtesy that prompted the offer, though the real reason was equally as simple. I had just spent the most enjoyable evening I'd known since the fire that changed my life, and I didn't want it to end.

"I wonder if that would be wise." I could tell by Arthur's voice that he was asking the question of himself.

"Not proper, you mean? Oh, Arthur, you and I are both past the age where we need to worry about that, aren't we?"

"You may be right, but there are rules of conduct in the teaching contract I signed."

"About carousing with loose women?"

"Something like that."

I reached around the man and pushed open the door. "Well, I give you my word there will be no carousing, not a single moment of it, even if Ruby Strunk stocked the kitchen with loose women when she was here this morning. It's just a cup of tea at the kitchen table, and not even Millie Winters would consider that improper." I was inside, turning up the oil lamp on the hall table and speaking over my shoulder to him, and he had no choice but to follow along behind me if he wanted to keep up with the conversation.

"She's got the perfect place to keep an eye on who goes in and out of this alley," Arthur said.

"I know. Right across the street from the end of the

alley." I turned to face him. "But you're inside now so take off your hat, come into the kitchen, sit down at the table, and enjoy a cup of hot tea before you make the long walk home. Millie Winters will not begrudge you a few minutes next to a warm stove."

In the kitchen, I slid out of my cape, then lit the lamp in the center of the table, added wood to the low fire in the stove, and put the kettle on the burner. Surprisingly, Arthur did as he was told – something he seemed to be getting better at over time – and after placing his coat on the back of his chair sat down. I thought that it had probably been a very long time since a woman, perhaps since anyone, had fussed over Arthur Stenton. That seemed a shame to me. Good men needed to be fussed over every so often so they knew they were appreciated. It was true of women, too, and of all human beings regardless of age, but I had a soft spot for good, faithful, hard-working men who did their duty and kept their word. I hadn't known all that many of them.

Finally, both of us seated at the table and clutching our teacups, I looked at Arthur across the table and asked, "What was your favorite from tonight, Arthur? I don't suppose any of what we heard was new to you, but was there one you especially favored?"

"It's hard to pick a favorite. Shakespeare was a genius with words, but I think Portia's words about mercy are worth remembering." He must have seen by my expression that I didn't remember them because he smiled and quoted, "'The quality of mercy is not strain'd / It droppeth as the gentle rain from heaven / Upon the place beneath: it is twice blest; / It blesseth him that gives and him that takes:'"

After a moment, I asked, "Do you think that's true? That showing mercy has some kind of special value?" If Arthur thought the question odd, he didn't show it.

"I do."

"I think there are some acts so terrible they don't deserve mercy."

He looked at me soberly. "I disagree. If it's like Portia said, and I think it is, that there's a return for being merciful, then the more mercy you show, the more return you'll get from it."

The conversation had grown too serious and deep for me, and I said lightly, "You might be right. I admit that almost everything I heard tonight was new to me, but I could tell it wasn't for you. Did you study the words of William Shakespeare in school when you were a boy?"

"Yes, but it was my grandfather who taught me to appreciate them. He loved good writing."

"'Deep in the man sits fast his fate,'" I quoted and at Arthur's sharp look said, "He wrote that inside the cover of the Emerson book you loaned me. He was a judge, you told me."

"Yes, and very well regarded in his day. He couldn't think of a higher goal for a man than to spend his life working with the law."

"He didn't convince you, though."

"My parents died when I was very young and my grandfather raised me. I owed him everything, but I couldn't be what he hoped I'd be."

I caught a hint of regret in his voice and said, "A teacher is every bit as valuable as a lawyer, Arthur. In fact, I could make a case that he's more valuable, at least in the lives of children. Was your grandfather disappointed in you?"

"He was never anything but proud of me, Caroline. He understood me."

"Understood what exactly?"

"That I didn't, that I couldn't, want what he wanted, that I wasn't him. So when I left Boston to teach in Denver, and then agreed to come to New Hope after that, he never asked why. He just – understood."

What had I said to Ruth? *A person who wants an adventure generally finds it*, and I thought that Arthur's story proved me right. I wouldn't have guessed he was an adventuresome man, but what else would you call leaving everything familiar behind for a new place and a new job? That sounded adventuresome to me.

"Is your grandfather still living?" I asked but knew the answer before Arthur shook his head.

"No. He's been gone a couple of years now," adding after a moment, "He put my welfare ahead of everything else in his life, the most selfless and honorable man I've ever known. Even now, I don't want to do anything that would make him disappointed in me. Maybe that's why I expect so much of myself. Because he did." A pause and then quietly, "I still miss him." I understood better now why Arthur had blamed himself for Henry's dangerous trip back to the schoolhouse. Understood, too, how it felt to lose the people who loved you, more so when there weren't that many of them to start with.

"I'm sorry," I said.

"I know you are." He set down his teacup and stood, reaching for his coat. "Thank you for the tea. I should get going." I stood, too, frowning.

"I wish it wasn't such a long walk for you to get home, Arthur. Will your leg be all right?" From the tone of his answer, the question had annoyed him.

"I'll be fine, Caroline. It's a slight limp, not an amputation."

Men are all the same when it comes to their pride, I thought, and went ahead of him into the hallway, saying as I passed him, "I beg your pardon. Of course, you'll be fine."

Behind me, I heard him chuckle, his irritation gone as quickly as it came. I pulled open the front door and turned to ask what he found so funny but didn't get to the words. He was closer than I thought and smiling and suddenly so irresistible that all I could do was put both my hands to his cheeks and lift my face enough to kiss him firmly on the mouth. We were of a similar height, and I didn't bother closing my eyes so I saw the shock – there's no other word for it – in his eyes and then saw the emotion change to something else, something warmer and more intimate before he put both hands to my waist and pulled me close enough to return the kiss, just as firmly. The moment was enjoyable and passionate enough that a part of me decided I had been foolish to speculate about the man's experience with women outside his family. He clearly picked things up fast and that had its own unique appeal. At last, I was the one who disentangled herself from the embrace, reached for his hat from the hall table, and handed it to him.

"I had a lovely evening, Arthur. Thank you for accompanying me to the Lyceum."

I thought he might be feeling, if not embarrassed, at least a little self-conscious, but there was nothing like that in his expression. He settled his hat on his head and took a step toward the door, where he turned to reply formally, "Good night, Caroline. I was honored to have your company," before spoiling the effect by meeting my gaze and saying with a grin, "Teaching contract or not, I can't regret a little carousing at the end of the evening. It'll warm me up all the way home."

I smiled and said, "Good night, Arthur. You watch your step going home."

"I will. I always do."

He left me standing and staring at the door as he pulled it shut behind him, surprised again by a man whose temperament I thought I knew. I cleaned up the kitchen – there was no need for Ruby to see two dirty teacups on the table – and found myself chuckling at Arthur's words. When had the serious, too dignified and rather dull schoolmaster turned into this other man, with his sly sense of humor and warm kiss and teasing eyes? When had he changed? At the thought, I stopped with one arm still uplifted toward the shelf, feeling a jolt of something very much like shock, suddenly aware that I might be seeing only part of the picture and Arthur Stenton wasn't the only one who had changed.

16

By the end of January, the Beef Convention was, if not the only, certainly the main topic of conversation among the citizens of New Hope. Joe Chandler chaired several committee meetings, somehow managing to keep the conversations headed in the same general direction. Everyone seemed to be clear on the part he was to play: Mort Lewis, attorney at law and stand-in for John Bliss, would make introductions and get the conversation started; Abner Talamine would give special attention to any agreements that might impact New Hope directly; Isaac Lincoln, resident meat expert, would make note of anything said about the beef markets whether East and West; and Benny and I would make sure our guests were all properly fed, lodged, and if they so wished, entertained. Val Copco came just the once to let us know that there wasn't one reason he could think of, barring another winter blast of snow, that would keep the trains from running true to their printed times. Val was a railroad man through and through, and his tone told us that he would consider any further inquiries about the integrity of the Union Pacific Railway schedule to be an insult. After that first report, no one felt a need to invite him back to any more meetings.

The names of those attending the meeting from the East included the owner and namesake of the Nelson Morris Company, two men – not owners and namesakes but second in command – from the Armour and the Swift Companies, and the president of the Union Stockyards and Transit Company, all from Chicago. Those were big names and everyone knew it.

Our four western guests were lesser known. Two ranchers from Colorado, Mark Saylor and Fritz Becker, the head of the Wyoming Stockman's Association, and Mr. James Irwin, the U.S. Indian agent from Wyoming attending on behalf of Mr. Pierce, the nation's Commissioner for the Indian Bureau. No one remembered inviting Mr. Irwin and there was considerable discussion about involving the government in our local affairs, most opinions being that it was better to keep the government as far away from New Hope as possible. Still, since no one could figure out how to uninvite the man and realizing that the U.S. government provided a lot of beef to Indian reservations, everyone decided not to make a fuss about the man's presence.

There was a current of enthusiasm and excitement that ran through New Hope at the time and a great deal of speculation about what if anything it might mean for the town's future. I think I'm as progressive as the next person, but having been in the heart of Virginia City during the silver boom, I knew that the result of sudden prosperity wasn't always what people hoped for or expected. When I said as much to Ruth one afternoon, she gave a sober nod, the wife of a peace offer no doubt more worried about her husband's safety than the possibility of financial benefits from the beef industry.

"It was the same when the U.P. started adding stops," she said. We sat across from each other at her kitchen table where Ruth was busy slicing carrots and potatoes into a large bowl. "It seemed like we were a comfortable little community one day and a town that bustled day and night the next. Before Silas came along, we didn't even have our own constabulary and now five years later, look at us. Silas has Lucas and Clayton and plans to ask the council if he can hire a third deputy." She paused and then shrugged. "Progress, I guess, and I shouldn't complain." Looking over at me, she asked, "Was Virginia City as wild as people say?"

"Oh, wilder," I replied. "A lot wilder. All those miners in and out of town all the time made it so there was always something going on, and most of it was carousing." I spent a moment remembering the noise of the place, the dirt, and the fighting and looked up to find Ruth studying my face.

"I can't tell if you liked it or hated it there."

"Both, I guess. I managed a gambling hall owned by a man I had to keep one step ahead of. He paid me well enough and I liked the work, liked having the say about how to run the place, but sometimes he got ideas."

"About you?"

"Mm-hm. I was a woman on my own and some men look at that as a kind of invitation. If you know what I mean."

"I do."

"It was to the point that I was thinking I'd have to move on when Davey came along. If I say he saved me, Ruth, it wouldn't be the way you'd think, not like he saved me from the unwanted attentions of some man. I was raised mostly in an orphanage and on my own by the time I was fourteen. When I got to Virginia City, I already knew how to take care of myself, and I didn't need anyone to do it for me. It was more like Davey saved me from myself, from a footloose and meaningless life, from moving from one town to the next and on to the next. Davey gave me a reason to be happy, to be alive." I thought about the first time I'd seen Davey, how bright he'd seemed against a backdrop of dirty miners, how full of ideas he'd been, how hopeful and determined and certain, how he made the future so real it seemed a person could reach out and touch it. "He was different from any man I'd ever known in all my life."

"Sheba said that's when you met John Bliss."

"In some ways, those two were closer than brothers, but they were like night and day, too. Davey so open and John so cautious. Closed off, in a way, though Sheba's changed him, I can see that. It took a long time for John to believe that I loved Davey for who he was and not for his silver mine. Longer than Davey had on this earth, sad to say."

"I'm sorry, Caroline. I know John is, too."

I shook off the past and said with a smile, "But life goes on, doesn't it? You know that as well as I do."

"I'd guess Silas is as different from Duncan as Arthur is from your Davey."

The words brought an abrupt end to my recollections and made me stand. "I should get back to the hotel."

"It will no doubt collapse if you don't." I caught an odd mix of laughter and irritation in Ruth's voice, not like her at all.

"I didn't say that."

"That's true. You didn't."

Still seated, Ruth looked up at me and said gently, "You don't like my bringing Mr. Stenton into the conversation, but I don't understand why. It's a courtship, Caroline. Out for the world to see. You know that. You weren't born yesterday. And I'm not saying how it will end, that's not for anyone but you and Mr. Stenton to say, but in all the years we've known the man, you're the first woman who's ever caught his eye. It's a wondrous thing, and there's not a person who isn't happy about it."

For a minute, I almost told Ruth Carpenter in no uncertain terms to mind her own business before I stalked out of her kitchen in a huff, but good sense took over and I replied in as quiet a tone, "It may look like a courtship to

New Hope and it may even feel like a courtship to Arthur, but for me–"

When I didn't continue, Ruth repeated, "For you?"

There were too many things unsaid, things she wouldn't understand or approve of, things that would almost certainly get in the way of both courtships and friendships. And even if that wasn't the case, I wasn't really sure how I felt or what I wanted to say about Arthur Stenton, which was why it was better to keep him out of the conversation.

At my continued silence, Ruth murmured, "Well, in for a penny, in for a pound as Duncan used to say," and asked, "Are you fond of this other man, then? This Mr. Saylor?"

"Mark Saylor?! Hell's bells, Ruth! Doesn't a woman have any privacy in this town?"

"No, likely not." Ruth's words were matter-of-fact. "The last person to keep a secret for any length of time in New Hope was Emmett Wolf, and look how that turned out for him."

I wavered for a moment and then couldn't help myself. I began to laugh. Ruth joined in, and we were suddenly two schoolgirls laughing over some improper and unsuitable foolishness with enough gusto to bring tears to our eyes.

Ruth hiccupped, managed to squeeze out, "Not that it was funny at the time," took a shaky breath, added in a steadier and more sober voice, "I don't know why I'm laughing. It was an awful, awful time," and wiped her eyes with a towel that lay on the table. I took a trembly breath myself and tried to sound just as steady.

"I've heard it was," I said, "so let's forget we ever had this conversation. Sometimes it's either laugh or cry," then, "I know Bliss House won't fall down like the walls of Jericho if I'm not there, Ruth, but I don't want John Bliss to hear that I was derelict in my duty so I need to get back. Thanks for the company."

Ruth might have said something as I left, but I couldn't tell for sure because a sudden cry, one so piercing it rivaled an approaching U.P. engine, interrupted her. Alex was awake and wet or awake and hungry or maybe just awake and ornery. Whatever the reason, anything Ruth wanted to say was drowned out by her son's loud unhappiness.

That night I thought about parts of Ruth's and my conversation again. How could I not? I hadn't forgotten about Mark Saylor, far from it, but what I felt about him was as different from my feelings for Arthur Stenton as summer was different from winter. Two men of opposite temperaments, characters, and ambitions, and what I expected from them was as different and contradictory as the men themselves.

Ruth was usually wise about people and their shortcomings, but she was wrong about any courtship. Arthur and I were slowly becoming friends and struggling to understand exactly what that meant for us. I don't believe either of us considered what we had – friendship, for want of a better word – to be a courtship. I thought we had too little in common, that I knew too much about men and he too little about women for us to enjoy anything more than friendship, for the time being, anyway, and maybe forever.

But it still gave me a little rush of pure pleasure if he had one of his students drop off a book he thought I might like or if he walked back to New Hope with me after Sunday church or if he showed up unexpectedly at the restaurant for supper and then stayed for conversation afterwards so late that the lights of the dining room dimmed around us, that time spent together something I especially treasured. Arthur did all those things and did them so naturally, so gradually that I began to take his attention for granted. His *friendly* attention because truly, it was like no courtship I'd ever heard of. Except for that one kiss the night of the Lyceum, we never had enough privacy to try for a second one, and while I sometimes held onto his arm if we walked over rough or slippery ground, there were enough layers of clothes between us to keep everything proper. An unfortunate situation, I thought more often than I'd have admitted to anyone, because kissing Arthur Stenton had stirred an enjoyable heat I believed I would never know again. Still, as Ruth had so practically pointed out, New Hope, Nebraska, was a small town and not a place that offered much privacy, not for friendship or courtship or any other kind of ship you could think of.

The afternoon before the Valentine's Day town dance, I slogged through the mix of mud and snow left behind by a few sunshiney days out to the schoolhouse. Everything would freeze again once the sun set, but despite the mud, it was a pleasant walk. There was the barest hint in the air that winter would not last forever, that days would warm, leaves sprout, beardtongue and tickseed and phlox begin to show along the roadways and paths. Ice at the edges of the river was already cracking enough to show the water moving beneath. For the moment it seemed that spring was right around the corner, though I had heard of snow coming as late as April. Not this year, I hoped. I was ready for spring to arrive sooner rather than later.

I stopped just inside the schoolhouse door and watched Arthur raise his head from his work. Though I might have imagined it, I thought that lately whenever Arthur saw me, his expression brightened. Not so grave. Not so serious. That's what I saw that afternoon, too.

"I'd come in," I said, "but my boots are a muddy mess and I don't want to track it on the floor."

Always the gentleman, he had stood when I entered. "It's nothing that can't be cleaned. I'm always happy to see you, but I have to ask – is there something wrong?"

"No." I stamped both feet on the threshold to get rid of loose dirt and then walked toward him almost on tiptoe, trying not to leave footprints along the floor. "There's a social tomorrow night in the Meeting Hall, a dance, I think I heard, and I wondered if you planned to attend. That's all." Watching my feet as I walked, I missed seeing his expression change, but I heard a difference in his voice.

"I don't attend dances, Caroline, because I don't dance," no more explanation than those few words, his tone expressionless.

"Surely not because of your leg." I stopped and gave him an innocently inquiring look of disbelief and got only a scowl in response. "Because," I went on, "that would seem vain on your part, and while you have many qualities, most of them admirable, I never thought vanity was one of them."

"I did not find dancing enjoyable before my injury, and it is even less so now. It's not something I choose to do."

"Is not dancing in your contract, too?"

"I beg your pardon."

"In the teaching contract the Merchants' Association had you sign. Does it put dancing on the same level as carousing with loose women?" From his sudden, quick smile, I knew I had the man right where I wanted him.

"No, Caroline, it does not."

"What a relief," I said and smiled back. "You don't have to dance a step if you don't want to, Arthur. No one will care, whatever you choose to do, but there's music and conversation and the winter's been long and gray. Your friends will be there. It won't hurt your leg or your dignity if you come. Please."

A pause followed, then, "All right," with nothing grudging in his tone. I considered the two words a victory of sorts.

"Thank you," I said and turned to go. "I promise you won't regret it. Chef Clermont is making some kind of sweet called a profiterole – I'm sure I'm saying that word wrong – and you wouldn't want to miss that. Come for a profiterole, if nothing else." He was quiet until I reached for the door handle.

"I'll be there," I heard him say so softly I almost missed

the words, "but you know very well that the reason I'll be there has nothing to do with the music or the chatter or even the profiteroles." He said the word as if French were a second language for him, as it might have been from what I knew of his educated background.

Another woman might have turned with a flirtatious look and said, "No? What then?" but I had never been good at flirtation, had never really needed it, and even if that weren't the case, I knew Arthur Stenton well enough to realize such a response would have disappointed him.

So instead, I turned long enough to say very clearly, "Yes, I know," before closing the door behind me and making my way up the sloppy path back to New Hope.

The evening of the dance turned out better than either Arthur or I expected. The Meeting Hall was draped with red banners from corner to corner and several members of New Hope's town band sat enthroned on a raised platform at one end of the room. Refreshments were spread out on two side tables and the rest of the large room was filled with people, many dancing, some just eating, and everyone talking. I kept one eye on the door, even as Ruth and I talked about this and that and saw Arthur before he saw me. Something about the way he entered, with his shoulders held back as if on his way to an execution, his lean face serious and determined, dressed in his good dark suit touched me in a way I hadn't expected. He was there, as uncomfortable as I knew he was, because I had asked him to come. I care a great deal about this man, I thought, but couldn't name it love. The only love I'd ever known had been for Davey Moore and that feeling had held none of the tenderness or warm compassion I experienced looking at Arthur Stenton. Could they both be love? All my experience dealing with men didn't help with an answer.

"There he is," Ruth said, following my gaze. "You'd better go grab him," adding in a voice she didn't bother to lower because of the surrounding din, "Be kind to him,

Caroline. The man's clearly lost, and I wouldn't be surprised if it's the first time in his life."

When I met Arthur at the door, I said, "Thank you for coming, Arthur."

"It's the draw of French pastries," he said with a smile.

"Then come along and have one before the band gets started."

"I warned you that I didn't dance."

"You also told me it was a slight limp and not an amputation, and I know for a fact that any man who still has both his legs can dance." I didn't give him time to argue with the statement but hurried on. "I didn't say dance *well,* I just said dance. I have a deal for you. If you dance just once with me and tell me you didn't enjoy it, I promise I won't say the word *dance* to you again. Not once all night. You can find a chair and spend the whole evening wishing you were somewhere else." He eyed me, still not convinced. "Arthur," I said, "you need to trust me. Just this time and just this once. You won't regret it." Arthur Stenton was a man who stood, who lived, on his dignity and as brave a man as I knew he was, I also knew a part of him feared the idea of appearing ridiculous. You're not alone, I wanted to tell him. We all have our fears and someday I'll show you mine, but I stayed quiet, waiting.

"All right," he said at last, which was all the invitation I needed.

At the end of the evening, as people started going home and the band packed up their instruments, Arthur was still there and I could still say the word *dance* to him if I wanted to. We finished the evening two doors down at a table in the restaurant where we had spent several evenings during the last few weeks, enjoying hot tea and comfortable conversation and shared laughter.

"I understand you won't want to admit that I was right," I told him, stirring my tea, "but I was right."

"About dancing?"

"Yes, that, but I was right about some other things, too. You're no better or worse on the dance floor than most men, Arthur, and believe me, I've danced with some real clinkers."

"Is that meant to be a compliment?"

I had to laugh. "I don't know. I don't think so. It's just a fact."

"What other things were you right about?" One of Arthur's finest qualities was the way he listened, the way he didn't get distracted or caught up in his own story but acted as if he was as interested in hearing what you had to say as you were in saying it.

"That it's been a long, gray winter and being with people who care about you is good for your spirits. That your dignity has nothing to do with your leg or how you look dancing. People respect you for the man you are, Arthur. Nothing more or less."

The flare of emotion in his eyes made my heart speed up, but all he said was, "Thank you. I think I knew that once, but time and being on my own must have made me forget it."

"Being alone can do that," I agreed.

When he spoke, I don't know what I expected to hear, but it wasn't the words he said. Nothing about the longings caused by being alone. Nothing about feelings, at all. Instead, he leaned back in his chair and said, quite gently, "Tell me about your husband, Caroline, and about your daughter. What were they like?"

In the years since Davey's and Jean's deaths, Arthur Stenton was the first person ever to ask me about them, and I was suddenly aware of how much I wanted to talk about them. It was a longing all its own that I hadn't recognized until that very moment. Once I started, I couldn't seem to stop, sitting, tea forgotten, caught up in a thousand memories, rattling on about all the big and little things that had made up my husband and my daughter, things that made me laugh and cry, and Arthur sitting across from me, eyes never leaving my face, listening to every word in that careful, concentrating way I thought I could easily learn to love.

When I finally ran out of words, it was quiet for what seemed a long time until Arthur asked, "The fire wasn't an accident, was it?"

"No," I said. "Some very bad men set the house on fire on purpose, left us to die, and stole our livestock. The Territory governor did his best, but it was too late and no one ever found out who was responsible."

"I'm sorry."

"I was laid up a long time, Arthur. Our place was out in the grasslands, far from the nearest town, and no one saw the fire, so by the time anyone found me, the herd was gone, Davey and Jean were dead, and I was almost dead. I have scars from the fire, inside and out. I still dream about it." I shook my head. "I can't let it go. Someone should be held responsible. Someone should pay."

"Yes," he agreed, "someone should," asking after a moment, "And you don't have any idea about the men who did it?" He waited for my answer with even more than his usual attention.

"No," I said, which wasn't the whole truth anymore but was all I was ready to say at the time.

Arthur didn't say anything, just nodded like he was thinking through some difficult problem and then reached to place one hand over mine on the tabletop. "Did it trouble you to talk about it? I didn't want that." I turned my palm up so I could lace my fingers through his.

"No, it was a relief," adding quietly, "It made me happy. Thank you, Arthur. It was kind of you to ask and even kinder to listen like you did."

He wanted to say something more, I could tell, but he didn't. Or couldn't. Whatever the reason for his quiet, he let go of my hand and stood. "It's late. I'll walk you home."

"You don't have to. I can find Lucas if I need company, which I don't. It's New Hope, not Virginia City."

That was the wrong thing to say apparently because Arthur glared at me, as much as the man is capable of glaring, before he went and pulled our coats off the wall hooks. He put on his own coat, said, "I am well aware that I don't *have* to do anything," and brought my coat over to where I stood. That pride of his again, I thought. I should have known better than to suggest he wouldn't do the gentlemanly thing. He held my coat as I slid my arms into the sleeves and then rested his hands on my shoulders for what seemed like a long time. It was all I could do not to lean back against him. I thought if I did, he would wrap his arms around me and I would be held safe and warm by someone I both trusted and admired. How long it had been since I had known the luxury of leaning on anyone and how attractive the idea seemed at that moment! But it was late and I was tired and Arthur still had a long, cold walk home. I picked up the two teacups and saucers, made a quick trip to the kitchen with them, and came back to take Arthur's arm.

"Let's go, then," I said. It was late enough that Kip must already have been asleep on his cot because there was no one behind the lobby desk. I leaned into Arthur a little during our quiet walk down the alley, sometimes holding onto his arm with both my hands for warmth and steadiness and for something else I wasn't ready to put a name to yet. On the front porch of the Blisses' house, Arthur kissed me lightly on the cheek.

"Good night, Caroline. It was a pleasure being with you tonight." He was a reserved man and always would be, but I could sense the emotion behind the formal words, could hear the words he didn't say.

"Good night, Arthur," I said in return. "You watch your step going home."

"I will. I always do."

Later, in my nightclothes, sitting on the edge of the bed, and brushing out my hair, I thought that talking so long and so earnestly about Davey and Jean, the ranch and the fire, would bring more dreams than usual or at least bring more fiery dreams than I had been used to lately, but I was wrong on both counts. That night I slept better than I had in a long time.

17

All the Bliss establishments were a beehive of activity the final few days before the big meeting. Extra help was brought on for the event, special menus worked out with Chef Clermont, linens for the dining room and the hotel rooms pressed and pristine and ready for the occasion. Mort Lewis called the last formal meeting of the convention organizers so he could practice his welcoming speech. When he finished, we all agreed it would do fine. He's a lawyer and if lawyers know how to do anything, it's talk. Mort also reminded Benny Tidwell that any entertainment provided to our guests was limited strictly to music and drinking.

After a sideways glance at me, Mort said, "You know what I'm talking about Benny. Now that the paper's put out the news that we'll be having some bigwig visitors in town for a couple of days, we might be seeing the wrong kind of entertainment show up. If you know what I mean. And we won't be having any of that in New Hope. We aren't Dodge City or Tombstone, and besides, we'd have every wife in town lined up outside your place if that was thc casc. No one wants that." Sober nodding followed Mort's words because he was absolutely right: that was something no one wanted.

The New Hope Union was growing a name for itself in the area and had a considerable readership, so Mort might be right to worry about prostitutes coming to his little town hoping to cash in on rich men with a commodity that was always in demand. Maybe it needed to be talked about further, and I wondered if I should tell Mort that he didn't have to worry about my delicate sensibilities. I didn't have time to speak up, however, because Benny immediately replied that he was surprised Mort felt the need to bring up the matter at all since John Bliss would have his head if he ever heard that loose women had been allowed to offer their wares at the Music Hall, Beef Convention going on or not. The meeting was planned for the Bliss Music Hall and not the town's Meeting Hall because of the availability of good whiskey. Men sometimes appreciated whiskey when they talked business, but loose women would only get in the way.

The words *loose women* made me smile, reminding me of Arthur and his school contract and distracted me so that I almost fell behind in the conversation. I had to give myself a little shake to bring my attention back to Mort, who was concluding the meeting with a few final instructions.

Everyone in the room and nearly everyone in town expected great things from the convention, although they'd have been hard-pressed to say what those great things would be exactly. I was looking forward to the occasion, too, but my reason had very little to do with the future of New Hope, Nebraska. For me, the fact that Ray Summerton had said he would return with information was what really mattered, information I was more than willing to pay for, information I had been searching for for years, getting ever closer to what I needed to know. Denver to Ogallala to New Hope. Following the cattle. Following the cattlemen. Town by town and always closer to an answer. Closer to peace of mind, as well, because I thought one must certainly lead to the other.

Ruth delivered an answer to the letter I had mailed the month before. With railroads crisscrossing the country, mail moved a lot faster than it used to, but my letter had to go as far north as Fort Maginnis in Montana Territory and in the middle of winter, besides. A reply in a month was nothing short of miraculous, and I took it as a good sign.

"I hoped there'd be a letter from Vera Ann waiting for me," Ruth explained, "so I walked down to the post office to check."

"And was there?" Ruth shook her head as she shifted Alex to her other hip and dug around in the pocket of her short coat.

"No, but there was something for you." She pulled out an envelope and placed it on the desk where I sat. "It looked important so I didn't think you'd mind if I interrupted you."

"You're not interrupting me." Ruth gave a skeptical look at the binder open in front of me.

"I know a ledger when I see one, Caroline, and with the first arrivals for the big meeting expected tomorrow, you must have a hundred chores to get done." I looked down at the envelope with its heavy black script and felt a stir of excitement.

"I think Bliss House is as ready as it can be, Ruth." I stared at the envelope a moment longer and finally looked back to her. "Why don't you have a seat and let Alex warm up while I read this letter? You look like there's something else on your mind."

"I just wanted you to know that if you run out of rooms for ordinary people because of all the bigshots you've got staying here, you can send people over to Hart's. We're a boarder down since Mr. Slate left for parts unknown, and I'll have room."

"All right," I said, but I hardly heard what Ruth said, being more intent on carefully slitting open the envelope and unfolding the letter contained inside, two large sheets of fine linen paper written top to bottom in the same bold script as the envelope. I was conscious of Ruth fussing with the baby, taking off his hat, smoothing his hair, rubbing his hands warmly between her own, but my real attention was on the words of that paper. I read it, then reread it to be sure I had all the details straight in my mind. For a little while, I sat holding the letter with both hands but not looking at it, thinking about it instead, thinking about what it said and what it meant and what it proved, if it proved anything.

"I hope it's not bad news, Caroline." Alex was being ornery about wearing his hat and had managed to snatch it off his head and toss it onto the floor. Ruth retrieved it, put it on the youngster's head again and added, "I know it's not my business so forgive me if you think I'm being nosy."

By then, my heartbeat had slowed back to normal, and I was able to respond with easy humor, "It's New Hope, Ruth. I think everybody's nosy. No, it's not bad news. Far from it. Years ago, my husband met a man named Granville Stuart at Fort Caspar and the two of them hit it off from the start."

"I've heard of him," Ruth said. "He's a big time cattleman, isn't he?"

"Over nine thousand head on eight hundred acres near Flat Willow Creek and Fort Maginnis in Montana Territory," I said. "There's no bigger name in beef west of the Missouri. Granville was at Fort Caspar trying to make a deal to provide the army in Wyoming Territory with beef when Davey met him. He helped us pick out our first herd. I don't think we could've done it without his help."

"And you've kept in touch with him?"

"Not very often anymore," I said, "but he did what he could during a bad time, and I'll always be grateful to him. Granville was up north in Montana so he didn't find out about the fire and Davey dying until nearly a month after it happened. When he did, he came down, found where I was, and asked what he could do. I told him all I wanted was to find out what happened to our livestock. He did his best, but too much time had passed. There were cattle moving across Wyoming Territory all that spring and summer, one herd after another. It wasn't Granville's fault that he couldn't find ours." Without saying a word, Ruth stood and lifted Alex back into her arms. She was like Arthur, a good listener who knew enough not to interrupt a story, especially one she hadn't heard before.

"I wrote him last month," I volunteered. Ruth hadn't asked the question, but I knew she was thinking it. "I thought he might be interested in coming to our little meeting here. It would've been nice to see him after all this time."

"But–"

"But he can't make it. He sent his regards and kind wishes but said he wouldn't be able to get to Nebraska anytime soon."

"That's a shame," Ruth headed for the door, one wiggly little boy squirming in her arms, "but maybe he can make it when the snow's gone. Is he a married man?"

I laughed at the words because my matchmaking friend had finally gotten to the question she'd been waiting to ask.

"He's married to an Indian girl and they have ten or eleven children. Granville always sounded perfectly happy with the arrangement whenever the subject came up."

Ruth looked at her son, whose fussing was getting louder the longer his mother stood talking to me. "Ten or eleven," she muttered. "Goodness. I've got another one coming, and I can hardly handle the one I've got now. I'd better get home, but if there's anything I can do for you over the next couple of days, just ask."

After they were gone and it was quiet in the office again, I read the letter with slow care one more time. It was true that when I wrote Granville, I had mentioned the Beef Convention in New Hope and had let him know he'd be welcome to attend if he chose, though I knew his DHS Cattle Company already had more customers than it had beef. But an invitation to New Hope's Beef Convention wasn't the main reason I wrote Granville Stuart. There was something I hoped he would remember from the time eight years earlier when he had followed and then lost the trail of our Rocking J herd and the men that stole them.

How far did you get before you lost their trail? I had written. *I know it's been a while, but do you remember?*

And he had replied, *We followed them clear into Colorado as far as the Poudre River and lost them there. The Poudre was a main crossing for a lot of herds from Oregon and Idaho and Montana Territories looking to reach the railroads in Colorado.*

There was more in the letter: the latest book he was writing – he was a man who always had a pencil in his hand – thoughts about the growth of Montana Territory and his DHS brand, even a comment about Trenton Saylor – *A good man I've known for years though his son has been a grief and disappointment to him for reasons better left unsaid* – but the words my eyes kept returning to were: *We followed them clear into Colorado as far as the Poudre River and lost them there.* The words *Poudre River* told me everything I suspected and everything I needed to know.

People still talk about New Hope's Beef Convention, though any number of more important things happened between then and now. A German man whose name I can't remember figured out what caused cholera, the disease that killed both my parents and eventually sent me to an orphanage. The painter Edouard Manet died, something I know only because Sheba told me, but she considered it a sad loss for art and I trust her judgment. Mr. Stevenson brought out a book called *Treasure Island.* I wouldn't ordinarily remember when a book was published, but Jem Fenway and Frederick Lincoln spent that fall dressing up as pirates and searching for buried treasure around New Hope, and those two boys with their pirate hats and wooden swords are hard to forget. New Hope saw its share of deaths and births, more of the latter than the former, I'm happy to say.

The Grubers' baby boy was one of the newcomers, a brother for Jem and Sheba's second nephew.

"Montgomery is a big name for such a little boy," I said, stroking one of the baby's cheeks with a finger, caught up in the wonder of him.

"It is a big name," Dee agreed, smiling at a memory she didn't share. "We'll call him Monty for short."

A new Carpenter baby came into the world, too, a curly-headed little girl named Dorcas. Her parents are still over the moon about it, Alexander not quite as much, but I imagine he'll get used to having a little sister in due time.

For all the things, both little and big, that have happened in between then and now, it's the Beef Convention that made the most difference in my own life. Unfortunately, the Convention didn't make a bit of difference to the future of New Hope. The Merchants' Association, after a great deal of heated discussion, decided that the town did not need and would not benefit from a slaughterhouse on its northern flank. The New Hope Union quoted Mort Lewis saying that stock pens were one thing, but the sights, sounds, and smells of a slaughterhouse greeting people as they got off the train was not what the Association saw as good for New Hope's future. Then the drought of '86 came, followed by the blizzards of '87, and cattlemen, even those as well-established as my friend Granville Stuart, ended up losing everything. Nobody regrets that slaughterhouse today.

All four eastern guests invited to our meeting arrived on the same afternoon train and showed up at the front desk of Bliss House at the same time. A clerk less capable than Lizbeth Ericson might have felt somewhat intimidated by four important men in business suits, each expecting to be given first attention. Not Lizbeth, however. I can never figure out how she does what she does, but in hardly any time at all, the four men had picked up their traveling bags and were climbing the stairs to their rooms, calmed and content and talking to one another as if they hadn't just traveled together all the way from Chicago.

The four men from the West weren't as accommodating. Mr. Irwin, the U.S. Indian agent representing the country's Indian Bureau, arrived by the early morning train, way ahead of when he was expected, which caused Benny Tidwell to laugh and say it was just like the government to come where it wasn't invited and arrive when it wasn't expected. Benny's comment is how I know Mr. Irwin was at the meeting. Otherwise, I have no personal recollection of the man at all, and from the meeting notes Isaac Lincoln took, it doesn't appear that the Indian agent contributed a single word to the discussions. To this day, no one's ever figured out why the man was there, and that includes John Bliss, who's certain he never invited him.

Both Fritz Becker, a well-known western rancher and longtime member of the Wyoming Stockman's Association, and the president of that organization came on the late morning train, so by mid-afternoon on the last Monday of February all but one of the invited participants had arrived – all but the most important one, if you had asked me.

Mark Saylor arrived in time for Monday's supper: Chef Clermont's brisket and all the trimmings, bread still warm from the oven, and apple pie, none of the chef's favorites as he was quick to tell me when we decided on the menu for those few days, but one which our guests were certain to appreciate. The table girls were quick on their feet, all smiles and apparently able to read minds. No coffee cup ever reached half-full and dishes were whisked away at exactly the right time. How they knew which man wanted to take an extra swipe of gravy with that fresh bread and which ones were truly finished I don't know to this day, but they did and continued to make the same wonderful impression at every meal.

I missed Mark Saylor's arrival though I watched for him all day, for Mark and Ray Summerton both, and especially made it a point to be in the hotel lobby after every eastbound train arrived, but there was no sign of either of the men. I remember wondering if perhaps they didn't take the train but for some unexpected reason rode in on horseback or came by buggy or wagon. But then, there Mark was after all. I had passed the front desk, getting a nod from Lizbeth that all was well – as if I expected any other message from her – and stopped in the doorway to scan the tables. When my gaze reached the table where Fritz Becker sat, I was startled to see Mark Saylor sitting next to Mr. Becker, and even more unsettling, Mark was staring right at me. At his direct look, I felt my stomach turn and my heart pick up and thought, even that early in the timetable, that something wasn't right. I managed a quick smile and when I didn't approach him because I thought it would be rude to interrupt his and Mr. Becker's meals, Mark said something to his companion, dabbed a napkin to his lips, and pushed back his chair. Becker looked over at me and turned back to say something to Mark that made him smile and nod. When he reached me, he took a gentle hold on my arm and pulled me to the side and out of the doorway.

"Caroline. You look lovely, as usual. I looked for you when I arrived but was afraid I'd miss supper if I waited too long to get a table. Forgive me for not taking the time to find you first thing." He held my hand in his as he spoke.

"There's nothing to forgive, Mark. Any sensible man would put Monsieur Clermont's brisket first. Any sensible woman, too, for that matter." He laughed and finally released my hand.

"I knew you'd understand. Having met Mort Lewis and

some of the other organizers, I don't have to ask if everything's in place for tomorrow's meeting. My only regret is John Bliss's absence."

"At the risk of sounding disloyal," I replied, "you won't really miss his presence. He filled Mort in on his opinions and not surprisingly, they agree with everyone else's in New Hope." Mark and I chatted a little longer, nothing of any importance, and then I asked with what I hoped sounded like casual interest, "Has Mr. Summerton already eaten and left, or did he head straight for the Music Hall?"

"Ray?" I knew by Saylor's tone, an odd mix of implied sadness and shock with an edge of unmistakable satisfaction, that I wouldn't like what he was going to tell me and that he knew I wouldn't like it. I experienced a slight shiver even before he continued, "Ray's dead, Caroline."

I couldn't contain the gasp that escaped me. "Dead?! I'm so sorry to hear that. What happened?"

Mark's attention never left my face, looking for something in my expression or listening for something in my tone. Whatever he hoped to see or hear, I tried to gather enough self-control that he didn't find it, although the news of Summerton's death, if true, would change everything.

"An awful accident. That damned bull."

"What?!"

"Ray said we should keep the bull stalled for a day or two, give him a chance to recover from being on the train and get used to his new home before we turned him into the corral and finally let him roam. We've got more snow than you have here so it made sense to keep him where we could see him close up and check on him. I don't know what Ray was thinking to get in that stall with him. No one'll ever know now."

"Your new Angus bull killed Ray Summerton?" I asked. The idea was so ridiculous I couldn't keep the disbelief out of my voice. The man I had watched load that same bull onto the train would never have put himself in such a spot. Never.

Mark nodded, acknowledging the same opinion he heard in my voice. “I know, Caroline. Nobody could believe it when we found him, but that’s all we can figure. His head was – forgive me if this is distressing – a mess. He was hardly recognizable after being under the hooves of that big creature all night, but we didn’t find any other wounds on his body.” Still Mark watched me. Did he want to know if I believed him? I didn’t, of course, but for a reason I hadn’t worked through yet, I knew it would be dangerous for me to act as if I doubted his story.

“I’m so sorry,” I managed finally. “What a foolish thing for Mr. Summerton to do! And I know how you counted on his know-how with the herd. You’ll miss him.”

“That’s true, but you know, Caroline, Ray Summerton wasn’t everything he seemed.”

“No? What do you mean?”

“Well,” Mark looked away a moment to nod at Fritz Becker as the rancher walked past us and toward the lobby stairs, “to say it frankly, Summerton was a liar and a cheat, and he didn’t possess an ounce of loyalty.” I couldn’t think what to say in response. “Ray had his good points, I suppose, and you’re right, he knew beef on the hoof like no one I’ve ever known, but he could be difficult. It got so there at the end that I couldn’t trust him any further than I could throw him.” I could hardly argue with that since I’d used those exact words weeks ago when describing Summerton to Lizbeth, but I knew Mark had recognized all of that in the man early on. Something else had to have changed if, as I suspected and dreaded, Ray Summerton’s death wasn’t an accident.

“I’m surprised to hear that about him,” I said with a calm I didn’t feel, “but as awful as the news is, if what you say is true, you’re lucky to be rid of him.” From the look Saylor gave me, he hadn’t expected that reaction from me.

Finally, he gave a slow smile and said, "Trust a practical woman like you to see the obvious. Yes, I think you're right, Caroline. I am very lucky to be rid of him."

I took a step back, suddenly wishing to get as far away from Mark Saylor as possible, desperate to think matters through and make some kind of sense of this unexpected change of plans. Behind me, I heard a voice I recognized and turned to see Arthur standing at the front desk talking to Lizbeth. The sight of his lean, dark-coated figure seemed to settle my confused mind. The nearer the Beef Convention got, the more I welcomed the companionship of this steady, reasonable, calm man, this trustworthy man who never asked anything more from me than intelligent conversation and an appreciation for the silliness of life.

Lizbeth gestured in my direction and Arthur turned toward me, raising a hand in greeting when he saw me and walking toward me. He must have been more tired than usual because his limp was very pronounced, and as I turned away from Saylor, I caught a look of pity in Mark's eyes as he watched Arthur's approach, pity mixed with the kind of scorn a strong and healthy man feels for a man he considers to be weak and because of that, of no importance. I felt a burst of rage burn its way up my chest at Saylor's unconcealed expression.

"Hello, Arthur," I said, with enough warmth in my voice to surprise both men.

"Caroline." Arthur turned toward Saylor and without waiting to be asked, extended a hand. "Arthur Stenton," he said in a firm voice.

"Mark Saylor." The two men shook hands.

"Are you here for the beef meeting, Mr. Saylor?"

"Yes."

"Welcome, then. I hope it's everything you expect."

"After seeing Caroline again, it's already better than I expected." Mark put a hand lightly on my arm. So he had heard something in my voice when I spoke Arthur's name that he didn't appreciate. Why else would he want Arthur to believe there was something between us?

Moving away from Saylor's touch, I said, "Arthur is the headmaster of New Hope's school."

"Oh?" A little more pity and scorn was in Mark's voice, but Arthur didn't seem to notice. Obviously, he felt no need to explain or justify his occupation. Instead, he gave Saylor another moment of his usual courteous and interested attention before turning back to me.

"I won't bother you any longer, Caroline. I know you'll be busier than usual for the next few days, but I thought you'd enjoy reading this. Not now, of course, but when you can find the time." The title on the cover of the small book he handed me read *WORK: A STORY OF EXPERIENCE BY LOUISA M. ALCOTT,* printed all in capital letters. "You may find that you and Miss Alcott have a lot in common." Arthur gave me his quick, attractive smile, murmured, "A pleasure to meet you, Mr. Saylor," and limped his way to the door.

After he'd left, Mark said, "You're a kind woman as well as a beautiful one."

"I beg your pardon."

He should have known by the tone of my voice not to pursue the topic, but Mark Saylor was a man unable to listen to a woman in any real or important way. I had recognized early on that when Mark complimented me or gave me his attention, it was because he hoped doing so would eventually get him something in return, an invitation to my bed no doubt his highest goal. Did he think he was so different from other men, so special, that I wouldn't understand that about him?

"Mr. – Stenton, was it? – seems to harbor feelings for you." Mark gave a quiet sigh. Pity again. I could have struck him. "Can't say I blame him, of course," he continued, "but he's a fool if he can't see that a cripple doesn't have it in him to satisfy a woman like you or give her what she deserves." The hot streak of rage I'd felt earlier blazed up again.

"You could never understand a gentleman like Arthur Stenton," I said when I could trust my voice, my words deliberate and as cold as my fury was hot. "Never. The two of you could be from different planets." I turned away abruptly, afraid I'd say too much when I was still so unsure what to do and how to act around Mark Saylor. The news of Summerton's death had thrown me off balance, inside and out.

Behind me, Mark said my name but I didn't turn back to hear his response. We would talk more later, I was sure of it, but for the time being I couldn't get away far enough or fast enough. As I walked quickly past the front desk toward the back office, I saw Lizbeth take a quick look at me, shift her gaze briefly to where Mark Saylor stood, and then bring her attention back to me. Hers was a thoughtful look that hadn't missed anything, even if she didn't hear a single word of our conversation. It was true that Lizbeth didn't miss much, but she also knew when the moment was right for a comment or a question and when it wasn't. At my challenging look aimed directly at her, Lizbeth gave me a small, innocent smile and went back to transferring the names from the last page of the sign-in book onto the list of customers' names we kept behind the desk. To the girl's credit, she did it without saying a word.

18

New Hope's eagerly awaited and carefully planned Beef Convention went off without a hitch. Mort's opening speech set the right tone and after that, the men began to carry the meeting along on the force of their own interests. At the end of the day, it looked like several partnerships between East and West, between cattleman and meat packer, might be set up. That was what Mort Lewis shared with me at the end of the meeting, anyway, since I had neither invitation nor inclination to sit in on any of the discussion. I can say that from what I saw, all the men involved were talkative and sociable over supper and decided to end their New Hope stay first by returning to the Music Hall for drinks and after that, by crossing the street for some friendly billiards. Considerable money changed hands – at least, that's what I heard. They were men intent on making money after all, and experts at turning a profit, whether in beef or billiards.

Mark Saylor didn't join the others when they left for the Music Hall but instead came looking for me. I knew he would, knew if I could show enough patience, he'd find me. There were things unsaid and matters unresolved on both our parts. I had had time to recover from news of the loss of Ray Summerton, or rather from the loss of the information Ray Summerton could have provided me. Late Monday night as I lay in bed, I realized with that clarity a person finds when staring out into a black room that I wouldn't be able to resolve matters as I had hoped. Without the evidence I needed and longed for, I was still on my own. I might be certain of the facts in my own mind, but I was just one woman and I needed more. A move back to Colorado might be next, and while the idea of leaving New Hope and starting fresh again in another town filled me with a kind of exhausted dread, I couldn't stop now. Some affairs a person must see to the end, no matter how long it took, and this was one of them.

Once the Beef Convention was in session, I made a quick trip to the jail. The marshal wasn't there, but Lucas was, and either of them would do.

"I need some help, Lucas."

"If I can, I will. I hope you know that by now, Caroline." Lucas Morgan was a fine man. In fact, New Hope, Nebraska, had more than its share of fine men. I wondered how that happened, or could I have said the same for any of the places I'd lived over the past eight years if I'd only taken more time to get to know the people around me?

"I heard yesterday about the death of a man I knew. His name was Ray Summerton, and I was hoping you could wire the nearest law to where Mr. Summerton died and see what happened."

"Was this Mr. Summerton a friend of yours?" Lucas asked.

"Not exactly a friend, but he was important to me in a special kind of way. I was told he had an accident that killed him, and I was wondering what the law thought about the matter." Lucas eyed me for a moment, knowing there was more to the story but accepting the fact that he wasn't going to get any more from me. "The accident happened somewhere around a place called Hot Sulphur Springs in Colorado, and as I recall from my days in Denver, Hot Sulphur Springs is in Grand County," I continued. "I don't know if there's any law in those parts, but if there is, I'd surely appreciate you inquiring on my behalf."

"I can find out about law offices from Lonnie at the telegraph office. Is there anything else I should know?" More to the deputy's question than the obvious.

"No. Thank you, Lucas." He nodded and I smiled and that was that. I didn't expect to hear anything different from what Mark Saylor told me, but I'm a woman who likes to have all her facts in order.

Mark showed up in the hotel office after supper and made a pretty apology using his best manners. "I'm sorry for sounding so crude yesterday, Caroline. I realized too late that that Stenton fellow was a friend of yours, and I had no business saying the things about him that I said. I hope you can forgive me."

"Of course. I was too quick to react. I doubt you meant any harm."

"No. Do you even need to ask?"

Looking at the man standing in the doorway, I felt such a rush and mix of feelings I thought they must all show on my face, but if they did, Saylor didn't say anything. He was looking at me with those striking blue eyes, the handsome and confident son of a rich and well-known father. If the circumstances had been different, I believe I could have been quite taken with him.

"The only man I've ever been sure of in that regard," I replied, "was my husband. Everyone else I've learned to take with a grain of salt." I smiled to keep the words light.

Mark stepped fully into the room, closed the door carefully behind him, and walked toward the desk.

"Am I interrupting your work?" he asked.

"Yes, but I'm glad of it. It's been a busy two days and

having you here gives me an excuse to forget about the Beef Convention for a while. Will you profit from coming to it, do you think?" He sat down across from me.

"It looks like it. Nelson Morris wants to talk further so I'll be making a trip to Chicago next month."

"Congratulations. I'm glad your trip to New Hope wasn't wasted."

"I met you, Caroline, so even if nothing comes out of this meeting, there's no way I'd ever consider the trip wasted." He sat back and crossed one leg over the other. "You mentioned your husband just now. You hardly ever talk about him."

"No? Well, if that's true, it isn't on purpose. My husband was a good man, and I hold his memory dear."

"How long has he been gone?"

"Too long," I answered.

Mark Saylor's questions could have been simple curiosity, but I doubted it. Had he learned something about me from Ray Summerton? Remembering the kind of man Ray Summerton had been, I wouldn't have been surprised to find out that he had tried to peddle what he knew of my past to the highest bidder. If I was willing to pay for the information, did he think Mark Saylor would pay him even more to keep the information quiet? It would be a serious mistake to underestimate the man sitting in front of me. Maybe Summerton discovered that but too late.

"Was your husband ill?"

"No. Davey was strong as a horse. He died in an accident."

"I'm sorry."

"Thank you," adding casually, "I think I told you that Davey was a good friend of John Bliss. That's how I came to know John, in fact, and how I ended up in New Hope."

"How well did you know Bliss back then?"

"Not well. The partnership didn't end happily, I'm afraid. John and Davey split up, over me of all things, and my husband and I moved away. It was a hard break for all of us, and it took us a long time to find a place that suited us as much as Nevada did. We were partial to mountains and blue sky."

"That explains Wyoming, then. That area around South Fork and Fort Caspar has mountains and blue sky to spare." He spoke the words easily, not realizing what he'd done, but I did, right away, and had to scramble for something to say, had to keep my voice steady and my expression unchanged.

"Yes, it does. We loved it the first time we saw it." I stood abruptly. "I appreciate your giving me an excuse to take a break from ledger sums, but I should check in the kitchen and make sure the dining room's ready for breakfast." I walked toward the office door. "You'll still have time for a drink in the Music Hall if you hurry." He reached for me as I passed him, grabbed me by one arm, and swung me around to face him.

"I'm not interested in the Music Hall. The only thing I'm interested in is you."

I pulled free, rubbing my arm where he'd grasped it, and said, "That's a compliment, I suppose, but you have a funny way of showing your admiration. A lady doesn't like to be manhandled."

"I'm sorry, Caroline, but you don't bring out the best in me." He reached for me again, and I sidestepped toward the door but not fast enough. Before I could sidestep again, he had backed me against the wall and was kissing me, his body pressed so hard against me I couldn't move, could hardly breathe with his mouth over mine and his hands fumbling at my body.

"Stop," I managed to gasp and surprisingly, he did, though he didn't free me.

"I can't, or I don't want to. Look at you. Eight years since your husband's gone and you without a man all that time. It's a waste of a woman like you." He bent his head to kiss me again and I thought if that happened, I'd die. This man's touch had the power to turn my stomach and buckle my knees, a prospect so unbearable that to stop him, as I knew the words would, I made myself calm, freed my arms, raised them around his neck hinting that I might have changed my mind, and drew his head close enough that I could whisper against his cheek, "I know who you are. And I know what you did." At my vicious hiss of words, every part of the man stilled.

"What are you talking about?" He pulled away from me as far as my arms would let him go and stared at my face. I freed him to move even farther away and somehow managed a smile that surely had no humor in it.

"You know what I'm talking about. The only person who knew that my husband and I ranched along the South Fork River by Fort Caspar was Ray Summerton, but somehow you knew it. You just said so. And how did you know how many years it's been since my husband died? I never told you. I never told anyone, but you said *eight years* like you knew. Which, of course, you do because you set up your own place eight years ago, set it up with the herd you stole from us when you murdered my family and burned down my house, so sure no one could survive the fire. That's how you knew it was eight years." He had moved several more steps away from me by then, eyes narrowed, arms at his side with fists clenched, still staring at me like I had snakes coiling from my head, his own Medusa come to life from ancient stories.

I knew my actions weren't according to plan, knew this might be the greatest mistake I'd ever made in my life, but at that moment, I felt powerful and satisfied. What pleasure it gave me to say the words! How I loved the stammer in his voice and the way he had turned pale!

"That's a ridiculous accusation."

"Did you think I was the kind of woman to be so impressed by a little sparkle that I'd be taken in by that damned stick pin you wear, that I couldn't see how easy it would be to turn a rocking J into an anchor? A line here, another line there, a circle at the top and just like that the J's an anchor. Burn your anchor brand over our J and who'll notice? Who'll care? Well, I know and I care, you murdering bastard. Couldn't you tell that your touch made me sick?"

Things had changed between us in the room. I was the one moving forward, he the one backing away. A glorious reversal, though it didn't last long because he finally came to a stop. The stammer was gone, and he had regained both his color and his thoughts. Mark Saylor was a man who knew how to play the odds and wasn't afraid to take risks.

"Even if it was true – *even* – I'm not saying it is – who would believe you? A woman who spent her early years in a gambling hall in Virginia City, making her living God knows how. A woman made crazy by grief chasing make-believe outlaws from town to town. A nobody." We both knew that part of what he said was true. I *was* a nobody.

"I'd rather be a nobody than a murderer and a liar and a thief," I retorted with defiance, "because they don't hang a person for being a nobody, but they do for murder and cattle rustling. I've heard that sometimes they even hang them without a trial. Fancy that. Exactly the way you killed my family, without warning and without a trial. You're right that I don't have a rich father who'll cover for me, Mark, but I have one rich friend, and he'll believe me, and between the two of us, we might be able to convince other people to take a careful look at you and your stock, ask for a bill of sale or the name of that man you said sold you the herd. That would make it difficult for you, wouldn't it?"

"And that friend would be who?" The question was little more than a sneer, but my words had hit home. He knew I wouldn't make something like that up.

"Granville Stuart." I pronounced the name of the most famous rancher west of the Missouri with a triumph Saylor didn't miss. "I know you've heard of him," I continued. "There's no more important cattleman in these parts. People respect him. I think they'll listen to him, too, but whether they do or not, you should know you'll never be rid of me. I'll always be as close as your shadow until the day you die." I shouldn't have allowed that final threat, but after so many years balancing on the edge of despair, I couldn't hold it back. To have answers, to be this close to seeing payment made for the deaths of the people I loved made the words bubble out even when my more sensible self cautioned quiet.

Mark had recognized the name Granville Stuart and stood considering what I said very seriously, nodding a little and chewing on his lower lip as he thought. I don't know what he would have said or what he might have done. If he believed my threat was serious, would he have tried to harm me then and there? I can't answer that question because just as Mark's eyes met mine in a coldly assessing, unblinking stare, Lizbeth knocked on the office door and pushed it open just enough to bump against Mark. He instantly stepped away from the door, straightening his coat and pulling at his sleeves as he did so.

"Oh, excuse me. I thought Mrs. Moore–" I came forward and pulled the door fully open.

"I'm here, Lizbeth. What is it?"

"I beg your pardon for interrupting," Lizbeth said, glancing at Mark and then bringing her sober gaze back to me, neither her expression nor her tone sounding at all penitent, "but Chef wants to change the dessert on tomorrow's luncheon menu before he goes home, and you know he needs your approval for that. Right now, he said. You know how he gets."

If the situation hadn't been so serious, I would have laughed out loud at the words. The idea of Monsieur Clermont needing my approval to change the menu at any given time for any given meal was outlandish. The man did what he wanted. My job was to smile, nod, and agree. Sometimes just agree, maybe, but everyone knew any role I held in the kitchen was in name only, and I suspected it was the same for John Bliss. Kitchen rules always meant Clermont rules.

"All right," I responded. "Thank you, Lizbeth. I'll be right there." I moved so that I stood between Mark and the open door. "Mr. Saylor was just leaving."

When the man turned to face me, it was as if nothing had happened behind the closed door. His face was pleasant; his smiled looked genuine.

"I don't want to get in the way," he said to me and to Lizbeth, "We were just saying our goodbyes. I leave first thing in the morning," and then back to me, "Good night, Caroline. The meeting went well. I believe I owe you for what happened here."

Equally as casual, I responded, "Nonsense. You deserve whatever occurs. It was all your own doing. I hope you have a relaxing trip back to Colorado. I'll come with you now, Lizbeth. Mr. Saylor knows his way out."

I was conscious of Mark walking behind us down the hallway and after we reached the lobby, I watched him ascend the stairs to his room. Did he remain as conscious of my uninterrupted attention as I had been of his? I thought it very likely.

When he was out of earshot and sight, the girl asked with quiet concern, "Are you all right, Mrs. Moore?"

I resisted the urge to hug her and instead simply answered, "I am now, Lizbeth. Thank you."

"Maybe it wasn't Mr. Summerton that we needed to watch out for," she said, remembering the day when Ray Summerton had stood exactly where we stood now.

"Maybe it wasn't," pausing a moment so she'd know I understood her and then continuing, "Why don't you go home? I don't expect the rest of our guests back from their New Hope adventures– " Lizbeth grinned a little at the idea

" –for a while yet, and I'm too restless to go home myself. I'll watch the desk until Kip's here."

"Are you sure?"

"Yes." As she passed me to get her coat from the hook, I added, "I don't know how you knew, Lizbeth, but thank you." She didn't pretend either ignorance or innocence, deception not being one of her traits.

"I probably know more than you think, Mrs. Moore, and you're welcome."

Walking through the empty dining room and kitchen, I thought briefly about Lizbeth Ericson and how easy it was to underestimate quiet people, but the rest of the evening and later, too, when I lay in bed, it wasn't Lizbeth who occupied my thoughts.

19

While the other westbound guests planned an afternoon departure, early the next morning on the last day of February, 1883, Mark Saylor checked out of Bliss House to catch the 8:11 heading west. I waited long enough for him to leave the hotel before confirming his departure with a word to Lizbeth at the desk and then walking down to the jail as soon as I heard the whistle of the engine announce its arrival.

Silas Carpenter looked up from behind the desk when I pushed open the jail door. Of course, he was the man who would be there, the one in charge of the constabulary and whose inborn authority somehow offered security to the start of each new day.

But I had expected to find Lucas and a touch of disappointment must have showed on my face because Si smiled and said, "Cranky baby at home. Seemed best for me to get out of the house so Lucas and I got our morning business taken care of earlier than usual. Sorry."

"No, that's fine. It was just that I asked a favor of Lucas yesterday and I wondered–" Si held up a piece of paper from the desk.

"It's right here."

Naturally, the marshal would know what went on in his own town and among his deputies. I thought it would be as hard to keep a secret from Si Carpenter as it was from his wife, in some ways two very different people and in other ways very much the same. How long did it take for husband and wife to get to that point? Davey and I hadn't had enough time together to find out.

Si didn't have to read the telegram again before telling me its contents: "Dick Sloan is the sheriff over in Grand County and he and I go back a ways. Dick says he had his doubts about what happened to Summerton, but nothing he can hang his hat on. Nobody saw what happened and that bull is more of a brute than Summerton was. That's the way Dick put it."

"All right," I said. "I don't think I expected anything else. I was just wondering. Thank you."

Si wouldn't, couldn't let me leave without saying, "If there's something I should know, Caroline, I'm here and I'm more than willing to listen. Lucas, too. Take your pick. Whoever you choose to talk to is fine. Ruth's worried about you." No one had worried about me in a long time so the words warmed my heart.

"That's kind, Si, but you can tell Ruth not to worry. I can take care of myself."

He gave a gentle shake of his head. "I didn't learn this before I got to New Hope, Caroline, but no one can take care of himself, not man or woman. We need each other in ways we don't expect." The engine gave a whistle that said the train was loading for departure, and I needed to see for myself that Mark Saylor got on board.

"You can still tell Ruth not to worry," I said with a smile and left, looking north as soon as I stepped outside. I hurried across the street, crossed the alley, and stopped at the door of the Freight Office with no plan to enter, only to watch the passenger car where it waited at the train platform.

And there he came, Mark Saylor, small traveling bag in hand, striding from the ticket window to the boarding steps and then into the car without a backwards glance. I waited in the chill morning air until the train began its noisy chugging, waited until the engine pulled away, waited even longer until both the sight and the sound of it had disappeared.

Then I walked to the platform and bent to ask Val Copco, who sat on his stool behind the ticket window, "Was that Mr. Saylor I saw get on the train?"

"Yes, ma'am." If Val thought my question was curious, he didn't look it. Maybe he was used to foolish questions from the great variety of people he talked to every day.

"And where was he headed again?" I asked,

"Denver." Val didn't have to look anything up. He was like Lizbeth and the sign-in book at the hotel desk. She didn't need to look there, either, to know a person's name, when they arrived, and when they left. Val and Lizbeth were people who knew their business.

I walked slowly back to the hotel with a mix of feelings stirring inside me: relief at seeing the backside of Mark Saylor for a while, but sadness just as strong and, unusual for me, a kind of anger – unusual because the anger wasn't directed at Mark Saylor but at divine Providence, the very same Providence that Pastor Shulte bragged on Sunday after Sunday for the way he said we were loved and cared for and forgiven and generously offered everything we'd need to start fresh. If what the preacher said was true, then why was Mark Saylor given free rein to do as he pleased? And why couldn't I rest here in New Hope, Nebraska, a place as close to home as I would ever find again in my life? Shouldn't the reckonings in life balance the same way the tallies in my ledger books did?

Even after the Union Pacific carried our Beef Convention guests off in opposite directions, Bliss House didn't have the luxury of slowing down. Rooms had to be cleaned, used linens gathered and sent over to Ruby for washing, and rubbish collected and taken out to be burned. The dining room had to be set for the next meal, and other guests still needed to be checked in and out the same as every other day. But among the citizens of New Hope, I sensed both satisfaction and leisurely relief. It's done and we did our best, was the main opinion, closely followed by wondering how, if at all, the results of the Beef Convention would affect New Hope.

There was a lot of conversation about both the past and the future, and I was thinking along the same lines, though my thoughts had little to do with the Beef Convention. I had a name now – Mark Saylor – but not the rest of what I needed: no proof of his murderous actions, no confession, and for all my boasting of a friendship with Granville Stuart, not even the assurance that Granville would believe me. I'd have to try, of course, but I also had to have a plan for what I'd do if he didn't believe me, if he thought I was what Saylor described: *a woman made crazy by grief, chasing make-believe outlaws from town to town.* I could find work in Denver, I supposed, since I still had friends from when I worked there, or maybe I would try to settle closer to Saylor, find respectable work, no matter how modest, around Hot Sulphur Springs in Grand County, Colorado. There was no way I'd let him out of my sight now. Now that I knew.

Arthur stopped at the restaurant after supper that night, surprising me as I walked through the dining room noting the table coverings that could last one more day before they needed to be replaced. I had an eye for it now and after assigning each table a number, I kept a list of all of the numbers on the wall in the kitchen with the day each particular table should get a new tablecloth. It was easy enough for me, and with all the other duties the girls had, my keeping track of something as small as a clean tablecloth meant they were one step closer to being able to go home at the end of the day.

When I made the final note in the little paper tablet I carried, I looked up to find Arthur standing in the dining room doorway silhouetted against the lobby lamps behind him. I thought I would recognize him anywhere with that upright posture, shoulders back and almost too straight, the way a soldier might stand. The natural dignity of the man, limp or no limp, was like no one else I had ever met. Yet when he smiled, which he seemed to be doing more of lately, he could look almost boyish, and he had a lock of hair that sometimes dropped onto his forehead in a manner I found endearing. An educated man without any airs, a man who thought himself as common as everyone else but certainly wasn't, at least from where I stood.

I dropped my tablet and pencil into a pocket and looked over at him. He had been watching me with great attention before I knew he was there but was too far away for me to read the look in his eyes.

"Hello, Arthur. I didn't see you standing there." He came into the dining room.

"You were intent on the task at hand. Do you need to finish it? Should I go?"

"No and no."

"I imagine you're busy getting caught up with your work after the big meeting. I should have waited. I'll come back another time."

The idea of Arthur Stenton walking away from me was more than I could contemplate just then. I had been thinking so much of goodbyes lately.

"No. Please stay. Are you hungry? I'll brave the wrath of the chef and heat you some supper if you'd like. Or are you just interested in tea? I could stand a cup if you could."

"Tea sounds good."

"Sit down, then, Arthur," I said and turned toward the kitchen before turning back long enough to say, "I'm glad you're here. It feels like weeks since I've had a chance to talk to you."

In the kitchen, Henry was working on the big frying pans, up to his elbows in water. I greeted the boy when I entered and chatted with him as I put the kettle on for hot water and got out the tea canister.

"Did you learn anything new today?" I asked as I puttered, a question that always animated the boy. For the Henry Strunks of the world, life overflowed with new ideas and inventions, new places to see and new discoveries to marvel over. I sometimes found the boy as endearing as Arthur but for entirely different reasons.

Henry stopped what he was doing and began to tell me about a bridge somewhere around New York City that was over fifteen hundred feet long and more than forty feet above the river.

"It's made of steel wire, not wood. I think that's got to be the smartest thing anybody ever made. It's called the–" Henry stopped and frowned in concentration "–New York and something bridge. I don't remember the *something*, but can you imagine how big that bridge is? I'd give anything to walk across a bridge that big."

"You wouldn't be scared?" Henry looked at me in astonishment at the ridiculous question.

"Scared?! No, ma'am. It'd be an adventure, that's what it would be!"

I put teacups, the teapot with its steeping leaves, and the sugar bowl on a tray, every once in a while looking over at the boy's expression as he talked and smiling at the glow in his eyes. He'll see that bridge someday, I thought with certainty, see it and cross it and make sense of how it stayed up. Then he'd make a bridge of his own, but bigger and probably covered with electric lights, besides. That's just the kind of boy Henry Strunk was.

With a hip against the kitchen door, ready to join Arthur in the dining room, I said, "Be careful going home, Henry." I nodded toward the shelf where Henry had set his eyeglasses so they wouldn't get spattered with grease from the pans. "And don't forget your eyeglasses. Good night."

Raised to be polite, Henry said good night in return and went back to finishing up the dishes, but I could tell his mind was nowhere near New Hope, Nebraska. It was busy imagining a bridge made of steel wire and how it would feel to walk across it big and bright as day.

Still smiling, I joined Arthur at what had become our table, along the side and under a wall lamp. As I poured the tea, I told him about my conversation with Henry.

"I think Henry should go on to high school," I said, "but I don't know where the closest one is."

"Henry can't go to high school, no matter where it is," Arthur replied.

I bridled a little at the words. "Are you saying the boy's not smart enough for high school?"

"Henry Strunk is the brightest boy I've taught in all my years, but you know as well as I that his mother counts on him for income and help with thc house and his siblings. It isn't just the extra income, it's having someone she can rely on."

Arthur was right, but I felt terribly sad about it, as if Henry was my son or it was my fault, neither of which was true. I stayed quiet as I sipped my tea.

"Caroline?" I raised my eyes and smiled at the concern in Arthur's eyes.

"I can't argue with you, Arthur, because you're right. It makes me sad to think it, but the week's taken a lot out of me and right now I'm a little tired."

"Everybody I've talked to says the meeting went well."

"Yes, I think it did, too. If nothing else, it brought important visitors to New Hope. Maybe they'll spread the word about what an agreeable group of people we are. I know I'll miss the town when I leave."

Looking under my lashes, I saw how Arthur's hand holding the teacup stopped briefly in mid-air before he lowered it back into the saucer. I should have warned him, I thought, but how could I? I could barely say the words once as it was.

"I didn't know you were leaving, Caroline," spoken in the same calm tone as usual.

"Well, not tomorrow," I said, "but John wired to say he and Sheba would be back in March, so I'll need to look for other work."

"Will you go back to Ogallala?"

"I thought I might at one time, but now I think I'll head back to Denver. I worked in Denver for a while – did I ever say? – and I still know people there."

Arthur nodded as if I'd said something very wise. Then he asked, so quietly I wondered if he were really asking me or just turning the words over in his mind, "Is there anything I could say to make you stay, Caroline?" The mix of longing and tenderness and regret I heard in his voice was almost too much to bear.

I'd stay here with you if I could, I wanted to tell him, but I can't. I have unfinished business with another man, and I won't let it go because he has to pay for what he took from me. I didn't put any of my thoughts into words.

Instead, I shook my head and answered, "No, Arthur. There's nothing anyone can say to change my mind."

He set down his cup and looked across the table at me, meeting my gaze to be sure I caught what he wasn't going to – or couldn't? – say out loud.

"You're a grown woman. You have a mind of your own and the right to make your own decisions." That out of the way, he said, "But it won't be the same without you. *I* won't be the same without you. You know that, don't you?"

"Yes," I said, the simple word nearly bringing me to tears, but not tears I wanted Arthur – or anyone else, for that matter – to see. Tears were too private a matter to have them on display.

"Good. There will always be a place here for you, but we can talk about that later. Like you said, it's late and you're tired and I've still got a lesson to prepare." He stood and reached for his coat on the back of the chair. "Good night, Caroline."

I stood but otherwise didn't move. "Good night, Arthur. You watch your step going home."

"I will. I always do."

After he left, I sat down again and stayed there a long time, sometimes lost in thought but other times simply lost. I was right when I told Arthur I was tired. I couldn't remember the last time I felt so exhausted that I couldn't think straight.

I must have fallen asleep because at the sound of Kip's voice, my head jerked up from where I had rested it on my folded arms, something I'd never done before at any place I had ever worked. How did it look for the woman in charge to be sleeping on the job? Never mind that it was past ten and there wasn't much of a job to do just then.

"I'm sorry, Mrs. Moore. I just wanted – well, I was worried about you." He looked very young, which he was, and uncomfortable.

"Thank you, Kip. I guess I was more tired than I thought, but I've got my second wind now, and I think I'll finish up the paperwork I left on my desk."

"It's late," still worried about me, apparently.

"I know. It won't take long."

Gypsy lifted her head from the basket by the stove in the office, opened one eye to see who it was that dared interrupt her last nap before her nighttime prowl, decided I was either welcome or unimportant – I had a feeling I knew which one – and resumed dozing. She was an independent creature who earned her keep and then some by the number of dead mice she left lying around the place. One of the first chores of the morning for the table girls was something they called "Gypsy clean-up," a chore awarded to the girl who drew the short straw. Just a few days ago, I had laughed when Darla shared that they had started a contest to see who would collect the most rodent corpses in any one day.

"Everyone threw a nickel into the pot," Darla said, "and I'm keeping a record for each day up until Easter."

"It seems to me," I told Darla, "that the winner is going to end up the loser, no matter how much money's in the pot." I liked the spirit and the loyalty I saw in each one of those girls and remembered being a little like them when I was their age but without a home to go back to as they all had. I would miss them.

Working on the hotel ledgers calmed my thoughts. It's satisfying when debits and credits balance, when the tallies in one column equal the tallies in the other. That was the way life ought to be, too, I always thought, balanced and fair. Sitting there in the cooling office, adding the figures and calculating the numbers, made me realize that was why I couldn't leave off following Mark Saylor wherever he went. If he got away with his awful deeds, then life would always be out of balance for me. If there ever was a reckoning, a final public reckoning, I believed I would be able to sleep without fire haunting my dreams. With my world back in balance, anything was possible, or so I hoped. Until New Hope, I hadn't realized how much I longed for the company of friends and the normal goings-on of everyday life. *There will always be a place here for you,* Arthur had told me. A promise, his promise, that I didn't mistake. Someday I will come back to New Hope, I promised myself in return. I will! And the first thing I'll do is tell that dear man exactly how much he means to me. I was only just finding that out for myself. What turns life takes sometimes!

When I finally placed the ledgers back into the top desk drawer, I stood, stretched, gave Gypsy a scratch behind her ears, and grabbed my cloak and scarf. Stopping at the lobby, I told Kip that it was late and quiet and he should head for his cot in the back room. Then at the last minute, I remembered the tea things Arthur and I had shared earlier in the evening, laid my cloak across the front counter, and went into the dining room to clear the table. With the tray balanced in one hand, I pushed open the door and walked over to the washing-up sink. Chef would know – he always knew – when someone uninvited was in his kitchen, but I should at least try to leave everything as I found it. On the shelf over the sink, I was surprised to see Henry's eyeglasses. Too busy thinking about that bridge in New York, I thought, smiling, and bent to place the tea tray into the empty tub.

Behind me, Mark Saylor said, "Hello, Caroline. I've been waiting for you here, seeing as you weren't over at the big house. You can turn around, but do it slow. Real slow."

I went still as a statue and I believe to this day that at the sound of his voice, my heart truly stopped beating for a long, long moment until I could once more feel its familiar thud and breathe again. The awful stillness brought on by the shock of his voice passed, replaced by a fluttering in my stomach and a curl of fear that made my hands shake. I did what he said and turned to face him.

I made no mention of the small pistol he pointed at me, glanced at it only long enough to see that it had two barrels so was most likely a double shot – something I thought might be handy for me to keep in mind – and then didn't look at it again.

"Well, here's a bad penny," I said and stared at him.

Mark Saylor grinned at the words, sure of himself, sure he had the upper hand and would, as he always had, land on his feet.

"It's nice to see you, too," he replied.

"What do you want?" I went on the attack with cold words, as I had learned to do when a man, any man, cornered or threatened me. Sometimes it worked, made them back up a step and reconsider, but I already knew that wouldn't be the case with Mark Saylor.

"I've been thinking about what you said, about you knowing Granville Stuart, and I can't have you talking to him, Caroline, I just can't. My father thinks the sun rises and sets in Stuart. He thinks more of him than he does of me, and he'll believe anything Stuart tells him, whether it's about me or you or that husband of yours. I can't have that."

"No? Too bad you showed up so late because I already wired Granville."

"I don't think so, Caroline, but even if you did, it won't matter. There's no way you could have put the whole story in a telegram and after tonight, no one'll be able to find you to get the whole story."

"Do you think you can just waltz in here and kill me in the restaurant kitchen, and no one will come asking you any questions? I gave you credit for being a smarter man that that."

"Everybody saw me leave on the morning train today, so as far as they're concerned I'm long gone. It was nothing to hop off after a few stops, get hold of a horse, and hightail it back to New Hope cross-country. It was a fast trip, faster than I expected, and when I'm done here, I figure I can catch up somewhere along the line. I'm good at hiding my tracks. You should know that." Saylor was sure he had everything planned out.

"Not that good. *I* found you."

"Yes. Yes, you did. I admit you were smarter than I expected. For sure smarter than that fool Ray Summerton."

"You killed him. Why? Did you find out that he was going to sell what he knew about you to the highest bidder?" We were carrying on the conversation with an unnatural calm, just two people who hadn't seen each other for a while and needed to catch up.

Saylor gave a short, sharp laugh. "What a fool that man

was! He had much too high an opinion of himself. He thought I'd be grateful that he kept his mouth shut and that maybe I'd offer him some kind of partnership in the Anchor in return. He understood beef, I can't deny that, and he was smart in his own way, but after all our years working together, he never did understand me."

"No," I agreed, "I guess not," and moved a step back from him, toward the carving table where the chef kept his sharpest knives. "You don't want to share that ranch with your father, let alone a grifter like Ray Summerton. And now you're going to kill me, too, like you killed Summerton, and you think no one will give either death a second look? Mark, does that really make sense? You being connected to two dead bodies is sure to make somebody somewhere suspicious." I took another small step toward the knives.

"You're a pleasure to be around, Caroline, that's a fact," his tone admiring, "and under different circumstances I'd enjoy spending more time with you, but I don't have more time." He used the barrel of the derringer to gesture toward the kitchen's back door. "You and I are going to take a walk outside, and if you make a sound, I'll kill you right where you stand. Do you believe that?"

"I believe it, yes, but I also believe you're not a fool. Who knows who's wandering around and might think a pistol shot coming from the kitchen should be looked into? Lucas Morgan makes his rounds all night. Are you willing to take that chance?"

Saylor smiled in appreciation. "You've got a good head on your shoulders, I'll say that. This little thing –" he waved the barrel of the pistol he held, "– is quiet as a mouse when it's held close enough, but you're right. It could make somebody curious. That's why it's better for both of us if you come without making a fuss. You get a little longer to live, and I don't have to drag your body outside and load it onto that nag I'm riding to lug you down to the river. A dead body's damned hard to handle. You know that, don't you, or wasn't there enough of your husband left after the fire for you to find out? There was a kid too, wasn't there? Don't move, Caroline!" At my jerk of fury and shock, his voice turned as sharp as the knives I'd never reach. "Let's go outside. Now."

I took slow steps toward the door, saying as I did so, "This won't work, Mark. People know we spent time together. Someone will think, maybe they quarreled and he killed her. Someone's bound to come knocking at your door."

But I was talking too much, taking too much time, and Saylor wasn't interested in conversation any longer. He wanted me outside and he wanted me outside now. I watched impatience turn his blue eyes almost black.

"Not if there's no body," he retorted. "Move. Now." We shifted toward the door at the same time, my left foot, his right foot, facing each other like we were going through the steps of an old-fashioned dance. The gun never wavered.

"But I have a body," I pointed out in a reasonable tone, "and someone's bound to find it."

"It's a shame about that body of yours," he said. "I mean that. A real shame. I'd have enjoyed a taste of it, but no one'll find it for a good long time, not until the river's thawed and the sun's warm again. Then something that doesn't look like you might rise to the surface. Have you ever seen a body that's been in the water a while? God, it's an awful sight, black and runny. Just awful. And you such a beauty, too. It's a real shame. Open the door, Caroline, slow and easy. Don't make me kill you here." His voice switched from easy-going and pleasant to sharp and menacing in a heartbeat. I'd never heard anything like it, and it was that, more than the small gun, that terrified me the most, how he switched from man to monster and back to man without any effort at all.

With my hand on the doorknob and still facing Saylor, I

said, "You do recall it's winter, don't you, and there's ice on the Platte?"

"Not everywhere. Not along some of the banks. I had time this afternoon to find a place or two where the ice is all broken up along the bank. You'll fit there fine. All I have to do is slide you under the ice and give you a push out into the water. God knows where you'll finally end up. The river will move you along. You'll appreciate being dead because drowning in that cold water trapped under the ice would be a terrible way to die." He stretched his arm so that his fingers rested featherlight on the back of my hand where it touched the doorknob. "Not as bad as burning up, though, am I right?" he whispered in a low voice colored by malice. "Not as bad as being burned alive." He met my gaze and grinned a little. Monster, again, I thought, and decided I'd rather die in the Bliss House kitchen than go anywhere with Mark Saylor. I'd rather die in light and warmth than spend one more moment in this man's gloating company, and I gave serious thought to throwing myself against him so that the bullet would kill me outright. How loud the shot sounded or how quiet wouldn't matter then. The idea of floating not-quite-dead under the ice in a black, cold river made me a little sick, and I decided to make sure I was good and dead before we got there. I suppose that sounds a little foolish in the telling, but our lives are made up of choices. A grown woman has a life of her own and a right to her own decisions, Arthur had said, and for one mad moment throwing myself against a loaded gun seemed like the best choice I had out of a lot of very bad ones.

Until over Mark Saylor's shoulder I saw the swinging door that led into the dining room open just enough for Arthur Stenton to slip into the kitchen. I looked away from the door immediately, hoping Saylor hadn't seen any change in my expression.

I knew what I had to do, even if the thought of it

disgusted me, and lowering my voice to a tone I hoped would sound husky and inviting, I asked, "Isn't there anything I can offer that would make you change your mind? Don't I have anything you want?" I held his gaze and ran a slow tongue along my parted lips. "Not anything?" A burst of triumph lit his eyes.

"I don't turn your stomach now, do I? And the idea of me rolling around on top of you doesn't make you sick anymore, either, does it? I knew it would come to this. You women are all the same when you want something from a man. Well, I admit it, Caroline, it goes against the grain to waste a woman like you, but you waited too long and you lost your chance. The only thing I'm interested in now is watching your pretty body disappear under the ice."

I made myself hold Saylor's gaze and not look past his shoulder to see how close Arthur was. I knew Arthur would be stealing forward, low and careful not to brush against anything that would give away his presence in the kitchen, but how far had he come and what could he do against a loaded gun, even if he reached us? In the end, that wasn't my business. My business was to keep Mark Saylor thinking about other things as long as I could.

Which wasn't all that long because Saylor had no sooner said *under the ice* when Arthur stood up tall. For a moment our eyes met before I turned my face in the direction opposite of where Arthur stood and shouted to an imaginary rescuer, "Lucas! Thank God you're here!"

Despite himself, Saylor turned quickly to see what I saw, and then two things happened at the same time. I yanked the kitchen back door open with enough strength to knock Saylor a little off balance and Arthur threw himself against the man's back, knocking Saylor forward. On the way down, he let loose with one shot from the pistol but it went wild, not close to me and certainly not close to Arthur, who at first was on top of Saylor, trying to hold the man down. He wasn't strong enough for that, however, and the two men began rolling on the floor, grunting, trying to land punches, bumping against tables, then rolling in another direction until it was impossible to see who had a hold on who and who, if anyone, would come out on top. I thought I should do something but didn't know what. If I swung one of the chef's heavy frying pans I could just as easily knock out Arthur as Saylor. The wrestling didn't last long, though, only until I heard another shot, not ringing like the first one but muffled. Muffled, I realized with a sick and sinking heart, because as Saylor had said, the bullet had found its target in close quarters, in one of the two men there on the kitchen floor. A stillness that seemed to last forever followed the second shot.

I stood as if glued to the floor, unable to move any part of me, hardly able to think at all because of the rush of fear pushing through my chest and against my heart, fear that the man to rise from that unnatural embrace on the kitchen floor wouldn't be Arthur Stenton, the one person in all the world I knew I could not live without.

I heard running footsteps through the dining room and someone push open the kitchen door so hard it banged against the wall, but I didn't look up to see who had entered the kitchen. Instead, I moved closer and would have dropped to my knees beside the two figures except one of them moved slightly, pushed the other body off with a heave, and got up as far as his knees.

With eyes only for me, Arthur asked, "Are you all right, Caroline? He didn't hurt you, did he?"

I wanted to hold out my hands and help him to his feet, but I couldn't move any part of my body. I could only stare. Lucas Morgan, who had just pounded his way into the kitchen, tried to grab hold of Arthur's arm and offer assistance, but he might as well not have been there. Blood trickled from a cut at the side of Arthur's mouth and one cheek was already beginning to show what was sure to be a large, purple bruise. He pushed himself upright and came close enough to put both hands on my shoulders. Several of his knuckles were skinned and bleeding.

"You aren't hurt, are you, Caroline? Tell me you aren't hurt."

I raised a corner of my skirt to dab at his mouth. "No," I said, "but I can't say the same for you," overwhelmed with a tenderness I couldn't contain.

For a long time, for years, my tears had been a private matter and no one's business but my own, but that didn't seem to matter anymore. I will not have any secrets from this man, I thought, not ever. I will keep nothing from him. He can have all of me, body, mind, and spirit for as long as he wants it. Out of nowhere I began to cry, holding onto Arthur's coat with two clenched hands, shaking, trying between gasps of breath to regain my previous calm, trying to say something, anything, that would make sense but not able to do anything but cry. Arthur put both arms around me and pulled me into his arms.

"Hush, Caroline. Hush now," his murmured words repeated the way you'd croon a lullaby to a restless child.

We stood like that a long while, so long that Lucas had time to bend down for a closer look at the body on the floor, stand, and say as if anyone was listening, "I'll go get Si. Looks like everything's under control here."

After Lucas was gone, I finally pulled away from Arthur to ask, "Is he dead, Arthur? Is he really and finally dead?" I nudged the body on the floor with the toe of my shoe.

"Yes."

"And like this." Whatever Arthur heard in those three words made him ask his next question carefully, as if he were sorting through a pile of words until he found just the right ones.

"Help me understand, Caroline." Pause. "What do you mean *like this*? Like what, exactly?"

I turned away to look down at what used to be Mark Saylor. It could have been Arthur, I thought, or I could be the one who's dead. For a moment I saw and felt the river in winter, black and rippling under the ice. The right man had died, I knew that, but I'm a woman used to ledgers and to balanced columns of debits and credits. I like everything to even out in the end.

"At night. In a back room. No one to see but you and me. He should've died in front of everyone with a judge reading the sentence out loud." I felt deprived and deeply sad. Saylor was the only one who knew the names of any of the men who had helped him and now they were all long gone. "No one will pay, Arthur. No one will ever pay for what that man did, not in a way that matters."

Arthur made a sound somewhere between a groan and a sigh and turned me back so he could look right into my eyes. What I saw in his took my breath away.

"Caroline," Arthur laid a palm so lightly against my cheek he might have been touching something fragile and priceless, "don't you see? *You* paid. All these years it's been *you* paying the price. My love, my dear love, haven't you paid enough?"

I stared at him. He was right, though I hadn't known it until that moment. For years, I had carried the cost and paid the price for loving someone, and for all the loneliness and grief, for all the sleepless nights lying in the dark stoking the fires of memory, I couldn't make myself regret any of it. Yet Arthur was right. Now it was time to set the past down, not forget it, but set it down and move on. Maybe it was like the good reverend said: that there really was a public reckoning for everything in the end, a reckoning that was completely out of our hands.

To answer Arthur's quiet question, I first came back into his arms and rested against him a moment before I said, "Yes, Arthur. I believe I have." He shifted a little as he held me, and I asked with quick concern, "Does your leg hurt? I thought you were limping more than usual when you left tonight." *Tonight*. It didn't seem possible that so much could happen in such a short time. "You should sit down, Arthur. Please."

"It's a limp, Caroline, not an amputation," a response that made me giggle into his chest despite the seriousness of the situation and having to share the moment with a dead body on the floor.

I reached up to tilt his head downward so I could get a better view of his face, then put two fingers to his chin and turned his head from one side to the other, all the while giving his injuries a serious examination.

"Arthur," I said, quite seriously, "You should know that your face looks like you've been in an awful fight, and it's only going to get worse. Do you think you'll be able to teach with one eye swollen shut? I can't imagine what your students are going to say." At the sight of his crooked smile and poor bruised face, the only thing I could think to do to make him feel better was to kiss him. It seemed to do the trick.

20

Naturally, there was some business to get out of the way before we were done with that night. Si Carpenter came and asked a few questions, not as many as I thought he'd ask but at the time I didn't know that he and Arthur had talked more than oncc about Mark Saylor and how he showed up in Colorado out of nowhere with a herd of prime beef.

"I taught at a school just outside Denver for a few years, until '75 when I moved to New Hope," Arthur told me the next day. "My students were the children of some of Denver's most prominent families, and I still keep in touch with some of them. I wondered if they knew anything about a man called Mark Saylor and his Anchor Ranch outside Hot Sulphur Springs."

Arthur and I were once more sharing a pot of tea in the empty dining room of the Bliss House restaurant. Not quite twenty-four hours had passed since the last time we sat there, and the bruises on his face were more colorful than they'd been the night before, a bright mix of purple, green, and yellow.

When I asked about his students' reaction, Arthur said, "Children are curious. I told them the truth." He'll make a fine husband and father, I thought, repeating one of the many thoughts that had crossed my mind when I had finally crawled into bed. I suppose it said something that going to bed made my thoughts dwell on Arthur Stenton. He'll give patient answers to trying questions, keep his head in an emergency, and always, always be kind. No monster in this man.

"I moved to Denver in '75," I told Arthur. "Granville found a doctor there who had experience in the kind of injuries I had, and he convinced me to make the move. I wasn't in any shape to argue at the time." I gave Arthur a thoughtful look. "It seems funny, doesn't it, to think that we were both in Denver around the same time but had to come all the way to New Hope to meet?" There was more I wanted to say on the subject but not just then. "What did you find out from your Denver friends?" Arthur's face settled into stern lines.

"People recognized Saylor's name because he got into the Cattleman's Association on that name, on his *father's* name. For the most part, Saylor stayed out of trouble."

"For the most part?"

"He beat a woman nearly to death, a prostitute. He never gave a reason and she left Denver as soon as she was back on her feet."

"Nothing was done about it?" Outraged, as I always was, by the helplessness of women and especially those women whose living depended on the needs of men.

"That was Denver at the time, Caroline. There wasn't much law and order to be found. It's one of the reasons I left Denver for New Hope."

"And you told Si what you found out?"

"Yes. We've been talking for a while about Saylor, even more after Si got the telegram about Ray Summerton's death."

"But how did you guess?" I asked. "What got you thinking about Mark Saylor in the first place?"

"Do you really not know?" Caught off guard by the quiet question, I could only shake my head. "It was Lizbeth who pointed Saylor out to me," Arthur went on, "but when I finally met him, it wasn't because of Lizbeth that I paid attention to the man. It was because of you and how you changed when he was around you." Arthur gave a little shrug at the memory. "I can't describe it and I can't explain it, but he turned you into a woman I didn't recognize. It might be as simple a thing as jealousy on my part, I suppose, but I don't think so."

I tried to remember how I acted when I was around Mark Saylor in those early days. At one time, I'd thought him handsome and charming, up until that moment when his diamond tie pin in the shape of an anchor had glittered in the lamplight. Maybe that was when the reckoning began.

"I didn't know I changed," I said. "Nobody else seemed to notice a difference in me."

"That's because nobody else loves you like I do," Arthur replied and would have kept talking as if he hadn't handed me the moon except I reached across the table and laid my hand on his arm.

"Are you sure?" I asked. "About the loving part, I mean."

"I'm sure," adding as if my question surprised him, "You're an intelligent woman. That can't come as a shock to you."

"Even if she's not surprised, a woman still likes to hear it said out loud." Lesson number one for the teacher.

"I'll say it as often as you want to hear it, but may I finish my story?"

I nodded. "Go ahead," but inside I was deciding what dress to wear to my wedding.

"When I left you last night," Arthur said, "I decided to stop by the jail before I went home and find out if there were any more details about Summerton's death. I was uneasy with how you sounded when you said you planned to leave New Hope. You weren't yourself, and it wasn't just because you were tired. Something was wrong, I could tell. At the jail, Lucas and I talked a while. I told him I was worried about you, that I knew something was wrong, and I asked him to let me know if he saw Mark Saylor back in town for any reason at any time. Then on my way home Henry Strunk came racing down the boardwalk and ran right into me. You know the rest."

"Oh," I said, suddenly seeing how all the events of the night before fit together. "Henry went back to the kitchen to get his glasses, didn't he?"

Arthur nodded. "He pushed open the kitchen door just enough to hear Saylor threaten you, and that was all he needed to go get Lucas Morgan."

"But he found you first."

Arthur nodded again. "Yes," was all he said. We were both quiet, remembering. I shivered at the memory.

"You took a terrible risk, Arthur," I finally managed to say, my voice shaky with the knowledge of what could have happened. Harold Sellers could be building a coffin for Arthur instead of Mark Saylor.

"Caroline." Arthur said my name and then stopped. All I could do was look at him. Finally, in as humble a voice, as human a voice, as I'd ever heard from him he said, "This is all new to me. I know I have a lot to learn about being a husband and pleasing a woman and making her happy, but if you're willing to teach me, I'm willing to learn."

"Arthur, are you proposing matrimony?"

"Yes. Am I doing that wrong, too?" A little bit of his normal amused thoughtfulness had crept back into his tone. Frankly, I found it much more attractive than humility.

"No," I said, laughing. I stood and went behind his chair, wrapped my arms around his shoulders, took a minute to nibble on one ear – I had somehow missed what attractive ears the man had – and whispered, "You are doing everything exactly right, my darling, and the answer to the question you didn't get around to asking is yes."

I married Arthur Stenton the Friday after Sheba and John Bliss returned to New Hope. They both looked tired from the trip but happy, making me think they had found a measure of peace during their travels, peace with their loss and peace with each other.

I waited to tell John privately about Arthur and me. We had both loved Davey Moore, and I thought John might take the news differently than the other citizens of New Hope, who seemed to a person to be delighted. Maybe John would think me disloyal for taking another husband, as if I were replacing Davey with Arthur, but I knew as soon as I shared the news that I had it wrong.

"You love Arthur Stenton?" I supposed I could understand the hint of disbelief in John's voice.

"Yes."

"And he loves you?"

"Yes." I was sure of that becausc Arthur had mastered lesson number one seemingly overnight.

At my single, firm word, John Bliss kissed me on the cheek. It almost looked like his eyes glistened, but I didn't know why the news would make him weepy, though I admit I've never fully understood the man.

"Good," John declared. "Davey would approve of Arthur Stenton, and I can think of at least two things they have in common." I gave John a questioning look because truly, Davey Moore and Arthur Stenton had temperaments far removed from each other.

"What could those two men possibly have in common?" I asked. My question made John grin.

"You," he said, dropping a kiss on my other cheek, "and having very good taste in women."

The night before the wedding, March daylight lasting later into the evening and just the slightest tease of spring in the air, I wrapped myself in my shawl and walked out to

Arthur's house. The house where we would sleep tomorrow night, the house where we would live together as man and wife for at least the next thirty years, please God.

He opened the door when I knocked, surprised and then again not surprised to see me. I was growing used to how much Arthur understood me. He'll always be a man difficult to surprise, I thought, and then smiled to myself. I had a few things planned for our wedding night that might more than surprise him.

Arthur's house was provided by New Hope as part of his teacher's stipend and while small, it was sturdy and warm. He had shelves of books everywhere, but otherwise I could see little of the man in the house. That was because he spent more time in the schoolhouse than here, something that would change over time. Knowing a warm meal and a warm bed are waiting for a man is often a strong draw for him to come home.

Once inside, Arthur and I stood facing each other. He had added a colorful rug to the living area and two new lamps, one on a table by the settee and the other on a stand by the bedroom doorway. We'll be the same two people tomorrow night, I thought, but we'll be different, too. What a change a few words can make in a person's life!

"I can't stay," I said. "I have to press my dress for tomorrow and get my things ready to move into your – into *our* – house, but there's something I have to show you."

Arthur heard the serious tone in my words and stood still in the way he had that meant he was listening with every part of his being. I started to unbutton my dress, my hands shaking now that a moment I had put off for too long had finally come. Arthur watched my face, not my hands as they moved from button to button. I had purposefully not worn either chemise or shift under my dress, and when I reached the last button I spread open the garment so that I was exposed.

"You should know this about me," I said. My voice and

my hands had stopped shaking as Arthur dropped his gaze from my face. "If you find it, find *me*, distasteful, I understand. I still do myself sometimes when I catch a glimpse in a mirror, but you wouldn't have to look at my scars in the daytime. Maybe that would make it more bearable."

Arthur made the same sound I'd heard the night Mark Saylor died: a groan, a sigh that came deep from his heart. Then he took one long step toward me and placed his hand on my breast. Or what was left of my breast. The fire all those years ago had caught the front of my dress and burned its way down until I'd had the presence of mind to fall to the ground and roll so that my weight crushed the flames. They had still caused terrible pain and left behind terrible damage. Ugly, red, thickened puckers of skin, some still taut and shiny in places, crisscrossed part of my chest and one breast. Over time, most of the scars had lost their bright red color but looking at them in a mirror, I thought that what was left behind had just grown uglier. It had taken a long while for the pain to lessen, but a tenderness still remained: a low ache in winter and the prick of pins in summer.

"The doctor wasn't sure if I'd be able to nurse a baby there again." At the time, with Jean and Davey dead, the doctor's words hadn't mattered to me, but now – well, time would tell, I suppose. "It's your right to see this, Arthur. I won't come to you as something I'm not. I have scars. Some you can see and some you can't, but you have a right to know about all of them." Arthur stood so close to me that I could sense his chest rising and falling, and his cool hand never moved from my ruined skin.

"'Each for the other they were born / Each can the other best adorn.'"

"Are you quoting Emerson to me right now?" I don't know how I thought he'd react to what I had just shared with him, but even knowing the man as I did, hearing him recite words from a poem by Mr. Ralph Waldo Emerson at such a time took me by surprise. I guess I still had a lot to learn about this man.

Arthur opened his mouth, paused, cleared his throat, took a breath that sounded a little trembly, and said, "I need Mr. Emerson right now because I don't have words of my own for how beautiful you are," his emotion deep. He wasn't a man used to those kinds of feelings so he had to take another breath before he sounded like himself again. "I thought women liked it when a man recited poetry to them. Did I get it wrong?" He sounded disappointed in himself, the teacher failing another test. Relief and love swept over me with the force of an ocean wave.

"You are a ridiculous man sometimes," I said, but I laughed when I said it and kissed him on the mouth. "I needed to be sure you saw for yourself what you were getting, but I knew you'd understand. You always do. I didn't want to start out our marriage with any secrets or surprises, though I imagine," I let my mouth linger for a nibble at his ear again, "we may still discover a few surprises tomorrow night."

Buttoning my dress seemed to go much smoother than unbuttoning, even with Arthur's rather awkward help. A husband never appreciated all the stays and fastenings his wife wore until he was in hurry to get her out of them.

"There's another thing you should know," I said, once I was finally put back together. The words brought him to a stop.

"Something else?" Was that a touch of uneasiness I heard in his voice? Lesson number two for the teacher: keeping a husband just a tad off balance makes for a happy marriage.

"Have I mentioned that I have a great deal of money."

"No, you haven't."

"It's from the sale of the silver mine Davey owned with John Bliss. They sold it for a lot of money. Davey used some of his share to buy our place in Wyoming and the cattle, the ones that Saylor stole, but there's still a good sum left. It's in a Denver bank. And I still own the land in Wyoming. It'll sell someday for a good price. I suppose you could say we're rich."

"Do you want a bigger house?" I looked around.

"No. I like this one just the way it is, though I admit I've gotten awful fond of the indoor plumbing at the Blisses' house. And it might be a little crowded if children come along. We'd have to add on then."

"It's your money and you can do with it as you please, but I still plan to teach."

"I know."

"Right here in New Hope, Nebraska."

"I should hope so. I like New Hope, and I wouldn't want to live anywhere else. I do have an idea about using that money someday, but now's not the time to talk about it. I should get back to the Blisses' house."

When the time was right, New Hope, Nebraska, would have a high school – for the Henry Strunks and the Lizbeth Ericsons of our little world, for the *Treasure Island* pirates and all the future Thomas Edisons just waiting to be discovered. I had the means to make that happen.

I hated the idea of Arthur having to walk me all the way back to town that night and then having to turn right around and make a return trip home, but this was the last time he'd have to do it. And while he was generally an agreeable man and always respectful, there were a few things that were useless to discuss with him, regardless of my powers of persuasion. One of those things was the idea that he would let me head off into the night on my own. A matter of courtesy on his part. Courtesy and love.

The wedding was a big affair by New Hope's reckoning, held in the church and attended by so many people we ran out of places for them to sit. Merchants put closed signs on the doors of their stores so they could attend the ceremony, an occurrence rarer than hen's teeth in the town's history. It was their way of honoring Arthur, and I loved them for it.

The Merchants' Association held a celebration in the Meeting Hall, and John Bliss along with Chef Clermont provided an endless spread from the Bliss House kitchen. I teased Arthur by making him say the word *profiteroles* and when he did, laughing at me and doing his best to imitate Monsieur Clermont, I kissed him hard and whispered, "There's more waiting for you at home, love." I wasn't talking about French pastries, either.

The citizens of New Hope knew how to celebrate and I wished them well, but I was impatient to be alone with my new husband and after that kiss, I could tell Arthur felt the same. As he and I gathered our coats to leave, Ruth Carpenter pulled me to the side.

"I'm so happy for you, Caroline, and for Mr. Stenton, too. The way he looks at you – well, anyone can see how happy you make him, and it's time both of you had the chance for it." Ruth hesitated. "This'll seem a strange thing to tell you on your wedding day, but I know what it's like to feel you're living in darkness that will never end, and I wanted you to know that it's all the brighter when you finally step out of that dark place. A woman doesn't forget; how could she? But that moment when you feel the sun again – oh, Caroline, it's like nothing in the world!" Ruth flicked a tear from her cheek and gave me a quick hug. Her final words – "I hope this is the start of a lot of bright days for you!" – stayed with me all the way home.

Sometime that night, I woke in the arms of my husband and lay very still, listening, wondering if my longtime companion waited in the shadows and out of sight. But I could tell there was nothing hiding anywhere. No whoosh or roar, no snap or hiss, no flash or flicker. Everything around me was softly dark and quiet, Arthur's steady breathing the only sound, and a warming glow of tenderness and love the only hint of fire in the room.

IF YOU ENJOYED *Through Seasons of Fire*, don't stop here. The first two books of the New Hope Series are available at Amazon.com and in the Kindle Store. Ruth Carpenter and Sheba Bliss each has her own back story and her own experience with heartbreak and danger, hope, risk, and love. Read about Ruth and her Silas in *What We Carry With Us* and John and Sheba Bliss in *Surprised by Shadows*.

All of Karen's books present characters and places you won't soon forget. With her writing described as "satisfying" and her research as "flawless," you can't go wrong. (Akron Beacon Journal, 2010)

The Laramie Series by Karen J. Hasley

Lily's Sister

Waiting for Hope

Where Home Is

Circled Heart

Gold Mountain

Smiling at Heaven

The Penwarrens by Karen J. Hasley

Claire, After All

Listening to Abby

Jubilee Rose

Stand-alone novels by Karen J. Hasley

The Dangerous Thaw of Etta Capstone

Magnificent Farewell

New Hope Series by Karen J. Hasley

What We Carry With Us

Surprised by Shadows

Through Seasons of Fire

~ Remarkable Women. Unforgettable Stories. ~

All in Historical Settings.

www.karenhasley.com

Made in the USA
Columbia, SC
23 December 2019

85530723R00186